Drawn In

Book One of the Paper Dreams Chronicles

by

Sioux Trett

First Printing 2015

ISBN 978-1505838718

Cover art by Leslie Willis

For information on distribution, please visit
siouxtrett.wordpress.com

The dedication of this book is twofold.

First, to my parents Sam & JoAnn Trett

who have always encouraged me to follow my dreams.

You gave me roots and you gave me wings, and the courage to use them both.

Second, to the two teachers who most infused me with a love of words—

Mrs. Marian Gregory & Ms. Michael Edwards.

Your lessons and gifts reach far, far beyond your classroom doors.

Forever thank you.

"Those who dream by day are cognizant of many things which escape those who dream only by night."

- Edgar Allan Poe

 Chapter One

*Y*ou know that ridiculous game you play at summer camp where one team has to race against the other and you have an egg in a teaspoon, and if you drop the egg you're out? Yeah, that's been me for the last five months. No, not the spoon-bearer—the egg. Held up carefully, delicately, everyone dancing around me on tip-toe, speaking in whispers and tilted heads.

I'm not as fragile as people think.

So having two whole months in California with my very best friend feels like I've been given a reprieve of sorts, like I've been granted a summer break stamped *NORMAL.*

"We're here!" Maia sings. Good to know, although it's really the part with the Jeep stopping that gives it away. She kills the engine (which interrupts Taylor Swift mid-chorus), flings her door open, and grabs her bag from behind the seat. She tucks a strand of perfectly wavy chestnut hair behind one ear and turns to face me. "Um, Rennie?" Her face has turned uncharacteristically serious in a way I don't like at all. She clears her throat and tilts her head.

Et tu, Maia? I know what's coming next. Not the words exactly, but I know this tone. I recognize the impulse to choose words carefully. My chest tightens, a small tremor starting in my hands. I won't cry. I stare at the silver ring on my index finger, twisting it around and around, the square blue gem playing hide and seek as it spins. So much for my normal summer.

"I just wanted to tell you before you meet everybody—no one knows. I mean, I haven't told anyone about the accident. If you want to talk, you know I'm here any time. But, well, I thought you should at least have the option of a fresh start here. Is that okay?"

The accident. It's the main reason Aunt Charlie agreed to let me come to California for two months. She knew I'd be more likely to talk to Maia than to anyone else, but just because I haven't talked about it out loud doesn't mean I haven't dealt with it. I don't see why everyone thinks I should be discussing it as if that will change anything. I brush a renegade tear from my face, resenting the sudden mood shift, but I appreciate the thought. "Thanks, Mai. When I'm ready to talk, you'll be the first to know. But not yet."

She reaches across and squeezes my hand. "I understand. You know I'm on call 24-7." She flashes me a brilliant (if slightly mischievous) grin and I know she's ready to move on. "Now, let's ditch the tears and have a little fun. There's more to see than the airport and my Jeep, I promise."

"Yes please." I hop out of the car and give myself a last look in the side-view mirror. No lip gloss on the teeth, check. Eyes remarkably un-smudged, check. In fact, they look pretty good. I don't even mind that they're such a pale blue they're barely even a color. The hair... well, it's as good as it's gonna get. After the trip here with the windows down, there's only so much taming my red curls will allow.

Maia is at the back of the Jeep urging me forward. "Come on, you look great." Her compliment is sincere but I can't help second guessing her judgment. Whatever. If I can't be confident, I can still act like it, right? Okay. Here we go. Never mind that Maia looks like she just stepped out of a shampoo ad, chestnut hair gleaming and completely unaffected by the wind that blew through the car only moments ago. Never mind that I'm going to be meeting all of her new California friends who are probably all tanned and skinny and perfect. Never mind that, despite the recent resurgence in movies and young adult novels, redheads are still only about two percent of the population, and I'm bound to be the *only one* at this entire shindig. No worries. I mean, it's not as if I'm too short, too skinny in some places and too curvy in others, and completely covered in constellations of freckles. Except wait, just kidding; I'm all of those.

I look up at Maia for one last vote of assurance. Yes, she is tall and tanned and perfect, but she's also the same girl who has remained my best friend through braces, bad haircuts and that one summer I listened to nothing but One Direction. She loves me regardless of all my imperfections, and the thought gives me real strength. I draw in a deep breath, give the legs of my shorts one last tug and join her, ready for anything.

We stop at the edge of the concrete to survey our surroundings before heading into the sand, and I can't hold back the gasp that comes to my lips. I feel like I've stepped into a postcard. The Pacific unfolds in front of us, the descending sun casting its light like thousands of tiny diamonds scattered along the surface of the water. A cove embraces the sea to our right, a small beach town opens up on our left, and the azure sky above us is so perfect it looks as though it's been painted by God himself. A long pier extends out into the ocean, seemingly infinite, its end lost in the bright sunlight. I soak in every last detail; I have to sketch this later.

"Nice, huh?" Maia says, grinning at my speechless reaction. After the miles of brown hills (which Maia says are generously called "golden" by the locals), it feels like we've stumbled into a storybook paradise.

"*Nice* doesn't begin to describe this. How does anyone get anything done when this is waiting right outside the door?"

She shrugs casually. "Oh we don't. That's why all Californians are independently wealthy, you know. We just lay around on the beach, soaking up the rays and letting servants bring us tropical drinks with little umbrellas in them."

I pull my eyes away from the horizon long enough to roll them at her.

"No really," she continues, all wide-eyed innocence. "We also surf to school." She breaks character to laugh with me, and hooks her arm through mine. "Okay, but honestly, this was the first thing that made it almost worth moving away from Pennsylvania."

Maia Cantrell has been my best friend since the second grade, ever since that fateful day when Dustin Bradford stuck his tongue out at me and called me Carrot Top. I'd like to think it was because of my red hair and not a reference to the comedian of the same name, but either way, it made me cry. Maia came to my defense by calmly explaining to Dustin that carrot tops are, in fact, green and if he was seeing my strawberry blonde hair as green then perhaps he should see a doctor. Then, just as calmly, she stuck her tongue out at him, grabbed my hand, and led me away to the swings. We've been inseparable ever since. Well, until last

December when her family moved to California. That definitely put a wrench in the whole *inseparable* thing. As if being almost seventeen isn't hard enough, being almost seventeen with a best friend all the way across the country is much, much harder.

A group of guys is hauling dried driftwood from the back of an old red pickup out onto the beach, presumably for the bonfire that tops tonight's agenda. Small groups of girls gather on beach towels and blankets, watching the boys appreciatively while trying to appear uninterested.

One of the guys looks over and lifts his chin in boy language for "hello" toward Maia. A blond with short spiky hair and khaki cargo shorts, he has removed his shirt for the task at hand exposing more muscles than I personally find appealing, but I know he's exactly her type. This has to be the infamous Seth.

"That's him," she semi-whispers to me, bestowing on him a flirtatious smile as he turns back to his work.

"I thought it might be. He looks like the one you'd pick."

"Hey!" She sounds cross, but I know she's not.

"It's true!" And she knows it. "Besides, I do the same thing. I'll find the dark haired, artistic one with a penchant for sci-fi films or comic books and I'll be ever-so-slightly more interested in him than he is in me."

"How is Danny, anyway?" she asks.

"Still a jerk." Danny was the guy I crushed on all last year until we finally went on a date and he turned out to be a creep. I want my first kiss to be with someone who's nice and sweet and actually likes me, not a self-indulgent chauvinist with too many hands and too few intelligent thoughts.

I look up to find we're almost to her friends who are waving us over and spreading out another blanket for us. I wave to them as we approach, and unfortunately my focus is so entirely on meeting these new girls, that I don't take notice of the large mass of driftwood that's about to run me down until it's hitting me square in the shoulder.

I let out a yelp and stumble into Maia, instinctively squeezing my eyes shut (yeah, like that'll help). Pain radiates from my injured shoulder, and Maia reaches out to save me from doing a full-on face plant as my first introduction to her friends.

"Alex, you idiot! Are you trying to kill us?" Her tirade sounds like it's happening in the next county, words carried away on the wind before they can reach me.

I open my eyes and look around so I can congratulate this jerk on his great impression of a bulldozer, but he's not there. No bulldozer guy, no Maia, no beach. Instead, I'm standing in the woods, my back pressed up against a thick oak tree. I gasp, the scent of fresh pine needles and clean damp earth filling my lungs. The pain in my shoulder is completely gone. Am I dead? No, that's stupid—get a grip. So where am I?

"Maia?" I whisper, my voice shaky and my pulse climbing. There's no answer. Come on, *think*.

I lean into the bark of the oak tree to hold me up, and study my lush green surroundings. Tall oaks and pines reach up for a misty sky, the light through the thick canopy of leaves overhead dancing on my skin. Farther into the woods, there's a dirt path lined in orange patches of poppies, and I realize with a start that I recognize this place. My recurring nightmares bring me to these woods over and over again, but never like this. Never when I'm awake. I *am* awake, right? Of course I am. I was just running down a dirt path, and tripped over an exposed root when I went to hide behind this—no, that's wrong. There was a... a beach? I hear footsteps on the road behind me, boots crunching into the hard dirt, and all other concerns swirl together to become one thought: *hide.*

My heart pounds in my chest, my breathing shallow. I take a step closer to the tree behind me, pressing my back into it like I can fuse myself into the bark. I try to hold my breath but it won't be stilled, coming in short gasps of fear. The footsteps continue uninterrupted, and their rhythmic sound travels past me enough that I risk a glance. I inch my fingers around the giant trunk of the oak and lean as far forward as I dare. A man in a long brown coat saunters down the road. I can just see the dark skin of his clean-shaven head, his hands swinging freely beside him. He begins to whistle a melancholy tune as he passes out of sight, and my breathing eases into a sigh of relief. I'm safe for now. I lean my head to the rough bark and close my eyes.

"Are you okay?"

I gasp, eyes flying open. He found me? But it's not the man in the overcoat. The woods are gone, and the bright light of the beach makes me blink several times as I try to regain my bearings.

Maia has her hands on my elbows, watching me closely. "Are you okay?" she repeats slowly.

I shake my head, trying to clear out the dull ache that's settling there. I don't know how to answer her. *Am* I okay? I don't even know what that was—a dream, a hallucination, a memory? But I do know the response that's expected, and I can deal with the reality later.

"Yeah," I say, nodding to reassure her (and myself). "Yeah, sorry, I just got dizzy there for a second. Jet lag, I guess." That definitely wasn't jet lag, but since I don't have a better explanation for why I was swept up into a dream when I wasn't asleep, I'll just go with that until I can sort this out. I'm getting really good at filing things away for later.

"Being run down by an idiot with a pile of driftwood can do that," she says, giving a not-so-subtle glance over her shoulder.

Oh right. Bulldozer boy. I look past Maia to give him a piece of my mind (or at least a stern lecture on Proper Walking Procedures When Carrying a Large Pile of Something), but my breath catches in my throat. You know how in movies when the hero meets the heroine, everything turns into slow-motion and music starts playing? Yeah, funny thing—that happens in real life too. I half expect to be transported back to dream world with the way my head has gone all woozy again, but it's not the weird vision thing this time. It's the boy.

Don't get me wrong. I've read dozens of books with the "insta-love" gimmick, and I've snorted derisively each and every time. And now, even with my heart pounding and words unable to form on my tongue, I'll say it again: Love at first sight does not exist.

Infatuation at first sight, however…

His eyes are stormy grey, vivid and bright. They make me think of those old *I Love Lucy* episodes where everything is variations of grey, but you know her hair is bright red even through the lack of color. I wonder what color his eyes would be if we weren't living in black and white. And there must be some Native American in his lineage, or possibly a Celtic warrior or I don't know, maybe Angelina Jolie and Benedict Cumberbatch had a secret love child, because wow—

cheekbones. Cheek. Bones. And on his left arm there's a tantalizing wisp of black ink that peeks out from the sleeve of his plain white tee-shirt, teasing me with the knowledge that there's some secret message hidden just out of sight. He's tall enough that I have to look up at him, and not overly thin (I'm pretty sure I'd still be able to hide behind him should the need arise); more of a swimmer's build as they say—lithe and lean and perfect.

"Sorry Maia."

He speaks! Glorious first words! Wait, why is he calling me Maia? Oh right. Other people. Aaaaand… I'm back. And as everything around me resumes normal speed, so does the pain in my shoulder. I rub at it, trying not to make a face despite the soreness there. And then those beautiful grey eyes fall on me.

"Are you okay? I really should have been watching where I was going." His voice is soft and poetic, a raspy quality that makes me want to lean in to hear him better.

"I'll be fine, it's problem. No! Problem. Fine." Was that me? That wasn't even a sentence! "I'm okay." Better. Keep it short, keep breathing. Maia's looking at me like I just grew a third arm and I realize too late that this is *so* not the first impression I would have wanted to make. When I was sane, I mean. I bite my lip and glance away. I'm just certain I knew how to form sentences this morning. Maybe I can blame that vision. I can't quite shake the eerie feeling of having just been somewhere else.

"I didn't catch your name," he says, gallantly rescuing me from myself.

"Rennie!" I say, just a little too loudly. I clear my throat and try to recover my wits. "Rennie Winters." Okay, not the vision then. What is wrong with me? He's only a guy. A perfectly gorgeous kind amazing guy. Oh, pull it together!

"Rennie." Coming from his lips, it sounds like poetry. It sounds whole and complete, not at all like a nickname I ended up with because my sister couldn't pronounce Serenity when we were little. He must come to some resolution or acceptance about it because he doesn't ask any of the standard follow-up questions about it being a real name and did I really say Penny or Randi or (as in one unfortunate incident) Kenny. He just nods and gives me a smile. A crooked, amazingly imperfect smile that makes my heart swell like the Grinch's on Christmas day. "I'm Alex."

I allow myself a real smile, the kind where the dimple in my cheek is fully displayed. "Nice to meet you."

"McKinley! Come on, man, we need that firewood if this thing's ever gonna get going!" One of the other nameless shirtless guys from the fire pit is waving his arms in our direction.

McKinley, he called him. Alex McKinley. I savor the name, rolling it over and watching it unfurl letter by letter in my mind.

"Sorry Rennie, I'm being paged. I'll find you later, okay?" Another smile, this one leaning toward apologetic, and he's gone.

"Okay," I whisper, long after he's out of hearing range. First the vision, then Alex. It's a lot to take in. And oddly enough, the two don't feel disconnected.

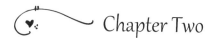 Chapter Two

I glance over my shoulder to appreciate Alex's departing figure one more time and find that he's turned to look at me too. Our eyes meet and we smile at each other, both a little embarrassed to be caught looking. When I turn back to Maia, she has one index finger pointed at me and her eyebrows are lifted sternly as she scolds "No" like I'm a puppy who just perforated a first edition Hemingway.

"What?"

"Listen, if you want to have a summer fling, I'm all for it. In fact, it would probably be really good for you. But not him."

My heart sinks down into my belly at her reprimand. She doesn't like Alex? What can she possibly object to? "But—"

"We'll talk about it later, okay? Just... don't. I don't want to see you get hurt."

Obviously she knows more about him than I do, and of course I trust her opinion (usually more than I trust my own), but how can she not like him? I start to reply, but she's busy pulling me over toward the girls. I'd forgotten all about them. I suppose a vision of another world and a first meeting with a potential soul mate will do that to you.

Maia grins as she pulls me down to sit beside her on the warm blanket. The three girls skootch around to make room for us and much to my relief, they look adorable and friendly, but not perfect.

"Introductions first," Maia says, taking the lead as usual. "This is Jane," she gestures to my left where a petite girl with a blonde pixie cut is smiling at me. She lifts a hand in greeting, but before either of us can say anything, Maia continues around the circle. "This is Kaela," she points to another blonde, the whole length of her platinum hair piled on top of her head in a mixture of messy bun and intricate braids. She's a bit bigger than the rest of us, but if she's self-conscious about it, I can't tell at all. I love that. I wish I had that kind of confidence in myself.

"And this is Ember," Maia finishes, gesturing to her right where a tallish girl with nearly perfect café au lait skin flashes me a smile. Her naturally curly hair is pulled back from her face with a bright pink elastic headband. Ember. Wasn't there was something about her that I was supposed to remember?

"Hallo Rennie. So glad you're here!"

That's right, Ember is British! The accent tickles me and my grin spreads even wider. I love that accent—must be all the time I've spent watching *Doctor Who* and *Sherlock* and every other BBC America show I can find. This is going to be fun. Oooo, what would Alex sound like with a British accent? I try to replay our meeting with the added element, but I'm quickly interrupted by other greetings from the girls. Too bad, that would have been good.

"Tell me a little about this place," I say when we've finished the typical how-was-your-flight kind of questions. "Maia picked me up at the airport and we came straight here, so I haven't gotten to see much. What have I gotten myself into for the summer?"

"You're gonna love it." Ember is the first to answer. "I've only lived here for two years, since my mum's job relocated her, which of course relocated all of us. But it's really fantastic—sunshine every day, no joke. As much as I miss home, I do not miss that London drizzle!"

"Yeah, Kae and I were both born here," Jane chimes in, "so the weather doesn't seem like a big deal to us, but we still love it."

"It *is* a big deal to me," I tell them. "If we were at my home in Lancaster right now, it would be well over 90 and we'd all be dripping with the humidity. But this is great; San Luis seems perfect!"

Ever since we started planning this trip, Maia has ended most every phone call by singing 'Meet me in San Lou-ie, Lou-ie,' and that's the way I pronounce it now (minus the singing). Jane cringes, and Kaela shudders so dramatically that her dangling earrings bat against her round cheeks.

"Sorry, was that wrong?" I ask.

"You committed a Cardinal Sin," Maia tells me with a wink.

"You're new, so you're allowed one error on this. It's pronounced San Lew-is," Kaela sounds out each syllable. "You can call it by the full name San Luis Obispo, or San Luis, or even just SLO. But *never* call it San Lou-ie. Seriously. You might get thrown out."

The others laugh, but Kaela looks deadly serious. Okay, noted. SLO—I like that. She says it like the opposite of fast, which definitely fits the restful pace that radiates here.

My terrible faux pas is quickly left behind and I find myself relaxing more than I have in months. The girls are so sweet and genuine, I feel like I've known them for years. And while they truly are great, I can't help another look around to find that dark hair and crooked smile that keep invading my thoughts.

But when I look over my shoulder, I see that the sky has been getting all gussied up for the evening's festivities. The sun is touching the horizon now, melting into the sea in bright golden waves. The sky around it is layered in watercolor strokes of pinks and oranges. The air itself has taken on an amber hue so saturated it seems like I should be able to smell it, or taste it; it's too much to take in with only one sense.

I fumble through my bag until I come up with the prize: my Canon Rebel. I wrestle the camera out of its case and toss everything else at Maia, tripping my way through the sand closer to the water. "Be right back," I shout over my shoulder. I weave my way through the crowd and begin shooting frames before I've bothered to stop walking. I've been dying to see the sun set over the Pacific, and I don't want to miss a second of it.

I take the standard shots, of course, the expected view of the horizon breaking the frame about a third of the way up, the painted sky filling out the rest of the picture. But when I have my fill of those, I let my more artistic side take over. I zoom in on a spot far out on the horizon, the water ablaze with golden light. A seagull diving through the tawny air gets the next shot. A couple hand-in-hand on the pier, simple silhouettes against a brilliant backdrop. Then a cloud formation that looks vaguely like a turtle. Another that resembles a dragon, pink and red and glorious.

A finger taps me on the shoulder, causing a little ripple of irritation to simmer through me. She knows I can't stop when I'm in the zone. "Just a sec, Mai," I tell her, capturing another shot of this incredible scene. "It lasts for such a short time, I can't afford to stop for a moment."

"There's no rush, I just didn't want to startle you," says Not Maia. I pause in mid-shutter-release, catching my breath and closing my eyes. Alex. I try to compose myself for a millisecond before I turn to face him. I give him my best smile and try to think of something clever to say.

"Ethan!" I greet him. Wait. Where did that come from? The smile freezes on his face. I expect him to look confused or maybe insulted that I've just called him the wrong name. But he doesn't look any of those things. He looks scared. Okay, whatever, I can fix this. I laugh, purposely letting my nerves take over for a moment. "I'm so sorry, that's wrong isn't it?" I hold a hand up to my face, allowing my very real embarrassment to shine through. "Alex, right?"

He visibly relaxes. "Right," he laughs with me but is still eyeing me cautiously.

"I'm sorry," I apologize again. "I've met so many new people today, I think my poor brain is on overload."

"I can understand that," he sympathizes, his manner easier now. "I was the new kid here not too long ago myself."

"Really? New? I mean, new area?" Crap! Breathe Rennie. Only a boy. "Are you new to the area then?" Better.

He shifts his weight and runs a hand through his dark hair, squinting in the sunset. "I moved here last fall, so I've been here for almost a year now. But since most of them grew up together, I still feel like the new kid sometimes."

"I understand. Well, I mean I understand second-hand. I mean, Maia. She went through the same thing when she moved here, too. But I guess you know that." Can I please sound a little bit lamer? Jeez!

"Oh right—Maia. I'm sure she's already made it clear that she's not my biggest fan." I take a breath to ask what that's about, but he glances away and continues on in a rush. "So anyway, I just wanted to see how your shoulder is holding up. I really am sorry about that. Is it doing okay?"

So I guess we're not talking about the Maia thing. I roll my shoulder around in the socket to test it out. I can't help a small wince as the dull pain spikes, and he's quick to respond.

He puts a hand out but stops just short of touching me. "May I?"

Wow. Such a gentleman. There's real concern in his face and I nod without hesitation. He steps in closer to me and lifts the short sleeve of my tee shirt carefully to inspect the injured site.

"Nice shirt, by the way." He gives me that crooked grin and my heart does a swan dive into my shoes.

I'm wearing one of my Nerd Shirts (as Maia calls them). This one is a soft celadon color with a drawing of the Cheshire Cat's smile hanging in the sky like a crescent moon, and below it, the words *That's no moon.*

"Let me guess," I say, trying to control my breathing with him standing this close to me. "You have a penchant for sci-fi films and comic books?"

He laughs, his focus still mostly on my shoulder, but that causes him to glance up at me. "I suppose you could put it that way."

I grin at him. "Good. Me too."

"It's starting to bruise already," he says quietly. Oh yeah, my shoulder. With a gentleness usually reserved for newborn kittens, he touches the darkening skin. Tingles radiate through my whole system and once again I find myself breathless, struggling to maintain an appearance of normalcy. I look over to watch what he's doing and find that he is mere inches away from me. In fact, without any effort at all I could lean over quite naturally and kiss that perfect mouth. The thought makes me blush but I don't move away. He's rolling my shoulder back and forth in the socket, but I'm feeling no pain. All I can concentrate on is that face so close to mine, the warmth of his hands on my arm, those beautiful full lips moving wordlessly mere inches from my own.

"Rennie?"

Okay, not wordlessly. I just wasn't listening. Crap. "Huh?" Quite the elocutionist I am. "I was thinking of, um, something else," I manage to get out.

He chuckles quietly. "Well I guess that means it doesn't hurt too badly then." He has no idea. "Still, I feel terrible. Let me at least get you some ice to put on it for a while, okay?" He turns to walk away, but to the surprise of us both, I reach out and stop him with a hand to his arm.

"Wait!"

He cocks his head to the side, waiting for me to finish whatever I was going to say. How cute that he thinks I had a plan before I opened my mouth. I look down and notice that I'm still holding my camera in one hand. "Sunset!" I blurt out. Then, less like a maniac, "I mean, the sunset's gonna be completely gone in a minute. Sit and watch it with me?" My heart is racing. Asking a guy to do anything is so totally out of the norm for me, I kinda feel like I might throw up. But in a good way.

"Sure, I'd like that." He smiles back at me, and those flutters swarm in the pit of my tummy again. Does he know how disarming that smile is?

I turn away and walk down the beach, breathing deliberately to calm myself and sit in the sand just a few feet from where the water is lapping up on the shore. He walks around to sit on the far side of me, shielding me from the light breeze.

"I've wanted to see the sun set over the Pacific for so long," I confide as we settle in. "I don't even know why. It just seems like one of those things everyone should see at least once, you know?"

He nods, taking in the scene with me. "I agree. It's something that gets taken for granted far too often. I mean, look at this." He gestures out at the horizon, the colors so saturated now that even the sand we're sitting on is blushing. "It's beautiful, it's right here at our doorstep, and not one of us is guaranteed that we'll get to see another."

I swallow hard, chasing away the thoughts that come up with that simple statement. "Yeah," I whisper, more to myself than to him.

His grey eyes are glowing silver with the dying light of the sun, and when he turns to look at me, I tuck a stray curl behind one ear and glance away.

"You must be quite a photographer," he says, shifting the mood deftly.

"What makes you say that?" I ask. "You haven't even seen the pictures yet."

"Your camera." He picks it up and looks it over. "Considering most people use their phones these days, I'm guessing you take this pretty seriously."

"True. It was a birthday gift." I let that rest for a moment and then glance up at him through my lashes. "From Charlie." I want to see if there's any reaction to casually throwing out a guy's name.

He flinches, just slightly and if I hadn't been watching for it I would have missed it, but that was an undeniable flinch. "Ah," he says in an annoyingly non-committal way. "Boyfriend?"

Shoot and score. I give him a smile, a token of reward for playing my game. "Aunt," I clarify for him, and he returns the smile. Is that relief in his eyes or wishful thinking on my part?

"Aunt Charlie?" He laughs. Definitely relief.

"Yeah, well Charlene really. But nobody calls her that—ever."

"Noted. She must like you an awful lot to give you a gift like this," he says, turning the camera over in his hands before setting it carefully next to me.

"She does. I mean, she's not like a normal *aunt* aunt like people think about when they say *aunt*, like I-only-see-her-at-Christmas kind of aunt." Stop saying Aunt! "I mean, I've lived with her my whole life. Well not my *whole* life, but ever since my dad died. My mom couldn't handle the loss and kind of flipped out. She dropped me and my sister Claire off at Aunt Charlie's, and she's raised us ever since." He looks at me with understanding, as though he's waiting for me to continue. "Sorry," I say, playing with the ring on my forefinger. "Those are major events in my life, you'd think I'd tell them better."

The sun has completed its exit and the night wind is picking up. I wrap my arms around myself and pull my knees in closer.

"There's no wrong way to tell a story," he says kindly. "Besides, I understand what it's like. I... um..."

He's staring just past my shoulder, back to where everyone else is standing near the successfully created (and now fully functioning) bonfire. I can't tell what specifically has his attention, but there's no mistaking the look of panic that just crossed his face. I watch as a word passes nearly soundlessly across his lips. I can't be sure, but it looks like *Enforcers.*

"Is everything all right?"

"Uh… yeah." His eyes volley back and forth between me and the bonfire. "Rennie? I realize that I've known you for all of fifteen minutes, and some of those were spent in pain that was due entirely to my own carelessness, but I need to ask you something that I wouldn't normally be asking at this stage in the game." The change in his demeanor is so sudden and so dramatic that I have to wonder for a moment if he's joking. But this doesn't feel like a joke.

"Okay…"

He shifts to his feet but stays squatting down so he's eye to eye with me, and he reaches out a hand to help me up. "Will you trust me?"

I hear Maia's warning reverberate in my head, but I take his hand without a second thought. "Yes."

He flashes me that grin I love. "Good. Then run."

Chapter Three

*W*hen I was eleven, I fell out of a tree in Maia's backyard and broke

my leg. We spent the whole rest of the summer cooped up in my house,

which could have been awful, but then we discovered *Alias.* And then *24.*

Aunt Charlie had the first few seasons on DVD (everything that was out

at the time) and our lives were forever altered. Obviously, it was our

destiny to be secret agents and save the world. I even came up with a

game involving stickers and the shoulders of strangers so we could

practice the fine art of sneaking up on people. This, however, feels more

like a spy game than that game ever has.

I run after Alex, dashing toward a rocky cliff wall several yards away.

I'm trying to move with some semblance of grace and assurance, but the sand is determined to make me look more like a drunken ostrich. I look towards the bonfire to see what it is that spooked him, but the only thing that seems even remotely out of the ordinary is the sight of two men wearing brown leather jackets and talking to a bunch of the guys. They don't seem particularly scary to me, but then again, maybe it's not them he's running from.

The rock wall stretches out in front of me, white and grey and unclimbably tall, but Alex is gone. A little prickle of fear starts to climb up my spine. Is there really some unknown danger out here and he just left me? A hand reaches out from what I thought was solid rock and grabs my arm. I stifle a cry of surprise as Alex yanks me into a small crevice, just big enough for the two of us to hide out of sight. My camera swings to the ground, (hopefully) landing safely on the soft sand at our feet.

He puts a finger to my lips and makes a shushing noise with his own. The space is so small that our bodies are pressed together, making me extremely aware of every single flaw I have. Can he tell that my ears stick out too far, or that my hips are too curvy?

I lean back as far as I can, but the rock stops me before I can put even a full inch between us. It's dark, lit only by the fading light from the opening, and the damp air makes it feel about twenty degrees colder.

More uncomfortable than that, however, is the little thread of fear that's trying to wriggle its way into my chest. I've never liked tight spaces, even when I was a kid. The first nightmare I ever remember having taught me that. As nerve-wracking as it is being this close to a guy I just met, there's something oddly comforting in it as well. Almost familiar.

"Sorry for dragging you into this," Alex whispers, so close his breath moves my hair. I'm not sure if he means the situation or the rocky crevice, but I don't open my mouth to ask. "Did you see anyone coming this way?"

"You mean the guys with the jackets?"

His eyes meet mine in a flash. "You did see them."

I nod. "Yeah, but they were only talking to some people at the bonfire. I didn't see them look over here."

"That's good news." He runs a hand through his hair, his elbow brushing against my arm. I try to disguise my shiver as a result of the cold. "I've just… I've never seen them here before."

"Who are they?"

"Would you believe me if I told you I owed them money?"

"Probably not."

"Too bad. That would have been a much easier explanation."

I try to remember the word I heard him mutter on the beach. "Enforcers."

His eyebrows climb into his hair and he inhales sharply. "How do you know that?" His eyes narrow, studying me more closely in the dim light. "Are you... do you know them?"

I don't know why this feels like a test. "No, I just heard you say it earlier. Are they really that dangerous? Should we call the cops?"

He's still studying me, like he's not sure if I passed that test or not. "We don't need to call anyone," he says finally. "I don't think they'd actually do anything here. I'm not even sure if they could."

He shifts slightly so that there's a breath of air between us and inches his head around the corner again. I have no idea what to do with my hands.

"I can only imagine what you must be thinking of me right now," he says. "Of this. Look, just so you know, I've been raised almost exclusively by my mom and I have the highest respect for women. I would never... I mean, even on a first date I normally wouldn't be this—what?"

I stop giggling before fully realizing that I'd started. "Sorry. I'm just glad to hear it."

"To hear what?"

"Well, being pulled in here is one thing, it may have even been chivalrous if there really is some danger out there, but having to go back to Maia and tell her she was right about you? Now that would have been unbearable."

He laughs, a warm comforting sound, like raindrops hitting a window pane. "Yeah, we can't have that." He looks over his shoulder, twisting so that he can see out of the narrow opening.

"Alex, I..."

He stops my words with a finger to my lips again, but only for a moment. His eyes widening, he seems to realize what he's done and draws the finger to his own mouth instead. "I think I hear someone," he whispers.

I strain to hear anything but my own heartbeat, but all that's out there is the sound of the waves sweeping up onto the shore and an occasional seagull. Even the music and laughter from the bonfire is out of range.

And then I hear them.

"He was supposed to be here." His voice is deep and dangerous and much too close. It makes my breath stop.

"It's not the first time we've had a faulty lead, and I'm sure it won't be the last." A less menacing voice, but I still wouldn't invite him in for cookies.

"Well, what now? Keep looking around like idiots? Asking children for their help?"

"What choice do we have?" After a moment of silence, he asks, "Do you really believe there's a long lost Heir out here somewhere?"

"You've heard the legend."

"Don't remind me. It's days like this I wish I'd never even heard of the legend."

Deep Voice lets out a long low whistle. "Talk like that will get you fired. Or hanged."

"Is there a difference?"

Deep Voice lets out a bark of laughter, their voices already fading into the distance as they pass us by. "I'm going to head into town for a little bit and have another look around."

"Another look around, huh?"

"Yeah. Maybe we'll catch a break and find that they're hiding at the bar."

We wait in silence for another few moments, but there's nothing more. When I see him relax, I figure it's okay to whisper again.

"Enforcers, Heir, legend… you want to tell me what's going on?"

He licks his lips and runs a hand over his hair again. "I don't want to get you involved in this."

"I'm hiding in a cave half the size of a broom closet with a boy I just met, and since you seem to think they're looking for you and here I am hiding with you, it kinda sounds like I'm already involved."

He's quiet for long enough that I question whether or not he'll answer at all. My mind uses the momentary silence to transition from *oh no someone's coming to get us* to *oh wow he smells really good.* A mixture of suntan lotion, fresh cut grass, and something spicy and unexpected— cloves maybe? I'm not sure, but it's intoxicating. Those same perfect lips that taunted me while he was checking on my shoulder are even closer now, his hair perfectly mussed, his bent knee resting against my thigh in the close, dark space.

Finally, he responds with a sigh. "It's a long story. And yes, I know that sounds like a cop-out, but it really is too much to go into right now. But as strange as this is, I actually hope I get to tell you sometime."

"If this was the movie version, we'd be making out right now."

His eyes widen and a startled laugh comes out of him, more like a snort, which is when I realize that I said that out loud.

"Not that I want to," I clarify, mortification making my voice speed up like a cartoon. "I mean, not that I *don't* want to, but I don't. I shouldn't. *We* shouldn't, but I never have and I don't think that now is a good time to start, I mean you're cute, *really* cute, and you smell so good. But I just meant that in movies, you know movies? When there's a couple and they have to hide and they always have to pretend to make out so that the bad guys will go past them and not notice because, you know, who wants to look too closely at people making out, right? And then they get away. Usually. In movies." I study the rise and fall of his chest, unable to look him in the eye, and I'm suddenly very grateful for the darkness surrounding us. At least there's a chance he can't see how red my cheeks are.

"I always thought it was because it hid their faces."

I glance up at him, and it's hard to see in the darkness, but it looks like he's genuinely interested in the conversation, and not making fun of me.

"You know," he continues, "because their faces are together, so their identities are more obscured."

"Huh," I muse. "That makes sense. I'd never thought about that."

"Either way, I think we're probably safe without that trick. Sounds like they're gone. And since I can't really see anything, we're not gonna know if it's safe unless we just go for it."

I nod, and he squeezes my arms in what I think is supposed to be an encouraging gesture.

"I'll go first," he says. "It's me they're after, anyway."

I put a hand to his chest to stop him, but withdraw it immediately. It feels too familiar, and much too bold for me. What is wrong with me? "That's exactly why I should be first. I'll be able to see if it's safe and you won't have to risk being recognized."

A little crease appears between his eyebrows, and it makes me smile to realize he's concerned about me.

I shrug. "Don't worry. No matter who is or isn't out there, I'm a stranger here." Trying to act much more confident than I feel, I move out of the safety of our hiding place. I look back at him over my shoulder as I step into the twilight. "I'll be fine."

And then I look up, and see how very wrong I was.

Chapter Four

I take a deep breath and a quick glance over my shoulder to make sure that Alex is still concealed. "Hey Maia," I greet her as she heads towards me, chestnut waves bouncing on her shoulders and a confused look on her face.

"Where did you go? I thought you were taking pictures of the sunset."

Relief feels like a balloon rising in my chest. Yes, the sunset. I totally have an out. "Right! I was, and it was really amazing. Very orange. And you know, bright. And then not."

She cocks her head at me, turquoise eyes scrunching up at the corners. I'm a terrible liar, and it's even worse when I'm trying to lie to Maia.

"Oh kaaaaay," she drags it out so it's two separate words. "And you're lying to me because...?"

I shrug pathetically and stumble over a few "Well I" and "You see"s, but she's still studying me.

"Where is your camera?"

I freeze, hearing nothing but an echo in the vast expanse that used to be my brain. "My camera?"

She nods, arms folding slowly over her chest. "Your camera. You know, the Rebel. The one from Aunt Charlie that you never let out of your sight?"

"Oh. My *camera.* Yeah, I thought you said, um, it's right over..." I start to point down toward the shoreline to stall a bit and draw her attention away, but then I see movement over my shoulder. It's my camera, dangling by the strap from a body-less hand coming out of the rock. "Oh. Here it is."

Alex steps out of hiding, attempting to appear casual. "Maia, nice to see you, as always," he offers pleasantly.

Maia takes a moment to process what she's seeing, wrapping her arms tighter around herself. Her lips press together into a thin line, holding back a wide variety of imaginative insults I'm sure. Maia and I don't fight often, but I recognize the signs and brace myself for the oncoming storm.

"Are you all right?" she whispers. Her words and tone are so contrary to what I expected to come out of her mouth, I can't quite form a response. In the silence, she looks me up and down and I see the moment her eyes catch on my shoulder. The bruise.

My hands flutter as though I should cover it up, but I stop myself. That's silly. She was there for the driftwood incident; I have nothing to hide.

"Yeah, of course," I reply, glancing at Alex for some kind of an explanation of her odd behavior, but he's not looking at me. His jaw is clenched tight and he and Maia are having some kind of staring contest.

"If he did anything—"

"No!" I interrupt before she can finish that alarming thought. "I'm fine. He's fine. Everything is perfectly fine."

"Uh huh," she mutters, and swings her attention back to me. "Well good. In that case, Ren, what I was saying is that I've been wondering where you'd run off to because I want to introduce you to some of those cute guys I was telling you about."

Alex nods in understanding. "Subtlety is an art, Maia." He hands me my camera and I sling the strap over one shoulder. "It was great talking with you, Rennie. I'll see you again soon, I hope." He squeezes my hand and calmly walks back towards the bonfire.

I watch him walk away before turning to face the chilly wrath of my best friend. And she doesn't disappoint.

"I thought you were going to stay away from him," she starts in full-on accusation mode.

"I never said that. *You* decided that I should, but I never agreed to anything."

"Well you didn't give me much of a chance to tell you my side of things before you let him make up your mind, did you? What were you guys doing in there anyway, or do I even have to ask?"

"Oh please, you know me better than that. We were only talking." On the rare occasions we do argue, my usual M.O. is to backpedal and apologize as soon as possible just to make the yelling stop. But I can still see Alex's retreating figure behind her, and a little part of me wants to scream that she's being ridiculous. A bigger part of me wants to follow after him. With a sigh, I ignore both parts and instead choose the path of least resistance. "You're right, Mai. I did imply I would hear you out.

You're my best friend, and I owe you that." She visibly relaxes, but I can't resist adding in a pitch on Alex's behalf. "To be fair though, he only came over to see how my shoulder is doing. It was actually very sweet."

"Yeah, real sweet considering he's the one who injured you in the first place. Oh, and you know where I always like to look at people's bruised shoulders? In dark caves." She's clearly not willing to give him an inch on this, but that was kinda funny.

I let out a small giggle, and she looks startled by the sudden change. But then her mouth twitches. And then we're both laughing together, because that's what we do.

"So..." I know what will turn her back to my side. "Who are these wonderful guys you're just dying to introduce me to?" I ask it with a sly grin, already knowing the answer.

She responds with the same grin. "That was a little mean of me, wasn't it?" She giggles at her own evilness and starts heading back towards the girls. "Okay, I *may* have overstated it a tad, but you really should meet some of them. You might find that summer fling we were talking about."

Funny. I thought I just did that.

Chapter Five

I sink down onto the blanket between Jane and Maia, pulling a bit of it over my toes to help keep the chill at bay. I inch closer to the fire. Yes, the night is cooler now that the sun has gone down, but I can't help but think that some of my shivers are from all of the eery things going on tonight.

When the girls begin a debate over which of two actors I couldn't care less about is hotter, I take the opportunity to nudge Maia.

"Hey," I whisper. "When I was gone earlier, there were two guys over here. I couldn't see them very well, but it looked like they were wearing leather jackets maybe. Did you see them?"

"Yeah, I saw them. They were kinda creepy."

"Did they talk to you? Do you know why they were here?"

She shrugs and twirls a strand of hair around her finger. "No, they were keeping mostly to the guys building the fire. There are some areas of the beach where you can't build bonfires, and I thought they might tell us to move. But then they just left, so I guess everything was all right. Why?"

I know better than to bring up Alex's name again so soon. "Just curious. They looked out of place, that's all."

She pauses and looks me over, trying to detect any untruth in my answer I'm sure. But before she can say anything else, Ember jumps in.

"You're talking about those men in the leather, aren't you?"

My pulse increases when I realize she's been listening. But that's silly; I haven't done anything wrong. "Yeah. I was just curious what they wanted."

Ember scratches her cheek, her dark skin glowing in the firelight. "I didn't talk to them myself, but Violet overheard them. She said they were asking some of the guys if they knew of a certain boy. Oh, what was that name? It was... Adam. Or Aaron. No, maybe Evan?"

"Ethan," I whisper.

"That's it," Ember agrees with a nod. "I don't know anyone called

Ethan. No one else seemed to either, so they left."

The chill is deeper now, settling into my bones and raising the tiny hairs on my arms. That name. I don't know anyone called Ethan either. At least, not when I'm awake. The only one I know is in my dreams. He saves me when I need it, comforts me when the dreams become too much, helps me to hold back the darkness and kisses away my fears. But he's not real.

So why are they looking for him?

Okay, Rennie, get a grip. Obviously, it's a coincidence. There are lots of guys with that name. I force myself to breathe normally, to act normally. Everything is fine.

As usual, it turns out my fears were unfounded. All that anxiety about meeting Maia's new friends, when in fact, they're pretty fantastic. I love the girls already, and quite happily, most of the others at the beach tonight are Maia's theatre friends. I've always been a Theatre Geek By

Association because of Maia, but being a geek in my own right, I fit right in. I say that with love, by the way. I own my geekdom. I'm perfectly content to discuss in great detail the pros and cons of the new Doctor versus the last Doctor, who would win in a battle between Dumbledore and Gandalf, how long of a mourning period was appropriate when we lost Wash, and whether or not Han shot first. So to find myself amidst a group of people happily discussing their own passions feels quite natural. It's like landing in a foreign country and discovering that by some miracle you speak the language.

I've already met more people than I'll ever be able to remember. Davin, the short blond boy that Jane may or may not have a crush on; Naomi, a doe-eyed brunette with an impossibly tiny waist; Violet, a beautiful Asian girl with a streak of purple in her dark hair; Morgan, a cute bubbly blonde with a bottle-cap nose and pink-framed glasses... I really am trying to file away all the names and faces in my jet-lagged brain, but for the most part they all fall into two categories: Alex and Not Alex. And unfortunately, the scales are greatly tipped to the Not Alex side.

So when a chill sets in and everyone huddles close to the fire, I can't help but seek out that dark hair and heart-stopping smile. I search each face glowing in the orange-hued light. Burning embers flit off into the darkness like the tiny fireflies I love so much back home. But no Alex.

Someone brings out a guitar and begins to play on the other side of the fire. It's a playful melody that I don't recognize, but several people cheer and start to sing along like we're in one of those old Elvis movies. Naturally, it would be the theatre crowd who feels the need to make life into a musical. No wonder Maia likes these people—she fits right in.

But for me, all I want right now is to find somewhere quiet so I can attempt to figure out some of the odd things that have happened to me today. Will my whole summer be like this? Full of frightening visions and mysterious leather-clad strangers and gorgeous flirting boys? Funny how that last item on the list seems enough to nullify the first two.

"You know," Ember says, addressing the girls and giving me a sly grin, "it occurs to me that Rennie is part of our inner circle now. Isn't it our sacred obligation as her new friends to make sure she has the best summer ever?"

"Yeah, of course," Jane responds, confusion knitting her brow.

"Well, there's only so much that *we* can do," Ember continues in a leading tone. "And therefore…" she gestures widely to the sea of people milling around us.

Kaela raises both arms in the air and exclaims, "Boys!"

"Oooo! Who should we set up with Rennie?" Jane rubs her hands together.

The question is like blood in the water and my new sharky friends are up on their knees now, all chattering at once, practically drooling as they scope out the selection across the way.

"What about Rick?"

"Too much of a jock. How about Lucas?"

"Nah, too weird. Andy?"

"Cute, but hello, wrong sandbox. Maybe Josh?"

"I think Rennie would like a guy with at least half a brain. What about Davin?"

"Wait, I think I might still like him! How about Seth?"

"Not. Funny." That's Maia, of course.

I'm not opposed to a "summer fling" as Maia put it, and I'm sure this would have been a fun game under different circumstances. But right now the possibility of Alex is much too alive in my brain to entertain the thought of someone else. True, I still know very little about him, and he could end up being not my type at all. Maybe once I get to know him, he's really a total jerk, or an arrogant snob. Maybe he kicks puppies. Maybe he has a girlfriend. Or maybe he's single and perfect and just waiting for someone like me to come along. But the point is: I'm not going to find out any of those things by being set up with someone else!

I shoot a desperate look to Maia, but she's too busy trying to select my soulmate. "Don't worry, Ren, there are lots of great options."

I have to wonder why all of them are still single if that's the case, but I keep my mouth shut.

"Speaking of Seth, where has he been all night?" Jane asks, still scanning the crowd.

"Yeah," Kaela throws in. "I thought by now you'd be snuggled up to him, all like 'Oh Sethy, it's so very cold out here! How ever will you keep me warm?'" She bats her eyes and raises her voice an octave in a truly terrible impression of Maia.

"Funny," Maia deadpans. "It's a good question though. I'll go find him. You are not leaving here tonight without meeting him," she tells me, then skips off into the shadows.

"Okay, back to business," Ember says. "Who might be Rennie's type?"

Kaela clasps her hands together and sighs dreamily. "This is going to be so great! It's the perfect first meeting. The sun is down, the bonfire is crackling away; it's so romantic! I bet it'll be love at first sight."

"You may have seen one too many Disney movies, Kae," Ember chides. "I'm cutting you off."

Love at first sight. There it is again. But now, instead of wanting to roll my eyes, I wonder if there's a way I could turn this to my favor and work Alex into their plans. I'm just working up the courage to ask them for their take on him when Jane stops all conversation with her hands out in front of her.

"Wait you guys, we are so dumb. What about Levi?"

"What about me?" says the voice behind us. My stomach does a small flip at the distinct maleness of the voice, but settles down quickly when I realize it's not Alex.

"Hey!" Ember greets him with a bright smile. "Well, speak of the Levi."

"You actor types are always on cue, aren't you?" Kaela teases.

"Well, I do try," he teases back before focusing on me. "Rennie, right?"

I nod, looking up at him. And up and up. Man, he's tall! And cute in a toothpaste ad kind of way. He has sandy blond hair and mossy green eyes. He looks like he's probably used the word *summer* as a verb and could easily fit into a name like Skip or Chet. "Mind if I sit?" he asks.

I don't miss the wink-wink-nudge-nudge going on between Ember and Kaela as I respond with a "Sure" and a pat on the blanket. He seats himself beside me, tanned legs stretched out in front of him.

"I'm Levi," he says, giving me a sheepish grin. "Levi Hart. Maia said she was going to come over and introduce us, but I decided not to wait. I hope that's okay."

"Sure," I say again. Great start yet again there, Rennie.

"She's told me so much about you, I feel like I should know you already," he continues.

I can't help but stare now. There is something oddly familiar about him. Suddenly it dawns on me. "Oh! You're Levi!"

He looks surprised for a moment, then laughs at my Captain Obvious declaration.

"No, I mean, you're the one from the play—Maia's co-star. You were in *Cabaret* with her!" I'm feeling very proud of myself for putting these pieces together.

"Guilty as charged," he smiles, giving a little half-bow. "Good memory, that was like two months ago." He sounds impressed, maybe even flattered. I guess I shouldn't tell him that I don't even remember his character's name, only that he was the one who's not the Emcee.

"For you it was months ago," I correct him. "But Maia sent me the DVD. I had a big viewing party with all of our PA friends just last week. We're all used to her being the star of every production, so it was hard not to get to see her in person, but we did the best we could."

"Well, it's good to finally meet you in person," he continues. "Not a day of rehearsal went by that I didn't get to hear some story about how fabulous you are and how much she missed you and how things would be so much more fun if only you were here." He's sing-songing this in a very Maia way, tilting his head back and forth with each new item on the list.

"Yikes," I cringe. "That's a lot to live up to."

"Don't worry about it. You're doing just fine." He smiles at me, and bumps his shoulder into mine. The sore one, naturally. "So how do you like our little town so far?"

"Well the beach is great, but other than that I haven't seen much. I got off the plane and Maia brought me directly here."

"Oh good. So you've seen our massive international airport. What did you think?"

"Very nice. You know, I'd never actually seen an airport with only one terminal before. And did you know there's a sign hanging on the wall that says the maximum capacity is 326? For the *entire airport*?"

He laughs, mouth open so I can see all the way to his back teeth. I like that he's so easy to talk to. "No, I didn't know that. But I'm not surprised." He looks me up and down for a moment, and I find myself self-consciously tucking a strand of hair behind my ear. "I have to be headed out soon, but I'm glad I got to meet you before I leave."

"I'm glad, too," I tell him, and I find that I mean it; he really is cute. I hear Jane giggle behind us and I make a concerted effort not to glare at her.

"You know, I was thinking. I'm gonna be downtown tomorrow running some errands for my mom, and I was hoping you might want to meet up with me for some coffee or something when I'm done. Maybe around 3:30?"

I hesitate to make sure there's no punchline. Did he really just ask me out? "Um, yeah, that sounds like fun. I'm sure Maia won't mind losing me for a while." I wait for the butterflies to hit me, but they don't show up. Maybe that's not such a bad thing. It might be nice not to be an idiot around a guy for a change.

"Okay, good!" he replies. "There's a great coffee place on Monterey Street called Outspoken. I think you'll like it. I could get you directions, or..."

"We'll get her there, don't worry," Ember throws in from behind us, making Levi jump. I guess he hadn't realized how closely we were being monitored.

"Okay then," he says with finality. "I guess I'll see you tomorrow at 3:30."

"3:30," I confirm, nodding.

"See you then." He stands and walks away, toward the parking lot. He barely gets out of earshot before the celebration begins.

"We are so good. Insert high five right here." Kaela holds up her hand and is met with the others swinging in her general vicinity, much more interested in the overall celebration than the aim.

"What are you going to wear?"

"Where is Maia? She's going to flip!"

"He didn't waste any time, did he?"

"He must really like you!"

"Now we absolutely must go get manicures tomorrow!"

"Okay, seriously… what are you going to wear?"

Everybody talking over one another is becoming the norm with these girls, so I just sit back and let it happen. I can count on one hand the number of actual dates I've been on, and still have three fingers left over. Aunt Charlie wouldn't even let me think about dating until I was sixteen, which is not even a year ago. And because I'm usually pretty awkward around guys I like, I'm not all that ask-out-able. So to be asked out by someone that good looking, on my very first night here? I'd say that is an excellent sign for the summer ahead of me.

Before I can answer even one of the girls' questions, Maia returns with Seth in tow. "What did I miss?" she asks.

"Levi asked out Rennie!" Kaela responds in a register that ensures all the dogs in the immediate area are now in the know.

Maia looks triumphant. "Already? Wow, I knew he'd be into you," she says with a grin.

I shrug. "It's only for coffee tomorrow."

"That's a good start," she insists. "This is so perfect; he's a really great guy." She looks over her shoulder to where Seth is standing, and grabs his hand to pull him forward. "Speaking of great guys..." she gushes, "Rennie, this is Seth. Seth, this is Rennie, the one I've told you so much about."

"Hi Rennie," he says, and puts his hand forward to shake mine. The gesture seems oddly formal, but I accept it as he continues. "It's good to meet you. Maia talks about you all the time."

"Yeah, I'm hearing that a lot tonight," I laugh. "I've heard a lot about you, too. In fact, just the other day she was telling me about the time—"

Maia hits my arm teasingly. "Rennie! You can't repeat what was told in strictest girl talk!"

"Oh right, what was I thinking? Sorry ... Seth, was it? Never heard of you."

Maia grins. "Much better."

Seth is still holding onto my hand and looking at me more intently than feels appropriate for meeting my best friend's whatever-he-is. I disentangle it from his with a weak smile, and he shakes his head like he's clearing his thoughts and smiles back.

"Sorry. Guess I'm more tired than I thought I was. I was up all night last night playing the new Halo with the guys."

Tired? That look said a lot of things to me. 'Tired' wasn't one of them.

Maia shakes her head at him. "Video games? Really? Do you have to be such a stereotype?"

"Oh right," he snorts. "Says the rich girl with 500 pairs of shoes."

"We're not rich, and it's only 87 pairs. Shows what you know." Maia turns to me. "Can you believe this guy? Wasting a perfectly good night indoors playing video games, when he could have taken me out instead." She gives him one of her signature winks.

"Actually, Halo is pretty awesome," I answer, rubbing at the headache forming behind the bridge of my nose.

Kaela gasps, Ember and Jane giggle, and Seth laughs out loud. But it's Maia's sudden pout that makes me realize my mistake.

"And what I mean by that is… Halo is pretty awesome, but *not* as awesome as going out with Maia would have been."

"Nice save," Maia mutters.

"I knew I was going to like you," Seth says through his laughter.

I run a hand through my wind-blown hair, trying to regain my composure. What sane girl would ever side with some random guy over her best friend? I blame the jet lag.

"So you're from Wisconsin, huh?" Seth asks me.

"Pennsylvania," I correct. "Same as Maia."

"Oh. Is there a difference?" He smirks like he's very proud of his little joke, and all the girls giggle.

Am I the only one who doesn't find him funny? For Maia's sake, I smile and attempt a graceful subject change. "It seems like everyone here is involved in theatre somehow. Were you in *Cabaret* with Maia too?" I don't know why I feel the need to keep bringing up her name. Something in the way he's looking at me is making a Red Alert go off in my head.

"Nah, that's not really my scene. I helped build the sets for some extra credit to help out my fine arts requirement, but I probably won't do that again." He leans forward, like he's about to tell me a secret. "Too many freaks," he half-whispers.

Maia hits him on the shoulder. "Hey!" she protests. "You know you had a good time. Besides, you got to spend all that time with me." She leans into him and slips a willowy arm around his waist.

He smirks at her, running a hand through his overly gelled hair. "Yeah,

I suppose I didn't hate that."

Maia giggles like that was funny, but it makes me bristle. I've seen them together for only a few minutes and I already don't like it. I take a deep breath and exhale slowly. She often chooses guys that I wouldn't personally go for, but it's not like her to choose a full-on creeper. It must be my long day catching up with me, and it's throwing off my perspective. It's not Seth's fault that I have a big old headache coming on, and it's not his fault that I've been up since 5am to get here. And it's certainly not his fault that I'm getting annoyed at the constant lack of Alex tonight.

So what is it that's bothering me about him? Okay, my brain is on overload, so let it rest. Word association then. Clear the mind and think *Seth*. Only one word floats back to me: *Maia's*. Not what I expected, but I suppose it makes sense. A reminder from my subconscious that no matter what I'm feeling, she likes him and he's worth giving a chance. Fine. So I smile and let it go.

The six of us are still chatting a little while later (Maia hanging a little sickeningly on Seth's every word) when a voice calls from the parking lot. "Garrison! You coming with us or what? You owe me a rematch, and you're not getting out of it that easily!"

Seth yells back in return, "Coming! Just hang on!" Turning to us, he gives a little salute and says, "Sorry ladies. The Master Chief needs my help to save the universe." Maia is ready to protest, but he leans over and kisses her cheek. "See you later, gorgeous," he purrs, effectively quelling any objection she was about to raise.

In spite of my misgivings about him I can't help but smile. She looks so happy, how can I not be happy for her?

She watches him walk away, then closes her eyes with a sigh. "And that," she says to me, eyes still closed contentedly, "is Seth."

I'm saved from having to make a direct comment on my opinion of him by Kaela jumping in. "You are so cute together! Why aren't you guys official yet?"

"I wish I knew," Maia answers, a trace of sadness in her voice.

"He'll come around," Jane says reassuringly.

"He better had," Ember agrees, patting Maia's arm.

I get the idea that this is not the first time this exact conversation has taken place, and they all seem to have their roles down.

"He will," Maia declares, shaking off her doubts with determination. "How can he possibly resist little ol' me?" We all giggle, and I'm glad to see that sparkle back in her eye. It's not like her to moon over a guy like that. "But we'll have plenty of time to talk about me and Seth," she says. "First things first—Levi asked you out already? Tell. Me. Everything."

Chapter Six

*T*he moon sits high in the sky, cradled in a nest of silver clouds by the

time we're headed back to Maia's house. My bare feet are resting on the

dashboard, toes tapping along with The Band Perry. I watch the ocean

for as long as possible out the window, then the side-view mirror until it

disappears. I already can't wait to get back to it.

Maia is going over our to-do list to accomplish before my date with

Levi tomorrow, and although I'm trying really hard to concentrate, my

day has finally caught up with me. Between the lull of the road and the

familiar sound of Maia's voice, I find myself starting to doze off.

It's the quiet that awakens me. There's no sound of the road or of

Maia, and as my eyes flutter open, I find that the reason for that would be the very distinct lack of both. I'm no longer in the Jeep. In fact, there's no sign of anything remotely road-like at all.

I'm sitting on the ground, cold rock and coarse sand beneath me. My eyes are adjusting to the darkness as I run my hand up the damp rock behind me. It extends far beyond my reach, stretching into blackness high above. A cave. The air is chilly and smells heavy with the ocean, like seaweed. Somewhere in the distance I can hear water dripping, and out beyond that the intermittent wwhhhsssshhhh of the tide rolling in and out. Something stirs in my sleepy brain. I was just at the beach with Maia, but we left. Didn't we? Is this another vision? It feels different somehow.

I get to my feet, clumsy on the damp rock. The ambient light grows brighter to my left and I head towards it. As I get closer, I can see that there's a wide space overhead that's open to the night sky. The moon shines in boldly, unafraid of the shadows. I wish I could say the same.

The cave twists and turns in both directions from where I stand in my safe patch of light. Indecision builds like a storm in my chest. I can pick a direction and hope that my instincts will lead me to an exit, or I can stay where I am and hope either someone comes to find me, or I wake up.

The thought swells into reality and I grasp at it. That's right, this is a *dream*. I've had this one before, so I know how to get out of it. Okay. Good. With new resolution, I turn to my left and head into the darkened corners. I remember now that it's never truly pitch dark, that ambient light will leak in from the holes above all the way to my destination. I can't quite remember where that is at the moment, but the memory that I've done this before comforts me enough to keep moving forward. I just need to keep moving 'til I hear the voices.

The whispers start in the distance, vague and unintelligible. The corridor of the cave becomes a larger cavern with two different paths. I know instinctively—the way you do in dreams—that the one to the far left will lead me outside to the beach. But the voices come from my right and I choose that direction without hesitation. As I move farther down the path, the voices get more distinct and I can pick out disconnected words and phrases echoing back to me. "She doesn't know..." "...how could you..." "...not ready..."

Both voices are male, but they're too echo-y to identify the speakers. Something in my heart leads me forward though, and I know that at the end of my path I will find Ethan. The thought makes me move faster, my bare feet stumbling on the shifting sand, my heart pounding in anticipation.

Finally, I come to a large room. The grey rock is rounded at the far end, curving up from floor to ceiling, creating a dead end. The two men are arguing about something, but they stop when I enter, much more surprised to see me than I am to see them.

I'm instantly drawn to Ethan, but something holds me back. There's a dense feeling of conflict, and I know that he's upset without knowing why. He's comforted me so many times when I've been afraid in this place, my only instinct is to do the same for him now. I reach my hand out to him.

"Ethan," I speak his name aloud, and it's as if that single word starts a maelstrom. The movement quickens in the small space, everything happening in a blur around me. There's a stone bench and an open book; a sudden, deliberate movement towards it fills me with both fear and a sadness I don't completely understand. I will my feet to move me forward, but they refuse. Everything seems to be in fast forward except for me, agonizingly rooted to my spot. There's a blinding flash of green light and I'm left alone in the cave with just one man, his laughter echoing all around us.

I'm jolted awake. For real this time, but I dig my nails into the palm of my hand to make sure. Yep. That definitely hurts.

I'm back in the Jeep with Maia and she's still talking about plans for tomorrow with Levi. I guess I was only out for a minute or two and she didn't notice. Not surprising, really. When she gets going, she can monologue for a good half hour without needing more than an occasional "uh huh" to keep her fueled. It's an attribute I'm very grateful for at the moment.

True to form, the music has transitioned to Beyoncé. (You never know what's coming next on Maia's mixed CDs. It could just as easily have been Michael Bublé or Imagine Dragons. But seriously, how did that not wake me up?) I lean my head back and try to shake the creepy, helpless feeling that comes after that dream. It's one of the recurring nightmares that have been plaguing me since January. There are no monsters following me, or zombies trying to chew on my brain, or weeping angels waiting to get me in the blink of an eye. Still, that terrible engulfing uselessness certainly meets the criteria for "nightmare" in my book. I know that in a few minutes, it will fade and I will be left with just a vague ickiness. I only have to be patient.

Having Maia here definitely helps. I look over at her and smile to myself, already feeling safer in her familiar presence.

She looks over at me and smiles back. "So what do you think? Sound good?"

I have no idea what she's said, but I do know one thing—whatever idea it is came from my best friend. "Yep," I tell her. "Sounds great."

Chapter Seven

*W*hen we get back to Maia's, she helps me lug my ginormous suitcase
out of the Jeep, and we wheel it as quietly as possible through the
wrought-iron gate, over the terra cotta tiled courtyard, and finally inside
the house, closing the heavy wooden door behind us. I'm too tired to
notice anything but a barrage of white. All the lights are off except for
the one just inside the door, and I still feel like I need to squint.

Thankfully, my room is just past the entryway and as we step inside,
Maia announces quietly, "This is your room!" and makes a gesture as
though showcasing a grand prize. And really, it kind of feels that way.

There's a large window to the left, blinds and gauzy white curtains
covering it for the night. Above that is another rounded half-circle

window—a transom I think you call that—and below it is a window seat that looks like a fantastic place to get lost in a good book. There's a queen-sized bed against the wall to our right, with a desk next to it on the far side and a night stand on the side closer to the door. In the corner by the window is one of those stand-up full length mirrors like they always show in old Victorian houses. I've always wanted one of those. The mirror, not the creepy old house. The room is all white with touches of a fresh leafy green, and so much cozier than I dreamed I'd find in a house run by Mrs. Cantrell.

"Oh Maia! It's so pretty; I love it." I walk around the bed, making a tactile connection with everything so it feels more like it could be mine. At least for the summer.

She points to the door in the corner nearest the nightstand. "You're closet is in here, and the bathroom is right next door. It's not really *your* bathroom 'cause it's the only one downstairs, but you can totally keep all your stuff in there."

"This is perfect. Thank you for this, for everything." I rush over to give her a hug, so grateful for this escape that it overwhelms me for a moment. I clear my throat in a pre-emptive strike against any tears, and hope that she won't notice. They seem to need no invitation these days, but pop up at the least opportune moments.

"What are best friends for?" She hugs me back, and then breaks the moment with a light laugh. "I'll help you unpack tomorrow, so don't even worry about anything tonight. I can tell you're about to fall asleep on your feet."

It's true. Now that my bed is actually in sight and sleep is so close, I can barely keep my eyes open. I start to respond, but it turns into a yawn instead.

Maia just laughs. "Good night, Rennie."

When she's gone, I take another look around and notice that Mrs. Cantrell has put a vase of fresh hydrangeas on the desk. She could seriously give Martha Stewart a run for her money. There's a little card next to the vase with perfect could-be-its-own-font handwriting.

> Rennie,
>
> So glad you could join us for the summer.
>
> Please make yourself at home.
>
> Sincerely,
>
> Mr. & Mrs. Cantrell

Not exactly overrun with warm fuzzies, but still very thoughtful. Even though Maia and I practically grew up at each other's houses back in PA, it would never cross my mind to call her mom Madeleine. And it would never cross her mind to ask me to. Aidan is another story entirely, always warm and wonderful and like a father to me. I know immediately that he had nothing to do with signing this "Mr. Cantrell." The very thought would have made him laugh out loud.

I take a quick shower to wash the sand off and put on my soft green Life is Good PJs. I set up my Macbook on the desk, carefully moving the flowers out of the way. When I turn to set them on my bedside table, my head spins for a moment, my vision going all blurry at the edges.

I'm back in the forest of my dreams, the transition so immediate and so complete, it can hardly be called a transition at all. One breath I was in my PJs in Maia's house, and the next breath I'm here... in a dress? What's that about? My head stops spinning enough that I can look around, but before I can notice more than the same trees and dusky sky as before, Ethan grabs my hand.

Ethan. Of course he's here. The world of my dreams is incomplete without him, and I'm instantly buoyed by his presence. I'll follow him anywhere.

"Come on. Let's get out of here," he says with a cheeky grin I know all too well.

We run for shelter beneath the canopy of trees, feet pounding against the packed dirt of the path, hands clasped tightly—a link that feels so solid and safe that the trees seem an unnecessary addendum. We reach the treeline, Ethan just ahead of me, and everything stops. Everything. Ethan is frozen, looking back over his shoulder at me, a smile barely starting to unfold on his handsome face. The light flickering on the muddy road behind us has halted in its search. Even the night breeze has stopped. Everything except me.

I squeeze Ethan's hand, trying not to panic. I've been in this forest with him dozens of times. This is new.

There's a sound like static from somewhere above me, the strangeness of it making the pit of my stomach turn into a knot. "Rennie," a voice says through the static. No, not through it, but from it. Unclear and fuzzy, as though created out of the static. "Rennie, you have to find Ethan."

I look around for the source, fear rising in my chest, making my limbs tingle. I look at him, that smile still frozen on his face. "Find him?" I whisper. "But he's right here." I finish the thought loud enough that whoever is addressing me might be able to hear.

"You must find him. Time is running out, and you're going to need his help." I reach up and touch his face with the hand that's not still clasped in his. And then I understand. She doesn't mean this dream Ethan; she means I have to find him while I'm awake.

"He's—he's real?" I step closer to his still figure, running my hand along his cheek, trying to memorize his face. I know that when I'm out of this world, the details will be lost to me, as they always are. But maybe this time I can make them stick.

"He's real, and he's near. You must find him Rennie, make him your ally quickly, or it will be too late."

I look around again, trying to find where the voice is coming from, but there's another loud shriek of static and then Ethan is running again, pulling my hand and subsequently the rest of me behind him. I stumble over my own feet, not ready for the sudden burst of speed, and he reaches down to catch me. We stop just inside the treeline and he pulls me close to him.

"Are you okay?" he asks, shifting his eyes to take in both my face and the searching lights in the distance at the same time. I don't know how to answer that, so I just nod. He flashes me a grin and gives me a quick kiss. "Good. Then let's keep moving."

I nod my head, the motion making me all woozy again. When I reach out to catch myself, I find that I'm back in my room at Maia's, the vase that was in my hands now on the floor, flowers and water strewn all over the plush white carpet.

I stare at the mess for a moment, trying to organize my thoughts. What is happening to me?

Find Ethan. How can I possibly find someone who only exists in my dreams? There's a memory nudging its way to the forefront of my sleepy brain. Alex on the beach today; I accidentally called him Ethan. I have no idea where that came from, but maybe my subconscious was trying to get me to connect the dots. Maybe that's why he feels familiar to me. Can it really be that easy? I'm supposed to find my dream guy, and he literally stumbles right into me?

I stand and stretch, my eyes immediately drifting to the water and flowers all over Mrs. Cantrell's perfectly cream-colored (and now perfectly drenched) carpet. At least this is a problem I know how to deal with.

I find my discarded beach towel and kneel down, soaking up every last ounce of stray water. Finally satisfied that I've removed all evidence of the Hydrangea Incident, I go back to my computer. As I wait for it to warm up and find a connection, I run my fingers over the hot pink swirls by the trackpad, smiling as my wallpaper comes up—Aunt Charlie and Claire are smiling back at me from the entrance of Hershey Park, a walking chocolate bar by their side.

I open my email as soon as it's up, too tired and confused even to stop by Facebook. There's a quick note from Aunt Charlie checking in on me. I reply with a simple message:

California's beautiful, Maia's great as always, sooooooo tired. Will send more soon (with pics). Love you!

I've never been this far away from home without her, and certainly not for two whole months, so I know that she'll keep a close virtual eye on me while I'm gone.

When I've sent that one, I sit back, fingers poised over the keys forming my next email in my head before I type. I email Claire almost every night and as tired as I am, I can't bring myself to skip this tradition. She and I had never been all that close when we were growing up, despite the fact that we're only thirteen months apart (or maybe

79

because of that fact, I'm not sure). But then she turned seventeen, and that all changed. I don't know what happened, but it was as if she finally *saw* me. Like I was a real person, and not just some annoying brat she had to tolerate in her space.

Claire Bear,

How do I find someone who may or may not exist? It seems like an impossible task, but I'm not sure I want to find out what will happen if I fail. What would you do?

Love you always,

Ser Bear

P.S. I think I met the boy of my dreams tonight. That first kiss I've been saving up? Yeah, it's gonna happen this summer for sure.

I take a deep breath and hit Send.

I sit quietly for a moment, letting my fingers rest on the trackpad. The tears that have eluded me for most of the evening find me again. When does that part stop? When does the huge crater in my chest become whole again? I turn off the computer and turn back the covers on my bed, slipping gratefully between the sheets. With sleep, there may be some bad dreams, but at least I can leave reality behind for a while.

Chapter Eight

*T*he next morning, I'm just about to finish unpacking my big suitcase when there's a light tap at my door.

"Rennie? You up?"

I poke my head out of the closet to greet Maia. "Yeah, come on in. I'm just getting my stuff put away."

She flops down in the chair at the desk and puts her feet on the bed. "What? You're telling me that you actually went to sleep last night with your bags still packed? I thought as soon as I left, you'd have to get everything in its proper place. All right, who are you?"

I have to laugh. She knows me way too well. "I know, I blame the jet-lag."

"Jet-lag schmet-lag, let's have breakfast! My mom is making her famous berry muffins," she trills in her most tempting sing-song voice.

"Oh I love those! And I'm definitely starving, but I'm almost done in here." I go back into the closet to finish hanging up the rest of my clothes. I'm so close to being done there's no point in quitting now, even though my tummy rumbles an entirely different opinion of my priorities.

"All right, at least let me help then." She stands and picks up the smaller bag from the floor. "Can I empty out your carry-on?"

"Sure, it's all books and stuff so it can go on the desk or nightstand, wherever. I'll organize later."

"Alphabetize, you mean," she teases. It's true, I arrange all of my books that way. And DVDs and CDs and even the spices in our kitchen. Maia used to tease me that I have "CDO," which of course is OCD but alphabetized, the way it *should* be. I can't help it, I just like to have things where I can find them.

"Yeah, I *might* get around to that," I confess. "But *you* can put them any old way."

"Don't worry. I won't ruin your fun." She takes a small stack of novels out of the bag, turning them to read the spines. "Okay seriously, I have two words for you: Kin. Dle. Get a Kindle, Rennie!"

"I have one," I answer, trying not to get defensive. "And I do use it, but it's just not the same as getting to hold an actual book in your hand. Flipping the pages one by one, using a bookmark or a concert ticket or a dried leaf to keep your place, underlining great quotes that you want to hold onto forever… you can't do that digitally, you know."

"Okay, I'll take your word for it." Maia likes reading the occasional novel, but she understands that my obsession lives on a whole other level. "But we *are* going to leave the house on occasion, right? You brought enough books to take you through Christmas!"

"Well, I never know what I'll be in the mood for, so I have to be prepared."

"Good thing too," she tells me as she draws out another stack. "You know we only have surf shops and day spas here. No book stores in a hundred mile radius."

"Ha ha," I reply. "It's not *that* many. I didn't bring the entire arsenal, only a couple of favorites, like comfort food, you know?" Mmm… food.

Still starving. I can see her from the corner of my eye through the open door, setting my belongings in neat piles on the desk. I just glimpse her pulling out a plain black book as I turn back to take another shirt from the suitcase. I pick up the light blue cotton and shake it out. It's only as I'm reaching for a hanger that it dawns on me what that plain black book was.

I drop the shirt to the floor and step out of the closet in one fluid motion. "Maia wait," I say, reaching toward her as though I can stop her from all the way across the room. It's too late.

She's sitting on the edge of the bed now, book open in her palms. She looks from the open pages to me, concern flooding her features. "Rennie," she says, barely more than a whisper. "What is this?"

My impulse is to run over to her and grab it from her hands—protect it. But I don't. Instead I walk over slowly and sit next to her, giving myself time to contemplate my next move. How much do I tell her?

"It's, you know, my sketch book," I hedge, careful to keep the defensiveness out of my voice.

"I can see that," she says, though what she means is *duh*. "I'm familiar with your sketchbooks, Ren. Faces, trees, birds, doodles, lists—I've seen those things a million times. But this is… new." She's choosing her words with care, and for once I don't mind. "This is just since the accident?"

"Yeah," I break in before she can finish the word (I hate that word), trying to sound nonchalant even though my heart is pounding. "I've been having these dreams, well, nightmares mostly. I don't like to talk about them, so I thought maybe if I started drawing what I could remember, it would help me to deal with it all." It's her prerogative as Best Friend to get to ask things that I wouldn't allow of anyone else, but I still hope that maybe she'll choose to let it go.

She's flipping slowly, page by page through the journal, taking in each image. Most are harmless enough—trees and pathways, a lake, not too far from the usual for me. Some, however, are much darker: a dungeon with bars and skeletons and dripping water, a cave full of shadows and shaded eyes lurking from the depths, an enormous metal door with a human bone as the handle, a figure in a cloak carrying a lantern through a dark twisted forest path, a dagger clutched firmly in the other hand.

The one Maia is studying now is the interior of a cabin and a woman in a wooden chair. Her head is lolled over to her shoulder, hair splayed across her face, her hand dangling lifelessly at her side. There's a pool of blood on the floorboards next to her. In the dream, I knew the woman. I had tried desperately to save her but I was too late. That happens to me frequently in these dreams, and that dull ache of uselessness eats away at me every time I wake up.

I draw one knee up and wrap my arms around it, tilting my head to use my bangs as a shield. I haven't told anyone about my dreams, much less let someone see the sketches. It makes me feel exposed in a way I'm not used to, and even for Maia, I don't like it.

"I don't know what to say," she breaks the silence. "I mean, they're amazing. Truly. You've gotten even better, which I didn't think was possible." More silence. Just the turning of thick white pages. "But these are kinda disturbed, Ren. I mean, it's not like you've gone all Goth and you're drawing decaying zombies or something. But I know you, and this isn't you. If you ever need to—"

My brain finishes the sentence in a half a dozen ways within the millisecond breath of a pause she takes. Talk? Cry? Scream? Run away? Create a time machine and fix it all?

"What I mean is that I'm here for you. Whenever you *are* ready to talk." She closes the book with a finality that lets me breathe a deep sigh of relief.

"Thanks. I know they're a little darker than usual, and I was going to prepare you before you saw them. I don't want you to worry about me. And, just for the record, the dreams aren't all terrible. Even in the worst ones, there's this guy. Ethan. I know it sounds silly, but he makes them better. Bearable. Even good sometimes."

"A dream boyfriend?" she teases, and I know we're past the danger zone.

I shrug, trying not to blush. "Something like that."

"Is he cute?"

"I think so," I answer.

"You *think* so? You don't know?"

"Well, they're dreams, so it's always a little hazy. I can never remember the details when I wake up. But yeah, I'm pretty sure that *cute* would be applicable."

Talking about him out loud is new territory for me, and it brings that vision from last night crashing to the front of my brain. *Find him before it's too late.* What does that even mean? I decide to skip that part. I don't even know how to explain how important Ethan really is to me. When my dreams get too horrible or too dangerous, or just too much for me to handle on my own, he's always there. Brave and handsome, and completely mine. It's a feeling I can't even describe without making her doubt my sanity, so I don't try. To think that he might really be out there somewhere in my real life seems too much to hope for. To think that he might be Alex... I can't even go there. Not yet.

I take the black book and set it on the desk behind me. As I do, I can't help but notice the scent of freshly baked muffin wafting in from the kitchen.

"And by the way, I'm not sure if I mentioned this, but I'm starving!"

She laughs with me. "Well, we do have a way to fix that now. And don't ever let it be said that the hospitality of the Cantrell family was found lacking!" She puts on a Southern Belle accent and fans herself with her hand.

"No ma'am!" I reply, trying my best to follow suit with the accent. "Lawdy, how folks would talk!" She giggles and takes my hand, pulling me to the door.

Now in the light of day, I can better see this remarkable place I'm supposed to call *home* for the summer. As expected, it looks like a professional decorator lives here. My room is situated just off the entry way, which has hardwood floors and a ceiling as tall as the whole two stories, rising above us like the inside of a castle turret. From the center hangs an elegant crystal chandelier. Narrow windows let in natural light that sparkles off of each crystal, sending rainbow prisms onto the surrounding walls. How wonderful to have a shadow made entirely of color and light.

To our left lies the family room, sunken down by a single step where the hardwood ends and cream-colored carpet begins. It looks like a Pottery Barn catalog. Or something fancier than that maybe, if I knew of any stores fancier than Pottery Barn. Little touches of red pop up here and there, but besides that most everything is white. Huge plate glass windows open up the far wall to show the green of the golf course in the close up view, and the mountains in the distance. It's a stunning entrance, but I'm having trouble picturing myself being comfortable actually living here. It feels too pristine to be lived in by mere mortals.

"Mom, guess who I found?" Maia sings, looking back at me over her shoulder as she darts through the dining room in front of us and out through an archway on the far side. The formal dining room is also white, but touched with purple: hand-painted Mediterranean-looking swirls on the walls, a runner on the dark wood table, shades on the sconces. I follow behind, trying to step carefully and lightly, afraid to touch anything.

Leaving the grandeur behind, I step into a brightly lit kitchen, again all white. Shades of deep blue and light aqua for the rugs and curtains provide a South American feel, which makes this room just a touch homier than the rest. The smell of those berry muffins doesn't hurt either.

"Rennie, you're up. So glad you made it in all right. It's good to have you with us for the summer." Maia's mom keeps her distance, but offers a warm smile, taking off her oven mitts as she turns to greet me. Homemade muffins, yet not a speck of flour on her beige linen pants or crisp blue oxford shirt. I think if any attempted to land on her, she just flat out wouldn't permit it and it would dissolve somewhere into the space-time continuum.

"Thank you so much for having me, Mrs. Cantrell," I say.

"I hope your room is suitable for you. You can make yourself at home and please let us know if you need anything at all." Little creases appear at the corners of her eyes and her head tilts to the side. I know that tilt. "Rennie, I'm so sorry for your loss. We were all shocked to hear the news. Are you doing okay?"

I try not to cringe. I hate this question. "I'm doing much better, thank you." We both know it's a lie, but she accepts it anyway.

It's a strange thing that happens when tragedy interrupts your life, not just *something bad* but actual Tragedy. People don't know what to say, and that's normal. I can't blame anyone for that. But it suddenly becomes clear who is on the outside of your life, and who is on the inside. Those on the fringe will ask 'How are you?' but it's purely out of courtesy, they are fully expecting you to lie. Those on the inside, who live right next to your heart, those are the ones who ask 'How are you?' and actually wait for a real answer. Like Maia tried to do earlier. She knows that the real answer is still buried underneath layers of tears and anger and covered up with a big hard numb shell. We'll dig through it all eventually, and the journey will be messy. But she won't mind.

"Is Aidan home?" I ask, hoping to change the subject.

"Mr. Cantrell is at work. He'll be home later this evening, dear." She picks up a plate from the counter and starts transferring the delicious-smelling muffins from their baking tin.

I can't help a small frown at his absence, but before I can reply, Maia grabs two muffins from the plate, shoves one into my hand and pulls me back through the living room.

"Okay mom," she tosses back over her shoulder as we cross through the breakfast nook (or whatever you call the room that is attached to the kitchen, which, by the way, is also white). "We're gonna get ready and head out." Maia opens the door to my room and ushers me in. "Sorry about that," she says quietly. "She doesn't really know what to say about the whole thing. She means well though."

"I know, it's okay." And I mean it. I don't know what to say about it either. That's why I don't say anything at all, just tuck it away for another time.

"But right now, I think it's time to get ready," Maia grins. "*Somebody* has a date!"

Chapter Nine

*W*hat was I thinking? Agreeing to meet up with Levi was one thing, but actually sitting here in the café waiting for him is something else entirely. I tap my newly manicured nails on the edge of my coffee cup, staring again at the door. This was a mistake, he's already late. Okay, only by five minutes, but still. He's definitely not showing. I can feel it.

I let a sigh escape, a rush of embarrassment and disappointment flooding my chest. Stood up on my first day in town, that has got to be some kind of record. But if I'm being honest, I'm most likely going to spend the whole time wishing I was with Alex anyway, so why am I stressing? The brief thought brings a smile to my face and I relax a bit. Might as well enjoy the afternoon, date or not.

I lean back in my wooden chair and cross my legs, straightening the shoulders of my sage-colored angel-sleeved top, and picking non-existent lint from my white capris. I pull a book out of my purse and take a nice long drink of my blackberry steamer. I've been sipping it since I ordered ten minutes ago, but this is the first sip I've actually tasted. Delicious. Setting aside the photo I use as a bookmark (Claire and me from many Christmases ago), I leave the world of the bustling coffee shop behind and enter Elsinore. It's one of my favorite locations, so I feel right at home.

A short time later, I'm completely engrossed in the words, words, words when a shadow falls across the open pages, making me look up.

"Rennie," says a breathless Levi. "I am so sorry. I'll bore you with my excuses in a minute, but first let me beg your forgiveness by buying you a coffee or something." He looks pathetic, poor thing. Eyebrows curving up in the middle of his forehead and lower lip slightly protruding, like a puppy who knows he's about to get sent to the doghouse. For a moment, I debate making him sweat it out, but before I know it I'm smiling and telling him it's okay.

"I'd love another steamer. Blackberry, please?" I tell him, handing him my empty cup. Relief puts the sparkle back into his green eyes.

"I am your servant." He bows dramatically and goes to the counter to order. I set my book aside and look again to my phone. 3:50—he does have some explaining to do. But really I'm just glad not to have been stood up.

I notice I have a new text message and can't resist opening it while I'm waiting. It's from Maia, naturally. It simply reads:

Sooooooooo??????

I glance at the counter to see if I have time to respond. Levi's still waiting; plenty of time.

He just got here. Will let u know more soon.

As I'm hitting Send, another message chimes in. An unknown number. My heart speeds up at the highly unreasonable hope that it's Alex. Right. He doesn't even have my phone number, but I'm sure it's him. Get a grip. I open the text and read:

Rennie it's Ember how is the date???

Of course Maia would have given my number to the girls. How else could they torment me all day? I smile to myself and write back:

He was L8 but so far so good. Details 2nite I promise.

I decide I better put the phone away completely before Kaela and Jane get in the mix and I spend the entire date texting. I'm just putting it back in my purse when Levi returns with two steaming cups.

"I was planning to get something iced, but your drink sounded so good I thought I'd follow your lead," he says as he sets them down and sits across from me.

"There's something comforting about it, even on a warm day. It's one of my favorites." I move the cup closer to me, enjoying the warmth on my palms.

"I fully agree," he says amiably. He leans back in his chair as though preparing for a long story ahead. "So, are you ready for my excuse?"

"Nope," I tell him lightly, shaking my head.

"What?"

"No excuse."

"But... really?" Clearly, this was not what he'd expected. "'Cause I have one. It's a good one too. And just in case you didn't buy the true story, I thought up a really good one as a back-up."

"Nope." I'm enjoying this now. It's not often I let myself have the upper hand in a conversation with a cute boy.

"But there are kittens involved. And a little old lady. And fire?" He grows increasingly desperate with each added element and by the end we're both laughing.

Finally I put him out of his misery. "Look, you're here now, so... clean slate, okay? I'm just gonna pretend like we were supposed to meet at 4:00 and you were so eager to see me again that you showed up ten minutes early."

"Wow." He's stunned. I like it. "You... wow." More stunned. "You realize that most every other girl I know would be screaming at me and throwing a drink in my face, right?"

"Then you really should have reconsidered that iced option," I tease.

He leans his elbows on the table, watching me with a smile. "I guess that'll teach me to think you're like every other girl."

Now it's my turn to be caught off guard and I find myself blushing. I have to be careful. I like Levi well enough, but I don't want to lead him on too much until I get the whole Alex thing sorted. I wonder if I have a great-aunt Scarlett somewhere in the family tree.

Levi lets his comment hang in the air between us for a moment, then breaks the silence. "So what are you reading?"

"Ah yes, the old 'what are you reading' approach. Unique." I find it easier to tease him than to have an actual conversation. He doesn't seem to mind and reaches across the table to flip my book face up.

"Shakespeare?" I keep finding new ways to shock him. "Just a little light summer reading, huh?"

I shrug, not letting myself get defensive. "I always carry a book with me, and I love Shakespeare. I'm working my way through the whole canon, but this summer I'm purely on vacation. I only brought my favorites."

"And *Hamlet* is your way of taking the summer off?"

"I brought other favorites too. Lighter things." I'm starting to feel that defense come up again, but I hold it back. Insulting my books is like insulting my friends, I don't take it well.

"Hey, don't get me wrong," he says, sensing my subtle mood shift. "I have nothing against a good book. I'm in AP English and I have never cracked the binding of a Cliff's Notes." The solemnity with which he makes this proclamation makes me laugh out loud.

"Well okay then. Besides, you can't make fun. Doesn't every great actor aspire to play Hamlet one day?"

"You think I'm a great actor?" He grins at the thought. Of course he would pick up on that part rather than the actual question. I'm no stranger to these fragile theatre egos.

"Well, that's not exactly what I meant…"

He makes a wounded face and grabs his chest. "Ouch!"

"Oh come on, I've seen you in one thing and that wasn't even live. I can hardly judge your entire theatrical worth on one performance I saw on a DVD."

"Fair enough," he concedes genially. "But to answer your question, I suppose a lot of actors do use that role as some kind of benchmark."

"I thought so," I say, bordering on smug.

"But not so much in musical theatre," he points out, deflating my smug.

"Oh. Right."

"Oh, don't tell me you're defeated that easily," he mocks good-naturedly. "I can't believe that someone who Maia calls her best friend would give up just like that. She and I used to have these sparring matches that would go on for hours back during rehearsals. This one time it actually went on for a day and a half when I dared to mention how one man couldn't possibly save the world as often as Jack Bauer did, and if they wanted to make a truly realistic episode, it should have been him sitting in traffic on the 405 for the whole hour. She got so mad that her mouth did that little twitchy thing that it does, you know what I mean? And then when I... what?"

Somewhere in there, it all clicked into place. I realize when he stops to question me that my mouth has dropped open with this insight. I snap it shut and put my smug back on.

"You should have just told me," I tell him, knowing I'm being cryptic.

"I should have told you what? That I'm not a big *24* fan?" He tries to laugh it off but he looks a bit nervous now.

"You know exactly what I'm talking about," I tell him smoothly, channeling my inner Maia. I'm never able to act this cool around cute boys so I know it's her influence. I take a lingering sip of my steamer and watch his body language over the rim of my cup.

He's eyeing me carefully but doesn't say a word. He licks his lips, darts his eyes to one side and back, rubs his hands along the denim of his jeans. I had no idea one little hint of information could bring so much power. His nervousness starts to make me uncomfortable. Poor guy, he's been nothing but nice to me, why toy with him this way?

I set my cup down and look him in the eye. "You like Maia," I tell him. It's not a question.

He laughs, trying to play it off. "Is that it? Well of course I do. I mean, everybody does, right?"

His denial doesn't ruffle me. "Levi," I say patiently. "You *like* Maia."

He blows air through his teeth, making a "tsss" sound of contempt for the idea. "Yeah, well if that were true then why would I... I mean, if I was going to be... Well, how could I..." After three miserable attempts, he finally lowers his head into his hands and moans lightly. "You must think I'm the worst person in the world," he says into his hands.

The response startles me a little. "Not at all! Why would I think that?"

He looks up at me, misery written on his face. "Because you're right. I do like her, I have for a long time. And yet, here I am on a date with her best friend! Come on, who does that?" The misery is replaced with a tone of discovery. "I am. I'm the worst person in the world."

This has the potential to go downhill quickly. I can fix this. "In the whole world?" I counter. "Well, okay. Let's test your hypothesis. Have you taken over a country and become a tyrannical dictator enslaving its people to work for your every whim?"

Confusion is written all over his face. "No?"

"Uh huh. And have you enlisted the help of small children and cute little puppies to assist you in a nefarious plot to undermine the world economy and collapse all capital, destroying life as we know it?"

"Not today." A slow smile starts to spread across his lips.

"I see. And have you begun work on an army of relentless cyborgs that are set to obliterate the earth and pillage the debris for resources to aid a cruel galactic overlord?"

"Well, maybe a few sketches, but no actual work has started." The twinkle is back in his eye and he's no longer feeling miserable. The power of nonsense never ceases to amaze me.

"See there? Not the worst person after all."

"You're really not mad?" he asks quietly.

I can't tell him that what I'm actually feeling is relief. "I'm not mad. Besides, I know how persuasive Maia can be. I'm sure she talked you into this."

"Well, she did suggest it," he admits. "But it wasn't that hard to get me on board. I mean, I'd be crazy not to want to get to know you better. You're funny and smart. You can carry on a conversation about something other than nail polish and shoes. And," he tilts his head in that charmingly timid way he has, "am I allowed to say you're really hot?"

A blush creeps into my face, and I try to stammer a response that comes out something like, "Eruhmphgll ee?"

"I'm sorry if that sounds creepy after I just told you I have a crush on your best friend."

"No!" I blurt out, forming words successfully again. "Not creepy." Amazing how quickly I lost that little bit of power I was feeling. "Not creepy, just... nice." Wow. Really nice. Maia's always been the pretty one. Don't get me wrong, I don't think I'm hideous or anything. I would say I'm cute in a Pixie or Elvish sort of way. But hot? I allow a moment to wonder if there's any chance Alex might share that opinion.

"Look, I'd appreciate it if you wouldn't say anything to Maia. I know that's pathetic, but with her hanging on Seth all the time... let's just say I'm not into setting myself up for rejection."

"No, of course, I get it. Your secret is my secret." I owe him that much after toying with him the way I did. Besides, I know exactly where he's coming from. I'm not all that anxious for rejection myself.

"Thanks," he says, relief making his green eyes shine. "So, now that the pressure's off, can we still enjoy an afternoon together? I'd love to show you around town."

"You mean so I can put in a good word for you later?" I tease.

"Well, you know. If the mood should strike you," he teases right back.

This could turn into a nice friendship. I'm not entirely convinced that he could keep up with Maia if she were ever to return his affections. But he does have one major thing to his advantage: he's not Seth.

We've been sitting at our table in Outspoken for almost an hour when he excuses himself to return a missed call from his mom. I can't resist taking a peek at my own cell phone as he's walking away. Thirteen new text messages. I smile to myself and put it away again. The girls are going to have to wait.

I pick up my book from the table and open to the bookmark. Might as well fill the time with my old friends while I'm waiting for the new. I'm not even through one good soliloquy before I'm interrupted though.

"Rennie?" I look up and my heart stops. I'm staring directly into the gorgeous grey eyes that I've been dreaming about for the last twenty-four hours.

"Alex!" I nearly shout, dropping my book to the floor as I uncross my legs and half-stand for some unknown reason. (What was the plan there? Was I going to curtsey or something?) I lean down to pick up the fallen book, but Alex has beaten me to it. He slips it onto the table top and smoothly slides into the chair across from me. My heart is beating again—apparently trying to make up for lost time. Surely he can hear that. "What are... doing? What... what are you here? Doing?" That's not a sentence! Come on, Rennie, breathe!

Amazingly though, he just smiles at me. That crooked smile is even better in real life than it was the million and a half times I'd replayed it in my memory. "I was on my way home and thought I'd run in for a little caffeine boost." He glances around, then rests his eyes back on me. "I better not stay long," he grins conspiratorially. "We don't want to upset Maia," he gives a little nod to the second empty cup on the table.

"Well actually, I mean, Maia isn't really..." My glance swings guiltily outside to where Levi is still on his cell phone, his back turned to us. He follows my gaze and his mouth drops open.

"Wait, Levi?" he sounds incredulous. "You're here with Levi Hart?"

This is not the way this was supposed to go. "I, um, sort of?" I get out lamely.

"You're sort of here with him?"

"It's not a date," I tell him quickly.

"Oh," he mulls that over for a second. "So you guys just ran into each other?"

"Well, not exactly."

"So he asked you out." There's no question there; he already knows the answer.

"Yeah, I guess he did, but…" I shift uncomfortably. I feel like I was caught cheating, which is highly unfair since Alex only had one conversation with me yesterday at the beach and then vanished for the rest of the night. For all I know, he was off making out with some surfer chick. And just as I'm about to tell him this (or some stumbling variation thereof), he surprises me with an apology.

"I'm sorry," he says simply, folding his hands and leaning his elbows onto his knees. He bows his head and sighs softly, that tattoo I'm dying to see more of teasing me from his sleeve again. It looks like two birds flying off a tree branch maybe? "I have absolutely no right to be jealous." Hang on, did he just say jealous? Focus, Rennie. He looks up at me through his bangs. "I guess I'll chalk this one up to a lesson in seizing the moment." He stands and rests a hand on the table top, looking down at me. "Levi's a decent guy," he says. "Have a good time, and I hope to see you around."

He turns to leave and I put my hand on top of his. "Wait." My pulse is racing again and I have no idea what I'm going to say to him, but I know that I can't let him leave like this.

He looks down at my hand on top of his. "You painted your nails," he says quietly. I pull my hand back as though I can hide the evidence. "And you look really pretty. And you're here with him."

"It's not a date," I insist.

He only chuckles. "The lady doth protest too much, methinks." He taps the cover of my book, and walks out.

My head starts to swim a bit, and I shake it to clear out the fuzziness. Did Alex really just confess to being jealous? And then he told me I'm pretty and then he quoted Shakespeare. No wonder I'm light-headed—I think I'm in love.

But this dizzy feeling isn't going away. The table top tilts dangerously to one side and I grab it to steady myself. Is this another vision coming on? The others happened so suddenly, though; why is this one different? I look outside, but Alex is gone and Levi is still on his phone, facing away from the door and my current plight. The windows are liquid, bendy, fading at the edges like a chalk drawing that's been smudged.

I feel like each of my limbs is being pulled in a different direction, and my stomach is trying to turn itself inside out. Whatever is happening, this is nothing like my previous visions. My hand knocks my book off the table as I stand. I pick it up and stumble to the back hallway. The restroom is locked. Of course. Another tremor has me reaching for the wall to keep myself upright. But it's not a wall; it's a door. I push through (ignoring the swirling Employees Only notice) and I'm outside —a narrow alley between the coffee shop and some kind of office complex.

I crumble to the ground and lean my back against the wall. My ears feel like they're stuffed with cotton, the sounds of traffic and distant voices muffled and hazy. My stomach is roiling, my head spinning so badly all I can do is close my eyes and wait for it to stop.

My fingers touch against something smooth—paper? I'm not sure. But when I open my eyes to see what it is, the alley is gone. Or more precisely, I'm gone.

And here I am, awake in my dream world.

Chapter Ten

*O*n the bright side, the spinning has stopped. But it's kinda hard to get excited about that when I'm sitting in the dirt in a place I've only seen in my dreams.

I'm on the ground, leaning against an iron post at what appears to be a bus stop. Yep—lamp post, stone bench, crossroads—looks like a bus stop to me. The lamp casts a warm flickering glow above my head, the only bit of warmth in a grey and misty landscape. I put a shaky hand on the seat of the bench and haul myself onto the cold stone to take stock of my surroundings.

In one direction, the road leads over a small rise, and farther into the distance to a glow shining through the gloom. A village maybe? The other direction leads into a dark forest, branches of tall pines and oaks reaching through the mist like skeleton arms.

I put my head in my hands, willing myself back to reality. I take two shuddery breaths, and then peek through my fingers. Still here.

Okay, there's no point in sitting here feeling afraid and sorry for myself. I can do that as I walk. But even after telling myself what a great idea it would be to go exploring, I find that I'm still sitting on the cold bench. There are a few birds singing from the distant trees, their voices hollow and echo-y in the mist. A chilled breeze chases dead leaves past my feet. But beyond that, all is still.

Where are my super spy skills now? Come on, Rennie. What would Sydney Bristow do? I get to my feet. The decision of which direction to choose is a simple one. Who would willingly head into a creepy forest when there's a perfectly good, warm, welcoming glow coming from over this hill? One foot, then the next. That's all I have to do.

The road is damp enough to keep the dirt down, but not so much that my shoes get muddy. I suppose that's a bonus. At the top of the rise, there's a stone wall running along the crest of the hill in both directions. Crumbling stones piled on top of one another haphazardly, as though they've been replaced at random intervals but not from the same stone, and not with the same level of care. In places, the wall is solid and strong, and in others, there are giant gaps, holes gaping, rocks leaning— it's a Jenga-player's nightmare. And the trees are actually very pretty once I stop with the freaking out part. Skinny pines and bit fat oak trees stand side by side, lining the road on both sides. Almost all of my dreams take place in these woods, so it feels strangely familiar to be here. Familiar, but not safe.

When I've visited here in my dreams, Ethan is always with me. In real life, I've never been a girl who needs a boy to feel complete, or who requires rescuing from a knight in shining armor. But here in this dream landscape, I can't help but feel he should be with me.

The fog grows thicker as I make my way down the road, nothing but trees and the occasional birdsong to keep me company. It's the kind of day that the zombies wouldn't feel at all foolish starting their apocalypse, and it's kind of freaking me out.

To keep my mind occupied, I play a game with myself. One I've played for as long as I can remember when I need to summon a little bravery and distract me from whatever is the cause of my fear. A visit to the dentist, trying to fall asleep again after a nightmare, a funeral I want to pretend isn't happening...

"Okay," I whisper aloud to myself. "A to Z. A is for Adams. B is for... Brontë. C is obviously for Carroll. C has never been more for Carroll than at this precise moment. D is for Dahl. E will be, um, Eco. F is for Fforde." Just as I've made it to *T is for Tolkein*, I hear it. Whistling from the fog behind me.

Panic seizes my breath, stopping me in my tracks. On the one hand, being able to get some answers from somebody (*any*body!) is tempting. But let's face it, I'm just not that girl. I run as quickly and quietly as I can down the road, veering over to the edge of the path where the woods begin. I'm not going in there, but at least I can hide until this unknown danger has passed.

I spot a big oak that is definitely hide-behind-able and dash towards it. A quick glance behind me reveals nothing but more fog. I can't see more than a few feet in any direction, but as annoying as that is, it's also working as my invisibility cloak at the moment. My toe catches an exposed root and I manage to catch myself on the trunk of the oak without tasting mulch. My foot is throbbing, but crying about it is not going to help anything. I ignore it and press my back into the bark of the tree.

Footsteps beat a slow and steady cadence on the road behind me, heavy and unhurried. All other concerns are replaced with a single thought: *hide.*

My heart pounds in my chest, my breathing shallow. I take a step closer to the tree behind me, pressing my back into it like I can fuse myself into the bark. I try to hold my breath but it won't be stilled, coming in short gasps of fear. The footsteps continue uninterrupted, and the sound travels past me enough that I risk a glance. I inch my fingers around the giant trunk of the oak and lean as far forward as I dare. A man in a long brown coat walks down the road. I can make out the dark skin of his clean-shaven head, his hands swinging freely beside him. He begins to whistle a melancholy tune as he passes out of sight, and my breathing eases into a sigh of relief. I'm safe for now. I lean my head to the rough bark and close my eyes.

Slowly I open them again, my fear morphing into something else now.

Something akin to wonder, maybe. I've been here before. I don't mean the dream world in general, but this. Right here, right now, my head against this oak. I saw—no, I *lived*—this exact scene when I was at the beach yesterday. Not only am I charged with finding someone who only lives in my dreams, but now my visions are showing me the future? What is happening to me?

As if in response, my stomach heaves and I sink to the ground. The same awful roiling sensation takes over again, but this time I welcome it. If this queasiness is accompanied by whatever brought me here, then I hope and pray that it's also about to take me home.

Who knew that a narrow alley and a dumpster could be a welcome sight? I'm so happy to be back here I practically have to stop myself from running over to hug that dumpster. My next impulse is to call Maia and tell her everything, but I squelch that as well. It's too complicated for a phone call, and I would rather make some sense of it in my own head before trying to explain it to anyone else. Even Maia.

My copy of *Hamlet* is laying on the concrete next to me and I scoop it up to put it away, but my bag is missing. Maybe I left it inside at our table.

Oh no. *Our* table. Levi.

I jump up and spin around, brushing the dirt off of my white capris and pulling an oak leaf from the bottom of my shoe. My hand is poised on the handle of the *Employees Only* door when I see it. There on the stucco wall, just above where my head was resting moments ago is a message hastily written in blue chalk: *Find Ethan.*

A chill runs up my spine. Someone was here—someone who *knows.* I look around, hoping there's another clue somewhere, or somebody watching from the shadows who I might recognize. Finding who wrote this would help to answer so many questions. But there's nothing. I snap a picture of it with my phone and use the palm of my hand to smudge the writing. Then I file this away under the ever-increasing topic of *Deal with This Later* and head inside.

Levi is sitting at our table, legs crossed casually, sipping from his oversized white mug. Still here. And thankfully facing away from me.

Plastering on what I hope is a casual, effortless, I-didn't-just-get-back-from-a-waking-dream kind of smile, I head over to him and touch his shoulder.

"Sorry to keep you waiting," I say, tucking a strand of hair behind my ear. "I had to, um... use the restroom. And take a call. I took a call in the restroom. Tacky, right? But it couldn't really be avoided, so I just... thanks for waiting."

He sets his cup on the table, green eyes twinkling. "No problem. Are you ready to continue our non-date?" He hands me a piece of wrapped bubble gum.

I turn it over, trying to figure out the joke. "What is this for?"

He grins. "First stop of our San Luis tour: Bubblegum Alley."

Chapter Eleven

*R*eeeeeeeeennnnnnnie." It comes to me from far away, hazy and distorted. "Reeeeeeeeennnnnnnie." Louder this time, my own name sounding foreign to my sleeping mind. Meaningless syllables. I swim upwards towards consciousness, breaking out of a blissfully dreamless sleep, and find Maia sitting on the foot of my bed bouncing it up and down to wake me.

"What time is it?" I mumble, not wanting to open my eyes long enough to look at the clock.

"Almost seven."

"In the morning?"

"Of course," she giggles. "Time to get up!"

I pull the pillow over my head and roll away from her. "Remind me again why I like you?"

"Because I am delightful!" She laughs and pulls the pillow away from me. I sit up groggily, and try to rub the sleep from my eyes.

"There's no such thing as delightful before 8am. Ten on vacation."

"Well, okay," she concedes. "If you want to go back to sleep, I guess I can't stop you." She stands up and opens the door before turning back to me. "Oh, but I did want to tell you that my dad is in the kitchen and he's headed to work in a few minutes, soooo…"

"Aidan?" I'm on my feet before my brain has fully processed that I'm mobile. I sway slightly, the sudden change in elevation making me lightheaded. For a moment, I fear I'm about to have another vision, but I shake my head and regain control. Maia stands out of the way as I dash into the hall and stop, completely lost. I turn a full circle before Maia gives me a push in the right direction. "Aidan?" I call, my voice cracking with morning-ness. I've been here for two days and still haven't so much as seen him. I'm not missing him again, even if it means I have to greet him in my PJs. I stumble through the living room and find myself in the brightly lit kitchen.

"There she is, the missing half of the Dynamic Duo," he grins and catches me as I launch myself at him. I throw my arms around his neck and he hugs me so tightly (complete with bear hug growly noises), that my feet leave the floor. I can hear Maia laughing and Mrs. Cantrell muttering what sounds like "Honestly!" but I ignore them both. He steps back to take a good look at me. I'm sure I'm a mess, but I couldn't care less.

"Well look at you," he says with that same boyish grin that will never age. "All the way from Philadelph-i-a, and safe and sound right here in Californ-i-a." He always thinks he's funnier than he actually is, but it still makes me laugh. "It's good to see you, kid." He ruffles my hair like I'm nine years old. "You doing okay?" he asks it quietly, honestly, dark blue eyes crinkling at the corners as he squishes up his forehead in concern.

I'm so glad to see him, it takes a second to wrap my sleepy head around what he's asking. I don't want to change the happy mood yet, so I just nod and respond to the easier part. "It's great to see you too."

I work my fingers through my tangled mess of bedhead hair, trying my best to make order of the chaos. I know from experience that this is a futile endeavor, but I hope that making the effort will stop the disapproving looks from Mrs. Cantrell. Apparently, my ensemble of tank top and Hello Kitty Stormtrooper pajama pants is not suitable breakfast attire. I glance down briefly, I just have to know. Yep, she's wearing heels at 6:45 in the morning in her own kitchen.

I pull out a barstool and sit at the kitchen island next to Aidan. He starts into all the expected questions while he sips his coffee, and I fill in all of the expected answers. I swing my feet happily and pick at a maple scone, feeling more normal than I have in a long time.

"So I heard you had quite an eventful day yesterday," he says nonchalantly, casting a sideways look to Maia.

I swallow hard, my mind a complete blank. How does he know about my dream excursion? I didn't even tell Maia about that yet. "You did?" My voice cracks a little and I clear my throat, hoping they'll think it's due to the early hour.

"In town for two days and already breaking hearts," Aidan says, shaking his head.

Relief floods through me and I relax. My date. Okay, *that* I can handle talking about.

"Oh, you heard about that already? Gee, I wonder where you could have gotten that information." I raise an eyebrow at Maia.

"Big news, small town. You do the math." She grins, and reaches across the island to break off a piece of my scone.

"These poor California boys won't know what hit 'em. So who is the lucky young man? Have I met him?"

"You know Levi, daddy," Maia explains. "From the play?"

"Oh right. Tall, good looking… nice kid."

"Yeah," I agree on all fronts. "Maia introduced us at the bonfire and we kind of hit it off. We just went out for coffee yesterday is all. He showed me around downtown a bit—the Mission and the creek. Bubblegum Alley. That was weird; very cool, and yet kinda made me want to shower."

He laughs. "I don't quite understand that one myself. Sounds like you had a good time, though. Do I need to have a talk with this Levi about his intentions?"

"Nah, I think we can save that. We had fun hanging out, but there's nothing between us."

"Yeah," Maia adds. "The poor guy never had a chance. Did he, Ren?"

"He's super nice," I say, shrugging defensively. "Who knows? It could have turned into something, but it just wasn't in the cards."

"Hmm… interesting," she taps her forefinger to her chin. "And I don't suppose there's any special reason for that. Like maybe you already had your eye on someone else?" Her eyes are twinkling mischievously, and I know she's thoroughly enjoying making me squirm. Does she have to embarrass me in front of her parents? Especially this early in the morning. She knows my defenses are low when the sun is barely up.

"Maybe?" I squeak, feeling the heat start to creep up my cheeks.

"And would you be so kind as to tell the court who that *someone* might be?" She has her hands clasped behind her, and she's pacing back and forth on the other side of the island, adopting her newest role with dizzying speed, as always. I seriously haven't had enough caffeine to keep up with her yet.

"The court?" I laugh nervously, glancing at Aidan who is watching us both with amusement in his eyes. "I know you don't like him much, but is it really worth putting me on trial?"

"Just answer the question please, Ms. Winters," she replies.

"Don't you have to go to work or something?" I plead with Aidan. I know Maia will stop if her audience leaves.

"I do," he says, "but now you've got me curious. I can't leave in the middle of a mystery."

"I'm sorry, but I have to interject."

I didn't expect a rescue to come in the form of Mrs. Cantrell, but I'll take it! I look to her gratefully, glad that she's about to take Maia to task for grilling me like this. I am a guest here after all, surely that's not proper etiquette.

"Rennie, dear." Uh oh. Me? "I know that you've had a rather unorthodox upbringing." She says *unorthodox* in a way that suggests I was raised by Gypsies or wolves or circus folk. "And I know that Charlene has done her best to be a mother to you girls. But for these next two months you're our responsibility, and I'm afraid that means that you're going to have to live by our rules." She pauses for a moment to let that sink in. "Now, as I'm sure you're aware, we have rules about dating. And while we're happy to let you have friends who are both girls and boys, we simply can't let you run around dating every boy you meet."

My jaw drops open. "But I... I don't! I mean, I wouldn't!"

"Two boys in two days, dear? Now, what am I supposed to think?" She purses her lips and crosses her arms, the very picture of maternal condemnation.

"You're supposed to think," Aidan says, standing to his feet and putting a hand on my shoulder, "that Rennie is our guest, not our prisoner. She's here to visit Maia and to rejuvenate for a while after a very difficult time. And if she's caught the eye of a couple of nice young men, then that's certainly no surprise."

"Aidan, please don't—"

"Madeleine, let me finish. If there's a sixteen-year-old with a better head on her shoulders anywhere, I ask you to name her. Present company included, sorry hon." He winks at Maia.

She nods. "True story."

"And as far as I can see, there is no reason that she shouldn't enjoy going on a date now and again. She's not going to go around dating the entire football team, and she's not going to pick some weirdo loner-type who will put her in danger. You should know her better than that by now. If it'll make you feel better about it, why don't you call Charlie and ask her. Get her opinion or her permission or whatever you need, and let the poor girl have some fun."

I smile at her and fold my hands in front of me on the counter, trying to appear as angelic as possible. I've never been in the room when parents were arguing before. It's both extremely uncomfortable and completely amazing to have someone come to my defense.

Mrs. Cantrell's lips purse so tightly together, I'm afraid they're going to disappear entirely. She lets the silence hang in the air, mixing with the smell of the scones and a hint of her Chanel. I never knew guilt had a scent. With military precision, she folds the dish towel she's been holding and sets it next to the stovetop.

"Aidan," she says quietly. "Laundry room, please." Without another glance to any of us, she walks out of the kitchen, her clacking heels the only sound until she's out of sight.

I turn to face Aidan. "I'm so sorry. I didn't mean to—"

"You didn't," he says gently. "No one did anything wrong. Not even you, little miss prosecutor." He smiles at Maia in an effort to lighten the mood. "Madeleine and I just have a difference of opinion which we will now discuss. In the laundry room, apparently." He pats my shoulder and heads off down the hall. "If I'm not back in ten minutes, send in the search and rescue."

With a sigh, Maia sinks down onto the newly available barstool. "Sorry, Rennie. I didn't see that coming."

"Does she really think those things about me?" I ask her quietly.

"I don't know how she could. If she's been paying attention at all for the last nine years, she should know that you practically put the *goody* in *goody two-shoes.* I mean that in the best possible way, of course." She bumps her shoulder into mine, and we giggle.

"For once, I'm glad to agree with that opinion."

We can hear bits of their discussion through the closed door down the hall, words floating by to snap at me. *Irresponsible. Fatherless. Promiscuous. Death. Accident.* Words that don't feel connected to one another, let alone to me. Words that push their way into my head, trying to find their way to my heart. But my armor is solid. I won't let them in.

The accident has nothing to do with those other things. And I know from my Psych class that there are countless studies to show how girls who grow up without their fathers around can spend a lot of time trying to find other kinds of love to fill that void, but that is not me. Promiscuous? Really? I've only kissed one boy in my entire life, and that was when Lincoln Blackwell cornered me by the jungle gym in first grade.

Maia grabs two fresh scones from the plate on the marble counter top, and stands. "Come on," she says. "They can be weird and parental if they want to, but we sure don't have to listen to it."

Maia and I sit on either end of the window seat in my room, our feet pulled up onto the seat and covered by a cozy green throw blanket. We pick at our scones and try to find some non-parental topic to discuss.

"Okay, so I have to ask," Maia blurts out, making me jump. "Last night, when Levi dropped you off at Jamba Juice to meet us, did he kiss you goodnight?"

I stifle a sigh. "Kaela asked me that last night, Mai. I told you he didn't."

"But I saw the way he looked at you, and I just can't believe that he wasn't feeling it." The look of hopefulness in her face is hard not to catch. I hate to keep bursting her bubble on this same subject. But…

"Believe me, there was no romance brewing at all. For *either* of us."

Pop.

"Okay, fine," she sighs. "It's because of stupid Alex, isn't it? You only talked to him one time, and you're really that hooked on him?"

"Twice," I correct without thinking. Her head snaps up. Mistake, Rennie. Big mistake.

"You mean twice at the bonfire, right?" she asks, eyes narrowing.

"Um yeah… the driftwood and then the sunset-cave-moment-thing. That was twice all right." I nod a little too vigorously. "Wow, these scones sure are good." I pop the last bite in my mouth as she watches me. "I wonder if it's safe to go out for some orange juice yet. That would go really well. With the scones, I mean."

"Rennie, what are you trying not to tell me?"

I swallow hard, the scone turning to dust in my throat. Why do I even try to lie to Maia?

"Did he call you?"

"No, I don't think he has my number," I tell her, grateful for something true to grasp onto.

"Then what happened? Spill."

I crumple my napkin into a tiny ball and rub it in a circle between my palms. She leans forward, arms encircling her knees in a deceptively casual pose. I guess I was going to tell her eventually anyway.

"While Levi and I were having coffee yesterday, he got a call from his mom and went outside. So, you know me, I had a book with me and I started reading while I waited for him." She nods to show she's with me so far. I take a deep breath. "And that's when he came in."

"Alex," she says flatly. Not at all how his name should sound.

"Yes, he thought I was with you and he was just going to say hi quickly so he didn't upset you when you got back, which was pretty considerate if you think about it. But then he saw Levi outside and figured it out. He was kind of upset. I think he was... jealous," I whisper this last word, still afraid to believe it. "He said it was a good lesson for him in seizing the moment, and that was it. He left." That wasn't quite all of it. First he told me I was pretty, and then he quoted Hamlet. But I don't think Maia's ready to hear that he hit two of the items on my list of Perfect Guy Qualities. And I'm not even close to ready to address what happened *after* he left.

"See, so I was right!" she accuses. "You didn't feel anything for Levi because you still had a head full of Alex. You just need to give it another shot, that's all. I know you two would be great together."

"It's not gonna happen Maia, you have to let it go. I know it's crazy, but I really like Alex. Or at least I like him enough to want to find out more." Another deep breath. "And I need for you to tell me what you have against him. I don't want this to be an issue between us."

"Okay," she leans back against the wall again, looking at me as though she's accepting a challenge. "You have to promise to actually hear what I tell you, though. You can't go into this already deciding that I'm wrong."

"I promise," I tell her solemnly, and then throw my wadded up napkin at her with a grin. "But I don't promise to like it."

She laughs and bats it away, throwing her own at me in return. "I'm serious," she tries to sound like it through her giggling, and then clears her throat again, returning to business. "I don't want you to get hurt by putting your heart out there for the wrong guy."

"I know. You always take good care of me, especially when it comes to guys. I trust your opinion, so let's hear it."

She nods. "Do you remember Violet? From the bonfire?" I sift through the sea of faces that I met that night, no one coming to the forefront. She sees me struggling and offers a description to speed up the process. "Asian, super pretty, purple streak in her hair?"

131

"Of course!" It comes back to me in a flash. "Violet with the violet hair. How could I forget that? She looks like an Animé character."

"Yeah, that's her," she affirms. "Well, the way I hear it, when Alex first got here last year, lots of girls had immediate crushes. I admit it, he's nice to look at."

I can't help but smile at that. She *does* think he's cute, that's a start.

"He didn't really seem to go for anybody at first," she continues, "even though there were girls practically throwing themselves at him. Cheerleaders slipping their phone numbers into his locker, the class VP writing her number on his hand in Sharpie... But still, no response. Then this last spring, not long after I got here, he started noticing Violet. Nothing big, he would just happen to be there when she was about to sit down to eat lunch. Or, he'd be waiting there when her class let out and would happen to be going in the same direction. Stuff like that. She was ecstatic. Even when the jealous girls started spreading rumors, you know the type, Violet never seemed to notice. She was way too far into the clouds to hear them."

I tug the blanket farther up my legs and lean in, totally lost in her narrative. I can't resist a good love story.

"So no one was at all surprised when word started to spread that he'd asked her to Prom. She was in my Acting III class with me, and all us girls got pretty close since it's a small class. I even helped her pick out her prom dress—white and purple slinky silk, one shoulder, absolutely stunning on her."

I feel a tug of jealousy. I could never pull off something like that. How can I possibly compete?

"And then came Prom night. I went with Seth, as you know, even though I practically had to hit him over the head with hints to ask me. And Ember was there with Isaac, and Kaela went with Hudson—you haven't met him yet. And Jane and Davin were there, and we were all having a great time, dancing and everything. And Violet and Alex were there, but not with us, just hanging out on their own pretty much, but still we could tell she was having the best time.

"We'd been there for almost an hour I think, and we were just dancing to a slow song and Seth was being all sweet, when I happened to notice Alex leave the dance floor. He was acting all weird, like he might have been drunk or something. Violet went after him, back into one of the hallways, and not ten minutes later, she was running out of the dance, her face totally streaked with mascara, and the shoulder of her gorgeous dress completely torn. The girls and I went after her, but she was crying so hard she could barely form words. She wouldn't even talk to us. She just kept shaking her head, and her hands were trembling—it was pretty obvious that he had tried something, and she ran. And the coward wouldn't even come out after that. He must have found a back door or something 'cause believe me, we all went looking for him. Now, honestly. Tell me this is someone that I should let my best friend date."

Her words leave me stunned. Poor Violet! I can see why Maia would have a hard time forgiving him for such a thing. And it definitely helps to explain her odd reaction to finding me alone with him at the beach. Still…

"Did you ever find out what actually happened?" I ask quietly.

Her jaw drops. "Seriously? *That's* your comment? You're going to defend him?" Each question gets squeakier than the last.

"No! I'm not defending him. Believe me, if he did what you think he did, then I'll be first in line to start tying the noose. But… well, she never actually said anything. I was just wondering if anyone ever asked. I mean, specifically." She continues to glare at me, but I can't seem to stop myself from talking. The memory of his gentleness is still so clear in my mind; I can't believe that this is true. "Obviously, everyone saw what it *looked* like, but... well I'd hate to jump to a false conclusion when it would be so simple to ask the question."

She starts to protest, but then slumps over her knees, shifting her glance out the window. There's a young tree in the middle of the lawn where a bird is singing a rather repetitive song. It's the only sound for the next full minute.

"I was there. I saw the look on her face. As far as I'm concerned, there is no other reasonable explanation. If it was all a big mistake, then why wasn't he out there with her, trying to explain what happened? It doesn't add up. And even if he didn't try anything, the fact that he snuck out still shows a cowardice, a flaw, that I don't think is worth your time." She snaps her gaze back to meet mine. "I'm not forgiving him," she clarifies. "But I guess it wouldn't hurt to find out what actually happened instead of just shunning him for life without an explanation." She gives me a half smile.

"So what does that mean exactly?" I ask hopefully.

"It means that if we happen to run into him again and you still think you might be maybe interested after everything I've told you, then I'll try to be mostly nice."

"Wow, how very… vague of you."

"And that mostly niceness only applies until we find out what happened that night. After that, well, I guess it depends on what brilliant story he can come up with. But I reserve the right to return to shunning."

"Fair enough." Maybe I'm being naïve, but it just doesn't seem possible that the sweet, gentle guy I met at the beach is capable of doing what she's accusing him of. Of course, that sweet and gentle guy didn't seem like the kind who would need to be hiding from anyone who calls themselves *Enforcers* either.

 Chapter Twelve

*S*o this is the infamous Farmer's Market," I say, enjoying that Maia is

so excited to show off her new hometown.

I got to explore some of the downtown with Levi on our pseudo-date,

but it looks completely different tonight. The main street is blocked off

to traffic and there are vendors and people everywhere. Music drifts on

the breeze from somewhere close by, people are talking and laughing all

around us, and the scents—oh wow, the scents! Grilled steak and freshly

baked cookies, cinnamon rolls hot out of the oven, the clean earthy

scent of fresh veggies—they all mingle in the air, reminding me like a

brick to the head that we skipped lunch today.

"You know, Rennie," Maia begins in a playful tone that I know all too well. "Even in this sunshiney paradise, not everything is always fun and games."

"You don't say," I respond as though I have no idea what she's about to say. After the morning tribunal and all its great fun, Maia and I spent the afternoon avoiding her mother and watching season one of *Alias* for old time's sake. Since that summer when I broke my leg and we first discovered it, it's been a tradition to re-watch at least the first few episodes every year. And now, I can tell it's inspired our next activity.

She nods, all business. "It's true. I mean, here we are traipsing around and having a good old time when there could very well be trouble afoot. I think it's time for a little recon, Agent Winters. Now, I realize that it's been several months since your last mission, so I'm going to give you an easy first target." She glances around, shading her eyes with her hand. I can tell when she's found one to her liking. "All right. Male, red polo, khaki shorts." She pauses while I take a quick look around and spot him at a nearby vegetable stand. "Are you ready for this?"

"Well, if I'd known I was going to have to save the world today, I'd have worn more practical shoes. But I think I can handle it."

"And Agent Winters? Be careful out there."

We salute one another in unison, and I head into the crowd. I weave through a sea of strangers, my focus solely on my target. I approach the vegetable stand, sidling up to the make-shift tent and taking my place right next to Red Polo Man. I pick up a tomato and smell it, shifting my gaze to see if anyone is with the target. With my other hand, I reach into the side pocket of my bag to extract my weapon of choice: a sheet of tiny star-shaped stickers that is always waiting to be called into action. I snag one easily, using just the tip of my index finger, years of experience guiding my way. I ease closer to him, his back turned to me as he talks to a cute brunette behind the veggie-laden table. They flirt and gush over one another, giving me my chance to move in. I put down the tomato, step behind him as though to leave, and pretend to fumble with the straps of my bag. I let it slip off my shoulder as I pass by and stumble just a little.

For the record, this worked out great in my head.

However, as I reach out towards his shoulder, sticker at the ready, my head swims and I'm no longer at the Farmer's Market. I'm in a clearing in the woods. I watch my own hand reaching out, trembling, but there's no sticker. I'm tip-toeing barefoot through soft grass, as silent as possible, and I'm reaching for a dagger. Not just any dagger though. This one is worn in the leather sheath on the back of a young girl who can't be more than nine or ten years old. It's only for a moment and when I blink again, it's all gone.

I gasp, recoiling my arm and throwing it up over my head, desperate to rid myself of the vision. But of course there's no dagger, no girl. Just Red Polo Man, who is now being completely mauled by my swinging bag as the heels of my cute but incredibly impractical strappy wedges flip to the side, and I go tumbling into this poor guy who only moments ago was the target in a harmless game. Fantastic.

As I regain my bearings, he's already standing upright. I apologize for my clumsiness as he makes sure I'm okay which only adds to my guilt for knocking him over in the first place. Maia has rushed over to help, and makes sure he's all right as he and Tomato Girl move to the other side of the stand, then she reaches a hand down to help me to my feet.

"Nicely done, Agent Winters," she says with a grin. "Is your ankle okay? That looked like it hurt."

"I..." I have no idea what happened, much less any way to explain it. Another vision? "Did you see..." I look around, trying to find any sign of what I thought I saw. There's nothing there, and Maia's worried expression tells me there never was, but I can't quite lose the eerie feeling. "I'm fine," I manage. "Just embarrassed. Guess I failed in my mission, huh? So much for saving the world today."

"That's okay, I've got your back. Or more to the point, I got *his* back." She winks and gives a little nod in Red Polo Man's direction. On the back of his shoulder is a small pink star. She never fails to impress me.

I grin at her in approval. "Just like old times."

"We make a good team," she says, laughing as she leads me back to the sidewalk so I can compose myself.

"Excuse me, girls, but we need a moment of your time," says a deep voice behind me.

I turn around, still laughing, and come face to face with a man in a brown leather jacket. He's tall enough that I have to look up, and his non-smiling, non-handsome face stares back at me. I swallow hard, feeling the blood drain from my head. Enforcers.

Maia is still laughing, and she responds first. "Yeah? How can we help you?"

The other man has caught up to Deep Voice now, and he pulls a leather-bound notebook out of the inside pocket of his jacket. He's shorter than the other one, with a fine-featured face and long lean fingers. There's something vaguely spider-like about him that makes me shiver. "I'm Agent Parker. This here is Agent Donovan."

"Really?" Maia leans her elbow casually on my shoulder. "I'm Agent Bauer, and this here is Agent Bristow."

The two men look at one another, obviously not knowing what to make of Maia's wise-cracking.

"She's kidding," I explain. "It's a game, a spy game. Bauer is... never mind. Um, what can we do for you?"

"We're looking for a young man about your age, name of Ethan."

"Wait a minute." Maia stands up straight again, eyes narrowing. "You two were at the bonfire the other night. You're still looking for this Ethan guy?"

"Do you know him?" Agent Parker isn't in the mood to answer questions, I guess.

"No. I don't know anyone by that name," she says.

"Is he in trouble?" I realize too late that I should have kept my mouth shut.

All three of them turn to look at me, and Deep Voice (I mean Agent Donovan) takes a step towards me. "If I said no, would that make you remember him?"

I raise my hands up. "No! I mean, I don't know him anyway, I'm just curious. You guys seem to be going to an awful lot of trouble to find him is all, so I wondered, you know, what he did."

Agent Donovan looks me up and down, his dark eyes squinting, and he must decide I'm telling the truth because he finally blinks and looks away. "He may go by another name, so be on the lookout for anyone displaying suspicious behavior."

"Is this guy dangerous?" Maia sounds serious now. Finally.

The agents exchange another glance. "Probably not, but be careful. He's unpredictable. We just need to locate him as soon as possible."

"Do you have a photo?"

A tiny ray of hope alights in my chest. A photo would prove beyond any doubt who my Ethan is. But they both shake their heads, and Maia flings her arms into the air in a way I know all too well. There's a rant coming.

"Hang on. You guys stop us in the middle of the street solely based on our age range, which is totally profiling by the way, and then you interrogate us about this Ethan guy, and *then* you tell us that oh yeah, he might not even go by that name, and we have no idea what he looks like. How is that any way to conduct a search? Are you guys even cops?" She's practically screeching by the end of this, and the two Enforcers waste no time in shutting her up.

Parker steps in close and twists my arm behind my back. Donovan charges at Maia, hand to her neck, and both of us are being propelled into a tiny gap between two buildings. My heart is pounding in my throat and pain is shooting through my arm like it could break with just the slightest pressure. Is this really happening?

Donovan leans in, his face so close to Maia's their noses are almost touching. Maia's eyes are huge with fear. "Listen here, missy. You want to play spy games? You want to act tough and run around here like there's not a care in the world and we're all just here for your amusement? Let me tell you something. You have no clue what's going on around you. You wouldn't know thing one about real trouble. But pull a stunt like that little tirade again, and I'll be happy to volunteer to teach you."

"Donovan..." Parker's voice sounds like a warning behind me, and it works. The bigger agent releases Maia and stands up tall. He straightens the collar of his jacket, then runs both hands over his dark hair. Parker gives my arm another tug for good measure, and I let out a yelp as he releases me.

I run over to Maia, where she is leaning with her hands on her knees, coughing and breathing heavily. "Are you okay?" She coughs again and nods, looking up at me with tears in her eyes. I throw my arms around her and we stand that way, trembling until she can speak again.

"I'm sorry," she says, voice coming out a little hoarse. "I should have kept my big mouth shut."

"That was *so* not your fault; no one could have seen that coming. Those guys are nuts!" I look around, but as I expected, they're long gone.

She rubs at her neck and I shake my arm out, my fingers tingling now that there's blood flowing again. "Well, whoever that Ethan guy is, I sure don't envy him," she says. "If they did that to us just for asking questions, I can't imagine what they'll do when they really get their hands on him."

"Yeah," I reply quietly. "Me neither."

By mutual agreement, we decide not to tell the girls about what just happened. Under normal circumstances, Maia would relish the drama of repeating a major incident like this, but this one was a little too frightening to relive yet. We also agree not to call the police, because really, what evidence do we have? But I convince her that when we get home, we *will* be telling Aidan. It just feels like some adult should know what's going on, even if there's nothing he can do about it now. So she links her elbow with mine and we make our way down the street. In only a few minutes, we're turning into a wide walkway between Express and the Gap and trying to act normal.

"Maia! Rennie!" Ember is waving us over to a table outside Pizza Solo, her toffee-colored skin glowing in the afternoon light. Jane stands up and hugs us both in greeting before we sit down. The evening is perfect for dining outside, and the aroma from the pizza ovens is enough to make my tummy growl its own greeting.

"We already ordered, I hope that's okay," Jane says, running a hand over her blonde pixie cut to smooth down strays that don't exist. "We got the usual."

"Sweet!" Maia replies, still rubbing absent-mindedly at her throat. To me she explains, "We always get the Guido. Don't worry, you'll love it." I'm not quite as adventurous as she is when it comes to culinary choices, but I trust her.

"Soooo…" begins Kaela, leaning across the table towards me, silver earrings swinging with her movement. Her blue eyes are wide and mischievous. "Have you heard from Levi again?"

I look to Maia, who is absolutely no help as she tries to twist the top off of her root beer bottle. "Actually, I haven't. I really think we're only going to be friends." Kaela's face falls.

"Oh no," Jane moans, sounding genuinely upset. "I thought you two had a great time together!"

"We did," I assure her.

"You guys," Ember cuts in, sounding as exasperated as I feel. "Leave the poor girl alone. They obviously didn't get on well; don't make her keep dredging it up."

Kaela leans back in her chair and folds her arms across her chest. "Well excuse us for trying to see that she has a fun summer," she says in full-on pout mode.

Great. This is exactly what I didn't want. I stretch my hands out in a placating gesture. "It's okay, really. He's a nice guy, he's just not the one I want to spend my summer with." I laugh, trying to lighten the mood.

All four heads snap to me, Maia slightly shocked and the other three brimming with curiosity. Did I say something wrong? I was only trying to get them off of the Levi issue.

"You mean there's someone else?" Jane asks, a sly smile spreading across her face. Crap. I did imply that, didn't I?

"You've only been here for three days!" Kaela sounds impressed.

"Well, aren't you the little vixen? It's always the quiet ones you have to look out for." Ember smiles and lifts an eyebrow.

This is not the topic I wanted to introduce, but at least I did succeed in bringing our mood back to normal. That must count for something.

"Who is it?"

"Is it someone from the bonfire?"

"How did you meet somebody already?"

"How long have you liked him?

"Do we know him?"

"What's his name?"

Yep, definitely back to normal. Maia sits back, watching the interrogation with a look that clearly says *You started this.*

I take a deep breath. "Okay, I'll talk!" They quiet down instantly. "I did meet him at the bonfire, and you do know him." I sigh as Kaela clasps her hands together, once again delighted at the prospect of potential blooming romance. "But I don't really know him yet, and he has no idea that I like him. So I will tell you everything, but you're gonna have to be patient with me. I'm not ready to reveal any details just yet."

"Awww,! The disappointment is an audible cry from all three of them. Sagging shoulders, protruding lower lips, and crossed arms all tell me how unfair I'm being for dashing their hopes of new gossip.

"I really am sorry, but I just—"

"Pizza!" Maia sings, pointing to the apron-clad server headed our way. We scramble to make room in the middle of the table and I take advantage of the chaos to whisper "thank you" to Maia for the interruption. She winks and hands me a plate.

We all dive in as soon as the pizza has landed, plates clattering and gooey strings of cheese going everywhere. It's an odd, very Californian, combination of toppings—something I never would have picked out for myself. Sweet fresh tomatoes, floral basil, creamy avocado slices, and tangy feta cheese all meld together in one delicious bite. It's quite a departure for my Pennsylvania-grown taste buds, but I love it. Maybe

I'm starting to grow up a little after all. Branching out and trying new things is supposed to be a sign of that, right? Or I'm hungry.

I'm just polishing off my second slice when a movement catches my eye. In a sea of people milling about, I have no idea what made me look up, but whatever the cause, there he is: Alex. I stop mid-bite, cheese dangling off my lip. He's across the way, pulling open the big glass door to the two-story Barnes & Noble. My favorite boy, my favorite store… It must be a sign.

"Rennie, what's wrong?" Maia whispers, not wanting to draw the girls' attention from their conversation. She follows my glance, and I can tell in her posture the moment she sees him. She sits a little straighter, annoyed, her face suddenly scowling. "Oh," is all she says. She studies me for a moment, and then sets down her bottle of root beer. "All right," she says, still just to me. "Let's do this."

"Do what?" I ask, only half-listening. I can't take my eyes off the door he just entered. I wonder how long he'll be here. What if he leaves and I miss my chance to talk to him again?

"You wanted to confront him about that night at Prom, right? Let's go get this over with." She's already standing when her words finally sink in.

"Wait, what? No!" I stand with her, grabbing her arm. The girls stop their chatter, and watch us with puzzled looks.

"We'll be right back," Maia tells them as she ushers me away. She takes me to the other side of a big planter, but I can still see them watching us, whispering to one another. As soon as we're out of earshot, she starts in. "You're the one who said we should find out what happened. You said we should give him the benefit of the doubt until we know for sure what happened with Violet. Well, here's our chance." She gestures widely to the closed door of Barnes & Noble.

"I... I don't think I'm ready yet," I stammer, panic starting to rise in my chest. "Maybe we could..."

"No way, Rennie," she interrupts. "According to our deal, I have to be nice to that jerk until we have this little conversation with him. And I am not going to drag that out any longer than absolutely necessary."

"Wow. Way to be unbiased there, Mai."

"I am biased, I can admit that. As far as I'm concerned, he could fall off the face of the earth and I'd be just fine, in fact I might do a little happy dance. But I agreed to be *mostly* nice until this is resolved, so let's go do it." She starts marching toward the bookstore, leaving me to gape after her.

I look back at the girls, but they're only three whispering heads at the moment. I guess I have no choice but to follow her. I duck inside the door, trying to be as inconspicuous as possible. I brush pizza crumbs from my shirt and run a hand over my hair. Am I really going to talk to Alex now? Like this? With Maia all wound up?

"Alex!" I hear Maia's voice up ahead; merely the sound of his name is an accusation. I guess we're doing this.

I dash forward to where she's found him in the Local History section. Briefly, I wonder what he was looking for, but I don't have much chance for idle curiosity. Maia means business.

He looks up and sees her, confused, then sees me rushing up behind her. "Hey Maia. Hi Rennie," he looks around her to give me my own greeting, eyes shining in the dim store light. He looks amazing: faded jeans, black tee-shirt, dark blue jacket, black Chucks. If I'd ever thought to sketch my perfect guy, this is what he'd look like. He gives me a half-smile, and brushes the bangs out of his eyes. They fall right back to where they were to begin with. I guess I can't blame them; if I was that close to his eyes, I don't think I could bring myself to leave either. Oh wow, when did I get this cheesy?

"Are you looking for a book?" he asks casually. "I bet I can help you find a good one."

I can tell from his expression that he's just messing with her, and I tuck a stray strand of hair behind my ear in an effort to hide a smile.

"We're not looking for a book, Alex," she spits his name out in a way I don't like at all.

"Be nice," I whisper.

She gives a big exaggerated sigh, letting me know how unreasonable my request is. "Fine," she says curtly, then turns back to him with a stiff smile. "My dear friend Rennie and I would be ever so appreciative if you could spare a few minutes for a question or two." She's dripping sugar now, so overstating the sweetness I'm afraid she'll draw ants.

He looks to me for confirmation, amusement shining on his face. I nod. Better than trying to formulate sentences while he's standing there looking all cute.

"Okay, shoot," he faces her squarely, planting his feet and folding his arms, ready for whatever's coming. I try to read his expression. Does he know what she's about to ask?

"If you'd be so kind," she continues in her sticky sweet tone, "would you please cast your memory back to the evening of May the 16th." He looks at her blankly. "Prom night," she clarifies, just a tinge of acid leaking in. He flinches but doesn't look away. "If you recall, you had a date with a mutual friend, Miss Violet St. Clair. Does this ring a bell?"

"Of course it does," he says evenly, his eyes never leaving Maia's.

"And, as you may also recall, you two looked like you were having a grand time together, dancing and laughing and having your portraits done. Prom memories last forever, you know." He nods, a muscle in his jaw twitching slightly. "But, of course, not everything went as planned, did it? At least not for poor Violet. You left a kind, beautiful girl sitting alone on the biggest night of the year, humiliated and crying her eyes out." Somewhere along the line she's switched from sugary sweet to accusing lawyer, but I don't step in. I'm willing to give him the benefit of the doubt, but as it turns out, I want to hear the answer too.

"It seems that I haven't been very nice to you since then, as Rennie was quick to point out. The way I see it, any guy who would do that is pretty much scum and doesn't deserve anything but contempt. However, Rennie is my best friend, and for some reason she's gotten it into her head that maybe you got the short end of the stick. That maybe, all the tears and Violet's dress being ripped from her shoulder, and you not even having the courage to show your face, was all circumstantial evidence. Just one big misunderstanding. Now I admit, I may not have given you the opportunity to explain your side of things. So here's your big chance. Explain."

He shifts his weight and clears his throat. Obviously we've blindsided him, but I admire the way he's taken it all in without getting defensive. His eyes drift to me, and I offer what I hope is an encouraging smile. "Everything you said is right on the money," he says quietly. "And I wish that I could defend my actions, but the truth is… I can't."

My heart sinks. Maia makes a dismissive sound through her teeth and rolls her eyes. "I knew it," she says. "Come on, Ren. I told you he wasn't worth your time." She grabs my arm and turns to leave, but I yank it away.

"No, wait." I turn back to him, a mixture of anger and desperation bubbling up inside me. "Let him finish," I say it to Maia, but I direct my glare at Alex. Was I wrong about him? Is he really just a jerk like Maia said he was? I'm not willing to believe that yet. "Something happened that night," I whisper so only Alex can hear me. "And I know it's not what they think it was. It's something to do with those Enforcers, isn't it? From the beach?" It's a shot in the dark, after the experience Maia and I just had with them, but this feels like the right answer. His reaction tells me I'm right. "I knew it; it wasn't your fault. So just... just tell us what happened."

His eyes search mine, and he opens his mouth to speak. I can tell that his defense is right there, ready to roll off his tongue, but he won't let it. "I can't tell you the details. I wish I could, but I can't."

I lift my eyebrows, waiting for more. Maia taps her fingers on her folded arms, still fuming.

He releases a sigh of frustration and continues. "All I can tell you is that I would *never* hurt Violet. Or anyone, for that matter. And I would never try to force any girl to do something that she didn't want to do. That's just not in my nature. It is true that I left, and she followed me. I wasn't feeling well, and..."

"You were drunk, you mean," Maia spits out.

"I wasn't drunk. If you knew me at all, you'd know how wrong you are about that. But things did get out of hand. She tried to help, but it wasn't... I couldn't..." He looks miserable, reliving the memory, trying to defend himself. I know what that feels like. "Listen, Maia. I admire that you stand by your friends. I never tried to offer an excuse to any of you because, quite frankly, I deserved the punishment. No matter the reason, the end result was exactly how you described it. Violet was alone and crying and I should have been there to help. I cared about Violet a great deal. I never meant to hurt her, and believe me, if I could take it back I would."

Maia's fingers have stopped tapping, and her face has softened to something that could almost be read as sympathy. But when she sees me notice this, she shoves her mask of disdain back into place. "Okay then," she says briskly. "Well, I promised to hear you out, and now I've done that. So... bye." She turns and walks quickly toward the exit without a backward glance to see if I'm following.

I reach out and touch his arm. "Thank you," I tell him. It seems an inadequate response, but he smiles. Before I can work up the nerve to think of something better, I hurry away after Maia.

I catch up with her outside, back at our table. She's grabbing her bag from the back of her chair and the girls are all gathering up their belongings as well when I run up to them. It's obvious she's still upset. She's never been one for hiding her emotions.

"What happened?" Jane asks, eyes wide.

"Nothing," Maia snaps. "Nothing at all. Are we ready to go get our tickets? We better get going if we want to catch a movie."

"Maia, please," I start, confused by her decision to dismiss this. "We talked to him, like you said we should. And you finally got to hear his side of things. Can't you at least... I don't know, acknowledge that?"

"Fine," she says. "Yes, I got to hear his lame-ass story. Great. It doesn't change what happened."

"Who did you talk to?" Kaela asks.

"Are you saying you don't think he meant what he said?"

"I'm saying that he didn't actually *say* anything. We don't know any more now than we did a month ago!"

"Know more about what?" Ember tries.

"We know that whatever happened, it wasn't intentional. That he would change it all if he could," I tell her, trying to be patient. My efforts are met with an ungraceful snort from Maia.

"Yeah, well what did you expect him to say? I could have told you he'd deny it."

"Well I believe him," I state firmly.

"And who's surprised? Anyone? Anyone?" she mocks.

"You believe who?" Jane attempts.

"I saw your face when you heard his story. You believed him too, at least until you talked yourself out of it again. Admit it."

"I admit nothing!" Maia throws her arms up. "If he felt so terrible about hurting Violet, why didn't he go to her immediately and apologize? Huh? Did you think of that?"

"Wait, Violet? You were talking to Alex?" Ember's mouth drops open in disbelief as she pieces the puzzle together.

"Do you know that he didn't?" I counter. "He said he didn't offer an explanation to *you* because he felt bad about it all. But are you sure that he didn't apologize to Violet personally?"

"Are you sure that he did?"

"I think it's very possible, yes!"

"We're talking to Alex again? I thought we hated him." Kaela's brow is furrowed as she tries to follow along.

Maia is silent for so long, I'm not sure if she'll even bother to answer. "Hate is a strong word," she says. "But unintentional or not, he broke Violet's heart. Maybe he's not a monster, but his actions still make him selfish and careless. But due to the circumstances, I suppose we don't *hate* him."

159

"Good," Kaela says with a smile. "I always thought he was nice."

Her kind comment is overpowered, however, by Ember exploding with, "Oh my giddy aunt, you like Alex!"

Jane is nodding along. "That's right! You met him at the bonfire, he's someone that we know, you didn't want to say anything yet because you knew we didn't like him… it's totally Alex!"

The blush creeping up my face answers for me.

"Nailed it!" Jane holds her hand up to Ember for a high five, looking very proud of herself.

"But what about all the prom stuff?" Kaela is still confused, and understandably so.

"I'll explain the whole thing while we're waiting for the movie," Maia offers, and leads the way down the steps to the theatre.

Picking a movie turns out to be about as successful as setting me up on a blind date was. We've ruled out the documentary, the slasher flick, and the animated 3-D (much to Kaela's dismay). Which leaves Ember searching her bag to come up with a coin to flip to decide between the romantic comedy and the superhero blow-up-all-the-things movie.

I'm happy with either one, so I stop paying attention and allow my mind to drift once again to Alex. Maia actually approves! Well, not *approves* so much as *maybe wouldn't throw him over a cliff if given the opportunity.* Close enough; I'll take it. Now I just need to find a way to talk to him again. Well, I know where he is now. I wonder…

The quarter comes up on the romantic comedy side and everyone but Ember is happy. I nudge Maia as the girls queue up to buy tickets for the next showing.

"Hey, Mai?" I pull her aside. "Umm… dinner was a lot of fun and well, we're going to get out of the theatre early enough that we can still do some window shopping, right? And during the movie, we're all sort of, you know, not really talking or anything. So I was thinking…"

"You want to go find Alex," she finishes for me.

"Would you hate me?" I cringe.

She stares at me, and folds her arms. Not a good start. "Hate is a strong word," she repeats, and I know I'm supposed to catch the comparison.

161

I don't know how to turn her to my side on this. "I know he's not your favorite, I get that. But—"

"You would really abandon me and the girls to chase after some guy you barely know? Not only is that incredibly unsafe, but it's also kind of pathetic."

I feel like she just slapped me. Did my best friend really just call me pathetic?

She must see that she's gone too far, because she immediately reaches out to touch my arm, softening her deadpan expression. "I didn't mean that. I just mean, well…"

"No, I think you said exactly what you meant." I'm shaking, but I'm not willing to let her see that. "Look, I don't want to fight about this, but I am going to find Alex. The timing stinks, I'll give you that, and I'm sorry to bail on you guys. But I know where he is right now, and I'm not going to lose this opportunity."

She nods slowly. We never fight, not for real. It couldn't feel more foreign if we both randomly started speaking in Japanese. I actually can't remember a time when I've stood up to her, and it makes the air thick around us.

"Okay, I respect that. But let *me* be clear too. Alex is on a very short leash. You don't know this guy at all, so just… be smart. If you can't find him, or he's already gone or he's a jerk—"

"Maia…"

"Or whatever, you come find us."

"I will. Thank you."

"Don't thank me. I still think you're being stupid, just don't get hurt doing it."

"Fair enough," I say. I don't expect her to love this idea, but I know she still loves me, so I let her be angry. "I'll meet you back here in an hour and a half. Now go on, you'll miss the previews. You love the previews." I nudge her toward the box office and she reluctantly heads in that direction.

"Rennie?"

"Yeah?"

She touches her neck again, and I know it's not only Alex she's warning me about now. "Be careful."

I nod. "You'll explain to the girls?"

"We got it already," Ember shouts from across the way. "Now go get your man!"

The girls all giggle. All except for Maia, of course.

Suddenly, I can't help the silly grin that spreads across my face. Get my man? That is exactly what I intend to do.

Chapter Thirteen

He must have come this way. I glance behind me, making sure I still know the way back. He'd already left Barnes & Noble when I got back up there, but I managed to catch a glimpse of him rounding the corner. And then the next corner. I feel like a stalker.

I stop walking and step into a doorway to get my bearings. There are still people all around—crowded around the Art Deco movie theatre across the street, down the block at the music store, across the way in a wine-tasting shop. Surely there's no danger if I keep going a little further, not with this many people close by. I stick my head out of the doorway and around the corner. No sign of him.

It's only now, as I'm contemplating yet another street that I have to wonder what in the world I'm doing. Am I really chasing after a boy I barely know just because he was nice to me?

"I really am pathetic," I tell myself aloud. This isn't like me at all. And yet, by the time I finish chiding myself, I look up to find that I'm halfway up the next block. "Well how about that," I whisper. Guess one more block won't hurt. To this next street sign and that's it—done.

A breeze blows across me and I shiver in the night air. Isn't California supposed to be warm? I stop and glance around me, suddenly unable to shake the feeling that I'm being watched. A quick overview of the area yields nothing. Okay, more carefully then; think like Jack Bauer. I narrow my eyes and check the shadows of the trees on the courthouse lawn, behind the car parked up the street, the windows in the building to my left. No one.

My heart begins to beat louder in my ears. Every sense is heightened and I know that my instincts are telling me something. This is the part where Maia always wins our spy missions. It's a fine line between good instincts and paranoia and I have a hard time settling on the right one.

Another breeze lifts the tiny hairs on the back of my neck—warm, like a breath. I spin around and find... no one. In fact, I find no street at all.

Instead, I'm standing in soft grass, looking out at the stormy ocean far below. Angry waves crash on jagged rocks, dark clouds gather overhead, and my hair whips wildly—an inferno of red flame. That same rush of fear that met me in the other flashes is quick to overtake me again, but there's no nausea. It's just a vision. It isn't real. Well, it isn't real *yet.*

I inhale deeply in an attempt to steady my nerves, and the salty sea air feels heavy in my lungs. Like my previous visions, I'm instantly thrown into the actions and emotions of where I am now. It's like stepping onto a stage and somehow knowing the scene I'm in without ever having read a script. There's a sinking feeling in my chest, sadness and anger that match the tempest surrounding me. A voice mingles with the wind, making it impossible to determine its origin.

"Serenity," she calls. But I won't look. "Serenity please, please come home. You must understand that I had no choice."

I grind my jaw, delaying my answer. If she knew me at all, she would know that those were precisely the wrong words to convince me. "No. This is not my home, I don't belong here."

"But you can, in time."

"Time?" I scoff. I turn my eyes to the roiling clouds above me, the grey and red of the castle's spiral tower intruding on the periphery of my vision. "Is that supposed to be a joke? There is no amount of *time* that will make me forget what you did." I shake my head, the motion making me all woozy again.

And just like that, it's all gone.

I grab my aching head in both hands, trying to steady my vision. These flashes have got to stop. Nightmares at night, visions when I'm awake, and now actually visiting my dream land for some unknown reason. Someone is definitely trying to get my attention. Either that or I really am going mad.

My breathing starts to settle as the headache fades. On the bright side, at least the visions are mercifully brief.

"Seriously Rennie," I say out loud, knowing that hearing my own voice will help to dispel the remaining nerves. "You're losing it."

"Do you always address yourself by name?" a voice teases me from behind. I spin again, heart racing.

"Ethan," I breathe before I can stop myself. I clear my throat, hoping that maybe he didn't hear me. "Alex," I say louder, trying to look him in the eye but suddenly finding my sandals quite interesting.

His eyes narrow, and he folds his arms across his chest. "That's the second time you've called me that." His voice is soft, curious. "Why?"

I'm sure that even in the light of the street lamps he can tell that I'm blushing. Do I dare to tell him the truth? That he may or may not be a guy I dream about, who rescues me from my nightmares and is completely in love with me? That I think he might be the one that I have to find and ally myself with before it's too late? Whatever *that* means.

"I guess... Maybe you just look like an Ethan to me," I stammer. Chicken, party of one. I try to play it off by shrugging and glancing up at him in a flirtatious way.

He smiles, and his shoulders visibly relax. I make a mental note to *think* before saying his name aloud from now on. Actually, thinking before speaking to him at all seems like a grand idea.

Alex turns and starts up the sidewalk, looking over his shoulder at me.

I know I'm supposed to follow but I suddenly have second-thoughts, Maia's warning reverberating in my head. I glance back toward the crowds and the cars on Monterey Street, and my moment of indecision makes him laugh out loud.

"Oh come on. You've been following me for the last four blocks and *now* you're worried?" He looks me right in the eye, those stormy grey eyes burning into me.

"You knew I was following you?" More great spy work, Rennie.

He tilts his head, amused. "Come on," he repeats softly, not a reprimand this time, but an invitation. "You're safe with me."

Another little itch of memory tickles my brain. Why does that seem to happen when I'm with him? We walk in silence up the block, his hands shoved into his jeans pockets, his eyes focused on the sidewalk in front of us. I look over at him, wondering what deep thoughts are causing that look of concentration. I open my mouth, ready to break the silence when he turns into a courtyard on our left. A few wooden benches sit at the edges, curving out of brick planters. To our right is a set of four wide cement steps. They don't lead anywhere, only up to a bigger brick planter, but it looks like a nice place to relax away from street traffic. I look up at the glass doors and windows. There's no name printed anywhere that I can see on the large, two-toned brick building.

"Where are we?" I try to keep my voice casual, but a small crack betrays my anxiety.

"The public library."

"This is what you wanted to show me? The library?"

"Yeah, I…" This time he's the one who looks unsure, and I instantly regret the sarcasm in my last question. He shuffles a foot nervously along the cement, and glances around us. "Let's sit."

He leads the way to one of the benches and I follow, my mind swimming. A guy I barely know, a place I don't know at all, and I can't see another soul in any direction. Was this a huge mistake coming here? What if Maia was right about him? I could be back with the girls right now enjoying some brainless comedy, laughing and eating popcorn. Instead I'm here with Alex about to be—what? Confided in? Kissed? Assaulted? Murdered? I have no idea and my mind won't stop sending out useless suggestions. Stupid brain, shut up shut up shut up.

"Why were you following me tonight?" Alex's direct question startles me. A thousand excuses and denials spring into my thoughts but I shove them aside.

"I like you," I answer, sitting beside him, heart racing. It's not like me to be *that* honest with a boy I like. Ever. "I thought you might be someone I'd like to know better."

"Even after everything Maia told you? About prom?" His voice is so soft, so gentle. Any lingering doubt I was harboring skitters away.

"I know that you didn't do what she thought you did. What they all thought."

"How? I mean, you're right. I didn't; I *wouldn't*. But... you just met me. How do you know that with such certainty that you're willing to be here alone with me?"

I study the silver ring on my left hand, twisting it around my index finger, the light blue gem flashing in the light each time it reaches the top. "I just know," I whisper. I was so sure I could be direct about this, but here I am blushing and playing with my jewelry as though I want to be somewhere else. I don't. I really *really* don't.

He places a hand over mine, forcing me to stop fidgeting. His eyes search mine, his pupils moving back and forth as though he's literally trying to read my thoughts. It's unnerving to be scrutinized like this and yet I can't bring myself to look away.

"There's so much I wish I could tell you," he says, his voice low and intimate.

"I'm right here," I whisper, trying to be reassuring. Maybe he's ready to reveal more of the details about prom, or maybe he'll finally tell me why those Enforcers are after him. "Tell me."

He's silent for the space of several breaths, his mouth opening and closing with indecision. "Books are important to me," he begins. "Stories and words and..." He shakes his head in frustration. "I'm sorry, I don't know where to start. I mean when I'm with you, even the moment I met you, I felt like maybe... like we could..." He lets out a blast of air, running a hand over his hair again.

I'm so lost. Why is he talking as though I should be able to fill in the blanks? What did I miss?

"Maybe we could start with what happened at the beach," I prompt. "The Enforcers—who are they, and why were we hiding from them?"

He shakes his head. "They're nobody. I shouldn't have dragged you into that nonsense, I'm sorry about that."

"Well, those nobodies assaulted Maia and I earlier today, right on the street in broad daylight. So whatever is going on, I think I'm right in the middle of it."

"They *what?* Are you okay? What happened?" He squeezes my hand tighter, looking me up and down for any injuries.

"I'm fine. We both are, but it was really frightening. One minute they were asking us questions, and the next they were pushing us into this little alley and the big scary one had his hand around Maia's throat, choking and threatening her. And the little one had my arm twisted up behind my back like they always do on those cop shows. It was terrifying."

"Rennie, I'm so sorry that happened to you." He licks his lips, looking like he wants to say more. He shakes his head, a small smile playing on his lips. "Once again, I find myself wanting to tell you more than I can. What is it about you that makes me want to reveal all of my deep dark secrets?"

"Why can't you? It looks like I'm involved anyway."

"I will tell you this: The Enforcers are no one to mess with. I've never known them to be here before this, so something has changed, and please just believe me when I tell you that it can't be good. If you see them again, get out of there. Lie, scream, fight, whatever you have to do, okay?"

I bite my lip, trying not to look as scared as his words are making me.

"Okay," I whisper.

"Do you know what they were looking for? What were they asking?"

Here's my chance. I can ask him more about Ethan without sounding completely crazy, because the Enforcers are already bringing enough crazy for all of us. "Well it's kind of funny, because I think I'm looking for the same thing."

He furrows his brow and opens his mouth to reply, but doesn't get the chance.

"McKinley." The name echoes across the courtyard, a harsh bark that makes me jump.

I lean back, not realizing how close I had been to Alex. Looking over my shoulder, I see the source of the call. Seth. There's a tightening in my gut that I can't explain. Something inside me instinctively does not trust this guy.

"Garrison," Alex answers, the obligatory guy-greeting of last names only. This doesn't feel like a greeting though, more like a warning. Alex's grip on my hand tightens.

"You guys are friends?" I whisper. Somehow I can't picture easy-going Alex voluntarily spending time with someone I've only seen as rude, and now bordering on volatile.

"Yeah," he explains quickly. "We started hanging out when I first got here, and we're both on the baseball team. But lately he's gotten a little more intense."

Seth is on the other side of the square making his way down the few cement steps from the sidewalk. His spiky blond hair doesn't even move in the night breeze. Way too much hair product. But I'm pretty sure that shouldn't be my main concern. His face is tight, head lowered as though he's heading into a confrontation. He stops several yards from us, eyes shifting down to take in the sight of our linked hands. "I need to talk to you."

"It'll wait; you can see I'm busy."

"Now." Seth's hands ball into fists at his sides. A blue vein in his neck is pulsing angrily with each heartbeat. Not a good look.

Alex is about to argue further when I speak up.

"It's okay, I don't mind." I smile at him, making sure my dimple is properly displayed. It makes him smile back at me, as I'd hoped it would. "Go ahead. I'll wait for you."

He looks at me gratefully and stands up, releasing my hand to take off his jacket. He wraps the dark blue warmth around my shoulders, holding on to the collar as he adjusts it to my form. His thumb sweeps against my jaw and he inclines towards me as though to whisper in my ear. I lean in to hear what he has to say only to be rewarded with a gentle kiss to my right cheek. He stands upright, gives me a quick smile and turns to Seth.

I can't seem to remind myself to breathe. He really kissed me? I mean, my cheek, but still. I close my eyes and savor the small bit of fire that burns where his lips touched my face, just at the cheekbone near my temple. I touch it with my fingers, lightly so as not to disturb the sanctity of the site. Somewhere deep down, I honestly do know that I'm being ridiculous, but I simply don't care. The huge swarm of butterflies that has taken over my insides has squelched any thought of decorum.

I pull the jacket closer around me, inhaling his scent. It's that same wonderful clean earthy scent I remember from when we were hiding in the cavern. I take in another greedy lungful and let my eyes flutter open, automatically searching for the source of this newest happiness. It's not until I see him arguing with Seth that I'm brought back to reality.

They stand face-to-face on the far sidewalk, their argument quiet but animated. Their bodies are flexed from head to toe as though ready for a physical fight to break out at any moment, but their voices are remarkably restrained. Seth leans in aggressively, muscles tensed and face drawn taut in anger.

Something Seth says makes Alex laugh and respond with a smirk. And that makes Seth respond with a fist to Alex's face.

I jump up from the bench and race towards them, screaming "Stop!" and waving my arms.

Alex staggers backwards clutching his face, but in a flash he has a hold of Seth's shirt, and Seth is winding up to hit him again. I dive in between them, pushing them apart with a hand to each of their chests. Seth makes a move like he's going to go around me (or maybe through me, it's hard to tell), but Alex steps away, hands up in surrender.

"This isn't over, McKinley," Seth growls, pointing a finger and breathing like a bull in the ring.

"Oh, I think it is." Alex's smile rests on me, and in spite of what's happening at the moment, it causes a little flutter inside me and I smile back.

"Unbelievable," Seth mutters. He flings his arms up to disengage me from his chest and turns on his heel, stalking off into the darkness.

In the space of a heartbeat, Alex is beside me and all is right again. He takes my hands in his and leans in close. I don't move away.

"You're okay?" he asks.

He's too close and smells too good for me to be able to form words yet. I nod.

"Sorry about that. Seth has issues, and for some reason he always feels a need to drag me into them."

"I'm just glad *you're* okay." I reach up, gently touching the bruise starting to form next to his eye. He inhales sharply, but doesn't pull away. "I thought you said you guys are friends. What made him do this?"

"Let's just say he's not very happy with some of my choices lately." I get the feeling he's trying to be diplomatic.

"He didn't seem to like that I was here with you," I venture.

Alex laughs humorlessly. "Well, I think he likes us together about as much as Maia does." The look on my face brings a genuine bark of laughter from him. "Don't worry about him. I like you enough for both of us."

He gives me a timid smile and I realize that my fingers are still lingering on his face. I pull them away and take a step backwards.

Alex clears his throat. Then he closes the distance between us in a single step and puts his arm around my shoulders. I find that I fit perfectly, like a missing puzzle piece that's found its home.

"Come on," he says lightly. "Let's get you back to your friends."

We're starting to round the corner when I stop. His arm slides off my shoulder with his unchecked momentum and he turns back to face me.

"What is it?" That little crease is back on his forehead and I'm momentarily distracted by the thought of how nice it is that he's concerned for me.

"What we were talking about before Seth showed up." I'm not sure how to go into this. I can't just ask him if he's Ethan. The chances of him having any idea what I'm talking about are slim at best, but the chances of him thinking I'm completely loony are pretty good. I don't like those odds.

He looks away, running his hand over his hair again in that nervous gesture that is suddenly so adorable. He takes my hands again. "I'm sorry, we were rudely interrupted, weren't we? Tell you what, let's just forget all of that for tonight. No Enforcers, no Seth, no distractions. Let's just figure this out as we go."

I smile up at him and put a hand to his chest. It's a daring move for me and I enjoy the fluttery feeling it gives me. "I like the sound of that."

He rewards me with that ridiculously cute smile and tucks me under his arm, once again moving down the street. "Now, tell me about you and Levi."

"Ugh!" I roll my eyes with enough over-emphasis to make even Maia proud. "He's a nice enough guy, but honestly? I've only been here for a couple of days, and I'm already sick of hearing his name." I laugh, and he laughs with me.

"That is a perfect answer." He pulls me closer to him, and we head off into the night.

Chapter Fourteen

*T*onight's dream is a new one. I know this right away because Alex is with me (sweet and adorable and perfectly knowable) instead of the shadowy figure of Ethan. It doesn't feel wrong at all, in fact it feels perfect. I still think that the only possible explanation is that Alex and Ethan are the same person. What else could explain why I'm so drawn to him? But those kinds of impossible thoughts belong in the real world, not here.

We're walking side by side, his arm wrapped around my shoulders. He leans over and kisses my cheek, a familiar gesture that suggests he's done this many times before. I grin up at him and silently wonder how I got so lucky.

"Do you like it?" he asks, leaning in so his voice is a soft purr in my ear.

"Hm?" I muse, not minding if I sound inarticulate. It is a dream after all. "Like what?"

He laughs. "The garden. You mean I brought you here to impress you and you don't even notice?"

I look around me for the first time and see that there's more to this dream than just Alex. Much more. We're standing in a beautiful Chinese garden. Stone pillars stand regally at the entrance, guarded by two lions carved in the Asian style with open mouths and fierce expressions. Gently undulating sidewalks wind in and out of view around the perimeter, and a shallow pond gleams inside, still as a painting in the fading sunlight. At the center of the pond stands a red and black gazebo, the five points of the roof rising at the edges and in the middle like fabric being lifted at each corner by invisible thread. The whole garden doesn't take up more than a half a block, maybe. It's secluded, intimate. Perfect.

There's a direct route straight ahead of us, but Alex takes my hand

and leads me along the path to our left. Back and forth along the gentle curves, past a wall of live bamboo that forms a barricade from the outside world. Somewhere in the distance, I can hear someone playing a guitar, people laughing, the completely incongruous sounds of cars passing. But it all sounds miles away. Here, there's only me and Alex.

He leads me up a few wooden steps and we're inside the gazebo. It feels like we've stepped into another world. He goes to the railing at the far side and leans his back against it, pulling me into him. Normally, being this close would make me nervous, stammering over my thoughts and losing myself in my own shyness, but I know that this is only a dream and the knowledge makes me bold. I lean into him and slide my arms around his waist.

"Tell me a story," I whisper, smiling up at him. He grins at me and kisses my forehead. My skin radiates with the heat. I close my eyes to enjoy the feeling and lay my head against his chest.

"Once upon a land, in a far away time," he starts, "there was a young lady of uncommon name, and uncommon beauty."

"I love fairy tales," I sigh happily, hugging him tighter.

He kisses the top of my head in response before continuing with the story. "And though this extraordinary girl was kind and brave and generous, the people did not know her. This was no fault of theirs, however. For how could they recognize her, when she did not recognize herself? You see, as is so often the way in tales such as these, there was a secret that the young lady didn't know: she was born of two disparate lands. And though she lived her life in the one, she lived her dreams in the other."

I shift my weight slightly. There's an uncomfortable prickling starting at the back of my neck and I shake my head, trying to force it away.

"And the dream land called to her, gently at first, for it had no cause to rush. But with each passing year, the need for her unique gifts became greater, and the calls became louder. And as she neared her seventeenth year, the calls became desperate cries, and the dreams more insistent. Louder and louder, coming to her not only under the cover of night, but breaking through at every opportunity, pulling her in and drawing her close for they knew her by name. Still she resisted, grievously unaware of her own value. But the dreams would not be silenced. The legend moves like a living thing, and it will not be ignored."

A shiver runs down my spine, and he puts his hands on my shoulders, gently lifting me away so I can see his face. But it's no longer Alex that holds me. It's Seth. I gasp, pulling away so quickly that I end up with my back against the railing on the opposite side. He can't be here, not like this, not this close; I won't allow it. I want Alex. Seth closes the distance between us, desperation twisting his face.

"You know what you have to do, Rennie. You're the only one who can fix this," he tells me through gritted teeth, sudden urgency making his eyes bulge. He looks over his shoulder as though someone may be listening, or coming closer. He grabs my arms and shakes me. "Tell me, Rennie. Tell me what you have to do!" He's frantic now, and I sense the turmoil building inside of him. Fear clutches at my throat. His ragged nails dig into my flesh.

"I have to..." I wrack my brain trying to come up with the right answer for him. I can't get this wrong. "I have to... I have to wake up."

And I do. My sheets are wrapped around my legs so many times I feel like a mummy, and I can still feel Seth's fingers digging into my arms. Sweat knots the hair at the back of my neck, covering my skin with a sticky sheen. There's a soft knock on my bedroom door, and I stifle a scream.

Aidan's head peeks in. "Rennie? Is everything okay?" Concern fills his dark eyes as he looks at me, sweeping the room in a single glance for any sign of what's wrong.

I'm so relieved to see his comforting, rugged face that all I can do is shake my head, trying unsuccessfully not to sob into my hands. He's beside me in an instant, sitting on the edge of my bed, the comforting father figure I've loved for so long. I dive into him, wrapping my arms around his neck and letting the tears flow onto his shoulder.

"Rennie, hush. It's okay, hush; it was just a dream." He pats my head and makes shushing noises. "It's okay," he repeats. "That must have been some dream, kid." I nod into his shoulder, still unable to speak properly. "I was just headed out to work and I heard you talking. At first I thought you'd gotten all crafty and snuck a boy in here. A soon-to-be dead boy."

I laugh, feeling the tightness in my chest lift somewhat, and pull myself away from him to wipe my eyes.

He hands me a Kleenex from the bedside table. "You want to talk about it?"

I sniff and shake my head. "I don't really remember," I tell him. "Something about… there was a garden. And Alex was there."

"Alex?"

"Yeah, that's the guy Maia was teasing me about in the kitchen the other morning."

"Ahh," he says, not committing to a response. I wonder what Maia has told Aidan about him.

"And there was… I don't know. It got all creepy and weird, and there was something I needed to remember. Something I needed to do." I sigh and turn my palms up helplessly. "Just one more in a long string of bad dreams, I guess. At least this one was new. It's good to keep it interesting." I rip at the corner of my Kleenex to give my hands and mind something to do while he mulls that over.

"You haven't had an easy go of things lately, have you?" he says kindly.

I shake my head, tears starting to well up again. Another side effect of the dreams—they make all of my emotions sit right at the surface where the tiniest ripple can bring up tears. Stupid, useless tears that don't change anything. He takes a breath to continue, but I cut him off.

"You probably better get going," I tell him, knowing he'll pick up the hint. "You don't want to be late for work. Sorry about your shirt," I gesture to his tear-soaked sleeve.

He just smiles. "No worries," he says. "That's what shoulders are for." He sits there for a moment longer, but finally he stands and pats my head again. "Okay," he sighs, resigned. He turns to walk toward the door, then suddenly changes direction and flings open the closet door with a loud "Ah ha!"

A genuine laugh breaks through my tears, dispelling them as quickly as they came.

"All right, no boys. Just checking," he grins slyly at me. "See you later, kid." He ruffles my hair one last time and opens the door to leave.

"Aidan?"

"Yeah?"

I rip at my Kleenex again. It's not too late just to say goodbye. "Does Mrs. Cantrell really believe those things she said about me?" I ask it so quietly, I'm not sure if he's heard me or not.

After a few long moments, he closes the door again and comes to sit next to me. "I forget sometimes how grown up you girls have gotten. To me, I think you'll always be that little freckle-faced girl who ran around our backyard, climbing trees and trying to convince us she could speak Whale."

I smile at the memory. "I still can, you know. That kind of skill doesn't fade."

He chuckles, but I can tell that he's pondering how to answer my question. "Madeleine is a bit of a mystery, even after all these years," he says, choosing his words with care. "She's always had to be the strict one when it came to Maia because, well just imagine what it would have been like if I was in charge." He gives that boyish grin, and I can see there's a small amount of shame that goes along with the joke. "Then there was the move to California, which has been difficult in some unexpected ways. And then, after what happened to Claire... well, she's just trying to hold on a little tighter than usual. In her own way, she's trying to keep you safe."

I stay silent for a moment, taking it all in. It does make sense when I think about it from that angle, even if I don't agree with her tactics. "I guess I understand. I'll try not to give her any reasons to worry."

He smiles gently. "You don't have to change a thing. You're a good kid, Rennie, and Madeleine knows that. Somewhere deep... deep down."

I laugh again. He always makes me feel better. "Thanks a lot." I roll my eyes and he stands to leave, still chuckling to himself.

As soon as he's gone, I take my sketchbook and pencil from the desk and lay back down on the bed. With careful, measured strokes, I begin to draw a five-pointed gazebo and a dark winding path.

Is it dumb that I miss you? says the little text bubble on my iPhone. I grab the phone from my nightstand and flop down onto my bed, but before I can even reply, it rings three more chimes announcing three more individual text messages.

This is Alex, BTW. Not Levi.

Ha ha

Is it dumb that I just wrote ha ha?

I flip onto my back, holding the phone over my head and text back, grinning from ear to ear.

None of that was dumb. I miss you too. And then, just

because I can't resist, I send off two more.

This is Rennie.

Ha ha.

My phone rings a moment later, Alex's picture coming up on the screen, the one I took on Thursday night when we exchanged phone numbers. He's giving that lopsided smile that melts my heart, and I take a second to sigh contentedly at it before tapping *Answer.*

"Hey there," I say, keeping my voice low. It's still early, and I've already heard Mrs. Cantrell in the kitchen. I definitely don't need her overhearing me talking to (gasp!) a boy!

"Hey yourself. I'm not very good at texting, sorry about that," he laughs. His voice is still groggy, and I love that he thought about me before he's even un-groggy. "I wasn't sure if you'd be awake yet."

"I've been up since about six," I tell him, the words sliding out through a full-toothed grin.

"6:00? Are you one of those early-to-bed, early-to-rise types?"

I laugh. "No way. I'm usually one of those late-to-bed, sleep-'til-it's-noon types, especially on summer vacation. But Maia's dad was headed out to work early this morning and the noise woke me up." It's only a partial fib; no need to bother him with my bad dreams.

"Ah ha. Got it." He pauses for a moment and I leave the silence untouched. I can tell he wants to say something else. "So I was thinking..." There it is. "I really did miss seeing you yesterday. Hanging out with you on Thursday night was a lot of fun."

"I agree," I say tentatively. *Hang out* is such a non-committal term. Is this a let's-just-be-friends speech? (Please oh *please* don't be a let's-just-be-friends speech.)

"But it wasn't really a date," he goes on.

"More agreement." My heart starts beating harder, anticipating the worst. It's taking some effort to keep my voice even.

"So, what I was thinking is... well, maybe we should fix that. I mean, not fix Thursday. I don't have a time machine or anything." He laughs nervously. He's nervous? How cute is that? "But maybe we should go out. You know, like on a real date."

I hold the phone away so I can do a semi-silent squeal and kick my legs up and down on the side of the bed in an impromptu happy dance. That was the polar opposite of let's-just-be-friends. "That sounds like a really good idea," I say, much more calmly than I feel. My insides are doing flips and the rest of me is about to join them. "When did you have in mind?" Very calm, very collected. I'm so impressed with me.

"Well, I know it's late notice, but I was hoping maybe tonight. Did I mention I miss you?" He is so freaking cute! He misses me? Me!

"Yeah, I think that would work. Maia's not up yet, but she didn't mention having anything planned." I stand up and start dancing around my bed, a tango for just me and my phone. I stop to pose in front of the mirror, and try my best Tyra *smize*.

"Great! I have some things to plan, but would it be okay if I picked you up around 5:00? Is that too early?"

"No!" I say a little too quickly. Come on, keep the cool going. "I mean, that should work."

"Okay, great! That's great."

"Great," I agree, grinning so hard it hurts. "I'm staying at Maia's house, in the country club. Do you know where that is?"

"Oh yeah, she's just a few streets over from Seth's house. I'll find you."

I love the sound of that so much, I'm not even bothered by the unexpected news that Seth is so close. "Okay then. I'll see you in a few hours." The giddiness starts to bleed through in a giggle. I cover it by clearing my throat, but I don't think he buys it.

"Okay. I… great. See you at five. Bye Rennie."

"Bye Alex." I hate saying goodbye already, but I love getting to say his name out loud—to him! I am very careful to hit the *End* button before letting a jubilant "Woo hoo!" escape. I throw the phone onto my bed like it's a football and do my touchdown dance around and around the open space.

"What in the world?" The interruption stops me in mid-twirl. My knee slams into the desk chair and I land in an ungraceful heap on my bed. I clutch my throbbing knee and hiss through my teeth, looking over my head at a very displeased Mrs. Cantrell. Even from my upside-down view of her, I can tell this isn't good.

"Sorry Mrs. Cantrell," I cringe, sitting upright but still holding on to my sore leg. "I guess I was louder than I meant to be."

"I should say so. What could possibly cause that sort of outburst at 8:00 in the morning?"

"It's nothing really; I was just being silly." I wave my hand dismissively.

"It's another boy, isn't it?" She puts one hand on her hip and looks around as if she's going to find some evidence of this.

I stifle a sigh, remembering what Aidan told me. She's only trying to keep me safe, be a good temporary guardian. "Well…" I stall.

"Honestly, Rennie. I don't know what has gotten into you!"

"Nothing!" I stand, hands out to defend myself. "It's only a boy. *A* boy. Just the one. The only one I like, and the only one I've liked since I got here."

"I see. So it's the one you went on the coffee date with then."

Oh crap. Of course she would remember that. If I was a better liar, I would just say yes and be done with this, but I know better. "That was Levi," I explain, "but he and I are just friends, I swear. This one is different." I don't know why I'm bothering, but for some reason I need her to understand.

She looks at me, the stench of her disappointment hanging like a cloud between us. After a pause that ages me at least five years, she finally says, "You're almost a grown woman now, Rennie. I would think that someone in your situation would have a clearer view of what is important, and what is not."

She closes the door before she sees that her words have knocked the wind out of me. My legs wobble and I sit back down on the bed, mouth hanging open and mind reeling. Is she right? Am I being somehow disrespectful for concentrating all of my energy on a guy right now? That's not why I came out here. A wave of guilt rushes over me and tears spring to my eyes. Maybe I am just being selfish.

But Aunt Charlie *did* say that I should take a break. Relax. Take some time away to remember what normal life is like again. And isn't that what I'm doing? Isn't that what Alex is helping me to do? I shake my head to dislodge the pallor of grief that tries to settle on me. I won't let it back in.

I push myself up and head to the closet. Every ounce of giddiness has left me, but I know the feeling isn't so far away that I won't get it back. I open the closet door and survey my options, allowing the trace of a smile to pass over my lips. Time to pick out an outfit suitable for falling in love.

"Nope, try another one." Maia dismisses me with a wave of her hand.

"Really? What's wrong with this one?" I've tried on at least a dozen outfits, full-on wardrobe changes with shoes and all. So far, nothing has worked.

"Hey, whoa now. I'm excited 'cause you're excited. And of *course* I want to help you find just the right thing to wear. But as far as I'm concerned, you could throw on one of your Nerd Shirts and be done with it."

We've reached a probationary truce where Alex is concerned. I told her how sweet he was at the library on Thursday night, and then this morning I broke the news about him asking me out for a real date. She took it calmly and refrained from any more warnings, but I know she's not happy with my decision.

"I know, I know. I'm sorry. I'm glad that you're lending me your expertise—you're so much better at this kind of thing than I am." I step in front of the mirror and twirl to make the soft fawn-colored cotton swing around my knees. "But are you *sure* about this one? I think it's kinda cute." I pull at the wide shoulders of the pink peasant blouse, and re-examine myself.

"It is cute, and you look adorable in it. But it's just not quite there." I can see her scrutinizing me from my view in the mirror. Suddenly her eyes light up. "I know exactly what we need! Hang on!" She jumps up from her seat at the desk and runs out the door before I can even think to question her.

I go back to the closet for another run through my wardrobe. I can't believe that only a few hours ago, I liked all of these clothes. What was I thinking? Apparently I have a closet full of nothing to wear.

Maia returns moments later, barely out of breath from the dash up to her room and back. She thrusts an armful of fabric and a pair of boots into my arms and pushes me inside the closet. She swings the door shut and shouts from the bedroom-side, "That's the one, I know it. Hurry hurry!"

I toss the boots to the floor and hold up the dress she's handed me. I'm skeptical at best. For one thing, it's off-white. I'm sure this color looks amazing on Maia, with her dark hair and tanned skin. But on my fair complexion, I'm going to look like a ghost wearing a sheet.

A few minutes later I emerge tentatively, already anticipating the look of distaste that will be on Maia's face. She's filing her nails and humming to herself when I step into the room, but both activities stop when she sees me. She cocks her head to one side, and a slow smile spreads over her face.

"I knew it," she says, very proud of herself.

"Really?" I hurry over to the mirror to see for myself, and my mouth drops open at my own reflection. Far from the sallow apparition I expected to see staring back at me, the cream-colored eyelet lace makes my skin look porcelain perfect, a lovely blend of peach and ivory that I never knew was there. I touch the simple rounded neckline and adjust the wide straps closer over my shoulders. I give a girly twirl, and the skirt billows out just the perfect amount before settling back down to hit just above my knees. With the wide brown leather belt and a pair of brown knee-high boots that Maia was smart enough to add, the whole effect is nothing short of...

"Perfect," I breathe the last word aloud.

Maia's grin appears next to my own in the mirror's reflection. "Told ya," she says, putting a long gold necklace over my head, a delicate blue teardrop that just matches my eyes dangling onto the ivory lace. "Oh I wish we were doubling tonight," she says wistfully. "Seth and I with you and Alex. They're good friends, you know; did I tell you that? How fun would that be?"

Yeah, such good friends that I had to step in to keep them from pounding each other to a pulp. I might have sort of forgotten to tell Maia about that little incident, so I'm careful to keep my face neutral, and to stick with the truth. "Well, maybe not on our first date."

She giggles. "Yeah, I guess that would be a bit much. Well, I think you look ready for whatever it is he has planned. Of course, it *would* be nice if he'd be courteous enough to let you know where you're going, at least. But that's only my opinion."

"Maia…" I warn.

"What?" she asks, all innocence as she fluffs my hair back out over the back of the necklace, copper strands shining in the light from the window. "I'm just stating an opinion is all."

"Well it just so happens that he did text a little bit ago, and asked what I thought of the restaurant he picked out for dinner. So there."

She perks up. "He did? Why didn't you tell me? Where are you going?"

"I didn't know the place so I just said it was fine." I get my phone from the bedside table and scan through to find the text. "Yeah, here it is. He says we'll be eating at a place called Yanagi. Ever heard of it?"

She starts laughing. "Yanagi?"

"Uh oh, what?"

"No no, I'm sorry. It's actually one of my favorite places. But you *do* realize that you just agreed to go out for sushi."

The tiniest feeling of nausea passes over me. "I what?"

"I have to say, I'm impressed. I've tried for years to get you to go to sushi with me. And yet, here comes Alex and after less than a week, all he has to do is ask once and there you go. I must ask his secret." Her faux-serious tone only highlights her amusement at my distress.

"I can't do this," I gulp, the oxygen suddenly depleting from the room. "My first date with Alex and I'm gonna throw up raw fish all over him? I *can't. Do. This.*" I'm starting to hyperventilate. Not a good feeling.

"Oh Rennie, I'm sorry—stop stop stop." She rushes over and puts her hands on my shoulders, turning my back to her so we're both facing the mirror again. "See how amazing you look?" I have to admit, I look pretty good. I nod. "And remember how excited you are to see… Alex?" I can tell that saying his name in a non-detrimental way has cost her something and I smile at her reflection, the tension in my lungs easing. "You're gonna have an incredible time, and there will be plenty of things that you can order that don't involve raw fish. I promise."

"You're sure?" She nods solemnly and I turn around to give her a big hug. "Thanks, Mai. I don't think I could do this without you."

"Oh, I'm pretty sure you couldn't," she teases. "Now, about your make-up..."

Considering my usual make-up routine consists of a little mascara and a lip gloss that's barely even a color, I know I'm once again at her mercy.

And after twenty minutes, three eye shadows, two shades of lip gloss, a blush, a highlighter, an eyeliner, and a mascara with the word Buxom blazoned across it... all I can do is hope I don't look like a street-walking clown. When she finishes, she sits back with a smile. She tilts my face from one side to the other, using the natural light from the window as her guide.

"I'm brilliant," she says with a shrug. "And you are gorgeous." She points to the mirror and I obey.

I bite my glossed lip, crossing to the full-length mirror with equal parts excitement and trepidation. But when I look up, I can't help but gasp. I still look like me, but much more put together. Like some kind of alternate universe me (except I've been her already and she doesn't know any more than I do). For once, when I see Maia stand behind me, I don't feel like the shadow to her sun. I feel ready.

That is, until the doorbell rings.

Maia gives me a quick hug and I take a deep breath. I can't stop grinning. I follow her to the front door, and she gives me a quick once over, then pats my arm reassuringly and opens the door with an overly grand gesture.

"You're on time," she says by way of greeting. "Score one for you."

"Hi Maia." He isn't at all flustered by her teasing; I love that. "Is Rennie here?"

I peek around her shoulder to see him, and give him a smile. "Hi Alex." I suddenly feel like my insides are doubling as an aviary. He looks amazing—crisp white button-down shirt, dark blue jeans, and that navy jacket (which I happen to know smells so incredibly like him). His hair is brushed neatly, but still manages to stick up in all the right places, bangs falling down over his forehead in that way I love. Even the small bruise where Seth sucker-punched him only manages to make him look tough and mysterious. His grey eyes widen when I step around Maia.

"Wow," he breathes. "You're beautiful." He says it so simply, he makes it a fact.

"So are you," I say without thinking. Stupid. You can't tell a guy he's beautiful!

But he just smiles and shuffles his foot nervously, the sole of one of his black Chucks making a soft scraping noise over the welcome mat. We look each other over for a moment, both grinning from ear to ear, until Maia can't take it anymore.

"Oh gag. All right, loverboy, let's have a little chat." She drags Alex out into the courtyard by his elbow.

"Wait, what?" My happy little bubble of bliss just burst. What is she trying to pull? She agreed to this date, she agreed not to fight this.

She looks back to me over her shoulder. "My dad isn't here to have a talk with him, and I don't have a shotgun to be coincidentally cleaning, so this is going to have to do. Just chill for a sec." She waves me back into the house, and I stand in the doorway, arms crossed, trying to glare her into submission. She ignores me.

She pulls him out through the iron gate and to the front lawn. How embarrassing. I can see their discussion, but can't hear anything. I tap my foot, trying to gauge how it's going. She doesn't seem angry, which is a good thing, but she does seem very determined. After a few moments, she gives a satisfied nod, then gestures for me to join them.

"Okay," she says with acceptance. "I think we understand one another. He'll have you back safe and sound by 10:00." She smiles at me, playing the maternal role very well now. "Have a good time, and call me if you need *anything*." She stresses the last word enough so I know it covers everything from advice, to a ride home, to helping to hide the body.

"I will," I tell her, squeezing her hand.

Alex has gone around to the passenger side of his shiny blue Focus to open the door for me.

"Nice touch," Maia says, nodding in approval. "Just keep her safe."

"With my last breath," he says solemnly.

I give her a silent look of girly joyousness when his back is turned, and get into the car. I can't believe I'm actually going out on a date with Alex! I've only known him for a few days, why do I feel like I've been waiting years for this moment? I fasten my seatbelt, literally and figuratively... ready for anything.

 *Chapter Fifteen*

1 have zero talent for small talk. Zero. (Am I required to disclaim that before I agree to a first date?) Add to that fact that my tongue currently feels like it's made of sandpaper, and my history of using non-linear sentences when Alex is around, and this could be a truly unpleasant evening. Instead, it's perfect. He's perfect. That's all there is to it.

It's only a twenty-minute ride to our destination, another smallish town just south of SLO called Pismo Beach, and he fills the time with easy chatter. In no time at all we're walking into Yanagi. It's lovely inside, all dark woods and Asian influences. A large aquarium catches my eye in the waiting area, and I silently wonder if I'm supposed to pick out my own sushi, but I don't have to wonder for long.

The hostess leads us to a table by the window. All of the windows face the west, and views of the Pacific are visible from every angle. It takes my breath away.

"I hope Japanese is okay," Alex starts as we pick up our menus. "I realize I wasn't very specific in my texts."

"Yeah!" I say, a little too brightly. "This is great! In fact, Maia said this is one of her favorite restaurants, so it has to be good, right? I think I might try the... um..." My eyes sweep the list of items, nothing sounding even vaguely familiar. Edamame? Gyoza? *Caterpillar* Roll? Oh jeez, what did I get myself into? I set the menu down and start playing with my ring. "Actually, to be honest, I've never had Japanese food. I'm a little scared of it, I guess." I know I'm blushing and I feel like an idiot, but telling him the truth now seems a lot easier that trying to bluff my way through ordering.

He wrinkles his brow, and sets his menu down. "We can go some place else if you'd feel more comfortable. I don't mind at all."

"No no no!" Way to start this off right. "The views are amazing, and it smells really good in here. Plus, it's good for me to try something new, right? But, well maybe I'll let you do the ordering for both of us. If that isn't too old-fashioned and weird."

He smiles at me, a twinkle in his eye. "You trust me that much?"

"I do," I reply without hesitation.

"Okay, then. I'd be happy to."

"Great," I sigh with relief. "But no raw fish, okay? I really can't face that."

"No raw fish," he echoes.

"And no caterpillar."

He looks confused so I point it out on the menu. He laughs, a mouth-open, eyes closed, full-bodied belly laugh, and any tension that was hanging between us melts. "I'm sorry," he says when he can talk again. "I don't mean to make fun, but you are just so cute. I promise there are no insects of any kind on the menu. It's just covered in avocado, so it *looks* like a caterpillar."

"Oh," I say, laughing with him. "I've seen those travel shows where they go to Asian markets and they have bugs on sticks, deep-fried as snacks. It didn't seem like such a leap."

"No, you're right. I've seen those shows too." He studies the menu again while I study him. He really is beautiful. Then he gives me a quick glance and I can tell he's trying not to laugh again. "Just so you know, the dragon roll doesn't contain any real dragon either."

I throw my napkin at him.

When the waitress has taken our order, Alex takes a sip from his water glass and I realize I have nothing to offer to break the momentary silence. I bite my lip and stare down at my hands, examining my manicure. Why can't I think of something to say? If I was having dinner with Maia or Ember or any of the girls this would not be an issue. I have opinions, I have ideas. Where are they all now?

"I'm terrible at this," I blurt out.

He puts a hand to his mouth to keep the water inside and gives a small cough, obviously startled by my outburst. "At what?"

"This." I make a vague gesture to encompass everything around us. "Dating. Small talk. I've only been on a couple actual dates in my whole life and I wasn't good at those either and I have no idea why I just told you that. For some reason, when I'm near you, I can't quite think clearly thoughts. Clear think...ings? Think *clearly.* Crap! I swear I'm not an idiot."

He laughs softly and reaches across the table to take my hand. "I never thought you were." His eyes melt into mine. So sweet, so genuine.

"I really do form complete sentences sometimes." I smile at him, keeping my hand impossibly still in his, afraid any movement will scare him away.

"I know, I've heard them," he says with a shy smile. "I know what might help. I have a topic that'll be easy for you." His grey eyes turn silver in the sunlight, twinkling at his own ingenuity. "Shakespeare. You were reading *Hamlet* when you were at Outspoken. Was that a summer school project or was that just for fun?"

"Oh that was definitely just for fun. It's one of my favorites. Well that or *Midsummer.* Oh, or *Macbeth*! I love *Macbeth.*"

"Really?" His eyebrows hide in his hair again. "I thought every girl's favorite was *Romeo and Juliet.*"

"Ugh, no way." I must make quite a face because he busts out laughing.

"Seriously? True love, clandestine meetings, forbidden romance—I thought you would like that kind of thing." He sounds genuinely surprised.

"True love? Are you kidding me? It's not about true love. It's about infatuation and obsession and making stupid choices and... okay, look." I take a breath to slow down. "Shakespeare only wrote three types of plays: Tragedies, Comedies, and Histories. There isn't even a Romance category. The ones that people usually think of as Romances are actually Comedies. You know, *Taming of the Shrew* and *Much Ado About Nothing*, all of those. *Romeo and Juliet* is a freaking Tragedy!"

"Okay, I get that *officially* it may not be labeled as a Romance. But are you telling me that what is arguably the best known love story in the English language is not about true love? You can't be serious."

"It's not! They get in over their heads and let things escalate faster than they can keep up, but if they took two seconds to look at what was going on around them and get the facts, they wouldn't have ended up dead. I don't think that two dead protagonists can be a romance."

"Fair enough," he allows. "So is this exclusive to Romeo and Juliet, or are you saying that any pair of star-crossed lovers aren't really in love?"

"No, that's not my point at all," I say. "I think that literature is full of couples who are destined to be together despite any odds—Elizabeth and Mr. Darcy, Beatrice and Benedick, Katniss and Peeta. But people always forget that if Romeo had his way about things, it wouldn't even be called *Romeo and Juliet*, it would be called *Romeo and Rosaline*. He went to the Capulet party because he was already obsessed with another girl before the story even starts." I lean across the table, getting deeper into my argument.

"True," he concedes, leaning across the table to match my posture, "but he forgets all about her the moment he sees Juliet, which is exactly why nobody ever remembers Rosaline. His whole trajectory is changed in those first few moments when they meet. Are you saying you don't believe in love at first sight?"

The question stops me. I know the answer to this question. Don't I? At least I know how I've answered it for AP English essays. But now, looking into those soft grey eyes, his perfect lips just inches from my own... My eyes travel over his face. Is he asking this on Romeo's behalf or his own? "I don't think I—"

"Lobster roll?" I sit back so fast that I nearly knock over my water glass and in my effort to save it, all of my silverware has managed to clatter to the floor in one thunderous crash. I know I'm blushing furiously, but the waitress doesn't seem to notice as she sets down our order and scoops up my fallen place setting. I sneak a glance at Alex and he's trying to hide a smile.

"Saved by the sushi," he murmurs.

"That's something I never thought I'd be able to say."

By the time we get back in his car, I'm feeling quite at ease with him. I let my hand linger on his arm as he opens the car door for me. Such a gentleman! Or maybe not. Maybe he's just done this hundreds of times with hundreds of other girls. Maybe what I think is easy conversation and good manners is only a routine for him. I glance over at him as he slides into his seat and shuts the door.

"Tell me about Violet," I say before I've had time to think through what I'm asking.

He freezes, one hand on the wheel, one hand on the keys just about to turn in the ignition.

I feel a rush of embarrassment at once again saying the wrong thing in the wrong way. "I'm sorry. I just mean, well, you must have been pretty into her—asking her to prom and everything. And then, well things didn't go as planned that night, but do you still... I mean, is there any..." I can't bring myself to ask him if he still has feelings for her. One of my rules is that you don't ask questions you don't want answers to. I don't think I want this answer.

He starts the car and backs out of the parking space before saying anything. I'm about to tell him to forget it, when he says, "It's a fair question, it deserves an honest answer." He stops at a stop sign and uses the pause to look me in the eye. "I like you, Rennie. I liked you the moment I saw you at the bonfire." He starts driving again, maybe as an excuse to look away as he starts to talk about her. "I went to the beach that night hoping to run into Violet. I'd already apologized over the phone and at school, but I wanted to try to explain what had happened and maybe, I don't know, maybe work things out." I look down at my lap, playing with my ring again. I was right, I don't want to hear this. "But before I even had a chance to find her, there you were." He gives me that crooked smile and looks at me out of the corner of his eye. "I guess you could say she's my Rosaline."

I smile back at him and my heart goes all gooey. I nod my

understanding, and shift my glance out the window so I can grin like an idiot without him noticing. "So tell me about you," I say, switching subjects to one I like much, much better.

By the time we arrive at our next destination, I've learned that he works at Barnes and Noble (fantastic hair *and* a discount on books? Swoon!), he's lived in five different states, he loves baseball (especially the St. Louis Cardinals), his dad was in the military like mine was (and he was also killed in action—a lot more recently than mine, so he doesn't talk much about that topic), he lives with his mom in a house downtown, and has a big brother named Robbie who's also in the military. I don't admit to him that I've done a little Facebook-stalking and already knew about his Cardinals obsession, but what he doesn't know won't hurt him, right?

He pulls the car into a dirt parking lot next to the railroad tracks as he's talking about his family. "Of course, she doesn't like having him away all the time, but at least he's not deployed right now, just living it up on a base in Hawaii. Hard to feel bad for the guy, you know?" He laughs. "What about you? You said you have a big sister, right?"

"Oh, yeah I do. Claire." I loved hearing him talk about his family, but mine is not exactly first date material.

"Are you close?" He turns off the car and shifts towards me. The sudden silence feels like a weight on my chest.

"We never were, growing up. She was always the rebellious one, and I like my rules and a proper order to things. She never got that. Plus the fact that she's gorgeous: blonde hair, blue eyes, like a living doll. She never lost an opportunity to tease me about my red hair and freckles when we were kids." I can't believe I'm telling him this. I pause to gather my thoughts for a second, and he has another question lined up for me. It's a relief to move on.

"And you said you've lived with your aunt since your dad passed away. He was in the military, right?"

"Yeah. Army, special ops. I have these visions in my head of what he was like, running secret missions and infiltrating enemy camps. It all seems so exciting and heroic, even knowing the outcome. I'm proud of him, but I hate that I never got to know him."

217

"He sounds amazing. What about your mom? Do you ever hear from her?"

"No," I answer, trying to regulate my breathing so I sound like this is normal for me, and not like I'm freaking out because I never talk about this. "I think technically that makes me an orphan, right? But I've never felt like one since Aunt Charlie has always been there for me. I think my mom is in contact with Aunt Charlie sometimes, though. Every once in a while, I see an envelope while she's sorting the mail, and I recognize the big swirly *A* in the return address before she can hide it. My mom's name is Ava," I explain, changing his furrowed brow to a nod of understanding. "It looks really cool and artistic. Aunt Charlie says I get that from her. My artistic side, I mean." I lapse into silence again, but he doesn't seem to mind.

"That's nice. It's good to have something of hers like that. I have my dad's eyes." He smiles gently, and I'm glad I took the risk of talking about this.

There's a buzzing sound from my purse, and it takes me a second to realize it's my phone vibrating.

"I'm so sorry," I say as I dig through my bag to find it. "I could have sworn I turned this off."

"That's okay. I don't mind." Alex waves a dismissive hand.

"Thanks, but I do. I promised myself no texting tonight. No status updates or calls or anything. Let me just..." I finally locate the offending contraption and start to turn it off, but the message alert catches my eye. A text from an unknown number? I can't help myself. I open it.

You're wasting time. Find Ethan.

My hand flies to my mouth. How did this person get my cell number? Another text chimes in and this one fills my screen.

Find Ethan Find Ethan Find Ethan Find Ethan Find Ethan Find Ethan Find Ethan Find Ethan

"What is it? Is everything all right?" Alex's eyes search mine for some clue to what's wrong.

I'm not gonna get a better chance than this. Time to find out if Alex really is my dream boyfriend. With a trembling hand, I show him the screen. "Does this mean anything to you?"

It takes him a second to decipher what he's reading, but I can see the instant it sinks in. His eyes flash to mine.

219

"That's... that's the name you called me," he says, his voice strained. "What does it mean? Who sent it?"

I sigh. So much for that theory. I guess that would have been way too easy. "I'm not sure," I tell him. "I keep getting these weird messages in different ways, all of them telling me to find someone named Ethan."

"But you don't even know him?"

I shrug. Know him? I only spend almost every night with him, running through forests and escaping would-be captors and kissing in secluded oak groves. This is much too complicated to try to explain, and I am not wasting my first date with Alex on being crazy. "Not really. I mean, I guess I know *of* him, but I can't say that I've ever actually met him. Face to face, I mean." That was sort of the truth.

He's watching me carefully, but I don't think he knows me well enough yet to know that I'm not telling him the whole story. "Then how are you supposed to find him?"

"I wish I knew." I stare at the message for another moment, then press the power button with more force than necessary. "But that is my problem, and not one that we need to worry about tonight."

He doesn't seem convinced. "Are you sure? Whoever sent that message seems pretty insistent."

I shake my head and flash him a smile. "What message? I told you, tonight there are no phones. Just us."

He relaxes and glances over his shoulder. "Okay, if you're sure. We probably should get inside." He points behind us, and I'm surprised to see a line of people waiting to get into a single story building painted quite uniquely in blue, yellow and red. Gold letters across the blue portion spell out *The Great American Melodrama*.

"A theatre?" I ask, pleasantly surprised.

He nods enthusiastically, then hops out of the car and runs around to hold open my door. I could really get used to that. "We came here on a class field trip, and it became one of my favorite places. It's relaxed and silly and... well, I hope you like it." He takes my hand to help me out of the car, and doesn't let go once I'm standing.

"I like it already."

A Scott Joplin rag greets us as we enter the theatre, a gift from the man in a straw hat rocking out at an upright piano. It makes the whole atmosphere instantly welcoming. Rows of wooden benches line three walls, and the middle of the floor is covered in sawdust and round tables, where people are already seated munching on hot dogs. Photos of actors past hang on the walls, and there's another line around the corner where actors present are taking orders and filling pitchers of soda and buckets of popcorn.

We're led to our seats by an actress in an olde timey saloon girl costume who speaks with a Texas accent as she tells us where to find the restrooms and how the bar line works. She hands us newspapers (which turn out to be our programs) and goes on to greet the next guests.

"Well? What do you think so far?" Alex is so excited, and it's adorable how badly he wants me to like it too.

"I love it," I tell him honestly, and relief floods his features.

"I'm going to get us some popcorn and soda. What would you like?"

"You've done a good job ordering for me so far tonight, so surprise me."

"Okay. No caterpillar. Got it." He ducks as I swipe at his arm, and dashes off to join the end of the bar line.

I soak in the atmosphere as I wait, unable to keep my toes from tapping to the piano's latest song. I can seriously see Maia working here one day soon. I wonder if she's been here yet. I feel an itch in my fingers, dying to text her to find out, but it'll have to wait 'til I get home. Even if I hadn't made that pact with myself to keep my phone out of sight tonight, those texts earlier are enough to make me keep it safely put away. I may be under orders from an unknown entity to *find Ethan*, but tonight is all about Alex.

My sides ache from laughing by the time intermission rolls around. It's a silly western with the standard stock characters—the hero, the villain, the damsel in distress—and the whole audience cheers and boos and sighs respectively. It's so much fun, I can see why Alex loves this place.

"Are you having a good time?" Alex asks me as the lights come back up and the piano player resumes his ragtime.

"Do you even need to ask? It's awesome!"

"I knew you'd like it," he says brightly. He slides his arm around my shoulders, pulling me closer to him on the bench. "I want tonight to be perfect," he whispers in my ear, his warm breath sending shivers through me. My stomach does a flip when he touches his lips to my temple, and I nestle in closer under his arm.

"So far, so good," I say, taking his free hand in mine. My heart feels so full, it could burst right here. I can't remember the last time I felt this happy.

"Well isn't this a cozy sight?" Seth's voice is enough to throw a big bucket of ice water on our moment. I look up and see his cold blue eyes watching us as he approaches. I make a motion to sit up straighter, but Alex keeps his arm around me, holding me in place.

"What are you doing here, Garrison?"

"Same as you, McKinley. I'm on a date."

"A date?" I echo, the word making my jaw drop. I didn't want to enter this conversation, but look at that. Here I am.

"Yeah." His eyes sweep over to me and he looks me up and down slowly. It sends a whole different kind of shiver through me. "Jealous?" He smirks in that mocking way, and I sneer back at him.

"With who?" I demand, sounding every bit the jealous girl he just accused me of being. Alex glances over at me, the briefest look of concern crossing his face. "I know it's not Maia," I clarify, stressing the syllables of her name. "She would have told me."

"No, it's not Maia," Seth says, stretching his arms in an arrogant, falsely nonchalant way. He waves over to a table in the corner, and a pretty brunette in a too-tight too-low-cut navy blue sweater waves back.

"You're here with Naomi?" Alex asks, sounding tired. He shakes his head. "You're an idiot."

"Oh, I'm the idiot?" Seth looks to me, then back to Alex. "So, you want to be the pot or the kettle in this argument?"

That would have been a mildly witty remark if it hadn't been directed at Alex and meant for me. "You do realize I can hear you, right?" I fume.

"And you just happened to bring her here," Alex continues, not falling for the deliberate jab the way I did.

"Well, you did say this was a great place to bring chicks," Seth says, leaning in like he's sharing an inside joke with Alex. All of my previous insecurities leap back to the forefront of my brain. Is this a routine with him, or is Seth just being stupid?

"I didn't say that," Alex responds, his stare never wavering. "I said I wanted to bring Rennie here tonight. And here you are, what a coincidence."

"Huh." Seth scratches a finger in his overly-styled blond head. "Must have slipped my mind."

"We don't need a chaperone," Alex growls at him. I can feel his cool is about to crack.

"Hey, Alex?" I put my hand on his knee, and it instantly draws his attention back to me. "Would you mind getting us some more soda?"

He looks from me to Seth and back to me again and shakes his head. "No way. I'm not leaving you alone with this loser. But I have a tab open at the counter, so if you want, you can just..."

"No." I don't even let him finish that thought. "The last time I saw you two alone together, you ended up with this." I cup his face in my hand, running my thumb over his bruise.

He leans into my hand, then turns his face to kiss my palm. "That's exactly why I can't leave you alone with him, Rennie," he whispers.

I can see Seth bristling out of the corner of my eye. "What's wrong, McKinley? Afraid she won't be able to control herself?"

Alex's jaw clenches and in a flash, he's on his feet looking down at Seth.

"Hey!" I take Alex's hand and it draws both of their attention back to me. "I am *not* breaking up another fight, so unless you guys are ready to go old-west-saloon-brawl on each other and start rolling around in the sawdust, one of you needs to get out of here." Was that really me? I'm never that forceful. I guess Alex brings out my bad-ass side. I take a breath and get my pulse back under control. "Please, Alex?" I whisper.

He looks more shocked at that than anything else I've said yet. "Me? He's the one who needs to—"

"Please. I have something I need to say to Seth. I'll be all right, I promise."

He sighs, clearly not happy with this turn of events. "Two minutes." He kisses my cheek and reluctantly slides out of the row, shooting warning daggers at Seth as he leaves.

"Couldn't wait to get me alone, huh?" Seth snakes under the blue wooden railing and eases down next to me.

"Listen," I hiss at him. "I don't know what your deal is, or why you insist on giving Alex such a hard time about us."

"Us?" He scoots closer to me, a sly gleam in his eye.

"Eww," I push him away, my hand to his chest. "I mean 'us' as in me and Alex. Obviously you have an issue with us being together, but I like Alex and I'm pretty sure he likes me too, so you're gonna have to get over it. So go back to Bimbo Barbie over there, who is not even in the same league as Maia, by the way, and leave. Us. Alone." My heart is beating wildly against my ribcage. I never talk to people like this; why does this guy get under my skin so much?

His look of shock at my outburst has become amusement. "Okay, I can take a hint." He slides back under the railing but then turns to face me again. "Just tell me this. Have you seen his tattoo yet?"

Just when I thought he couldn't get any more random. "Uhh no? Why would that matter? Like that's some yard stick to measure if he trusts me or not?"

Seth shrugs. "Maybe. You tell me." He leans over the railing so he can smirk right in my face. "Bye Rennie. I'll see you... in your dreams."

I feel a need to shower. My dreams, right, as though I would *ever* dream about Seth. Although, as he walks away, all swagger and arrogance, I can't help but think I did dream about him recently. Something about a garden. Sometimes I wish the details of those dreams would stick around just a little bit longer.

The lights dim as Alex returns with a fresh pitcher of RC. He slides his arm around my shoulders and leans in close. "You okay?" he whispers as the Emcee welcomes us back and introduces the vaudeville revue coming up.

"I'm fine," I tell him with a reassuring smile. I love the way I can see his jaw relax, the muscles there unclenching as he smiles back at me. I put my hand to his face, rubbing my thumb along that perfect jawline. My heart races as I lean in and kiss his cheek. "I'm so much better than fine," I whisper. I feel him sigh as he relaxes, and we sit back to enjoy the rest of the evening.

He's merging the car back onto the freeway when we finally stop laughing about the show we just saw. I reach across and take his hand, turning so I can face him.

"I'm having the best time," I gush. "I wish we..." I stop mid-sentence, giggling at my own stupidity.

"What?" He smiles encouragingly.

"No, I... I was about to say that I wish we had done this a long time ago. But that's silly. I've only known you for a few days."

He looks at me from the corner of his eye. "That's funny. You know, when I first met you on the beach that day, I wanted so badly to ask you if I'd met you before. But that would have sounded like the worst line ever."

He laughs, but my throat is suddenly tight. He *does* know me. I suppose it would make sense that he could be Ethan and just not know it. After all, they're my dreams, not his.

"That is funny," I reply, stalling for time. How can I find out for sure?

"I wonder why it is that both of us feel like we know each other."

He lifts my hand and kisses it. "Must be fate."

Sweet, but not helpful.

"Have you ever..." I don't even know how to finish that question. What do I tell him? *I've had these disturbing dreams for months, and then when I got to California I started getting visions of that same place while I was awake. And then, to top it all off, I somehow ended up going to that same place, all without any reason or explanation. And by the way, I think you might have been there too.* How about no?

"Have I ever what?"

Time to dive in. "Sometimes I have these dreams," I say, looking at our linked hands. "And they're so real, it feels like I could grab hold of whatever I wanted and bring it back with me. It's like even calling them dreams is wrong somehow. Like it's another life, and it's just waiting for me to be a part of it."

He's silent, staring out at the sea of red tail-lights and bright white headlights flowing around us. I wait a moment for him to respond, but he doesn't. He's just listening. Waiting.

"Have you ever had any dreams like that?"

He squeezes my hand and releases it to hold onto the steering wheel. "They sound really intense," he says, sympathy coloring his voice. "I'm sorry you have to go through that. Dreams can be so ambiguous sometimes, can't they? It's hard to know what they mean."

I sigh. I can't be frustrated that he didn't understand what I was trying to ask. I'm not really sure I get it either.

"It's nice that you're starting to talk about yourself a little bit. I like getting to know you," he says and gives me that heart-stopping smile. "Tell me three more things I don't know about you."

I smile back. "I did warn you I'm not good with the small talk. How about you ask me three things and I'll answer. But make them easy."

He laughs and runs a hand over his hair.

Okay, first thing you don't know about me? I love it when you do that. But I manage not to say that out loud. Yay me.

"Okay, I can handle that. First question... I've been meaning to ask you this. Rennie is an unusual name. Is it a nickname?"

"Yes," I reply, being deliberately vague. "Any guesses?"

"I've given this some thought," he confesses. *Mmm... love that.* "I was thinking maybe it was a play off of Renée?"

I shake my head, enjoying this now. "Nope."

"Okay, how about Renita?"

I shake my head again.

"Reynaldo?"

I laugh. "I'll give you a break on this one, 'cause there's no way you'll ever guess it. It's sort of a nickname, but *Rennie* is actually the middle syllable." I take a deep breath, praying he won't laugh too much. "It's Serenity."

He doesn't laugh. He just looks at me out of the corner of his eye with a soft smile. "Serenity Winters," he repeats softly. "Beautiful."

I feel myself blushing, and rush to cover up the compliment with chatter. "My mom named me Serenity and my big sister Clarity. You

232

think maybe she was feeling a little lost?"

It was sort of a joke, but he tilts his head, pondering the question. "Maybe. Or maybe she just knew that the world needs a little more of both."

Wow. He's good. I whisper a shy thank you, feeling that blush creep back up in my cheeks again. He clears his throat and rubs a hand over his chin in thought. I straighten the hem of my dress over my knees, giving my hands something to do besides reaching out for him like they want to be doing.

"Okay, next question. What's your favorite color?"

"Oh good, a nice easy one. Pink," I tell him, relaxing again.

"Favorite movie?"

"*Alice in Wonderland.* The Tim Burton one, even though the animated one is infinitely more quotable. Oh, but I also love *Star Wars.* They all have their merit, but *A New Hope* will always be my favorite. And—oh jeez, you did know that I'm a geek, right? I mean with the whole sci-fi, Star Wars thing. Well, *Star Wars, Lord of the Rings, Avengers, Doctor Who...* I kind of like it all. Most people just know that about me, like it's a tattoo on my forehead or something, and I know that the whole *fangirl* thing can be a little overwhelming for some people, and it's not just gonna stop. Believe me, it runs too deep. But I can at least *try* to tone it down for you. I like other things, too." I'm rambling so fast, he can't get a word in, but his laughter finally stops me.

"You can *try* to tone it down?" he teases. "Oh please. 'Do, or do not. There is no try.'" He grins at me and my mouth drops open.

"You can quote Hamlet *and* Yoda?" I marvel. "You really are perfect." I did not mean to say that last part out loud. I really should have my inner monologue checked for leaks.

"I'm definitely not perfect. But maybe I'm perfect for you."

Which, of course, only proves how perfect he is. What do I say to that? *I hope so? Let's find out? Marry me?*

He continues before I come up with an audible response. "But I like movies too, so maybe we can do that for our next date."

"I'd like that," I say, slightly giddy at the idea.

"Okay, so... favorite TV show? Or should I say shows?"

"You're learning," I tell him, impressed. "Let's see—Oh wait! I thought you only got three questions."

"Aww, caught in the act. Come on, give me this one. You know you can't resist."

"Okay fine, you're right. It's like you know me already." I pause to see if there's any reaction to that, but he just smiles at me, eyes sparkling. "Well, *Alias* and *24* are my two all-time favorites. Maia and I are a teensy bit obsessed with those, even though they've been off the air for ages now. You should have seen the party we had when they did the new half season of *24.* There were fireworks, let me tell ya. *The Unit* falls into the favorites category too, I guess, although I still have unreasonable hopes that they'll bring that one back since the ending was literally the only bad episode. Oh, and *Doctor Who* of course, and *the Big Bang Theory* and *Once Upon A Time* and *America's Next Top Model*—don't judge me," I say when he laughs.

"No, no judgment," he says, raising a hand off the steering wheel like he's taking an oath. "Actually, I bet you could give most of those models a run for their money."

"Oh right," I scoff. "Maia and I used to take pictures all the time—full make-up and wardrobe changes and everything—it was so much fun. But I'm usually the photographer. Things are much easier behind the camera, you know? Especially when you have a best friend who looks like Maia."

He glances at me again as he changes lanes. "What does that mean?"

"Oh you know," I say vaguely. I didn't mean to open this particular can of insecurity. "She's just always been the pretty one, I guess. And no, I'm not fishing for compliments, so you can keep quiet about this one. I know what's what, and I'm fine with how things are."

He does keep quiet. For half a minute anyway. "Okay. But you are seriously crazy if you think that she's prettier than you are."

I don't know how to respond to that. "Levi said that I'm hot," I blurt out, and then my hand flies to cover my mouth. "I don't know why I just said that. I'm sorry, I guess I'm not used to people saying—I mean, having cute boys think that I'm—I mean, not that Levi's cute! I mean he is, but you, *you* are so much more... oh what is wrong with me?"

"Not a thing as far as I can tell," he replies.

I blink at him, slightly surprised that he's still in this conversation. "Huh?"

"Listen, Rennie. I'm glad that Levi said that to you if it helped you to realize how amazing you are. But that isn't something I can tell you."

I study my manicure, feeling like a complete moron. "Oh. Of course, I wouldn't expect you to."

"No, Rennie, let me explain. You know that my dad was away a lot when I was growing up, and much of the time it was just me and my mom. She's raised me with some very definite ideas of how to treat a girl, especially a girl I really like. Opening doors, offering you my jacket, these things may seem old-fashioned but it's how I was brought up. They're ways for me to show you that I respect you. And calling you *hot* just doesn't fit in with that. That's something that you say about some woman in a movie or in a video; someone that you only have a hope or intention of ever knowing from a distance. It labels them in a way that anyone walking down the street can do." He pauses to look over at me, making sure I'm still with him. "But *you* are gorgeous. You're cute and funny and smart; you're a million different things which can't possibly be contained in a tiny three-letter word that only cares about your appearance. So yes, every single day that I'm lucky enough to be with you, I will remind you that you're beautiful. But not hot. Don't settle for hot."

I look at him, but I can't form words. Beyond him, the ocean blurs past the windows. A boy I'm seriously falling for just told me I'm gorgeous, the moon is shining like a painting over the Pacific, and I haven't had any of those weird visions all day long. This really could be a perfect moment.

"Thank you," I whisper, knowing it's both inadequate and all I have to give. "Next question?" I ask quietly.

 Chapter Sixteen

*W*e have seven minutes to spare before Maia's imposed curfew of

10:00 when Alex and I arrive back at the house. He pulls into the

driveway and turns off the ignition.

"Well, here we are," he says.

"Yep. Here we are," I agree. Could I sound any more awkward? I've

never been on a date where I actually wanted to get a goodnight kiss, but

this one is definitely in a whole other league. Aunt Charlie always drilled

into us that kissing on the first date is not acceptable behavior for a

young lady who wants to be treated like a young lady. She has a lot of

rules of this nature, all of which Claire did her best to ignore when we

were growing up. I always paid attention, but didn't really have occasion

to either obey or disobey. Now that I'm faced with the option, well, I'm just glad Aunt Charlie isn't here.

"Can I walk you in?" Again, the perfect gentleman. Surely Aunt Charlie wouldn't object to that.

"Yes, of course. Please." Get it together, Rennie.

I'm too antsy to wait for him to come around to open the door, so I meet him on the front lawn. He's already taken his jacket off and is waiting to place it around my shoulders. I whisper a grateful thank you, and he takes my hand, rubbing a thumb across my palm.

I take a deep breath, inhaling the perfume of freshly mown grass and night-blooming jasmine. Nearby crickets serenade us with their evening lullaby, but I can barely hear them over the sound of my own heart beating.

"Can I ask you a weird question?" I say before I lose my nerve.

"Anything. After all of my questions on the way home, you've earned it."

"Can I... Can I see your tattoo?" It sounds even dumber coming out of my mouth than it did in my head, and his reaction proves how strange he thinks it is. Eyebrows raising, head jutting forward a bit as though he misheard me. I shouldn't have asked.

"My... Um, can I ask what brought that on?"

I shrug, feeling foolish. "Something Seth said tonight, that's all."

His face takes on a serious look. This is going downhill fast. "What did he say to you?"

"Oh, he just asked if I'd seen it yet. He made it sound like it was some rite of passage or something. Never mind, it was dumb."

But he's already rolling up his sleeve. "There's no rite of passage here. You already know that I trust you, and of course you can see it. That just caught me a little off guard. Here you go." He leans his arm out towards me, and I can finally see the whole thing.

It's much more involved than I'd originally thought. It's a compass, or most of one in a deconstructed sort of way. And the letters of the directions are all normal sized except for the W for West, which is so big it's coming off the side in a big fancy font, the ending flourish turning into the tree branch I'd seen before and the two birds flying away from it.

Without even thinking about it, I reach up and trace the W with my finger. I hear him catch his breath, like he wasn't expecting me to do that. I guess I should have asked first, but I didn't know I was going to do it either.

"What does it mean?" I ask.

He lowers his arm and rolls his sleeve back down before answering. "When my dad was killed in combat, a lot of things changed. One of them was that we moved here to California. I guess part of me felt like the move westward and the freedom of being here was some kind of reward for living through losing him. This was my way of celebrating that. Celebrating him."

"That's really nice," I say. "It's a wonderful tribute. I bet he would like that."

Alex just smiles at me. "Thank you for saying that. So, my turn to ask a question. Did you have a good time?" The raspy quality of his voice is brought out by his soft tone.

"I did. It was almost perfect."

He takes a step back in mock despair. "Oh ouch, and I was so swinging for the fences on this one. What did I miss?"

"No, that's not what I meant." Nice one, Rennie. "It was an incredible night; thank you so much for everything. Truly, I had the best time."

He's unconvinced. He pulls me in close, his hands on my waist. I return the gesture, looping my forefingers through two of his belt loops.

"But I did miss something," he whispers. "Tell me."

I look down at the narrowing space between us, studying one solitary button on his shirt to avoid eye-contact. "It's really nothing. Nothing that you could fix, I mean. Just me being silly."

"I like silly," he coaxes. "Tell me. I want to get the next date just right."

I look up into his shining eyes and bite my lip. He's going to think I'm an idiot. Finally I take a deep breath and just tell him. "Fireflies," I breathe. "I miss the fireflies back home."

"Fireflies? The little lightning bugs?" His lips crook into that half-smile I love so much.

I nod. "I know it's childish, but I didn't think about them not being here. This night was so perfect, it just doesn't seem right without them. They're magical."

"You believe in magic?"

"Well, I'm not waiting for my letter from Hogwarts any more, if that's what you mean. But I do think there are magical things all around us if we look for them, things that are wonderful for no apparent reason. And fireflies definitely qualify."

He sighs and draws me into a hug I could happily die in. "Rennie," he says my name with so much affection it makes my head spin. "I have to tell you something. You know how I told you I was practically raised by

243

my mom? Well, she's instilled a rule into me never to kiss a girl on the first date."

I nod understanding. "My Aunt Charlie taught me the same rule. Except with guys, I mean."

He's silent for the space of several heartbeats. Then, "I suppose if we're going to avoid having two very disappointed guardians, I need to leave." He stretches his arms out, removing me from his warmth in one swift motion. "But before I go, tell me when I can see you again. Because the next time I see you, it will no longer be our first date, and that rule won't apply."

I smile up at him, displaying my dimple. "I like the way you think."

"I have to work late tomorrow, but is there a chance I could see you on Monday?"

I'm pretty sure wild horses, an earthquake and Armageddon couldn't keep me away. "I think Maia mentioned going back to the beach on Monday afternoon. Where we had the bonfire?"

"That's perfect. I guess I'll see you there."

"That sounds good," I tell him. I want to tell him so much more. I want to tell him that this is the best night of my whole life. I want to tell him to forget the rules, forget Aunt Charlie and his mom and fireflies and just kiss me already! But I don't. I'm certain now that Alex is my Ethan, and I know for a fact that those kisses are worth waiting for.

"Good night, Serenity." He puts his lips to my temple, and when he pulls away, I reluctantly turn towards the house.

"Good night, Alex." I slowly walk into the courtyard, not wanting this to be the end. I look over my shoulder when I reach the porch and he's still there, watching me. I wave my fingers at him, and close the door.

Maia grabs my arms almost as soon as I'm inside, her black yoga pants and bright green tank top standing out boldly against the assault of white everywhere. She must have been waiting for me.

"Where have you been? I've been texting you for *hours!*" Her complaint is friendly enough, but it is still a rude interruption into my Alex-filled head.

"What?" I ask, confused. "I told you I was going to leave my phone off."

"Oh," she replies simply. "You were serious about that?"

"Hi Rennie."

I look over to the sofa and am pleasantly surprised to find Levi there, ankle casually crossed over his knee and arm laying along the back of the couch.

"Hi Levi." I lift an eyebrow at him and shoot a glance over at Maia. What did I walk in on?

"Oh yeah, Levi came over to bring me a monologue he found that he thought would suit me. Wasn't that sweet?"

"Extremely sweet," I agree. Good for him!

"I was just getting up to get us some Cokes. You want one?"

"No thanks, I'm good."

She prances off into the kitchen and I sit next to Levi, nudging him with my elbow.

"Look at you! Making your big move on Maia?" I waggle my eyebrows at him and he laughs.

"Not hardly. But maybe laying a little ground work."

I roll my eyes. "Ground work? You worked side by side for all those months! You need to make your move soon or she'll end up being with Seth forever. Come on, no one wants that."

"You can say that again," he says, his smile fading.

"Say what again?" Maia comes back into the living room and hands Levi a tall glass.

"Nothing," we answer at the same time.

She looks back and forth between us. "Yes, very convincing."

I stand and stretch my arms over my head. "All right, well I think I'm headed to bed. I'm still a little off on my time zones. Nice to see you again, Levi. See you in the morning, Mai."

"Wait, you're not even gonna tell me about your date?"

Levi's mouth drops open and he grabs his chest. "You had a *date*? So soon? How will my poor ego ever recover?"

These two really could be good together. "Oh please, I couldn't possibly compare to our bright and burning love, Levi, but I had to take a chance. Get back on that horse, as they say."

"Well okay, I suppose that's fair," he says, mossy eyes shining with this new game. "Be strong, Rennie. You'll find love again."

"Are you two finished? My best friend just went out with a guy that I don't exactly approve of. I need details!" Maia waves her arms, her Coke sloshing dangerously close to the rim of her glass.

"Later, Mai. Levi doesn't want to hear this. You two have fun, and in the morning I'll give you every detail you can stomach, okay?"

She puts on a pouty face, which I take to be a good sign. She only pulls that face when cute boys are around. "Okay, fine. But you better tell me everything. Even the bad stuff."

I put one hand on my hip and give her the haughtiest expression I can manage. "Sorry, but there *was* no bad stuff. He's perfect." My told-you-so attitude melts into a silly grin, but I don't care. My skirt billows out as I spin around and head to my room. I wave sweetly to them from my door, and shut out everything but my memories of Alex.

It's not until I'm ready for bed and reaching for my journal that I see the note. A small white note card leans against the lamp on my bedside table, the gold embossed letter C on the front so fancy it's barely recognizable. Looks like Mrs. Cantrell has gone all out again.

But it's not from Mrs. Cantrell.

Serenity,

I have made a very simple request of you, and you continue to ignore it. Consider this your formal invitation. Present yourself to the Citadel before the date of your *seventeenth birthday. Please believe me when I tell you that you don't wish to make me angry.*

The Commander

Chills run up my spine. I read it over several times, but it doesn't change. I flip over the thick white card, hoping to find some evidence that I'm missing a joke, but knowing that I'm not. This is a threat. *In my bedroom.* A threat left for me on an embossed card in my bedroom.

Who does that?

The Commander, apparently.

 Chapter Seventeen

1 run into the clearing, the searching lights of our pursuers fading into

the distance. Panting, I stop to catch my breath, and lean back against

one of the tall pines. My lungs want to expand more than is physically

possible, the result being this wretched pain in my chest and side. But I

don't care. We got away.

"Are we really safe?" I gasp out, still looking past the treeline and

back towards the castle grounds.

"We are. We left them wandering around, headed in completely the

wrong direction," Ethan manages, hands on his knees to try to recover

his own breath. To my surprise, he's grinning.

"What can you possibly be happy about right now?" I wonder aloud.

"That was terrifying!"

"Oh come on, admit it. That was fun."

"Fun?" I echo. "What is fun about running for our lives?"

He shrugs one shoulder and saunters towards me, eyes locked on mine and his smile crooking impishly to one side. "Out here in the woods, alone under the stars, already flushed and breathless... what's *not* fun about that?"

"Ethan!" I exclaim, pretending to be shocked, even though I know he's just teasing. Well, mostly teasing. He wraps his arms around my waist and pulls me close. My hands linger on his chest before I slide them up around his neck. "We should probably gain a little more distance before we stop for too long, don't you think?" I let my fingers rest on the back of his head, playing idly with his hair in a way that completely contradicts what I've just asked of him.

"Probably," he purrs, his eyes flicking down to my lips. "But sometimes, I just can't resist a little danger."

Like every other time, the dream fades much too quickly. I grab my sketchbook from the nightstand and rub the heel of my hand over my eyes. I'm fairly certain now that Alex is Ethan, but a little confirmation would go such a long way. If I could even draw the outline of Ethan's face... but it's gone. It always is. I close my eyes, trying to relive the last moments. Something about running, and then needing to run but stopping, and the kiss. Always with the kiss. I may not know what Ethan looks like, but I'm certain I'd know those lips anywhere. Maybe I could go door-to-door, some bizarro version of Cinderella. The thought makes me laugh, but it turns into a yawn.

It's still early, just after 7:30, but there's no way I can go back to sleep. This impossible quest I was given has taken a personal turn. Whoever this Commander is can now access my subconscious, my cell phone, and my bedroom.

I take my journal over to the window seat and pull my knees up. Opening to the next clean page, I let my mind wander and my pencil doodle. All down one side I draw big swirls that melt into clouds, leaves that turn into birds, dandelion seeds that become raindrops. I don't try to make any sense out of it, I just let myself draw unedited and unencumbered by reality. At the top of the page I draw out Ethan's name in big bold bubble letters, adding dimension and texture as I go.

When the creative side of my brain is satisfied, I let my CDO take over. Time for a list.

1) How can I know for sure that Ethan is Alex if he can't remember?

2) Who is the Commander & what does he want with me?

3) How did the Commander find me? Is someone feeding him information?

4) What does the Commander want with Ethan (Alex??) ?

5) Is Ethan really Alex????

"Oh, thank God!" Kaela gushes when Maia and I arrive at the beach on Monday afternoon. "Somebody else in a one-piece bathing suit!" She throws her arms around my neck in a hug of relief, blond braids swinging wildly.

"Are you kidding?" Maia responds. "Rennie wouldn't be caught dead in a bikini. What was that motto that Aunt Charlie always used? It isn't rude to be a prude?"

"Modest is hottest," I reply, striking a pose and giggling.

"I love it," Kaela exclaims, laughing with me.

"You do realize that Aunt Charlie only made up all those rules to keep you from going out on a date before you're like thirty, right?" Maia teases. She's as familiar with all of the rules and mottos and helpful sayings as I am, but naturally they don't apply to her. Me however, they have shaped and molded. Aunt Charlie's voice is always in my head.

"Oh I know. She does her best, but this particular rule is a necessary one. I would burn to a crisp in a two-piece suit."

We set up our towels next to Kaela and Ember's things. I pull my sunglasses out of my bag and slip them on, pulling my hair out of the way and wishing I had put it up in a ponytail. I adjust the straps on my blue and white striped suit, and tug at the legs of my navy shorts before settling down onto the towel. Maia pulls her tee shirt off over her head, revealing a turquoise bikini top that perfectly matches her eyes. She leaves her cut-off jean shorts in place for the time being, and sits beside me. I feel the usual twinge of jealousy, wishing that I could wear something like that and feel comfortable in it. But there is no way. I'll leave that particular brand of confidence to her. I smile, remembering Alex's comment from our date. *You're crazy if you think that she's prettier than you.*" He honestly believes that? Let's see if it holds true after he sees Maia in her bikini.

The sun is blazing hot this afternoon, and the beach is packed with people of all ages, shapes, and sizes. You can tell by the various stages of sunburn who has been there the longest. The sky is an exquisite shade of blue that just can't be duplicated on film. Believe me, I've tried. Still, it won't stop me from trying again.

Kaela is standing directly in the line of sunlight, casting a cool shadow down on both Maia and me. "You want to go in the water with me? It's hot out here!"

"Sure!" Maia hops up, shimmying out of her shorts with no hesitation at all. "Is Ember already down there?"

"No, she's over at Fat Cat's with Isaac and Hudson," she replies, pointing to where there's a burger shack down the road. "She's gonna bring me a milkshake."

"Oh okay. You coming, Ren?"

"Actually, I think I'll just wait here for a bit. I want to catch up with my sketchbook."

Maia shades her eyes from the sun with her arm. "More bad dreams?"

"Only the usual," I answer. "I'll let you know if you need to worry."

"Promise?"

I try not to sigh. I love that she worries, I really do. "Being here is helping," I tell her. "Like yesterday. Back home, a drizzly Sunday would have meant an excuse to stay in my pajamas all day feeling depressed and sorry for myself."

"We did stay in our pajamas all day."

"Yes, but who could possibly be depressed with you, popcorn, and an *Iron Man* marathon? I mean, come on. I'm having a great time."

She shifts her weight, still unsure. "Okay, but if you need anything..."

"Come on, Maia!" Kaela's already halfway to the water, hopping up and down impatiently.

"I'm fine," I tell her. "Go have fun. Besides, I'm on the lookout for a certain someone."

"Of course you are." She winks, and runs down the beach to where Kaela is dipping her toes into the tide. I pull out my sketchbook, and draw the forest copse that's been haunting me lately.

Almost two hours have passed and my sketch is long finished, along with two acts of *Midsummer,* a game of *Settlers of Catan* on my phone, and a valiant attempt at sandcastle-building with Ember when I finally start to get frustrated. Alex did agree to meet me here today, right? I mean, we weren't all that specific as to time, but I know we said afternoon, and it's now almost 3:30. Isn't this like the peak of afternoon? I know how eager I am to see him again, is he not as excited to see me?

I set my book and my phone aside and watch the tide roll in and out, trying to match my breathing to its steady pulse. It helps. A little.

"He'll be here," Maia says, watching me through her sunglasses. She's laying on her towel, trying to enhance her already glowing tan, and keeping an eye out for Seth at the same time. I left out the part about running into him when I recounted the date to her. I didn't know how to tell her about Naomi Tight Sweater without totally crushing her. I hope it was the right decision.

"I know," I sigh, picking at the fringed edge of my beach towel. "I'm just being impatient, that's all."

"I hate to say I told you so, but..." Maia leads.

"Then don't," I finish. "Please. I know he's not your favorite person, but once you get to know him, you'll see how good he is for me. I promise."

She shrugs and looks at me through her champagne-colored lenses. "Maybe," she says evasively. "He sure seems to make you happy, anyway. Tell ya what, if he can get through the summer without breaking your heart, I will be more than happy to give you my blessing."

"Thanks, that means a lot to me."

A shadow comes over our towels, interrupting Maia's sun rays. My heart leaps. He's finally here!

"Hey!" she protests, looking for the source.

"Oops, sorry Maia. Hi Rennie." It's Levi.

I sink back onto my elbows and try not to be annoyed. "Hey Levi, have a seat." I tap my foot at the end of my towel as an invitation.

He sits down with us, leaning back and lifting his face to the sun. "So how do you like our little town so far, Rennie?" He's talking to me, but I notice that his eyes keep drifting over to Maia's bikini-clad form. Story of my life.

"It's great. I really feel at home here," I reply.

"Good, good," he says, nodding. I can tell he's not really listening. Levi's a sweet guy, but when you come down to it, he is still a guy. I could have told him that I like SLO except for the fact that it's overrun with R.O.U.S.es and I think I would have gotten the same response. "So Maia, did you hear about the auditions coming up for the theatre downtown?"

She sits up and hugs her knees, giving a little gasp. "No! Tell me, tell me!"

His face brightens at the attention, green eyes sparkling. Poor guy, he really is smitten. I'm surprised she can't see it, she's usually so clued into these things. I blame Seth.

"They just announced it this morning. They'll be doing *Into the Woods,* and auditions are in two weeks."

Maia throws her arms into the air in celebration. "Yes! I've wanted to do that show for *ever!*"

"Me too! Do you know that show Rennie? *Into the Woods?*" It's nice that he's trying to include me in this, but he's having trouble keeping his eyes off of Maia.

"Only from Maia and seeing the movie," I say.

"Mmm," he attempts to acknowledge my response, but it proves too much for him. "You know, you would be a perfect Cinderella." Now I

259

know that's not meant for me.

Maia freezes, giving him a withering stare. "Cinderella?"

He looks at me nervously, wondering what he's said wrong. I shrug.

"Cinderella is my fourth choice." She counts off on her fingers, holding them up high so he won't miss it. "In order, I want the Witch, the Baker's Wife, Little Red, and *then* Cinderella. You think I couldn't play the Witch?"

I refrain from saying that she's doing a pretty good job of that right now.

"I think you'd be fantastic in any of those roles," he sputters. "I was only thinking that I really want to be Cinderella's Prince, so it would be great if you were Cinderella, that's all."

She shifts moods again, her features softening in a flash. "Awww, that's so sweet! That *would* be fun, wouldn't it? You know, you'd be great as the Baker, too."

"You think so?" He blushes. I stop listening. I make a mental note, however, to point out to Maia how cute they are together.

I sit up and grab my camera, shooting frames without even bothering to stand. I try to capture everything. Kaela and Ember at the shoreline, playing in the tide; Maia and Levi completely absorbed in their talk of future stardom; the pier, the water, all of it. I zoom in far to my right and notice a shallow inlet of water where some smaller children are playing without fear of tides or undertows. On the other side of that inlet is a cluster of huge grey rocks rising out of the sand.

It's here, amidst the rocks, that I first spy Alex. My heart lifts at the sight of him, until I notice that he's not coming towards me. He's stumbling through the sand, hurrying toward the rocks. He goes between two of them, and when he doesn't re-emerge, I realize that there must be a cave entrance hidden there. My heart skips a beat. Some of my sketches are of rocks like these, and I know my fear stems from the bad dreams I've been having, but I shake that off. If I want to see Alex, it's time to face up to that fear today.

"I'll be back in a few minutes," I say, setting my Rebel aside and pushing myself to my feet.

"Did you find him?" Maia questions, a sly smile on her face.

"I'm not sure, I think so. You'll know soon enough," I grin down at her. "You'll see the sky-writing."

Chapter Eighteen

*M*y bare feet slip in the sand as I wind my way through the giant

rocks. I know he came this way. This is more than the pursuit of a first

kiss; I can't fight the feeling that something is terribly wrong. I've

entered a world of shadow and light, the cave entrance appearing

suddenly, yawning around me, ready to swallow me whole. I open my

mouth to call his name, but nothing comes out. I swallow hard, forcing

down the fear that's rising in my throat. I should turn back. But of

course, I don't.

I take a hesitant step into the darkened opening, the cool air greeting

me with its chilled breath. I wrap my arms around myself, trying to

convince my own mind that my goosebumps are from the sudden

change in temperature and not fright. I take another step inside, reaching out to grab the rock wall for balance against the slipping sand under my feet. Why am I doing this? Go back, go back, go back.

I don't.

I take a deep breath and plunge in boldly, counting my footsteps for comfort. Three, four, five... There's light up ahead around the next corner. Eleven, twelve... natural holes in the ceiling above me are letting in sunlight. I can do this. Seventeen, eighteen...

I come to a larger cavern with two different paths to follow, and stop. Here would be a great place to turn back. I tried to find him, I conquered my fear by coming this far, it was a good effort. I turn to retrace my steps, when I hear voices—hushed tones speaking quickly, urgently. I stop to listen, trying to find a source, or at least a direction. They seem to be coming from the path farthest to my right, and I find myself following them before I realize that I'm doing so.

I round corner after corner, a maze of rock, sand, sunlight and shadow. The whispers echo off of the rocks, carried away on the wind, coming at me from all sides. It doesn't make finding the speakers an easy task, but as I listen I begin to understand the words.

"She's not ready! *I'm* not ready; I need more time." That's Alex.

"And what exactly do you think I can do about it?"

More hushed whispering that I can't make out, but I don't have to think about it for very long. As I come around the next turn, there they are. The two of them stand in a rounded cavern, the brown-grey walls curving up around them, framing their tensed bodies. One whole side of the ceiling is filled with holes, sunlight filtering in at dramatic angles. And in one of these natural spotlights, Alex and Seth stand facing each other, squared off like they're about to duel in an old Western movie.

Seth is the one facing me, but I can tell that Alex knows I'm there. An ugly smirk twists Seth's mouth. He glances at me and then back at Alex, cocking his head slightly in an arrogant way that seems to suggest he's just won a game. Alex's shoulders sag under a weight I can't see. What have I walked into?

"Alex?" It comes out as a plea, soft and vulnerable. I have no idea what is happening but I'm afraid. He turns to face me and my heart aches. His beautiful grey eyes are filled with a sadness I've never seen before.

"You shouldn't be here," he says, voice cracking under the weight of his emotion.

"You're wrong," Seth's voice rings out. He's leaning against the opposite wall now, arms folded across his chest. "This is exactly where she should be."

"What's wrong? Please just tell me." I ignore Seth and take a hesitant step toward Alex, my hand extended to touch his shoulder.

He recoils, tripping over his own feet in his haste to get away from me. I snatch my hand back, cradling it as if I've been burned. What is going on? Alex turns his back to me, leaning his weight on his outstretched arms against the stone wall. I push aside the feeling of rejection that's starting to swell in my chest and take another tentative step towards him.

"Alex please—" I stop.

There, half-hidden in the shadows, is a stone bench, and on top of the rough grey surface, a book lays open, pages fluttering gently. The hair on the back of my neck stands up and I stumble back a step. Suddenly all the pieces click into place. I've seen this before—in my own sketchbook. This isn't possible. I saw my vision come true, when I found myself awake in my dream world that day with Levi. But this feels different—bigger. This dream that has been haunting me for half a year just found me. And not only me—Alex.

265

I look to him, my blood pulsing in my ears, but he faces purposefully away from me. I want to say something to comfort him, to remove that sadness from his handsome face. But I remember this scene. I know my line.

"Ethan." It isn't a question; it isn't even a statement. Just a breath, a simple exhalation that changes everything. "You're Ethan," I repeat. His head drops down and he makes a noise in the back of his throat somewhere between a sob and a plea.

"Well, well." Seth sounds... amused? Impressed?

I don't care. All that matters is Alex. Ethan. I know it doesn't make any sense, but here we are. My dream has taken on a life of its own, and we're only the players.

Alex turns slowly and looks at me, an overwhelming sorrow coloring each of his features. "It's not fair," he whispers. "I wanted more time." He gives me a half-hearted smile and I love him for the effort. Then, sadly and deliberately, he stretches out his hand, closes his eyes, and touches a drawing on the open page of the book.

A noise like a windstorm crashes through the silence. Instinctively, I cover my head and turn away, but not before I see a bright green flash of light, the book snapping shut like hungry jaws. It's over as suddenly as it began, and when I lift my head Alex is gone. Just as I knew he would be.

I run over to the bench and pick up the book, flipping desperately through the pages. I don't know what I was expecting. Somehow I'd thought it would be warm to the touch, still seething with some internal power. I'd thought the pages would be fragile and aged. Maybe I even thought I could find that drawing and bring him back. But it's none of those. It's only a book.

And then from behind me, I hear Seth begin to laugh. "Well, that's not how I expected that to go down."

I whirl around, clutching the book to my chest. My bare feet fly across the damp rock, quick strides propelled by fear and anger, and in the space of a single heartbeat I'm on him, pushing his back into the stone wall with my free hand. The abruptness of the movement startles him into sobriety, but only for a moment. I raise myself onto my toes so that I can look him dead in the eye.

"Tell me what just happened here." I try to make it sound menacing but my voice quavers. My pulse is racing with what I've just seen, my stomach in knots at having to be this close to him. The familiar feeling of helpless dread that always lingers after waking from my dream is so real now that it hangs in the air like a toxin, seeping through every pore.

I feel Seth's muscled chest move under my hand. He's laughing again, but softer now. He reaches a hand up like he's about to touch my face, and I bat it away. Oddly enough, that's exactly what I needed. Anger overtakes the despair rising in me and I push him again—harder. His head snaps sharply against the rock behind him.

"Augh!" He rubs his head, no longer amused.

"Good, now you're paying attention. Tell me what happened. Where is Alex?"

"You were right here. You saw the same thing I did." He brings his hand away from his head checking for blood, which of course is not there. Big baby.

"But it doesn't make any sense! People don't just disappear into books!" Maybe I shouldn't have said that out loud. Can you say things like that without having men in white coats take you away to a padded room? But a memory leaps up, unbidden. The alleyway behind Outspoken and my own disappearing act. When I arrived back in the alley, my copy of *Hamlet* was on the ground next to me. Is that was made me vanish as well? If Alex really is Ethan, then right now he is in the same place I went to that day. The same place I visit almost every night. Alex is in my dream world.

I take a deep breath and try to steady my nerves. I have no idea how much Seth knows, or what I can say to him. He's watching me closely, like he's waiting for me to say something else. But my dream never extends this far, and I have no clue what comes next.

"Okay, at least tell me what we're supposed to do now."

"Well, I have a few ideas," he smirks.

"Rennie?" Maia's entrance takes me completely off guard. "Seth? What are you doing?" She stands there by the opening, staring at us.

I look at Seth and realize in an instant what she must be seeing. Walking in on us alone, standing so close, my hand on his chest, my bare feet on tip-toes to get nearer to him. As my brain is still processing this image through her eyes, Seth is already acting on the same realization. I feel his arm snake around my waist.

"What does it look like we're doing?" He pulls me closer and I lose my balance, falling into him.

I push myself away, calling after her as I regain my footing. She's already gone. I can hear her sandals flip-flopping across rock and sand, racing away from us. From me. "You idiot!" I yell at him, my voice echoing back a chorus of agreement. "Why would you do that to her?" I don't wait for an answer. I hear him yelling after me as I run after Maia, but I don't bother turning back and he doesn't pursue. At the edge of the overhang I stop, blinded by the bright sunlight. By the time my eyes are rid of the purple blinking spots, she's already back at the main part of the beach where we'd left our things. "Maia!" I yell after her but if she can hear me she doesn't let me know it.

"Fantastic," I mutter, setting out after her. The cold Pacific bites at my ankles as I step into the shallows. I suck in my breath as the water gets deeper, chilling my calves and knees, but I ignore the cold and push through, trying to get to Maia before this gets too far out of hand. I step out of the water and run up the beach, my wet feet turning to mud, and reach her just as she finishes gathering up our belongings. "Maia wait," I pant. "Let me explain."

Her dark hair flies around her as she spins to face me, eyes flashing. "Explain what? I know what I saw."

"No you don't. Seth was lying, I don't know why he said that."

"Seth didn't have to *say* anything. The picture was pretty clear." She starts up the beach, heading for her Jeep. I follow behind her, trying to get her to hear me, but even I know how pathetic I sound. If I'd walked in on that scene I would have thought the same thing.

"Maia, wait up!" I stumble my way through the sand, bits of rock and wood scratching up my bare feet. She's slamming the back door when I finally reach the parking lot, our towels and bags strewn carelessly across the back seat. Still I take it as a good sign that she thought enough to grab my stuff along with hers—maybe she's not *that* mad.

I put a hand to her shoulder, still warm from the sun, and turn her to face me. I know instantly that it's a mistake.

"Don't touch me," she hisses. Her chin is starting to tremble and I fear the onslaught of tears that's about to start. She folds her arms and stares at the horizon instead. "How could you do this?"

"Maia," I try again, quietly and calmly, like Jack Bauer trying to negotiate for hostages. I want to tell her that she's being ridiculous, that we don't have time for this conversation right now when we should be trying to figure out what just happened to Alex. But I can't. "I know that looked bad, but I promise it's not what you think. You're my very best friend, and you know that I wouldn't hurt you by going after the guy you like, right?"

"I thought I did," she mumbles. "But honestly, I don't know anymore."

"What is that supposed to mean?"

Her eyes meet mine, cold and distant. "I keep telling myself that you're acting differently because of Claire. You're not ready to talk about it, and that's fine, but I know you. You're hiding something. We've always told each other everything. And now you're running after some guy you barely know, a guy I warned you was not only kind of a jerk but could actually be dangerous. You won't talk to me about the nightmares, or the sketches or any of the awful stuff going on in your head. And now I find you in a secluded cave, pressed up against the *one guy* I've told you I like. None of that sounds like the Rennie I know."

Her words take the air from my lungs. I gape at her, trying to process what she's just thrown at me. I was expecting to calm her anger and explain what happened and hug and move on. It's what we do. But this is much more difficult to navigate. "You're right, Maia," I say. "I am keeping things from you. There are awful things going on in my head sometimes, just like you said, and I'm not sharing them with you. I'm not sharing them with anyone but my sketchbook. I wish I could tell you everything, there are things happening that I can't explain. But I don't feel like I can drag you into it until I understand it better myself. I guess having you gone for the last six months has made me realize that there are some things I have to deal with on my own."

"I get that. It's been hard on me too, you know. And I had to start completely from scratch. When I was here, alone and feeling lost and so crazy-stupid lonely I thought I might as well crawl into a hole and stay there, do you know who the first person to talk to me was? The very first person to be nice and act like I wasn't an outsider freak?"

"Seth," I whisper, remembering the story she's told me a half a dozen times.

"Seth," she echoes with a nod. "And you know what? I love you like you're my sister, Rennie, but I will not let you steal him from me. I just won't."

"I don't. Want. Him." I say each word slowly and clearly, trying to get them through to her. If I could physically imbed them inside her brain, I would.

"Okay," she says quietly. "But if that's true, then what were you doing in that cave with him?"

I clearly hadn't thought this through to its inevitable conclusion. How do I explain this to her? *Remember that dream boyfriend I told you about? Well, a funny thing happened...* Yeah, I don't think so.

"I was looking for Alex, and I thought I'd seen him go in there, but when I got into the cave, Seth was there." I can't tell her what happened, not yet. But there is one thing that I can tell her, and she's not going to like it. "So I decided that I needed to confront him about something. Something that I should have told you before." She unfolds her arms, concern crossing her face. "When I was on my date with Alex, Seth was there at the Melodrama too. And he wasn't alone."

Her eyes widen as she grasps what I'm telling her. "Who?" she whispers.

"Naomi." I let that sink in as she takes a breath and starts picking at her fingernail polish. "Maia, I'm sorry. I told him that night that he was being a jerk, but I thought it would bear repeating since I saw him again today. That's when you walked in; I was so close to him to try to be, I don't know, threatening I guess. Then Seth pulled me into him as a stupid joke or something and I lost my balance and fell against him. That's all."

There's enough truth in what I've said that I hope she won't be able to tell where I mixed the stories. "I'm sorry, Maia. I should have told you right away, but I didn't know how. I don't like to see you get hurt." That part is definitely true, and while I feel bad about telling her like this, maybe it's better that she knows so she can be done with him. I need her back on my side quickly, because if I'm going to figure out any of what is going on, I'm going to need my best friend. Playing spy games is one thing, but the chance to solve something real is frightening beyond belief. I'm going to need her.

"Thank you for telling me," she says, still fixated on her nails. "I know he's not perfect, but I really do see potential in him. He and Naomi have been friends since they were kids. They've grown up together. So they were probably just out as friends." She looks up at me, the hint of a smile coming back to her face. "After all, he didn't take Naomi to prom, did he?"

I smile tentatively back at her. She still likes him; what else can I do? "No, he didn't. He took you." I lean over and give her a hug, still holding onto the book in one hand.

After a moment, she breaks the hug and steps back to look at me. "Wait a minute. If Alex wasn't there, then you still haven't gotten your kiss?"

That brings a genuine smile to my face. "Not yet," I answer, clutching the book to my chest. "But I have a feeling it'll happen soon." At least, I hope so. I just have to keep believing that he's okay, and that he's coming back to me.

 Chapter Nineteen

$\mathcal{T}$here has to be something here. There *has* to be.

I'm sitting cross-legged on the window seat in my room, the book from the cave open on my lap. I've been through it cover to cover four times since I got back from the beach. There is nothing at all unusual about this book. Leather-bound, maybe an inch thick, small enough to fit in a purse or a back pocket, and the pages completely blank. No text, no drawings, nothing. I've held them up to the light, looked at every last inch of every last page. There is *nothing* here.

I pinch the bridge of my nose and sigh, once again replaying the scene in my head. I can still see that look of sadness in Alex's eyes, feel the rush of wind from nowhere. I could get out a giant box of crayons and show you the exact shade of green from the flash of light. But I don't know what any of it *means*.

I set the book down carefully and go over to the desk to get my journal. While I'm pondering what my next step is, I run my fingertip along the spines of the books on my desk. It settles my churning brain just to see them there, all lined up and neatly ordered; each one in its proper place from Adams to Yolen.

I sit down with my journal spread open across my lap and close my eyes. When I'm feeling this lost, sometimes some good old-fashioned word association will help. Okay, clear my mind and think… Alex. *The cave, those eyes, sushi, that smile, those perfect lips, kissing those perfect lips…* Okay, this isn't working. Maybe if I try from another angle. Ethan. *Dreams, forest, running, laughing, hiding, find Ethan, find Ethan, find Ethan…* and I'm stuck again.

I've been charged with the impossible task of finding the Ethan of my dreams, and the second I do, he vanishes. I wonder if there's a way I can go to him. I landed in my dream world that day at Outspoken, maybe I can replicate that somehow. Trouble is, I don't have any idea how I did that. It felt like something that was happening *to* me, not something that I was causing. Why is my life suddenly this complicated?

I skip any kind of doodling and go straight for the list.

1) The book caused Alex to disappear. How? Did my copy of Hamlet do the same for me?

2) My dream of the cave came true. Does that mean all of the recurring dreams will eventually come true?

3) When I disappeared, I was only gone for maybe 10 minutes. So where is Alex??

I stand and stretch my arms over my head, allowing a yawn to break through. I've been denying myself the luxury of being tired since we got home. My brain is absolutely fried, but I can't stop thinking about this. What if Alex is in trouble? Maybe that's why he looked so sad, he knew that he was headed into something dangerous and he didn't want to go. And what about me calling him Ethan? He and Seth both seemed to know that was coming, even though Alex flat-out denied that name meaning anything to him. Is it possible that he didn't remember until that moment? I'm seriously questioning what *possible* even means anymore.

There's a light *tap-tap-tap* at my window and I jump, my heart leaping into my throat. I imagined it. It was a tree branch, or the wind, or a really lost bird. I wait, sitting as still as I can, praying that it was my imagination. *Tap-tap-tap.* No such luck. I stand quietly and creep across the soft carpet on tiptoes. Measuring curiosity against fear, my fear will win most every time. But there's a tiny piece of me that thinks *What if it's Alex?*

I kneel on the window seat and reach out a trembling hand toward the blinds, but pull back at the last second. I know what happens in movies when someone does this. They part the slats only a few inches, and that's *exactly* where the monster-alien-zombie-serial killer is peering through. I pause with my hand on the turny-stick that opens them and take a deep breath.

"Rennie come on, I know you're still up. I can see your light on."

Seth? I bypass the turny-stick and yank on the string, the blinds flying open with a shrill whine. I sit on the window seat and inch open the glass. Seth is at my window. Seth. I can't quite wrap my brain around this.

"What are you doing here?" I demand.

He stands in the dark, just on the other side of the carefully manicured rose bushes that line the front of the house.

"Minnie Mouse?"

I'm too stunned to respond at first. Is that a code? A password? "What?"

"Nice PJs." He looks me up and down, and I do the same. Well crap. I cross my arms across my chest and try not to blush. "Can I come in? It's freezing out here." He shoves his hands deeper into the pockets of his hoodie and grimaces, dancing back and forth from foot to foot. It may be like 50 out there, but it's not freezing. What a baby, he has obviously never lived where there are actual seasons.

"No way. What are you doing here?" I repeat.

"You come out here then, we need to talk."

"It's two o'clock in the morning. I am not going anywhere, and I'm about ten seconds from closing this window if you don't tell me what you're doing."

"I would think you'd be a little more inviting, considering I'm the only one who has the answers you're looking for." He looks so sincere, blue eyes catching the light as he tilts his face to look at me. Without the smirk he usually wears, he's actually very good looking. Not that I care, of course, but it's good to note. For Maia's sake.

"I do want answers, you know I do. But this isn't my house, so I can't exactly go inviting strange boys in at all hours of the night. And do you have any clue what kind of trouble you caused me with that little stunt you pulled in the cave? Maia was livid. But was she mad at you? Oh no, of course not. She still thinks you're the bee's knees. She was mad at me, and it took all my powers of negotiation to talk her down."

He smiles. "The bee's knees?"

I refuse to be side-tracked. "Yes. The bee's knees, the cat's pajamas, the snake's hips. Pick a random Prohibition phrase and insert here. The point is, she was mad and it was your fault. So you can stand there and freeze, and tell me what I need to know from there."

"She never could take a joke," he mutters with a nervous glance over his shoulder. "Okay, look, I don't have a lot of time. My dad will kill me if he finds that I've snuck out of the house again." He stomps his feet and blows air through his teeth, either cold or frustrated, I can't tell which. "We may have gotten off on the wrong foot, and it's probably my fault. But I don't want anything to happen to you. So just be careful, okay?"

I take in a breath of the cool night air to ease the knot forming in my stomach. "Wow, um, thank you. I don't really know how to respond to that. I mean, you haven't exactly been the nicest person to me, and now you come all the way over here in the middle of the night to vaguely warn me about being careful? I don't really know what to make of—"

"You're smart, Rennie," he interrupts. "When you found us in that cave, you didn't just happen to wander by, did you?"

"No, of course not. It took some stalking and a little luck to find you."

"Exactly. So did you even ask yourself how Maia just happened to pop in?"

I hesitate. In truth, that had never even crossed my mind. "Not really. I was more worried about getting her back than how she got there. Wait a sec, you don't think that Maia is involved in Alex disappearing, do you?"

He rolls his eyes. "Of course not. I'm suggesting that she got her information from somewhere."

This is one puzzle too many; I just maxed out. "Seth, please. I'm so tired of trying to guess at things that don't make sense. Just *tell me* what this is all about."

He looks over his shoulder again before answering. "I want to help you, Rennie. I want to be... I mean earlier today you said... " He puts his face in his hands and lets out a strangled sound.

Normally, I would find him stumbling all over himself a refreshing change of pace, but right now I'm tired and my patience is gone. "Seth, stop. It's late, we're both tired. Honestly, I only want to know if Alex is safe. The rest of it can wait."

His face hardens into that sneer I've come to know and despise. "Alex will be just fine; he's really good at taking care of himself." He shakes his head and releases a snort up to the stars, muttering, "Why did I even waste my time?" With a sharp look back to me he growls, "Just don't do anything stupid." And with that, he turns to walk away into the night.

"Seth! Seth, wait," I hiss, whispering as loudly as I dare. There are so many things I still need to ask. I put my hand up to the cold glass and lean as close to the screen as I can without risking a tumble into the bushes. "What about the book?"

That makes him hesitate for a moment, his feet coming to a stop on the dew-wet lawn. He gives me a look over his shoulder that's even colder than the temperature outside. "Keep it safe," is all he says. Then he's gone.

I watch him walk away before closing the window and lowering the blinds. Well I'm not exactly sure how, but I blew that all to pieces. A perfect opportunity to get some of the answers I need, and I know nothing more than I knew before.

It's approaching 2:30 when I crawl into bed. My mind is so overwhelmed, it's finally ready to power down for a while. I've left the book over on the window seat, and briefly wonder if I should put it somewhere more concealed, but before I can even form a coherent response to that, I'm drifting off to sleep.

It's the hand covering my mouth that wakes me.

Chapter Twenty

My eyes fly open and I'm struggling for air, trapped between the pillow behind me and the hand pressing over my mouth. A familiar voice comes from the dark above me.

"It's okay, it's okay. It's just me. It's Alex."

I stop struggling and let my eyes adjust to the moonlight. "Alex?" I mumble into his palm.

He relaxes, sitting next to me and releasing his hold on my air supply.

"Sorry about that. I didn't want you to scream, and I didn't know what else to do."

"Next time, how about a nice code word or something?" I say, stretching my mouth and rubbing at my face.

He smiles, white teeth shining in the ambient light. "Good idea. How about *caterpillar*?"

I swat at his arm, and then stop, looking at him more carefully. "You're back." I want to touch his arms, his face, his hair. I have to make sure he's really here. I reach out and run my fingers over his cheekbones and down his chin. "You're safe, and you're back."

He closes his eyes and leans in to my touch. And then all at once, we both seem to notice that he's sitting on my bed. In the dark. In the middle of the night.

He leaps to his feet and I tug the blanket higher over me.

"I'm sorry," he says, turning his back to me and holding onto the desk chair. "I should probably go. I only needed to—"

"No way," I tell him, throwing the blankets off and blocking his exit. "You're not going anywhere. Last time I saw you, you were in the cave, looking so incredibly sad for a reason I still don't know, and then you vanished into that book. Seth has been less than helpful (not really a shock there), but even if he won't tell me what's happening, *you* are going to."

His eyes narrow, and he slowly closes the distance between us. "Seth didn't tell you anything?"

"No. He was kind of taunting me with the fact that he had information, but wouldn't actually tell me any of it. Very annoying. But none of that matters anymore, because you're here."

He touches my arm, sliding his hand down until it rests on mine, our fingers intertwining like Tetris pieces. With a sigh, he leans his forehead to touch mine, and it's only then that I notice his hair is wet.

"Your hair…"

He leans back and touches it self-consciously. "Oh. It started to rain just as I was coming back."

"Right. From… the book." Oddly enough, this actually makes sense to me, since I was there myself and came back with an oak leaf stuck to the bottom of my shoe.

I'm suddenly acutely aware that I'm still in my pajamas; the same ones that Seth made fun of a few hours ago. (Was that even real? This night is getting curiouser and curiouser.) I silently will the legs of my shorts to be longer than they are, but they don't comply. So I tell my insecurities to stuff it and I wrap my hand more tightly around his. He's back. He's safe. Now I can finally find out what's going on.

"Tell me a story." The words are out of my mouth before I have a chance to think of what I actually want to say. *Tell me a story?* What am I, three?

Alex's reaction surprises me though. He draws his hand over the back of my head, drawing out a single red curl with his fingers. "Finally," he whispers under his breath. He looks toward the door to the hallway. If there's going to be any kind of conversation happening, we have to move somewhere that doesn't require whispering and apprehensive glances.

"Go through the dining room into the kitchen," I tell him, feeling very cloak-and-dagger. 'There's a back door, wait for me on the deck."

He nods and then takes a moment to rub his wet hair with the bottom half of his tee shirt. Anyone who can quote Yoda should not be that ripped. I'm not staring at his abs, I'm not staring at his abs, I'm not...

"I'll be waiting," he whispers, giving me a small smile and heading out into the dark hallway.

I take a deep breath and try to recover my wits. Alex. Here. Waiting for *me.*

That thought is enough to push me into action. I fly to the closet and grab the first things that come to my hand: jeans and an oversized icy blue sweatshirt to throw on over my tank top. The neck part is ripped so much that is hangs off my shoulder but it's still one of my favorites, so I don't mind.

I dart over to the mirror and run a brush through my hair, trying to tame some of the strawberry curls that are obviously more interested in finding new and exciting shapes to portray rather than lying flat in any normal hair-like fashion. *Fine. Have it your way, hair, but in the morning it's the flat iron for you.* I dab on a bit of clear lip gloss and mascara (*why yes, I do always look fabulous at 4am. Thanks for noticing*) and make a quick and quiet dash for the door.

For being such an obviously expensive home, there is hardly any yard to speak of; just a small patch of grass blocked in on one side by the driveway and surrounded by a wooden fence. At the back of the grass, there's a redwood deck, which Maia tells me her dad built himself. I find it hard to picture erudite Aidan swinging a hammer and measuring two-by-fours, but it's a job well done nonetheless. On the deck are two Adirondack chairs with a little cocktail table between them and a free-standing porch swing.

It's here on the swing that I find Alex, rocking gently back and forth dragging one foot as an anchor, petting Maia's cat who is purring rather contentedly.

"That's Lily," I say as I approach him. "Maia's had her for years; I even got to help name her." I sit down next to him and he releases the kitty to the ground. She swishes her tail in his general direction and looks back over her shoulder with a look that clearly says she was not done being fawned over.

"Lily," he repeats. "That's nice."

"Thanks. We were feeling very grown-up for not choosing Snowball or Fluffy."

"I don't know, those seem like viable options to me too," he says, brushing white hairs from his black tee-shirt. His cheekbones are even more pronounced in the moonlight, his dark hair glossy and sticking up around the edges from being dried so hastily. I'm dying to run my hands over it to smooth it down, but I don't dare.

"So, um..." How do I start this? I don't want to scare him off by jumping in with crazy questions, and I'm not quite brave enough to start swapping stories about my own disappearance. But at the same time, he *did* just appear out of a book. That may warrant a little bit of crazy.

"You wanted a story," he says, smiling gently.

"Yes," I agree. "I'm sorry, I don't know why I phrased it that way. But yes, I would really like an explanation."

He nods and takes my hand across the bench. By all means this should be very romantic, even a setup for a Perfect First Kiss. But curiosity trumps romance. I have so many things I want to ask him, it's hard to let them simmer.

"I know that I owe you an explanation and I promise you'll get it, but I need you to tell me about Ethan. Before the cave, you called me that twice. And then in the cave, you said it again. Why?"

I blink in surprise. I knew we'd get around to this eventually, but maybe the fact that he just got back means that he remembers. Maybe he knows now that he's Ethan and he's waiting for me to connect the dots.

"I'll warn you first, it doesn't make any sense."

"What part of this does?" He gives me an adorable little half-smile, and I relax. I can trust him with this.

"For the last few months, I've been having these recurring dreams, and in most of them there's this guy—Ethan." I search my memory for something solid that I can describe, but it's all so hazy and fluid and frustrating. "I can never really see his face, or I guess it's more accurate to say that I can't remember it when I wake up; everything fades pretty quickly. But in my dreams I definitely know him—like *really* well—and when I met you, there was, well there *are* these moments when I feel like I know you. I feel like my memory is trying to connect you to something else, something more."

I can see the wheels of his brain turning, trying to absorb this. "And then in the cave, it seemed like you figured it all out."

"No, I wish I could say that, but it's all so confusing. I'd dreamed it all before, so I wasn't shocked really, but it was a little scary to watch one of my dreams come to life—that's never happened before."

"Wait, you'd dreamed what before? The cave?"

I nod. "The whole thing. The cave, the bench, the book, you, Seth—everything."

His eyes meet mine in a flash, staring at me as though he's never seen me before, like a stranger just plopped down next to him and started spouting complete gibberish. Which, of course, I have.

"And your other recurring dreams," he continues. "Is Ethan in those too?"

"You are," I say, looking him right in the eye, not shying away from the crazy this time. I'm sure enough to share my hypothesis with him now. I let that sink in for a moment, and I can see the lines of his face change as he accepts what I've said. Oddly enough, he doesn't seem to be scared off by my revelations. Exactly the opposite in fact. He's holding my forearms now, leaning in so closely that I can feel his breath on my cheek.

"You think I'm Ethan," he whispers, his eyes searching mine for my answer.

I nod. "The man of my dreams." I smile shyly at him, and he relaxes just a bit. "I know it's weird. My head says it doesn't make sense, but my heart thinks it knows better."

He takes a shuddery breath before continuing. "No, it does make sense. That very first day when I ran into you with the driftwood, and I heard you speak—somehow my heart knew you too."

I reach up and touch his face, tracing his jaw with my finger. The tension building in my chest is replaced with sudden and overwhelming joy. He knows me. He's not running away, or finding a butterfly net; he's just accepting it. Accepting me.

He takes my hand from his face and kisses my palm. "So what does this mean?" he asks. "That text you showed me when we were on our date, it said you were supposed to find Ethan. So, what now?"

I shrug. "I honestly don't know. I've gotten that message in several different ways, but I still don't know what it means. I'm supposed to *ally* myself with you before it's too late." I give him a smile. "You wanna be my ally?"

He waits a long moment before answering. "More than anything."

He's so sweet, I'm not sure how to respond.

"Do you have any idea who is sending you these messages?"

"The last one I got was a little different. To be honest, I'm not sure it was even from the same person, but it's the only one that was signed. It was from someone called the Commander. Sounds kinda full of himself if you ask me, but I still don't know what it's about."

Alex's face has gone slack. "I think I do."

I gasp, leaning forward. "You do?"

"Yeah, I think I do. So... you wanted a story, huh?" He runs a hand through his hair and moves to the far end of the swing where he can lean his back against the arm rest. He shifts so that one foot is up on the seat with him, and his arm is draped over his knee. It's a casual pose for what I'm sure is not going to be a casual conversation. "We call it Traveling; I guess I should start there. This isn't something I'm used to talking about, and things tend to be fuzzy when I come back. Unclear. It makes it hard to remember the details. So I'm sorry if I don't have all the answers."

"That's okay, I'll take what I can get. Do you know why I would know you as Ethan in my dreams?"

He clears his throat and scratches the back of his neck. He must be freezing, his shirt just starting to dry out and his dark hair still slick and shiny in the moonlight. "Every Traveler uses an alternate name, both for anonymity and for safety. There are those on both sides who would do just about anything to exploit this ability."

"Like the Enforcers?"

He nods. "Enforcers are part police force, part militia, part bounty hunter. They are a nasty breed, and I wasn't kidding when I told you to do whatever you have to do to stay off their radar. They work for the Commander."

I bite my lip, fighting a smile. Even with every bit of evidence pointing to it, this is the first time he's actually confirmed that we are in fact talking about the same thing. I suddenly have so much more that I need to tell him; comparing notes about this other place and questions about the people who seem determined to bring us there together.

"The same Commander who sent me an engraved invitation to meet him, and to bring you along for the ride? That Commander?"

"Seems like it." He pauses, swaying the swing gently back and forth with his foot on the deck. "Do you have any idea why he would single you out?"

"I don't know how he would know me at all, it doesn't make any sense. For all I know, he's been stalking me the whole time I've been here and I'd never know it. Do you know what he looks like?"

Alex shakes his head, his forehead creasing in concern. "No. Nobody does."

"Wait, what?"

"No one sees the Commander. The closest you can get is the Council, and even that is by summons only."

I rub my hands over my arms, feeling the cold a little more distinctly at that thought. "That's creepy, like he's a ghost or something. I guess that confirms my instinct to avoid him." I lick my lips and turn my ring around my finger, letting the little blue gem catch the light. I know it's time to tell him that I Traveled too, and I know he of all people will understand that. But I still can't quite bring myself to say it out loud.

"Come here." He reaches across the bench and pulls me to him. He kisses my forehead, then turns me around so my back is to him and slowly leans me against his chest, wrapping his arms around me. I don't even mind that his shirt is still damp from the rain. I could stay like this forever. "Thank you," he whispers, his lips just above my ear.

"For what?"

"For still being here, for not running for the hills. You're taking this really well. Guess it's a good thing I picked a sci-fi geek to fall for, huh?" He gathers all of my hair to one side and kisses my neck. I feel like electricity should be shooting out my finger tips like the Emperor.

"I have to ask you something," I say, trying to get back on track. It's really difficult to stay focused with his arms wrapped around me. "Why did you pull away from me in the cave?"

He hesitates, just long enough to make me wonder if he's about to tell me the truth or not. "I panicked. I knew I was about to be pulled through and I didn't want you to see me like that; to know that I'm a complete freak with some unexplainable ability. And on top of that, I'm not exactly an expert at this yet. I wasn't sure what would happen to you if we were in contact at that moment."

I hadn't considered that. The thought makes me cringe, but it also makes another mystery very clear. "That's what happened with Violet, isn't it? At Prom?"

"Yes," he says. "I knew that I was about to Travel and I was able to get away from her, but she followed me. She reached out to me and in my attempt to get away, I guess my cufflink got caught in the shoulder of her dress. I was desperate to get away, so I just ripped it and ran. I felt terrible, of course, but what else could I do?"

"So you didn't sneak out some back exit. You were quite literally *gone.*"

"Exactly. I wonder sometimes if she saw more than she tells me, but I don't know. I suppose by this time she's come to whatever conclusion she's going to and moved on."

"I see why you couldn't tell us that when Maia cornered you about it.

I'm sorry about that, by the way."

"No. Really, I get it. But I'm glad to get to tell you the truth now."

I'm glad for that too, and I lean my head into his shoulder happily, feeling like another barrier has come down between us. And it's time for another.

"Okay, so... I have a confession to make." I take a deep breath and close my eyes. "When you Travel, where do you go?"

He releases a breath that comes out as part sigh, part laugh. "Rennie, that's not a confession. That's another question. I can tell 'cause it started with a question word and your voice went up at the end. I'm pretty bright that way."

I laugh and run my fingers over his arms, his hands. I trail one finger up his left arm and trace the inked W that hides there. I can feel it even with my eyes closed, the slightly raised flesh warm under my finger tips. "Okay, okay you caught me. But just answer this one more, and I promise I'll confess all."

"It's probably a terrible idea to tell you that I can't resist you when you're doing that with my arm, so I'll just answer your question instead. Once you remind me what it was." I can feel him smiling against my skin, his lips against my shoulder.

"Where do you go when you Travel? Do you start out at the crossroads?"

I feel him nod. "I do, almost every time. There have been a few exceptions, but mostly..." He goes very still, but I keep drawing with my finger. "Rennie, how do you know about the crossroads? I didn't mention that part yet."

"I know." I open my eyes, staring at my toes tapping on the wooden slats of the bench, and dive in. "I think I Traveled. Actually, given everything you've told me tonight, I'm sure of it." I explain everything that happened to me that day at Outspoken. The intense dizziness and feeling like I was being pulled apart, landing at the crossroads, hiding behind the tree just off the dirt road—every detail I can remember.

When I'm done, I can feel him shaking his head, his bangs sweeping against the back of my neck. "Rennie," he says softly. "This is huge. I mean, it's amazing that we're both here and both Travelers, and I can't even imagine what the odds on that must be. But..."

"But what?" My stomach sinks at that one small word. Maybe he's reconsidering dating me now, maybe this just became too much to handle and he's remembering what a nice uncomplicated girl Violet is.

"But this changes everything." He gently removes his hand from mine and nudges me to sit up.

I knew it. Only one date and he's already breaking up with me. I tuck my legs underneath me and turn to face him.

He has his serious face on. "There are a million things you need to know, and you need to know them fast. Have you Traveled at all since that first time?"

"What?"

He puts his hand on my knee. "I need you to focus, Rennie. Have you Traveled since Wednesday?"

I can't stop looking at his hand on my leg. "Umm, no. Wait, you're not breaking up with me?"

He sits up straighter, obviously surprised by this. "Break up with... no! Why would I... Okay look, I can't exactly break up with you since I haven't actually asked you to be my girlfriend yet, which I fully intend to do, by the way, and I *really* would have loved for that to be a much more romantic moment, but all the romance in the world won't matter if we don't get some of these basics down and you end up getting imprisoned by Enforcers or stuck in the other timeline or—or worse."

I nod and try to concentrate, but something he just said stops me.

"The other timeline? Are you saying that we're talking about *time* travel?"

"Yes, I'm sorry. I guess I should have started with that."

"Yeah, ya think?" My mind is spinning. Time travel? I traveled through time. I'm dreaming of the future, and I'm traveling through time. I can't wrap my head around that. "So you're saying the book acts as a time machine?"

"Sort of, but not in the H.G. Wells, *Back to the Future* kind of way. It's more of a portal that transports you between two fixed points. You can't choose where you go, so there's no going back in time to kill Hitler or re-take that Chem test. Only here, there, back. We're pretty sure we're not even moving locations, that it's taking us right back here but in some kind of alternate timeline. And the book is more of the vehicle, the actual portal is the drawing. No matter what book you're using, or how many pages you turn, a drawing will be there. That's the portal." He tilts his face up to the stars, and I know he's having trouble processing all of this as well. Somehow, that makes me feel better. "Your instincts were good. Hiding when you heard somebody coming towards you, I mean.

The Traveling times are usually short, especially at first, and your best course of action is just to keep yourself safe. I know that doesn't sound very exciting, but trust me, you don't want to get tangled up in anything going on over there. It's a mess, on the verge of war... you don't want to get involved."

I've never seen Alex so stern before, and I do my best to match his urgency. I guess it's time to stop thinking of these incidents as dreams now that I'm living them.

"There are so many things you need to know, I don't even know where to start."

"My brain takes things better if they're in some kind of order; it's too bad we can't, I don't know, alphabetize it all." I giggle nervously, but tamp it down by clearing my throat.

"That actually helps. There are a few rules we can start with. Will that make it easier?"

I sigh gratefully. He does get me. "Yes. Let's start with that, please."

He wipes his hands over his jeans. "Okay, the first rule of being a Traveler is that you can't talk about it to anyone. The only reason I was telling you is because you saw it happen, and you deserved to know the truth. But that is a huge exception. We do not talk about Traveling. Ever."

"Got it," I say. "There is no Fight Club."

He cocks his head to one side. "Rennie, this isn't a game. I have to keep you safe, and this is the only way I can do that right now."

"Sorry," I mutter.

"That's okay. And also, that was pretty funny." A small smile breaks through his seriousness and he looks like Alex again. "Rule two, never 'out' another Traveler. We all have alternate names on the other side, and those names need to stay on the other side. This one is easy to follow at first, because you won't remember even your own name most likely. Everything will be too fuzzy when you get back the first few times. But it can be a difficult rule to follow once you start learning who the others are, and it's vital that this not be compromised, so be careful."

"Others. Wow, I wasn't even thinking about others. Do I know any of them?"

"Rennie..." He draws my name out in a chastising way.

"Oh right. Sorry."

He smiles. "Now you're getting it. Rule three, we have to have each others' backs in both timelines. Once you learn who the others are, you'll know what to watch for. This gets complicated and has spawned a lot of sub-rules along the way, but for the most part, it boils down to look out for each other."

I nod again. "I can do that. How many of these rules are there? Should I get a notebook or something?" I'm dying to get this all into my journal in a nice ordered list so my brain can start making sense of it. I was kidding about the Fight Club thing, but I really do feel like this is a movie, like it's happening to someone else and I'm just watching.

He takes my hand, holding it in both of his. "Only two more. I'm sorry to have to throw this at you all at once, but Traveling is very unpredictable and if you haven't been pulled through again in almost a week, then you are way overdue."

"You're talking like I could just vanish at any moment."

"That's because you could," he says gently, his stormy eyes shining with intensity. "Typically, once you start Traveling, it will happen two or three times within the first week. So if it hasn't happened again..." He doesn't have to finish that sentence out loud. I get it, and I'm suddenly very much focused. "Make sure you have a book with you at all times," he continues. "And a Kindle won't work—it has to be paper and ink. When you feel it starting, try not to fight it. That will help with the sick feeling."

"Got it. Rule four?"

"Rule four is a little outdated, but it says that if another Traveler saves your life, they can name their reward. I've never heard of that one being put into play before, but you never know. And the last rule is that you can only Travel when you are summoned. I don't know how you would even manage to go through if you weren't, but there must be a way or that rule wouldn't exist."

"What happens if you go through on your own?"

"Legend has it, you stay there, stuck in the other timeline."

I feel a shiver snake up my back. Trapped in another time with no way back; no family, no friends, nothing familiar at all. I can't imagine a worse fate.

I use the momentary silence to venture a question of my own. "Do you know how this corresponds to my dreams? Why I was able to dream about this other place before I was ever there?"

He shakes his head. "I've never heard of that happening before. But it is funny, because there actually is a correlation between dreams and Traveling. The way it was explained to me is that we are finite beings, and we can only view time in a linear form. Anything outside of that automatically gets processed as a dream. It has to; the brain simply can't deal with it any other way. And, well you know how it is when you have a really vivid dream, but when you wake up it fades away? And the harder you try to remember it, the quicker it vanishes? It's like chasing a rainbow. You think you should be gaining on it, but it always stays just out of reach."

"That happens to me all the time," I tell him, feeling like he's just summed up a good deal of my own life.

"It's the same thing. Your brain is already processing it as a dream, so when you get back to your regular timeline, the experience is discarded. Most often, you're left with the general feeling, but none of the substance. In fact, when we come back to our own time, we refer to that as 'waking up.'"

That stirs something in the back of my brain, but I have too many questions to allow it to the forefront just now. "So I should expect to have fuzzy memories of my experiences then."

"Exactly. Don't worry when that happens, it's normal."

I laugh. "Normal? Want to try again?"

He gives me that lopsided grin that I adore. "How about... expected?"

"Better," I say. There are so many more questions I need to be asking, so much more I need to learn. Only I'm too distracted to pay any attention to any of it at the moment. I reach out and touch his face, tracing the line of his jaw with my thumb, and lean in just slightly so his face is mere inches from my own. My heart starts to race again, my breath coming quicker. He puts his hands on my waist, pulling me towards him. This is it. Alex is actually going to kiss me! I feel like I've been waiting for this forever.

I tilt my head to one side, hoping I've picked the right direction and we're not about to bump noses (definitely not the facial feature I'm going for). I close my eyes, already anticipating what those perfect lips will feel like, when there's a loud crash on the other side of the deck.

We both jump up, completely startled out of the moment, eyes searching for the mysterious intruder. Alex has stepped in front of me, arms spread wide to shield me from... a shovel. It was apparently standing in the corner of the railing, and is now lying prostrate on the wooden planks with Lily hissing at it as though it tried to attack her.

I breathe a sigh of relief and lean my head into Alex's chest. I can feel him laughing and I join in, the magic of the moment completely broken. I look up at him, and he smiles at me, pulling me into a tight hug. Disappointment floods through me at another lost opportunity for the Perfect First Kiss. But I can't be too upset. How many times does a girl get to hear that the boy of her dreams has fallen for her?

"I better get going," he whispers, his cheek resting against the top of my head. I hold him closer, not wanting to let him go yet. "If that crash woke anyone, we're going to have some serious explaining to do."

I can just imagine what Mrs. Cantrell would have to say about finding me alone with Alex in the middle of the night. "I hate to see you go, but I guess you're right." I try not to pout, I am so not one of those girls. *You hang up first. No, you. No, you.* Gag. "Aidan will probably be leaving for work soon. I think it's almost morning."

He looks at the lightening sky above us and takes my hand, walking me back toward the kitchen door. "You're right, it is. And yet I have more care to stay than will to go." He gives me that crooked smile again.

"Really?" I tease. "You're going to quote Romeo to me now? When you're about to leave?"

He chuckles and ducks his head apologetically. "Sorry, I couldn't help myself." We stop by the door and he kisses my cheek. "Stay safe, Rennie. Good night."

All I can do is grin in reply, and watch him walk away. As much as I hate to admit that Juliet was right, parting really *is* sweet sorrow.

Chapter Twenty-One

I had every intention of sleeping in late this morning. After Alex left last night, I finally crawled into bed around 5:30, only to wake up again when I heard the front door shut as Aidan left for work. That was 6:30, a whole hour of sleep. Whoopee. My brain is whirling with everything I learned from Alex, and everything I still need to learn. I found my Ethan. The thought makes the butterflies awaken in my tummy again. We may have a long way to go before we're as close as we are in my dreams, but the thought that he's alive and real and here with me is overwhelming. I'm not crazy. Somehow, my seemingly impossible task of finding him has become reality. He's here, and he's definitely my ally so now maybe those visions and messages can stop.

When I watch my alarm clock app change over from 6:59 to 7:00, I realize I'm not going back to sleep. So I take a quick shower and throw on some shorts and another of my Nerd Shirts. This one is icy blue with a picture of Starbuck (from *Battlestar Galactica*, not the coffee) hanging on a lamppost à la Gene Kelly, and the caption says "Nothin' but the Rain" in big musical-theatre font.

I start up my laptop and go immediately to my email. Time for a note to Claire.

Hey Eclair,

Guess what? Treasure hunts can be solved. And you'll never believe the treasure I found.

But that's all I get out. My brain is still too squirrelly to do this right now. So I abandon the email mid-paragraph and quietly head for the stairs. I can hear Mrs. Cantrell in the kitchen and I definitely don't want to run into her, so I tip-toe up the steps and around to the far side of the open space overlooking the living room.

"Maia?" I knock softly on her door. Nothing. I knock again. "Maia?" I hear a mumble on the other side that sounds enough like *Come in* that I go ahead and open the door. "Hey, Mai. You up yet?" She's sitting up in bed, rubbing her eyes. Her usually perfect chestnut hair is tangled and wild on one side of her head, and smashed flat against her scalp on the other. It makes me feel better to remember that even she can look flawed sometimes.

Her room is twice the size of the guest room I'm staying in downstairs. Her bed and nightstands occupy the far area by the windows, and an entertainment area closer to the door has a love-seat and a big cozy armchair, clustered together with a TV on the wall and a bookshelf filled mostly with knickknacks and DVDs. And of course, front and center is her prom picture with Seth. She's gone completely against the white of the rest of the house by painting most of the walls a brilliant deep purple, and the one behind her bed a pale blue. It's a very Maia thing to do, but I'm surprised her mom let her get away with it.

"Rennie?" Her voice is gravelly. "What's going on? What time is it?"

"It's about 7:30," I say, keeping my voice low. "Sorry to wake you, I couldn't sleep." I sit on the edge of her bed, the satiny fabric crinkling under me.

"I thought we were sleeping in today so we could go out with the girls

314

tonight," she yawns. It's more of an observation than a complaint, but I still feel the need to apologize.

"I know. I'm sorry, but... I kinda need to talk to you."

"Sure, you can talk to me anytime, you know that. What's up?"

I look out the big picture window on the far side of her bed. The view of the mountains is really pretty once you get used to the lack of green. Dark clouds are moving in from the north; maybe we'll get a little rain today. I'm stalling and I know it. Yep, definitely stalling. That's a weird word: *stalling*. Stall. Ing. If you're stalling and you know it, clap your hands. Okay, enough.

"Not here. I know it's early, but maybe we could go out to breakfast or something?" I'm not hungry at all, but it seems like a good excuse to get us out of the house. Maybe a little anonymity among strangers will help me feel like I can open up. I have no idea how to do this, but I have to tell her what's going on.

"Okay, sure. Give me twenty minutes to get ready, and I'll meet you downstairs, okay?"

"Thanks, Mai." I don't know why I feel relieved. How do I possibly tell her this without having her think I've lost my mind?

I sneak back down the steps, trying to be as quiet as I was sneaking up them. No luck.

"Rennie? You're up early this morning." Mrs. Cantrell's voice makes me jump, and I'm sure I'm wearing a guilty expression even though I've done nothing wrong. She glances up the staircase. "Did you wake Maia?" She asks it as though Maia is still a baby and I've woken her from nap time.

"Good morning, Mrs. Cantrell," I say politely. "I was just making sure Maia is awake. We're going out to breakfast this morning." The fact that I say it as though it was the plan all along isn't *technically* a lie. We are going out to breakfast.

She crosses her arms. "I don't think so, dear. Maia has obligations to take care of today."

My heart sinks. Why did I have to run into her? In twenty minutes we could have been out of the house and gone, but nooooo, of course not.

"Obligations?" I ask, trying not to sound annoyed. If Maia had plans, I'm sure she would have told me.

"Yes. Chores, dear. They've been sadly neglected this last week, and we let it slide since you had just arrived. But it's time to get back on schedule. Her room isn't going to tidy itself."

"Oh, well I can help her with that. We can have it done in no time."

"Not at all, I wouldn't hear of it." She purses her lips, looking at me as though I'd just suggested she wear white after Labor Day.

"But I—"

"You are a guest in this house, Rennie. I will not have you pitching in with housework as though you live here."

Ah. So that's it. "Yes, Mrs. Cantrell," I reply as evenly as I can. I go back to my room and flop down on the bed. Great. So much for my big plans. I grab my iPhone from the nightstand and swipe my finger angrily across the screen to unlock it. 7:40. I'm not just gonna lay here, I guess. I grab a hoodie and my copy of *Hitchhiker's Guide to the Galaxy* and head for the back door. A few chapters in the early morning air on the porch swing where my life changed ought to pass the time.

But when even Ford Prefect and Zaphod Beeblebrox don't keep my attention, I know it's time to pick another activity. One of the best books ever written and a perfectly good excuse to do nothing but sit and read, and I can't enjoy it. All I can think about is Alex. Alex in my room. Alex with his arms around me. Alex and our almost-but-not-nearly-close-enough kiss. Alex and the Traveling revelation. How am I ever going to explain this to Maia?

I glance up into the huge window that now has the wooden blinds and curtains open to the living room. I can't be certain, but I think that was Maia heading into my room. Perfect. She must be done with chores and ready to head out.

I jump up and dash across the dew-damp grass and into the back door. Mrs. Cantrell is nowhere to be seen, so I make a bee-line for my room. Maia is sitting in my desk chair, a pen poised over a fluorescent green sticky note but not writing anything. She's just staring at my laptop screen.

"Maia? Are you ready to go? I can be ready in... Maia?"

She's staring at me now, mouth slightly open like she's in shock. I rush over and sit on the bed, close enough that I can put my hand on her arm.

"You're emailing Claire," she says, her voice shaky.

I reach across her and close the lid of the computer, the little apple on top still glowing as if to mock my efforts. "I told you that I email her most every night."

"Emailed. Past tense, Ren. Emailed." Her eyes narrow as she looks at me, trying to decide how to proceed, I'm sure. "You know that—I mean, Aunt Charlie told me that you weren't dealing with this very well, but I didn't realize... You *do* know that Claire can't email you back, right?"

My heart is pounding, my breathing shallow. I can't do this right now. I can't. If this was anyone but Maia, I'd already be gone. "I told you. I'm not ready to talk about it."

"Okay, I get that. You don't have to talk. But I need you to hear me, okay?" She sets the pen down, puts her hand on my leg and leans in close so her eyes are level with mine. "I'm worried about you. It's been five months since the accident, and I won't pretend to know what it's been like for you, and I won't presume to tell you how you should be working through this, because I have no idea. But this..." She gestures to the computer without breaking eye-contact with me. "This can't be good for you. She's gone, Rennie. She's dead. I mean, I know you know that, but... I mean, you *do* know that, right?"

I can feel the tears welling up in my eyes, a few making their escape over my lashes, but I don't even try to wipe them away. Let them stay there, a salt-water monument to show Maia the pain she's causing me.

"I know it every second of every day," I say. "I knew it when they called in the middle of the night to tell us that our lives would never be the same. I knew it when they couldn't explain how her car got in that ditch, or why she didn't seem to have a mark on her body. I knew it when they assured us that she didn't suffer. And I've known it every holiday and birthday and snow day and weekend, and every time I look at the ring that's too big for my ring finger but I can't take off because it was hers. And I know it every time I hit *send* on an email to her, knowing there will be no reply. Yeah, I know it. But you can't make me say it. I won't say it out loud, because that won't fix it. It will only make it more real, and I'm not ready for that."

Her tears are stronger than mine, coursing down her face in beautiful liquid sympathy. She hugs me tight, holding me so close I can feel her necklace digging into my chest. But I don't mind.

Chapter Twenty-Two

*M*aia's intervention had some positive side effects. First, it made me

realize that even though I'm less ready to deal with the reality of Claire

being gone than I thought I was, I do feel a little better just knowing that

Maia's on my side no matter what. And second, she felt so terrible for

bringing it up that she convinced Aidan to let me borrow his car to get

me out of the house.

So she's home doing chores, which is so completely annoying, but

here I am driving a cute little silver Audi through downtown SLO,

volume up, windows down, feeling very Californian.

I already know where I want to go for some thinking time alone, and

with Maia's help on the directions, I make it without incident. It's early enough, I actually find a decent parking space too. Must be my lucky day.

I walk down the street and head into Mission Plaza. The Spanish Missions are all over California; I remember hearing about them in school. Getting to see one up close feels like a piece of history coming to life. I don't know what they all look like, but this one is big and white, with brown shingles on the roof and three bells set in three individual arched windows just below the roofline. Those same arches are echoed in the three separate doorways below them. There's a simple white cross at the apex of the roof, and the number *1772* in silver just above the windows. I take my Rebel out of my bag and snap pictures of each detail.

The plaza is laid out in front of the Mission; large slabs of concrete bordered in red Spanish tiles repeating over the spacious area. To the far left there are huge white columns supporting an open trellis roof for no particular reason, and some benches for weary pilgrims to rest. Or tourists. You know, whatever. And directly to my right is my destination: a large-ish square of natural rocks set at ground level, filled with water and a bubbling fountain in the middle. There's a bronze statue of an

Indian boy sitting in the far corner, next to him is a big bronze bear on all fours with one paw reaching into the fountain, and next to that are two smaller bears frolicking in the water. I remember seeing it when Levi took me around town, and now that I have time to myself, it's the first place I want to be.

I walk directly over to the big mama bear, running my hands along the smooth, cold metal. I slip my camera back into my bag and step onto the stone perimeter, easing myself up to sit on the bear's back. The sound of the water trickling below me is so soothing, I'm sure this is someplace I can think clearly. I swing my feet up to the bear's head. She doesn't seem to mind, so I settle in to work out the mess in my brain.

An hour later, I have a very sore, very stiff bum, but no more answers than I had when I arrived. Alex is wonderful and beautiful and he likes me, and we happen to have a very unique secret in common. Aye, but that's the rub. How do I tell Maia that I figured out my dreams are coming true, without telling her that the dream I saw come to life involved Alex disappearing into a book? How do I tell her that he's helped me figure out I can Travel to this other timeline, without telling her that he only knows this because it happens to him too? I can't possibly betray him, not to mention that I would also be breaking rule number whichever-it-was on my very first day of knowing the rules. But how can I figure this out if I don't have my best friend by my side? I need her analytical thinking and calculating mind. She's always been the better spy.

I sigh in frustration, kicking the bear's side with my sandal-clad foot. It does nothing to wound the bear, but it throws me off balance and I stumble to the ground, flailing my arms to avoid landing in the water.

I land in a crouch, expecting the palms of my hands to scrape along the cement, but instead they're met with the spongy softness of raw earth. Moss-covered rocks and damp mud, trees that are so tall they fade into the inky blackness of the night sky above me, and instead of the burbling fountain that was next to me moments ago, a pond. The panic I feel at the transition fades quickly, and unlike the others, this flash isn't accompanied by fear or desperation. I feel perfectly at ease, taking in deep lungfuls of damp air, the kind of clean that only occurs after a storm has passed through. I lean against the nearest tree, the scratchy bark biting through the thin silk of my dress. I don't even try to calm the butterflies in my stomach, but just smile and let them come. In a few moments, I know that Ethan will be here with me. My protector, my love. I hear a movement in the branches behind me, and turn to find him in the darkness, my heart rate rising in anticipation.

"Nice move," I hear from the street entrance. "You practice that, or are you just naturally talented?" Seth. My head spins unpleasantly, and I fight to stand upright as my vision returns to the present. So much for this being my lucky day.

"What do you want, Seth?" I can't keep the sneer out of my voice. I'm tired and stressed and these flashes are really messing with my head. I had almost convinced myself that they were done with me.

"Oh, hey now," he says, feigning injury. "Is that any way to speak to someone who is only here to help you?" He's closer now, his blond hair as ridiculously spiky as ever, and his face painted with a snide smile. His white tee-shirt is also way too tight over the muscles in his chest and arms; not that I'm noticing, of course but it's a little tacky.

"Help me?" I snort. "Yes, I'm sure that was number one on your list of things to do today."

He's level with me now, standing on the other side of the statue, his blue eyes staring into mine. "Our little rendezvous was fun last night. Of course, it would have been more fun if you'd let me into your room, but all in good time, right?"

"Right," I deadpan. "All in good time, just exactly what I was thinking. Why, it's all I can do not to throw myself at you right here." I lift one eyebrow at him, ignoring the knot forming in my stomach. I shouldn't have skipped breakfast, I need my strength to deal with this guy.

To my surprise, he laughs, his face softening from that sneer I'm so used to. "Funny," he laughs. "But you know what I find a little confusing?"

"The plot of most Spongebob episodes?"

He smiles, but ignores the jab. "When Alex talks about you—and he does; it's kind of sickening—he mentions how sweet and gentle you are."

"And that's confusing? Gee, thanks."

"It just makes me wonder which of us is getting to see the real you."

I open my mouth to reply, but snap it shut again when I realize I have nothing to say. Is he right?

"And I have to admit, I'm a little surprised that you're using your time to make jokes. Aren't you forgetting? I'm the only one who knows what happened in that cave."

I smile back at him, not afraid of a little confrontation. In fact, it may be precisely what I'm in the mood for. "Actually, I think *you're* the one who's forgetting. You weren't the only one in that cave."

His smirk falters for a moment, then slips entirely. "Alex is back?" He sounds completely surprised by that, even a bit nervous. I like it.

"Yes, he is. We had a nice long talk this morning, and he filled me in on *everything*. And also? He didn't make fun of my pajamas. So unless you have something to add...?"

"What did he... Did he tell you... I mean, wh-who else knows this?" Hearing him stumble over his words makes me smile. It's funny when it's not happening to me.

"You know that's not up to me." I cross one arm over my chest, holding onto my elbow in a semi-protective stance. Let him wonder how much I know.

"You didn't tell Maia?"

"No, I didn't. I also didn't tell her about your little midnight escapade to my window. For some reason, she likes you so I thought I'd give you a chance to make things right with her." I step around the bear, putting a finger in his chest and glaring up at him. "Maia is my best friend. I can't do anything about who she decides to like, but I will *not* sit by and

watch her get hurt. So stop toying with her. Either ask her out officially;
be a decent human being for once and make her your girlfriend. Or stop
messing with her head and just end it already. Those are your choices.
Pick one." I jab my finger into his chest again for emphasis, and walk
away.

The trouble with walking away dramatically, however, is that I don't
really know where I'm going. I'm not used to talking to anyone that way,
and it kinda makes my head swim. I'm not sure where that strength just
came from, but I think I like it. Maia deserves way better than him. I
hope he makes the right choice, whatever that is.

Maia and I meet up for lunch at a cute place called Big Sky Cafe. There
are booths all through the middle of the restaurant, and a bar on one
side. By the window are round bar tables, the kind with the high stools
where you have to step up to sit in them. There's jazzy music playing in
the background, and stars painted in a field of deep blue all over the

ceiling. It's so cute, I wish I was calm enough to enjoy it.

We sit down at our table in the window, and I don't tell her about last night.

We order delicious salads and beignets, and I don't tell her about last night.

We sip our iced tea and pay our bill, and I don't tell her about last night.

I suppose this means I'm not telling her about last night. She's so kind and understanding, and I realize early on that she still feels bad about this morning, and she's hoping that I'm finally ready to talk about Claire. Which I'm not. But because she's working under that assumption, she doesn't push me to talk about anything of consequence. She can tell I'm holding back, but it doesn't seem unnatural under the circumstances.

We head back out to the street and my phone chimes in with a text message. I pull it out of my pocket and smile.

"Alex?" she asks.

"Yeah," I respond, trying not to sound too mushy. "He wants to meet up tonight."

"Well it's about time!" She flings her arms in the air, her bag swinging dangerously. "He's been so absent since your date Saturday, I was beginning to think he was pulling another disappearing act!"

If she only knew. "No, he was just out of town is all. But he's back now." Not exactly a lie, and I can't tell her that I already saw him in the middle of the night in her own house.

"Good, I'm happy for you. When does he want to meet?"

"You mean you won't mind? I know we were supposed to meet the girls tonight. And I already bailed on you all last Thursday."

"Are you kidding?" Maia slides to a halt in the middle of the sidewalk, and clutches my arms. "First of all, the timing couldn't be better. You need a good distraction, even if it is Alex. And let's be honest, if it was Seth calling, I'd be bailing too, so don't worry about that. I caused a fuss last time, but I promise I'm okay with this. Because more importantly, we're talking about your first kiss!"

I look around, embarrassed. A couple passing by giggles over their shoulders at us. "Thanks for the announcement, Maia. But I've been kissed before."

"Oh right. How could I forget What's-his-name in first grade?"

"Lincoln Blackwell," I tell her, sounding defensive for some reason.

"That doesn't count," she says kindly. "I'm talking about the real deal, and you know it. Now you just tell me where and when, and we'll get you there."

We spend the next couple of hours looking through cute shops downtown. Of course, about half of that time is spent solely on Sephora. (A girl's gotta have her priorities, and now that I have someone to impress, I hope maybe I can be influenced by Maia's make-up genius.) The sun is just starting to go down when Alex calls. I take a second to grin at his photo before I answer.

"Hi Alex," I say.

"Hi Alex," Maia mimics in the background. I lean over and swat at her, and she giggles as she ducks out of reach. It doesn't stop her making kissy faces while I'm trying to talk to him though.

"Hey Rennie." Is it possible to *sound* cute? "Are you about ready? I can meet you wherever."

"Are you downtown already?"

"Yeah, I was working on a project, but it's done now."

"Oh great! Well we're at Sephora on... Osos Street, I think?"

"Okay, yeah, I know where that is. I'm not very far from there. See you in just a few minutes, then."

"I can't wait," I tell him. Maia rolls her eyes at me and picks up a new Urban Decay eye shadow palette.

"Me too." I can hear him smiling. "Bye Ren." It's the first time he's used the shortened version of my name, and it makes my heart flutter, like I just swallowed a butterfly. But in a good way.

"Bye Alex," I say, pressing *End* reluctantly. I give a great big sigh and lean onto one of the stools they use for make-overs. Maia is by my side in an instant, fanning herself with the make-up palette and batting her eyelashes.

"Oh he's just so dreamy!" she squeals and swoons into the chair next to me. I laugh out loud, not even caring that she's causing a scene. Let them look. I'm going to meet Alex.

True to his word, Alex arrives only a few minutes later. I'm waiting outside on the wide steps, and I stand when I see him approach. I wish I'd worn something else, something better. Maia always looks adorable, why can't some of that rub off on me?

"Hi Rennie." He greets me with a smile, reaching out to encase me in a warm hug. He looks amazing: Jeans and Chucks, a grey fitted tee-shirt, that wisp of ink peeking out of his sleeve. So simple, yet so perfect. "You look nice," he says in my ear. I melt. I want to say that I didn't know I would be meeting him tonight, that I would have worn something better than jeans and a tee shirt if I'd known. But I just smile.

"Thanks. You too," I say. He puts his arm over my shoulder, tucking me into that safe nook where I fit so well, and we head down the street. "Where are we going?" I ask, not that I really care.

"It's a surprise," he whispers, eyes twinkling.

"Ooo, I do love a surprise." I put my arm around his waist, twisting my thumb through a belt loop.

"I know it's been a stressful couple of days for you," he tells me. "Not knowing what was going on, where I was, what had happened to you, wondering if you were going insane."

"The thought did cross my mind several hundred times," I admit.

"I'm sorry you had to go through that. Normally when someone Travels for the first time, they have a guide. I don't know why that didn't happen for you, but now that you know more of what's going on, we can help each other figure this out. No more secrets."

"That sounds perfect."

After just a few blocks, we're away from the busy downtown area, and I suppose I haven't been paying enough attention because suddenly he stops and leans in close. "Do you like it?" he asks, his raspy voice just a breath in my ear.

"Like what?"

He laughs. "You mean I brought you here to impress you, and you don't even notice?" I take a look around us. It feels like we've left San Luis behind entirely. California, even. We've stepped into our own private Chinese garden. Stone lions guarding the entrance, little winding paths along the perimeter, and a five-pointed pagoda-style gazebo in the center. It's the gazebo that makes my breath catch in my throat. Why do I know it?

"It's lovely," I tell him, trying to get rid of the uneasy feeling that's creeping up inside me. It truly is beautiful, why can't I just enjoy it?

He takes my hand and leads me along one of the undulating paths, all the way around to the center and up inside the gazebo. It rises out of a small pool of water, so still in the night air that I can see the reflection of the moon painted in the water. My heart is racing. I know he brought me here for our first kiss. I love that he's put this much thought into it, and yet I can't shake the feeling that we shouldn't be here.

He leans against the railing and pulls me into him. I wrap my arms around his waist and rest my head on his chest. His heart is beating faster than normal too. I count the beats, trying to steady my nerves.

"I told you before that I was working on a project today, remember?"

"Mm-hmm," I say, nodding against his chest.

"I wanted tonight to be especially perfect. So I... well I made something for you." I lift my head and lean back in his arms so I can see his face. He looks so pleased with himself, I can't help but return his smile. He reaches one hand into his pocket and pulls out a small black box with a switch on it. "Ready?" I don't know what I'm getting ready for, but I trust him enough to nod. He holds out the box to me. "You do it. Just flip the switch."

I hold my breath in anticipation and do as he asks. A gasp escapes my lips and my eyes widen as I stare all around us. In every tree that surrounds the small park are fireflies—twinkling, blinking magically in the dark. He's grinning at me, watching my reaction with pride and affection.

"How... How did you—no one has ever—" I can't seem to catch my breath. "Thank you," I finally manage. And then I put my hands on either side of his face, and I kiss him.

I'm not dressed the way I'd like to be. There's no string quartet or fireworks, but it is absolutely, one-hundred-percent perfection.

 Chapter Twenty-Three

I lean back, letting his arms support me, and look Alex in the eyes. "I can't believe you did all of this just for me. How did you do it?"

"Magic," he replies, eyes shining.

I laugh, a giddy, girly sound that takes me by surprise. I like it. "Come on, really?"

He ducks his head close to mine and my heart flutters again. "Well, I'd like to think I know you well enough now to suppose you'd prefer that answer to some technical jargon about fishing line, LED lights and individual dimmers."

I grin and plant a kiss on the tip of his nose. "So, magic huh? Impressive."

"I'm glad you like it, but this is nothing. I would do anything for you,

Rennie." He brushes a stray hair from my face, tucking it behind my ear. I honestly believe he means that.

My heart is pounding, my head is swimming, my stomach is trying out a new gymnastics routine. I'm deliriously happy. "This is so much better than the way I dreamed it." I lean my head into his chest again, his arms surrounding me, warm and safe.

"Me too," he replies, running his hand over my hair and down my back. We stand this way for a moment in silence, enjoying the closeness of one another. "Rennie, I have to ask." His voice has taken on a different tone now. "When you say 'the way you dreamed it,' you mean that figuratively, right? I mean, this wasn't one of the dreams you were telling me about. Like the cave?"

It takes me a second to get into the mind frame that he's in now, out of la la land and into some semblance of reality. The dreams—right. "Actually, I think I did dream something about this. I have a sketchbook that I draw some of the images from my dreams in, just to try to keep track. I drew this gazebo the other day."

He leans back so he can look me in the face. "A sketchbook," he repeats. Not what I expected him to be shocked by. "You draw? I thought you were into photography."

I smile up at him. "Don't put me in a box, Alex," I tease. He still has a strange look on his face, waiting for me to respond. I shrug. "Yeah, sketching and photography go hand-in-hand for me. I love all kinds of art. I also took a year of tap lessons and can pick out some tunes on the guitar. Is that weird?"

"No, not at all." He shakes his head, so sincere over something so trivial, I can't help but smile. "Have your drawings ever done anything... unusual?" I tilt my head, waiting for him to hear what he just asked me. Finally, he closes his eyes and smiles. "That sounded a little odd, didn't it?"

"You could say that."

"Okay, how about something easier? Your sketch—are you positive that it was this gazebo? This park?"

I take another look around us, again marveling at the beauty of the fireflies he's created for me. "It has to be; I've never been in a garden like this before. And when we first got here, I had a strange feeling, kind of like at the cave." My head starts to ache a little as I try to remember why I felt that way. I look down at the reflections in the water below us, trying to dredge up more details. "And I'm sure you were there, but something was wrong. It was you, but then it wasn't. I don't know, it doesn't make any sense." I look up at him again. "I think maybe it was only a dream. I've never had that one before, so it's not one of the recurring nightmares. In the cave, when all the pieces came together, I knew it. There was no doubt that it was my dream. There are familiar elements here, but I'm not getting that same feeling." I search his eyes. He still looks worried, but he relaxes a bit at that.

"Okay, good." He runs a finger over my cheek, looking at me intently. "I don't know how you dreamed about something that hadn't happened yet, but I don't know why we're Traveling into an alternate timeline either. Maybe we can help each other figure it all out."

"Do you think other couples have discussions like this?"

He gives me that crooked smile that melts my heart. "I'm gonna go with no on that one. I'm afraid we're a couple of freaks."

"Good thing we found each other then, huh?" I say, holding him closer.

"A very good thing," he replies, and I lean my head back to his chest.

"Alex?"

"Yes?"

"Tell me a story."

He runs his hand over my hair again, leaning his cheek to the top of my head. "Always," he whispers, and begins. "Once upon a land, in a far away time..."

My head jerks up. "What did you say?" He looks so startled, I almost apologize. Instead I disentangle myself from him and take a step back to force myself to think clearly. "What did you say?" I repeat.

"I—I said, 'Once upon a land, in a faraway time.' It's how I always start my stories," he explains, reaching out to touch my arm. I pull it away. I get all woozy and stupid when he touches me. I have to think.

"I know," I tell him. "I know! *How* do I know that?" A rush of memory hits me, and I grab his arm urgently. "The legend moves like a living thing, and it will not be ignored," I quote from my dream. He goes pale. Not a little pale like he just saw a spider. I'm talking just-saw-the-ghost-of-your-dead-father-walking-on-the-battlements pale. "You do know what I'm talking about, don't you? You were going to mention it in the story you were about to tell me."

"How could you know—" he starts, but I don't let him finish.

I grab his hand and pull him toward the steps. "We have to get out of here. Now." He follows after me as I lead him down to the walkway, but then pulls his hand back and stops in his tracks.

341

"Rennie, what's going on? What are you talking about?"

"I was wrong. Before when I told you it was just a dream and didn't mean anything, I was wrong! It *was* a dream like the cave. You told me a story about... oh I don't know, it doesn't matter. But then, you were gone. You were just... gone. And I don't know exactly what went wrong, but I know that we need to *not be here*."

I pull again at his hand and he follows me back to the lions. I pull the small black box out of my pocket and reluctantly turn off my magical fireflies. I hate to see them go so soon but I can't risk leaving any clues behind if I'm right that there's soon to be trouble. I dash across the street, and duck behind a parked van, Alex right behind me.

"What are we doing?" He looks so confused, but I love that he trusts me enough to follow me even when I sound completely crazy.

I run my hand through his dark hair. It's incredibly soft and smells a little like cloves and I wish I had time to get lost in this moment, but my pounding head and heart bring me back to reality. I lean my forehead close to his, cupping the back of his head in my hand, our breath mingling in the small space between us. "In my dream, you told me a story. I'm sorry, I'm fuzzy on the details, but at the end you mentioned something about a legend. That's when you became someone else. Or someone else took your place, I guess? I don't know. It was a dream, and things get weird in dreams, so I didn't think too much about it at the time. But you completed the story before the danger came. So I thought that maybe if we got out of the garden before the time when you would have finished—I sound insane, don't I?"

"Well, no crazier than I sounded last night." He smiles at me, trying to be reassuring, but I can see he's struggling to keep up with my thought process on this one.

"Maybe I'm overreacting." I sigh, letting my hand slip down to my side and lean back on my heels. "I do that. I don't always have the best instincts when it comes to covert operations, just ask Maia."

"Shhh..." He ducks his head lower and touches my shoulder, urging me to do the same.

"What is it?" I whisper.

He points across the street to the garden entrance. Two men in brown leather jackets are standing between the stone lions, looking in to where we were just standing. Enforcers. And not just any Enforcers, of course, but Parker and Donovan. I can tell that they're arguing, but I can't hear the words exchanged. Parker holds up a finger in a sign for silence, and they both look around. Alex pushes me gently so I'm more hidden, and puts a finger up to his own lips. As if I would say anything right now. As if I could even form words.

"They're coming this way," he mouths, pointing toward the front end of the van. Staying in my crouch, I run to the front, Alex directly behind me. We duck around the corner as the two men hit the sidewalk, right where we were just hiding.

"He said she would be here," Donovan growls, his voice as deep and dangerous as I remember.

"Well she's not," Parker answers, clearly annoyed with life in general.

"So now what? This is the only good lead we've had in days. If she finds him before we get to her..."

"Don't remind me. Why are we even working this hard to bring them in? Do we really need another unstable toxin running around?"

"Careful now," Donovan warns, their voices growing more distant as they pass. "You don't want to talk about the Heir that way."

"Yeah, I know. But how is one seventeen-year-old girl this difficult to bring in?"

"Sixteen," corrects Donovan. "We still have a few weeks before she reaches seventeen. We can still get to her in time."

"Yeah, that's what we thought with the last one."

Their voices are past hearing now, gone down the street, but Alex and I don't move. I can barely even breathe.

After a few moments I dare to whisper, "They want *me* now. They were talking about me," I whisper back.

"We don't know that for sure." He shakes his head, moving over to peek around the side of the van. When he confirms that they're gone, we stand leaning against the front bumper. My knees feel like they could give out at any moment.

"Well I'm sure. Why else would I have dreamed this? It was some kind of a warning to get us out of there. Plus they said that the one they're looking for turns seventeen in a few weeks, which I do. Plus they said that someone told them they'd be able to find her here, and we're the only ones here. I think the evidence is kind of piling up, don't you?"

He swallows hard. "Yeah, you're right. I should have seen this coming, I guess. I should have been more careful."

"This isn't your fault, but we need to figure out what they were talking about. They want to bring me in to the Commander obviously. But what was that he said about a toxin?"

Alex nods, grey eyes serious and steely, darting around us as he speaks. "Travelers. Those who don't like what we can do refer to us as temporal toxins. We infect their timeline."

I shiver and run my hands over my arms. "Kinda rude. It's not like it's our fault. And wait a minute, Donovan said that someone told them where to find me. Someone I know just tried to hand me over to those guys. Who would do that? Who else even knew we would be here?"

He scrubs a hand over the back of his neck. "Well, I did sort of tell Levi."

"Levi?" I can't keep the shock out of my voice.

He ducks his head, unable to look at me. "I admit it's a little weird. But I knew he was good with lighting from the theatre productions we've worked on, and for the sake of our friendship, I wanted to make sure he was okay with, you know... us."

I put my hand on his arm. "That's so cute."

"But I'm sure he wouldn't be working with the Commander; he must have told someone else."

"The Commander. Maybe *that's* who told the Enforcers where I'd be. That would make sense, right?"

Alex nods and looks over his shoulder, paranoia still running high.

"He does seem to know more about you than I'd like. I just wish I knew why." He reaches out and touches my face, raising my chin so my eyes meet his. "Are you okay?"

"Yeah," I answer automatically. He raises an eyebrow, seeming to realize that my answer was on auto-pilot and waiting for a real one. I smile and touch his hand. "I'm okay. A little freaked out, and a lot confused, but basically I'm fine."

He folds me into a hug. "I don't know exactly why this is happening to you, but I do know one thing: if they want to find you, they're gonna have to go through me."

We wait another half hour before walking back downtown, and even then we take a different route. I don't feel afraid anymore, but the confusion remains fully intact.

"Alex?" He looks over at me with lifted eyebrows, waiting for me to proceed. "Tell me about the legend." He looks straight ahead again. A muscle shifts in his jaw but he stays silent. "You were the one who said no more secrets." It's a cheap shot, but it works.

"I suppose you should know about it anyway. Now that you're Traveling, you'll learn about it soon enough." He sighs, that muscle twitching again. He seems unsure how to continue, so we walk in silence for a bit and I try to wait patiently. I have no idea where we are now. We've passed some stores and office buildings, but nothing all that memorable. I try to pretend we're just out for a nice evening stroll, but it doesn't really work. Finally, he begins.

"Once upon a land, in a faraway time there was a great castle on a great hill," he says, his voice taking on a distant quality that tells me he's told this story before. "They called this place the Citadel, a solitary fortress on an oceanside cliff, its Spiral Spire looming over the waters like a sentry. And for generation after generation, the gift of time travel was bestowed solely on its residents. The True Heirs they were called, royals of their own making who ruled from this great castle and guarded their secrets and their bloodlines ruthlessly.

"But one day an outsider appeared. A Traveler. To this day, no one knows where or when he came from, or why he chose that particular land in that particular time, but choose he did. And, as the story goes, he managed to capture the heart of the youngest True Heir. Some say he was a future warrior, sent back to bring the royals to their knees. Some say he was an emissary, sent to ensure that the gift of time travel be granted to the common people. I say he was just a boy who fell in love with a girl and wanted to give her the normal life she craved.

"But we'll never know the true story, for while they managed to hide their love for a short time, her family soon found them out and demanded his execution. You see, not only had he seduced their youngest daughter, but his arrival in a timeline that wasn't his own produced a crack in time. A temporal toxin that could only be healed by removing him from time itself. And so it was that late into the night before his sentence was to be carried out, they both vanished, lost to the pages of some other history.

"Time flows differently from one side to the other, and I like to think that they're still alive somewhere, free of their past and allowed to write their own happy ending. But the crack in time has never been healed from that day to this, and it continues to grow. Someday it may even break entirely, the catastrophic effects of which we can only imagine. But there is hope. The legend tells of another who will be found, who will possess the ability to heal time. She is a daughter of the True Heirs, and she alone can restore what was lost."

I'm stunned to silence, both at the thought that this legend could somehow apply to me, and at the fairy tale that just sprung like magic words from his lips—a foreign language I didn't know he was fluent in.

"That was beautiful," I whisper, not wanting to break the spell with common words.

"Thank you, but..." He blows out a breath and looks around us. "I'm still working on how this applies to us. The Enforcers mentioned the legend earlier, and I know that there are people on the other side who spend their whole lives studying it, trying to find the last True Heir. I've never paid much attention; I find it's better to stay out of their politics as much as I can over there. But it looks like that isn't an option anymore."

"And the Enforcers, or at least the Commander, think that I could be this long lost Heir?"

"Sounds like it."

I bite my lip, trying to wrap my head around this. "So one of my ancestors was the one who broke time on the other side. And now, they think I can fix it?"

"I don't know. I have to admit, there are things about you that fit the profile I've heard, but it still seems a little far-fetched."

"What profile?" We turn the corner and there's the bright neon glow of a movie theatre just down the block. It's the art deco theatre I saw when I was stalking Alex at Farmer's Market. I know where we are now, and we're not far from where I parked the car, but I'm not ready to let this go, not by a long shot.

"It's always seemed like things that could apply to anyone, or no one, like it was all just an excuse to go to war. And I'm still not convinced that isn't the case." He looks at me like that was supposed to be reassuring, but I'm not sure how. "The popular theories change, but there is one description that gets cited so often, they've made a rhyme out of it."

"Like a nursery rhyme? Tell it to me."

He stops and turns me to face him. We're almost directly under the old-fashioned marquee, and although there are some people in the restaurant behind us, and a few people milling about the lobby inside the theatre, this spot right here is only for us. He traces a finger through my hair, pulling one curl out to its full length, then quotes,

"Hair of fire, eyes of ice,

with her family she's all alone;

She's been drawn in to a time forgotten,

but paper dreams will lead her home."

I watch his lips forming the pretty words and have to remind myself to focus on their meaning rather than their source. "Fire and ice, that could describe me physically, but certainly not *only* me. There are lots of proud gingers out there."

"Red hair, blue eyes. It's the rarest combination in the world," he says, running the back of his finger across my cheek. "Also the prettiest."

I smile at his shoes, and try to focus. "Thanks," I whisper. "But what does the rest of it mean?"

"I'm not sure," he says. "The *all alone* part seems to imply she's an orphan, or maybe she just doesn't fit in with the rest of her family."

I nod, taking this all in. "It could be either of those. And the part about being *drawn in to a time forgotten* sounds like maybe she's a Traveler. It definitely felt like being pulled in to another time."

"True. It's also said that a True Heir can create portals simply by drawing them, so the *drawn* part could be a double meaning. But the last line has always been my favorite; I just like the sound of it, even though I don't know what it means. Any guesses?"

I shake my head, even though something about this last line is digging at my memory. Someone out there thinks this rhyme applies to me, and it's my dreams that have led me to this other place. That can't be a coincidence. "It's all very cryptic, isn't it?"

"It is, which is why I've never given it much thought." He takes my hand and we start walking again.

"You told me before how the people on the other side are on the verge of a war, and this legend may just be a way to provoke that. What is the conflict about?"

"Several things; I don't think war is ever about only one thing. But one of the main issues is that time truly is broken on the other side. There's no predicting how long anything will last; things that we take for granted have been stripped away from them. A day is rarely twenty-four hours. The seasons don't obey the rules. One day could be six hours of spring and the next is thirty hours of winter. One day it's sunny and hot and it's followed by a week of perpetual twilight. Crops can't grow in nature anymore; only the greenhouses on the grounds of the Citadel grow anything worth eating now, which means that the Commander decides how it gets distributed. It makes people a little edgy at best, and at worst, it makes them angry enough to start a war."

We turn into the parking lot and we both lean against the door of the Audi, facing each other. "And the people think the Commander can fix time, but he's not doing it?"

"Oh, the Commander has said there's a plan, but the people don't trust him anymore. There's only so long you can follow someone who refuses to show themselves. That's why there's such a big push right now to find the True Heir. If there's any chance that the legend is true, then people are willing to try it. I've always thought it sounded like nonsense, but who knows? Maybe she is coming to heal time and save the people."

I give him a side-long glance. "So I take it you side with the Rebels then, not the Empire?"

"I always root for the underdog." He pulls me over to him and holds both of my hands in the space between us. "I hope this goes without saying, but I need you to tell me if anything unusual happens, even if you don't know what it means, or you aren't sure if it's significant. *Anything.* I just need you to trust me."

"I do," I tell him without hesitation. I bite my lip and look down at our linked hands. "Alex, I'm so glad that we can do this together. But..." The words stop on my tongue. I don't know how he's going to take this. "I need Maia's help too."

His eyebrows shoot up in surprise and he drops my hands. "No. No way. We can't pull someone else into this; we don't even know what we're dealing with yet."

"But that's my point. You don't know her like I do. She is great with puzzles and secrecy and spy stuff."

"Spy stuff?" he repeats, incredulous.

"Maia and I have a game that we play where we have to—well never mind. My point is that she would have a clear perspective and could really help us out. I know it."

"Rennie, this isn't a game!"

"I know! Don't you think I know that?" This is not how I wanted this conversation to go. I take a deep breath, trying to calm my nerves. Come on Rennie, keep it simple. I take his hand again, and run one finger down his arm, stopping to sweep my thumb over his tattoo. "Please?"

"I... You can't..." He lets out a frustrated sigh, then chuckles. "That's not fair. You can already change my mind with one word? I really am falling for you, aren't I?" He pulls me into him, looking down into my eyes, his face just a breath away from mine. "Are you absolutely certain you can trust her with this?"

"Absolutely," I swear, my head going all swoony again.

"Well, you trust her. I trust you. Looks like she's in." He doesn't sound convinced that it's a good idea, but he agrees and that's enough for me. "But Rennie, be very careful." He leans in closer and my breath catches in my throat. "Please?" He gives me one of those lopsided smiles, and then he kisses me.

As I drive back to Maia's, the danger of the garden situation is forgotten for the moment, my head entirely full of fireflies and lips and whispers and sighs. I can't stop smiling. Despite all the strangeness happening, it feels worth it. Because I have Alex.

When I get back to Maia's house, there's a note on my pillow. My heart stops for a moment. Another threat? A different impossible directive now that I've completed the first one? But it's just a note from Maia.

Gone to bed –
will need DETAILS in the morning.
♡ —m

I have to smile, despite the apprehension growing in the pit of my stomach. She's going to get way more details than she ever thought possible. I just hope she's ready for them.

Finally yawning, I pull on my PJs and get ready for bed. I don't even bother to brush my teeth. Instead, I fall asleep with a huge smile on my face and the taste of Alex still on my lips.

"You're seriously telling me that Alex McKinley is a good kisser?" Maia giggles, setting her styrofoam Jamba Juice cup on the bench between us.

"Hey, I don't have much in the way of comparison," I giggle with her, "but all I know is, he blew Lincoln Blackwell out of the water." We collapse into a fit of girly laughter that would have made me gag a week ago, but now feels completely natural. I *must* giggle, it is my female obligation.

"Well, I'm glad to hear it," she says, taking another sip of Caribbean Passion. "I'd hate to have your first real kiss be a dud."

"It was definitely not that. It was *amaaaaaazing.* Did I mention the fireflies?"

She shakes her head and groans. "Not in the last 30 seconds," she says with a smile that tells me I can mention them again if I need to. "I could have told you he was a lighting geek. He helps out on all the theatre shows, you know."

"Well I know that *now,*" I tell her, nudging her with my elbow.

"So other than the continual lip-lock, what do you guys talk about? Do you have stuff in common?"

"We do!" I practically leap up from the bench in my enthusiasm. I look around to make sure I'm not making a total spectacle of myself. We're seated on one of the benches in Mission Plaza, under the random lattice roof by the white pillars. I don't know why, but this plaza has become my favorite spot lately. It's such a peaceful place to think, or talk, or you know, tell your best friend that you've discovered that you and your new boyfriend can leap into books, that kind of thing. "We both love movies; he's even a Star Wars fan."

"Great, another nerd," she teases.

"And he loves to read," I continue, deliberately ignoring her comment. "He can even quote Shakespeare in everyday conversation without it sounding all stiff and boring. Oh, and both of us have fathers who were soldiers killed in action. His was a lot more recent than mine, so it's not something we really talk about, but still we have that in common. And, oh I don't know, lots of stuff."

"That's great, Ren," she says sincerely. "I'm happy for you. Now if I could just get Seth on board, maybe we could both have our summer romances."

I look down at my cup, tracing the design with my fingernail to avoid eye-contact. I definitely do not want to talk about Seth right now. I still haven't told her about him appearing at my window the other night, or again at the plaza the last time I was here. (How does he always seem to know where I am, anyway? Jeez!) It does make me wonder though, if Alex told Seth about Traveling, it would make sense to think he's a

Traveler too. He obviously knows about Alex's... ability? I don't know what to call that yet. Super power? That makes me smile—I like that, even if it's not exactly accurate.

"What are you smiling about now? More memories of last night?" She makes kissy faces at me 'til I laugh.

"No, not exactly. I was just wondering..." I guess now is as good a time as any. I look around again, making sure no one is within earshot and readjust the strap of my pale yellow sundress. There's still a part of me that's on the lookout for two men in leather jackets, but I don't see anyone even giving us a second glance. "Maia," I begin, picking up my bag from the ground. I pull out my sketchbook and hold it in my lap. "You know how you said I could talk to you—about anything?" She nods, eyeing the black book I'm holding. "I think I'm ready."

She takes both of our nearly-empty cups and goes over to the trash bin, tossing them inside before coming back to sit by me again. "No distractions," she says solemnly.

I nod, taking a deep breath. "When the accident happened, I started having dreams. Bad ones. I told you how I've been recording images in my sketchbook—when I remember something from one of the dreams, I draw it. At first I thought it was just to help me sort out the dreams in my head. Like maybe I could make sense of them or something. Like therapy."

"I remember," she says simply.

"But now..." I lick my lips. I don't know how to proceed. How do I tell her what's happening to me? To Alex? "Here, let me show you this." I open the book and turn to the drawing of the gazebo. I turn it around, and hold it out to her. She looks at it without understanding. "Do you know where this is?"

She shakes her head. "Should I?"

"It's the Chinese garden where Alex and I had our first kiss last night."

"Oh," she says, comprehension making her turquoise eyes bright. "So now, you've started drawing *good* things to replace the bad dreams. That's a great idea, Rennie. I think that's a really positive step." She puts a hand on my arm to show she understands, but I shake my head at her, loose hairs flying in my face. I brush them aside impatiently.

"No, that's not it, look at the date." I hold it closer to her so she can see the bottom corner of the page. "I drew this on Saturday morning. I dreamed of this exact place—before I was ever there."

"Well, you must have passed by at some point, and it stuck in your subconscious is all. It's not that uncommon to dream of things we don't realize we've seen."

I sigh and close the book, hugging it to my chest. I feel like I've exposed it to scrutiny for no good reason. "There's more," I continue, trying very hard not to be frustrated with her. It's not her fault she's not crazy. I flip through the book until I find a sketch of the cave. There's a shadowy figure in the background and a bench with an open book lying on it in the foreground. I show her the page and just start talking, not waiting for her to catch up this time.

"This one I drew back when I was still home in Lancaster. I've had this dream probably a dozen times. I'm in a cave and I hear an argument. I go toward the voices, and I find two guys. One of them is the dream boyfriend you teased me about, he's in almost every one I have. In my dreams, his name is Ethan. When they see me, they stop arguing, and Ethan turns to me. He seems really sad." Something about that scenario picks at the back of my brain. Am I remembering it right? "Then he goes over to the book on the bench, touches a drawing on the page, and disappears. Just... vanishes." I pause. She's looking at me with sympathy but nothing more. "This cave is the one you found me in with Seth. This dream—this *whole* dream—came true. Right here. Just a few days ago."

She looks back to the sketch, then to me, puzzlement all over her face. "You're saying that you met this guy, Ethan? And he disappeared into a book?"

"Yes," I breathe with relief. "Ethan is actually Alex, and the book is sort of a portal. He doesn't really go *in* to the book, it just takes him somewhere else." As if that makes it better. Focus, Rennie. Facts. Details. Don't let her panic or call the funny farm. I stand up and lean on the railing just a few feet away from us. She comes with me, looking at me with trepidation. "And there's more. The place that the book takes him to—I've been there before too."

She goes very still. "You have?"

I nod. "I've been there in my dreams, and in some visions I've had which happen to me when I'm awake but feel like dreams. And I also, well I think I accidentally went through one of those portal things too, when I was out with Levi. I know it all sounds insane, and I don't blame you if you can't believe me, but I swear to you I'm telling the truth. And it's okay if it takes you some time, but I'm really going to need your help to figure this all out. So please Maia, do you think you could please please believe me?"

Chapter Twenty-Four

$\mathcal{M}$aia sits down on the bench across from me and draws her legs up, hugging her knees. "Do you remember when you broke your leg that summer?"

That is so far from what I expected her to say that it takes me a moment to form an audible response. "Sure," I manage. "You stayed with me the whole time I was healing and that's when we started our obsession with *Alias* and *24* which eventually turned into the spy missions. Why?"

She smiles at the memory. "That did turn out to be an epic summer, but that's not what I meant. I mean, do you remember actually breaking your leg? Like, what physically happened?"

"I fell out of the big tree in your backyard and my leg snapped in two different places. I think that would be hard to forget." There's a prickling sensation at the back of my neck and I swat at it in irritation. Why is she asking these random things now? Didn't she hear what I just said to her?

"We *told* everyone that you fell out of the tree. We agreed it would be easier that way." She's watching me carefully for my response, but I don't have one. I have no idea what she's talking about.

"So I didn't fall? Then what, you pushed me?" I'm half joking, but I don't know what other logical conclusion to come to.

She rolls her eyes and tilts her head in that Maia way she has. "Seriously? That's what you're going with?"

"Well what else am I supposed to think? I know I didn't jump on purpose." I laugh it off, even though I'm not really finding this funny.

"Think Rennie," she urges. "This is important. Tell me what you remember."

I let out a deep sigh and try to comply. "All right, let's see. We were up in the big tree, like we always were back then. And you were… painting your nails?" It's a guess, but she nods encouragement. "Right. And I was drawing. Oh that's right, it was only a few days after my birthday and you'd given me that really cool sketchpad with a whole set of fine tip Sharpies. I loved that!"

"I recognized your talent even way back then," she grins at me and shrugs one shoulder. "It's a gift." We laugh, enjoying a moment of almost-normalcy before she gently asks, "What else?"

"Well…" I'm trying to remember, I really am. But it's as if there's a physical wall built up that won't allow me to pass through to this particular memory, and the more I try to think about it, the worse my headache gets. "Is this really necessary right now? Isn't there any part of you that's curious about what I just said about Alex and me?"

Her face is suddenly filled with sympathy. "I'm sorry, Rennie. I know this isn't your favorite topic. But just humor me, okay?" For anyone else, I would get up and walk away right now. My head is pounding, the tiny hairs on the back of my neck are all standing straight up, there's clearly some part of me that doesn't want to proceed. But this is Maia. I close my eyes to focus my thoughts.

"You have to remember on your own," she says. "But maybe I can at least get you started. We were talking about your parents."

That catches me off guard. While it's true that Maia and I can talk about practically anything, I can count on one hand the number of times my parents have been a topic. It's not that it's a particularly sore subject or anything, there's just not a whole lot to discuss.

'*So your mom's still gone, huh?*'

'*Yep. Still gone.*'

'*And your dad?*'

'*Yeah. Still dead.*

Just not a lot of material to work with there. So when Maia tells me that we were talking about them, it narrows it down. A lot. A little spark of memory makes the first chink in that wall in my mind.

"I remember that. We were playing MASH, which led to us planning our weddings, as usual. And you made some comment about how you knew you were going to cry when Aidan walked you down the aisle. And I said something about Aunt Charlie walking me down the aisle when I get married and you told me that she couldn't do that because it has to be your father."

"A comment I still regret to this day," Maia adds quietly.

I glance up at her with a smile. "Don't worry about it. We were kids, what did we know?" I laugh, but she doesn't.

"Thanks, but honestly I've always wondered… if I hadn't said that, if you hadn't started crying…"

That sparks a new memory. "That's right, I started talking about how unfair it was that I didn't have a dad, and how it wasn't his fault so I couldn't blame him but I was still so angry at him for leaving. And my mom *did* have a choice and she chose to leave Claire and me and go off on her own. Like we were some kind of baggage she could just drop off. I started sobbing, and I was so embarrassed to be crying like that in front of you but I couldn't stop myself. The grief was too powerful, I felt like I was drowning in it. And I remember thinking that I didn't want to be there anymore. I didn't want to be in that tree where you could watch me. I didn't want to be anywhere. I just wanted…" I stop. "Maia, what happened to me?"

She shakes her head, not looking away from my gaze, not even blinking. "I've wanted to ask you that for the last five years."

I stand, hugging my sketch book to my chest, and look down over the railing. The creek goes by slowly beneath us, slipping peacefully over moss-covered rocks and twigs. Its pace feels wrong. In the movie version of my life, it would be a raging torrent, rushing and falling over itself in tumbling rapids to match the pace of my racing thoughts. This tiny, slow creek is obviously miscast.

There are a few guys horsing around on the wide rocks that cross the expanse of water. Two of them are on the biggest rock in the middle, trying to push each other into the creek. Their laughter carries up to me, disrupting my miserable mood. As I watch, one of them slips, falling into the shallow water and is moved by the current down the rocks into a deeper pool, soaking him quite thoroughly. They all laugh, Drenched Boy included. The victor, on his very dry rock yells down to him, "What are you doing way over there, loser?"

Their laughter and any witty response he may have had fade away as a memory rushes back to me. Just a flash, a still-life photo of that day. I close my eyes, trying to capture the image, working my mind over the details to try to come up with what's bothering me about it. I was lying on the ground, looking up at Maia. She was so scared, but that's understandable. Even though her fear feels disproportionate to me simply falling, that can be accounted for by our young ages, right? So what's troubling me about this memory?

I try to look beyond Maia, but nothing seems out of the ordinary there either. Her backyard. The tree. The sky. Something tugs at the back of my mind. And then it hits me: the tree. It's not above her, as it should be from my angle lying on the ground. It's behind her—by several yards. Just like the boy who fell into the creek and was washed downstream.

"I Traveled," I say out loud before I realize that I'm speaking. Maia's head snaps up to me.

"Yes," she breathes. I try to sit on the bench but I don't quite make it, my legs folding beneath me so I'm on the cold concrete, my back leaning against the wooden seat behind me. Maia sits beside me, eyes wide.

"I was only eleven," I say quietly, "and I Traveled."

"When you told me what happened to you and Alex, it sounded exactly like what I saw in the tree that day. Can you tell me what happened?"

I nod, trying to find my voice. Alex told me that those who can Travel don't start until they're sixteen or seventeen. How did I Travel when I was only eleven? "I was in the tree with you," I start, trying to remember. "And then, just like that, I didn't want to be there any more so I wasn't. And then I was, I don't know, somewhere else. Is that what you remember too?"

371

Maia's nodding. "Yes, that's it exactly. There was a flash of light and you vanished, and I had no idea what had happened. But then, just a few seconds later, you were there again, but you weren't back in the tree. You just showed up in mid-air, and you crashed down so hard it's a wonder that only your leg was broken."

"And all this time, all these years, we never talked about this?"

"You hit your head pretty hard when you fell. I don't think you remembered what had happened by the time you woke up in the hospital. We agreed it would be best just to act like you'd fallen from the tree." She says it with a slight shrug, as though she feels a need to defend her actions from so long ago. Something about what she's just said picks at the back of my brain, but I ignore it.

"All this time, I've thought it was a dream. I thought that was my first nightmare—running, scared, alone. Then being pulled into a tight, enclosed space. It was dark and humid and there were muffled voices above me. And I think... oh my gosh, I think Ethan was there. Is that possible? I don't even know anymore. But I kept thinking that it had to be a dream, and that if I could just wake up I'd be in your backyard again."

The breeze picks up and blows some stray hairs across my face. I take a moment to make them behave and as I look around, I can't help but feel vulnerable out here in the open. I can hear the babbling of the creek below us, and voices and traffic noise coming from the street just outside the plaza. It's all very normal, but something feels off. The tiny hairs on the back of my neck start to lift again. Here we go, decision time: paranoia, or danger?

"So what happened next?" Maia asks impatiently, interrupting my thoughts.

I answer without looking at her, my eyes still sweeping the plaza, trying to find something out of place. "You know, now that I think about it, we probably shouldn't be talking about this out in the open. Maybe we should head back to your car."

Her eyes sharpen instantly, her gaze sweeping with mine. "You think someone might be listening?" I love that she doesn't even question me, she just falls into step with my thinking.

"I'm not sure," I admit. "But I do think that we should move to somewhere less exposed."

She's on her feet before I'm even done speaking, gathering up both of our bags in one fluid motion. I grab my sketch book and we head for the street. We haven't gone more than a few steps when she clutches my arm, halting me in my tracks.

"Wait," she whispers, peering over her shoulder.

"What is it?" I whisper back.

We're both silent for the space of several heartbeats, but I don't hear anything out of the ordinary.

"I thought I heard footsteps behind us," she says, doubt creeping into her voice. "Maybe I'm just being paranoid." We take a few more steps, both of us on the alert now. A car horn honks around the corner in front of us. A couple sits on the steps in front of the Mission across the way, holding hands and whispering to one another. Music plays softly from the patio of a nearby restaurant. And there are definitely footsteps matching our own from behind us. We both hear it at the same time and whirl around as a single unit.

Maia lets out a little shriek as we discover we were right.

"Hey ladies, what's going on?" It's Levi.

I exhale so much oxygen I feel like my lungs might just collapse right there on the spot.

"Levi!" Maia chastises, smacking his arm. "You scared us half to death!

What are you doing sneaking up on us like that?" There's an edge of panic to her voice, but also some excitement. The thought of someone *actually* following us is terrifying and thrilling all at once. But mostly terrifying.

"I'm just hanging out downtown, same as you. What's with the third degree?"

"We have our reasons for being a little on the paranoid side," Maia says defensively. She hands my bag back to me now that the danger has passed and I put my sketchbook away. "Suffice it to say there are some strange things going on."

"It's funny you should say that," he whispers, glancing over his shoulder and then leaning in. Maia and I lean in too. "I found something over here that seems a little... unusual. I didn't really think too much about it, but maybe it'll mean something to you."

She looks at me, eyebrows raised in silent question. The hairs on the back of my neck are still at full attention. Something isn't right, but maybe whatever Levi found will help us find the answer.

He leads the way over to the stone wall, and we follow him around a corner. It's still open to the plaza around one corner, and the street around another, but this little square is mostly secluded with only a bench set apart for privacy. He kneels down and pulls a folded-up piece of paper from a gap between two rocks in the wall. Wordlessly, he hands it to me.

She remembers. It's time.

My blood goes cold. I look up at him, and find that he's watching me. I see his face change. It's subtle—just a small shift in the way he's holding his smile, like suddenly it weighs too much to keep up anymore.

And now I can't shake the feeling that this is more than coincidence. Levi is here at the very moment we were talking about Traveling? He was the one who knew where Alex and I were going to be last night. He was with me when I first Traveled and the mysterious blue chalk writing showed up on the wall directing me to *Find Ethan*. He's the link to the Commander.

"Maia," I say, trying to keep my voice even.

"What? Let me..." She's trying to read the note, but I've folded it back up, still watching Levi.

"Maia, you need to run."

Her eyes meet mine in a flash, but it's too late. Levi gives me a sad look and grabs her from behind, holding one hand over her mouth and keeping the other on her shoulder. I've seen Jack Bauer in that position often enough to know what he could do to her if provoked.

"You shouldn't have done that, Rennie," he says. He has a wild look in his eye, like this is not how this was supposed to go and he's not fully prepared to play this role. "You know it's only you they're after. Why did you have to tip her off?"

I hold my hands up, my heart beating in my throat. "Levi, let her go. I'll go with you if you want me to, but you have to let her go. Okay?" I can see his shoulders relax and I know I'm on the right track. "You and I both know you don't want to hurt Maia."

That sadness passes over his face again edged in desperation. "No, I don't. It shouldn't have come to this. I even tried to give you a clue at the beach that day, but you didn't pick up on it. If you had, we wouldn't be here right now. So here we are. You have to know that I don't want to hurt either one of you."

"Unfortunately," says Donovan from behind me. "You won't get the same promise from me."

Chapter Twenty-Five

*W*hichever one of you screams, the other one dies first. Got it?"

Donovan illuminates the point with a hand on his hip, moving his leather jacket out of the way just enough to expose the shining metal of a gun.

I look at Maia. She's trembling and she looks like she's trying to decide between screaming, running, or crying. But she also looks uninjured and right now that's all that matters. We both nod to answer Donovan's question (not that he left much room for debate).

"Good," he continues, putting a hand on my shoulder. "See Parker? I told you we wouldn't have to break out the chloroform today."

"Too bad," Parker says, taking his place behind Maia. Levi's standing to the side now, licking his lips and shifting his weight from one foot to the other. Parker slaps his back. "Nice work, kid, but we've got it from here."

Levi hesitates. "You're not going to hurt them, right? You said we were just going to take them in to the Council—unharmed."

Donovan shrugs a meaty shoulder. "We'll see how the mood strikes us. If they behave themselves, we should get along fine. Commander's only interested in the redhead, anyway. That leaves us a little wiggle room with the brunette." Levi bristles, but Donovan continues over any objections. "Don't try to be a hero, kid," he says, his voice deadly quiet. "You don't want me to have to tell the Commander you don't know how to follow orders."

Levi gives one more look to Maia, his green eyes imploring her to understand, or forgive, or simply acknowledge him, but she refuses. I don't blame her. With a sigh that's almost pathetic enough to earn a bit of sympathy, he turns and slinks away.

"Isn't that sweet? The young protégé has a crush on the brunette," croons Parker.

"Touching. Let's hope that when we're done, there's enough of her to save for him. Come on ladies; step out of line in any way at all and I swear to you, you will regret it."

They lead us out of the secluded nook and out onto the sidewalk where a tan-colored SUV with deeply tinted windows is parked at the curb. Maia and I both look around, trying to find anyone to make eye contact with—anyone who's even looking remotely in our direction—but everyone is either engrossed in conversation or staring at their phones. Fantastic.

Fear starts to morph into panic, and it's quickly taking over all the space in my chest leaving precious little room for oxygen. This is really happening. Not a dream, not a vision, not a game. Maia and I are being abducted.

She climbs into the backseat first and I follow, growing dread filling each moment that takes us closer to being alone in an enclosed space with these thugs. Parker leans in and casually zip-ties my hands together while Donovan does the same to Maia on the other side.

"You don't have to do this," I whisper. Parker's eyes shift up to meet mine, his spidery fingers skittering over my wrists. His movements are precise, measured, but perfunctory; like he's done this so often he has the routine down to a science. It's chilling to think about. "You can still let her go. It's me you want."

He gives the end of the zip-tie another tug to make sure it's tight.

"Hair of fire, eyes of ice," he whispers.

My mouth drops open. The prophecy? Of course he would know it since that's why he's been sent to kidnap me in the first place. But why is he quoting it to me now?

"Don't forget her phone," Donovan says, holding up Maia's and shutting the door.

"I'm not an idiot," Parker growls, looking through my bag.

I haven't even let myself wonder where they might be taking us. I know eventually they plan to take me to the Commander, but Maia... I don't allow my brain to dwell too long on the word *expendable.*

"No weapons; they're clean," says Parker and he tosses my bag at my feet, slams the door and locks us in.

The windows are so dark, it's like we've just had a sudden eclipse. There's a tinted partition between the front seat and us and there are no controls of any kind on either of the doors in the back. No window control, no locks, not even a door handle. (Who would make a car like this? Seriously, is the model called The Kidnapper?) These facts do not help my rising panic, so I'm more than a little surprised to hear Maia whisper, "This is good."

I can't help but stare at her. "Good? Which part of this is good?"

Her eyes never leave the front seat, trying to determine how closely we're being watched now that we're tied up and locked in. "Can you reach your bag?"

I glance down, trying not to draw attention, and nod. I hook my foot through one of the straps and then shift like I'm trying to cross my legs. It's not exactly working, but then we go around a turn just a little too fast and the bag swings high enough that I can grab it with my bound hands.

Maia smiles at me, still watching forward, and then in a flash she changes her expression to one of defeat and remorse as Donovan gives us a cursory glance in the rear-view mirror.

As soon as he's not looking anymore, she says, "Rennie, show me that sketch again. The one of the gazebo in the park."

"What? Now?"

She nods urgently. "Hurry!"

I flip through pages as quietly as I can, trying to come up with it.

"Here it is," I whisper triumphantly, laying the open book on the seat between us. She looks at it, then at me. Out of the corner of my eye, I see the pencil lines of the drawing shimmer, a strange prism effect cascading from one corner of the page to the other. I blink, and it's gone. Odd, but I don't have time to wonder about it at the moment, because Maia is giving me that *trust me* smile.

"I'll be okay," she says, which makes zero sense to me. Shouldn't we be making a plan, discussing our escape? "Be safe." She reaches over and squeezes my hand, then presses it to the drawing.

I'm sitting on a dirt road, my head spinning. Bright sunlight blinds me and I blink several times to try to make my eyes adjust. There's a bench behind me, and a street lamp whose three candles flicker unnecessarily in the sweltering heat. What happened?

I scramble to my feet and look around, trying to clear my head. I'm in the middle of a crossroads, at what appears to be a bus stop. There's a sudden sinking in my stomach. I'm back? But how? The answer hits me like a slap in the face: the sketchbook. Maia used my sketch to create a portal for me, trusting that it would let me escape. Which means that she's still back there, alone in the car with the Enforcers! I search behind the bench, both sides of the path, the weeds all around the lamppost. The book has to be here somewhere. I *have* to get back to Maia!

I take a deep breath. Panicking will not help her right now. Better start with getting out of this zip-tie. I never thought the often-uttered phrase *I saw this thing on You-Tube* would save my life, but here it is. I picture the steps in my mind, suck in a breath, and raise my arms over my head. With a silent prayer that I make it out of this without any shattered bones, I squeeze my eyes shut and slam my elbows down to my sides while pulling my wrists in opposite directions. Pain shoots up my arms, but it works. My hands break free and I rub at my sore wrists, taking the time now to look around me.

It's just the way I remember it, wooded in one direction, a rise in the road in the other direction. The difference now, however, is that there is no fog. For the first time, I can see beyond the creepy trees that have always looked like a skeleton army in the haze. Off in the distance, against the brilliant blue sky, is the silhouette of a castle. It's too far away to see any real detail, but I can see that the tallest spire is jutting out at an odd angle, an exposed staircase wrapping around it like a snake. The Spiral Spire. This is the Citadel—the Commander's stronghold. Just the thought that I'm close enough to see it sends me scurrying in the opposite direction.

I head toward the rise in the road as I did last time, when I remember what Alex told me: Stay hidden and wait it out. Excellent advice in most cases, I'm sure, but there are two major problems with that. One, I need to get back to Maia *now*, and two, I wasn't summoned here. And according to Alex, if I wasn't summoned here, that means I won't automatically be sent *back* either and I could very well be stuck here forever. And that is not an option.

I shield my eyes, wishing I'd known to bring along sunglasses, or maybe a hat. Does being a Traveler mean I need to dress in layers now? Carry a book at all times, bring a sweater in case it's cold and foggy, some suntan lotion in case it's blazing hot, have some jogging shoes in case I need to run away—I might as well walk around with a packed suitcase.

Okay, focus. Thinking about sweaters and books and even Maia isn't going to help me right now. Think. What do I know about this place? It's run by the Commander, there's some kind of conflict brewing among the people, and there's a legend about a girl who will be able to heal time. Well okay then. Guess I'm all ready for anything except, you know, if anyone should actually talk to me or anything. I guess it didn't occur to either of us that there might be a scenario in which I *don't* want to hide.

There's a smaller path that breaks off to my left, and I stop to consider it. A smaller path could mean less chance of running into someone helpful, but it could also mean that it leads to a smaller location like a village or a house. I close my eyes and wish I had my sketchbook so I could make a pro-con list. Guess I'm gonna have to trust my gut and wing it. Small path it is.

It's darker here, the light dappled and sporadic as it filters through the trees. The path is lined with wildflowers on both sides, and their presence makes me feel better somehow. Like maybe this isn't such a terrible place after all. Bright orange poppies, and something tall and blue that kinda look like upside-down lilac on stems—pretty.

Well off the path to one side is a large pile of logs, and I suppose that means there must be a dwelling of some kind nearby. Something new mixes with the earth and pine scents as I get a little farther down the path and it makes me think of Alex, but I'm not sure why. It's clove, I realize—the same scent that lingers on his jacket and in his hair.

There's a noise of some kind coming from up ahead, something I can't quite identify. I stop and listen, my heartbeat speeding up again in anticipation. *Thwack. Creak-creak.* Silence. Then again. *Thwack. Creak-creak.* The rhythm of the noise tells me that it must be man-made, and the thought brings butterflies to my stomach. Hiding suddenly sounds like an excellent plan again. But I know the price of that this time. I have to get back, and soon.

I creep forward along the path, the steady cadence of the sound growing louder, until I come to the edge of a clearing. I step into the sea of wildflowers and finish the last few paces behind the safety of a tree. Peering carefully around the side, I discover the source of the sound. A man is on the outer edge of the clearing, wielding an ax to make firewood. *Thwack*, it comes down, splitting a log in two. Then *creak-creak* as he pulls the edge of the ax free from the tree stump and sets up another log. Sweat pours off of his face, his dark skin shining with the effort. He's wearing simple clothes, a button-down shirt that probably used to be white, brown cloth pants, boots. Over a nearby tree limb hangs a long brown coat.

I'm resigned to the fact that I need some help, or at least some answers. But approaching a stranger who may or may not be loyal to the Commander and who happens to have an ax? I'm pretty sure this is a whole chapter from the book of Nope. I turn to leave, but don't get two steps before I make myself stop. Maia is counting on me. Somehow she put together enough clues to send me here. She got me out of that car, putting herself in even greater danger to do so. Now it's my turn to do something brave.

I take a deep breath to steady my rising pulse and step back onto the path. With a confidence I am definitely not feeling, I walk towards the ax-wielding stranger.

Chapter Twenty-Six

$\mathcal{A}$x Man does a double take as I saunter over to him. He looks me

over from head to toe, dark eyes narrowing. "Well, would you look at

that?" He seems to be growing exponentially as I get closer to him. He's

much taller than he looked to be from behind that tree, maybe 6'-5"? 6'-

6"? I feel miniscule by the time I get close enough to attempt a

conversation. At least his smile seems genuine enough. "Where did you

come from, miss?"

"I... I hardly know, myself." Feeling very much like Alice at the

moment, I can't help the irony of answering like her. But I have to

remind myself that the Cheshire Cat always gets lumped in with the

villains for a reason, no matter how friendly the smile may be. "I was hoping you might be able to help me," I say. It takes a lot of effort to make my voice sound normal, but I hope I'm faking it enough not to tip my hand too badly.

Thwack. The ax hitting the stump startles me right out of my bravery. He takes a blue rag out of his back pocket and wipes the sweat from his face and clean-shaven head before dropping it on top of the ax handle. I'm glad he's unarmed now, but when he takes a step towards me, I take an answering step back. He lifts his hands in a harmless gesture.

"I have no desire to hurt you," he says. His voice is deep and warm, like honey. "But it seems to me, you took quite a risk approaching me like this. You must need something awfully bad. How is it I can help you?" That smile again.

I want to believe him, but I don't even know where I am, much less who to trust. Was this a huge mistake? "I need to find my way back home." Great. I'm Dorothy now too. I swear if I find out months from now that I just had to click my heels together, I'm gonna throttle someone.

"Well now. That is a problem," he says, looking genuinely distressed by that. "I don't know where your home is. But I do know how to find my home, and I know that my wife will have a delicious supper waiting there for me. We don't have much, but there's always enough for one more." He holds a hand out to indicate the other side of the clearing. A large pile of firewood is visible, and beside it, a well that looks ripe with wishes. I can think of a few I'd like to make just about now.

"That's very kind of you. Thank you." I'm not going to get anywhere if I don't trust someone. And the thought of being indoors instead of out here in this heat sounds very appealing.

"Name's Hollis," he says as he reaches over to collect his coat from the tree limb. "You got a name, too?"

I don't know what to tell him. Alex told me that all Travelers use alternate names, why didn't I think to come up with one before now? "Paige," I blurt out, then smile at my own pun, since I got here by way of a book.

"Nice to meet you, Paige," he says. "My wife's called Siobhan, and if the wind was coming from the other direction, you'd be able to smell a venison stew that could bring a grown man to tears. You like venison?"

"That's deer, right?"

He chuckles, a warm sound that makes me smile. "That's deer."

"I don't think I've ever had it," I say, feeling a bit foolish that I had to ask. Of course I know that it's deer, duh. We're headed toward the well now, and I have to take two steps to every one of his.

"Is your home part of a village?" I ask, just to say something to break the momentary silence.

"It's not," he replies with a side-long glance that tells me he's probably trying to weigh my ignorance. "Most everyone lives in one of the villages these days. But there are smaller groups about too—foresters and whatnot."

I nod and keep moving forward, trying not to think about this too much. I've been here before, Alex has been here before, we both survived. I can do this—just one step at a time 'til I can figure out a way to get home.

"Forgive me for asking, but what is a nice young lady like you doing out here in the woods all by yourself? And hardly dressed for an adventure."

I tug the strap of my sundress back up so it sits straight on my shoulder, and then shrug which only causes it to slip again. "I guess you could say I wasn't really planning an adventure today." If he only knew.

"But I was hoping I might meet a friend of mine, now that I'm here."

"Ah ha. A young man, I see. No need to be embarrassed. Me and my wife are going on ten summers together, and I'm still madly head-over-boots for her."

"His name is Ethan," I volunteer, a little giddy to get to call him that without being wrong, and surprised how readily the name comes to my tongue.

"Ah. I see there's a little romance brewing there. Am I right?" When I just blush and look away, he chuckles. "That's okay, no need to answer. Those roses in your cheeks tell the story just fine." He kicks a rock out of the way with his worn boot, and it goes skittering off the path into the poppies.

In just the space of a few minutes, clouds have moved in and the heat has been replaced by a cold wind. I cross my arms and try to hold off the chill, but I'm grateful when we come around the treeline and Hollis announces, "Here we are."

There's a cabin with a front porch, and a hewn-log front door. Smoke emanates from the chimney, and a soft glow shines through the bottle-glass windows. It looks like Snow White herself could be a resident.

"This is home," he says with a smile as he opens the front door for me. "I'm home, Shae," he calls. No need for much of a call though, there are only two rooms. She comes out of the back room, a reply dying on her lips when she sees me. "This here is Paige," he says over my head, leaning in to give her a kiss on the cheek.

She's about the same age as he is, I would guess somewhere in the late 30s, early 40s. She has pale white skin, mousy brown hair, and suspicious blue eyes that look me up and down. "Hollis?" she questions, not taking her eyes off of me. "Is she…" She lets the unfinished question hang in the air.

"Paige approached me in the clearing. She's looking for a little help finding her way home, and I thought she could use a safe place to stay and a good meal in her belly while we talk out her predicament. I told her your venison stew is not to be missed."

She's still staring at me.

"Thank you for inviting me into your home like this. It's lovely," I offer, looking around at the small space. It's simple and extremely rustic, but immaculate. Woven rugs in muted colors dot the floor, and each surface has been recently scrubbed clean, the scent of fresh lemon mixing with herbs and wood smoke. I have to wonder if a wooden cabin resents smelling of its own demise. "It's a pleasure to meet you," I put a hand out to shake but she doesn't move.

"Shae?" Hollis puts a hand on his wife's shoulder, shocking her out of wherever she went. "Siobhan? It's time for supper, our guest is hungry."

Hungry isn't even on the list of things that I'm feeling at the moment, but it does smell good. She nods, and finally moves into the living area. There's a wooden table with four chairs around it situated next to a cozy fireplace. A hand-carved mantle holds a small earthenware vase of rather wilted flowers and a single book that looks like it's seen much better days. Below, there's a metal grate over the coals that holds a dented iron pot, the origin of that delicious smell.

Hollis hangs his jacket up on a peg next to the door and sits in one of the chairs, gesturing that I should join him. "Now Paige, I suppose a few questions are in order, if that's all right with you."

I nod. "I'll do my best, but to be honest, it's been a very strange day for me."

"I'm sure it has. Weary traveler like yourself, must have some stories to tell. Suppose we start with how you happened upon me."

His use of the word *traveler* makes me watch him a little more carefully. Did he mean it the way that Alex uses it? I know how the Enforcers feel about Travelers, but I didn't think to ask Alex about other people's viewpoints.

While I'm still trying to formulate a suitable response, Siobhan sets steaming bowls in front of each of us, and sits down in the chair across from me. I put my nose into the steam and inhale deeply. I can pick out the gamey meaty scent of the venison, and some of the herbs— rosemary mostly, a little black pepper, and something unexpected. Cinnamon maybe? I pick up my spoon and take a mouthful to avoid answering for a few moments longer. I don't know these people. They definitely seem nice enough, but how much can I tell complete strangers in a place I know so little about? They seem unfazed by the silence, however, and merely wait for me to finish chewing.

"Just luck, I guess," I answer. "I knew I'd need to ask someone for help, and there you were. So I took a chance."

"Very brave of you," Hollis says, nodding knowingly. "And your friend —Ethan, was it? Ah yes, the one whose very name brings a blush to your face," he chuckles warmly as I do exactly as he claims. "Don't worry, I'm not one to pry. I only wanted to ask where he is? I would have thought he'd be here to escort you, show you around a bit. If I'm not mistaken, it seems like this is your first… adventure?" There it is. He knows. He raises an eyebrow at me, smiling like we're in on the same joke. Which in a way, I guess we are.

"Well, I didn't exactly know I was coming. The journey was a little unexpected," I explain, taking another big mouthful of stew.

"I see," he says with a nod to Siobhan.

"This is delicious, by the way. Thank you for taking me in like this," I tell her, hoping that she'll relax enough to enter the conversation. She doesn't; she just stares at her bowl, moving the stew around with her spoon. I clear my throat and turn back to Hollis. "I have a few questions of my own, if you don't mind."

They share a glance before he answers. "By all means."

"I need to find my way back home. I've left a friend in terrible danger, and I have to get back to help her. Have you ever heard of a way for… for someone like me to go back on purpose, at a time of their own choosing?" It's pretty obvious he knows I'm a Traveler now, but I can't bring myself to say the word to him, just in case.

Hollis' eyebrows lurch up his creased forehead. "You weren't called here?"

"Not exactly," I confess, tipping my bowl up to scrape the last bits out with my spoon. I was hungrier than I thought.

"Well now," Hollis says, a smile slipping slowly onto his face by degrees. "So it is you."

"We've been waiting," Siobhan speaks up, eyes shining in the firelight. "We knew that you would be coming soon. We've studied the legend of the lost Heir very thoroughly and all the signs pointed to it. Hollis here has been making trips to the crossroads every day for the past five months. And finally, here you are."

I look from her to him and back again. What have I gotten myself into? "And you think that I have something to do with this legend?"

"Oh, we know you do." She nods several times quickly. "We've studied the texts and read every proclamation that the Commander has written about finding you. We've prepared for this day for a very long time."

I try to remember everything Alex told me about the Commander, but my thoughts won't quite line up. I stifle a yawn. How, after everything that's happening around me, can I possibly be tired? And yet suddenly, I can barely keep my eyes open.

"Proclamations? Declaring what, exactly? Why do you think the signs are pointing to me when there must be dozens of Travelers coming and going?" I ask, trying to focus.

"Those are some good questions," Hollis says, rising to his feet. "But why don't we save them for tomorrow? Don't you worry about a thing now." He moves behind me and helps me stand.

"What's wrong with me?" I slur. My gaze drifts to the table where our empty bowls are still sitting. No. Only mine is empty. "The stew—you poisoned me?" I can't believe I fell for that. Sydney Bristow would never have fallen for such an obvious trick. My eyes feel so heavy. Maybe if I just close them for a few minutes, I'll be able to think clearer.

Hollis laughs as he leads me to a cot in the corner, already made up and waiting for me. "Not poison. Why would we go to all this trouble only to kill you? No, you'll just sleep well tonight is all. Can't risk having you run off while we're still waiting for your sister to arrive."

Wait, did he just say something about Claire? That doesn't make any sense. "My sister?" My tongue feels too big for my mouth.

"Oh yes," Siobhan says, fluffing the pillow before Hollis helps me down to the bed. "The legend is quite clear on that point. It has to be both of you."

I start laughing, a tired, drugged, slightly manic laugh that I can't quite control. After all this time of running from the truth, here it is. This is how I'm forced to deal with it. My body folds in half, contorted with the laughter that claws at my heart.

"What is it?" There's a note of anxiety in Siobhan's high-pitched voice. "Do you think we gave her too much?"

"It's not the drug," I say between fits of laughter, tears now careening down my face. "You've gone through all of this—waiting, preparing, drugging me—and for what?" My eyelids are closing against my will now. I ease myself back onto the cot, knowing that sleep is about to overtake me, ready or not. "For nothing," I spit the word at them. "You're waiting on my sister? Well here's a wrench in your plans: She's dead. Killed in a car accident months ago. So take that to your Commander." My words are so slurred I'm not even sure they heard me, but I don't care. I lay my head back on the pillow and let the darkness consume me.

Chapter Twenty-Seven

I awaken near dawn, daylight coming through the window above my head. It's so grey and shallow, I suppose it can hardly be called *day* or *light*. There's a pounding in my skull, like a tiny little man is trying his best to push my eyeballs out from the inside, and my mouth is so dry I can hardly swallow. (When did my teeth become fuzzy?) I crack open one eye at a time, afraid that movement will only make it worse.

My eyes finally focus after a few scratchy blinks, and my breath catches in my throat. Not my bedroom in Pennsylvania. Not Maia's house in California. I'm on a cot in a log cabin, a hand-crocheted blanket thrown over me. Hollis and Siobhan. They drugged me. They drugged me so they could wait for…

Claire. I put a hand to my mouth, choking back a sob. I've said it out loud now. The first time since the accident and I screamed it at strangers. She's dead. Gone too quickly, too soon. No goodbye and no coming back. I spin the silver ring around my finger, gently running my fingers over the smooth metal, the raised gem. The only piece I have left of her. I want to curl up as tightly as I can, pull the blanket up over my head and cry myself back to sleep. But I can't.

I shove the emotion down to its hiding place again, take a deep breath, and stretch my arms and legs. My joints are all stiff from my drug-induced sleep, and it takes me a moment to comprehend what I've just done. I stretched. I'm not tied up, or handcuffed, or in any way restrained. Hollis must have over-estimated the effect of the drug.

I look around cautiously before moving again. No one in sight and the only sound I hear from the other room is a light snoring. A very good sign. My heart is beating way up in my throat as I sit up as quietly as possible. The cot creaks a little under my shifting weight, but there's no break in the steady rhythm of snores. I grab my sandals from next to the cot, and ease myself up.

I cross the room in light, quick strides, stepping from rug to rug to avoid any floorboards that might tattle on me. I pause for a moment at the door, and before I have a chance to second-guess myself, I'm through it and breathing in the damp morning air. I shut the door as quietly as I can behind me, not daring to feel relief yet. I slide on my sandals and take a brief look around to weigh my options. Back to the crossroads? Straight out into the woods? I'm anticipating the moment when I'll hear one of them wake up. Hear my name shouted, or feel hands grabbing at me. But it doesn't come.

I run.

And once again, here I am with the wrong shoes on. Obviously it's too late to do anything about it now, so I just keep running, useless brown sandals and all. The fog is so dense, I can only see about a yard around me in any direction. I'm crashing through tree branches, leaping over rocks and fallen oaks, but more than anything else I'm just trying to stay upright.

I know the lead I have on Hollis and Siobhan is minimal at best. Even though they were sleeping when I snuck out, I can't rely on that, which is why stealth is definitely not my priority. Not yet. Speed—getting as much space between their deceptively cute cabin and me as possible—is the only thing that counts. I shake my head in an attempt to clear out the remaining fuzz from the drug they gave me. The action causes me to stumble over something, but I don't take time to look back. That stumble cleared my mind way more than the shaking did. I cannot fall. I cannot get caught.

The beads of fog on my skin have turned to beads of sweat by the time I pause to catch my breath. I was not cut out for this. Maia and I may wear the same size clothes, but she is in way better shape than I am. Not that I would ever wish for her to be the one running away from mad people who tried to drug her and take her to their leader. All I'm saying is she would be handling it better than I am.

I lean against one of the big oak trunks and put my hands on my knees, attempting to breathe normally. The stitch in my side and the wheeze in each ragged breath mock my efforts. Stupid TiVo. That's right, TiVo, Netflix, Hulu… you're all to blame for my lack of interest in jogging with Maia all those times she asked me to join her. Oh and I can't let my books off too easily either. Jane Austen, J.K. Rowling, Veronica Roth I'm looking at you. If I get caught…

Wait, what was that? I try to hold my breath so I can listen closer. My heart is already in my throat, but my adrenaline pushes it up another notch. Was that a twig snapping? Footsteps? My lead can't be gone already!

I'm not taking any chances.

Without wasting another moment in my habitual indecision, I begin scaling the tree behind me. It's not perfect, but it will have to do. I dig my fingertips into the bark, not even caring that I'm ruining a perfectly good manicure that's only a few days old. My sandals don't exactly help the process, but at least I'm not wearing my wedges. Yay me. Within just a few scrambling seconds, I'm perched halfway up on a very sturdy branch, looking down through a veritable afro of green leaves. Suddenly, I'm quite grateful for all those summer days Maia and I spent climbing trees in her backyard.

There's a small window through the green where I can see the dirt path below me, and I watch it for any signs of life. Path. Rennie, you idiot! Why was I sticking to a *path*? If I get out of this, I'm heading into the woods away from any sort of easy route.

I'm up here long enough that I regain my breath, and start to feel like maybe I let paranoia win out over actual facts. Again. I wonder how long

I've been up here? For that matter, I don't know how long I was running before that, or how far away I might be from Hollis's cabin. I could be using this time to gain some more distance.

I shift to begin climbing back down, when I hear them.

"She must have come this way. You saw all of those broken branches, just like I did. What else do you think caused that?" That's Hollis, his voice deep and musical, like velvet. Why did he have to turn out to be a bad guy? I so wanted to trust in that voice. He sounds angrier than before though, adding an edge that doesn't seem as trustworthy as before. This Hollis I might have been more wary of.

"I know what we saw," says Siobhan, going all squeaky in her irritation. Like a rat, an annoyed and whiny rat. "But if she's really the one the legend describes, don't you think she'd be smart enough not to follow a path to run away?"

See? Even she knows I'm an idiot for that move.

"She *is* the one we've been waiting for. She's the Heir," Hollis growls, no room for argument in his tone.

How can he be so sure about something that makes no sense? Reading about prophecies and oracles and all of that might be really fun, but having it suddenly pointed at me is a whole different story. So far all it has gotten me is betrayed by Levi, captured by Enforcers, dropped into another world that seems entirely made of fog and trees and bad people, and drugged to sleep by strangers. Yeah, good times.

"Fine, fine, she's the one. And now she's running around loose, and she has no idea where she is or who she can trust. Good lord, Hollis, she thinks we were going to turn her in to the Commander!"

"Woman!" he barks, then continues quieter, more in control. "I'll thank you to keep your peace. She may have gotten away, she may still be half-drugged, and she may have a poor view of us. But she's not deaf. So save your plentiful objections for later and help me look."

They've moved past me now, out of earshot, but there's no way I'm moving for a good long time. I close my eyes and try to focus on what just happened, gripping the rough bark on either side of me to steady my balance and my nerves. So they weren't going to take me to the Commander after all? Then what was that all about?

I wait until I can no longer hear any movement, then I count to a hundred. When my feet touch down on the winding path, I don't even hesitate. I head off the path and into the woods, oak and pine trees crowding together to block out the sunlight. It's darker here, but it suits my mood. I don't know how, but I am going home.

Chapter Twenty-Eight

There's only so long a person can wander in the woods alone before they start to lose it. Turns out my cap is about ten minutes. For someone who practically grew up in the 100 Acre Woods, Middle Earth, *and* Narnia, this is a little disappointing. Don't get me wrong, it's a stunning landscape. More shades of green than I knew existed intermingling on all sides of me, tree limbs bowing gracefully under their burden of leaves, even the earth is covered in a soft spongy moss. I wanted off the path and I officially got it. I have no idea where I am.

I stop and lean against a big oak, tendrils of mist trailing after my movements as I yank off my sandal. As expected, a small pebble falls out. I rub at the sore spot it created on my little toe, and wonder again how

I'm supposed to get out of here. Back to the crossroads, maybe? I guess it makes sense to think that if that's where I came in, then there should also be a way to get back.

I stick my sandal in my armpit and pull my iPhone out of my pocket. Naturally, I know I won't have a signal here, wherever or *when*ever I am, but I can at least start a Note to keep track of any clues and questions while I'm here. Alex said that not remembering clearly is normal for Travelers, and just in case that's true for me, I want to have a foolproof way of keeping that information intact. As I'm typing in key words to remind me of Hollis and Siobhan, I hear a snap. I hold my breath, waiting to hear if the sound will come again. I don't have to wait long. Within moments, there's a *rustle rustle snap.*

Someone is out here. Hollis? Or maybe just a rabbit. (Please be a rabbit.) I slip my sandal back onto my sore foot, my phone back into my pocket, and creep toward the noise. If I'm not mistaken, it came from just past this next line of trees. Gingerly, I reach out and move a branch from my view, peering around a tree trunk that is big enough to conceal about six of me. Please be a rabbit, please be a rabbit, please oh please oh please...

There's a small clearing just ahead, and in the clearing is definitely not a rabbit. It's a young girl, maybe nine or ten years old I'd guess, and she's sitting on a rock facing away from me. She has her dark hair pulled up into a messy knot, and she wears a short floral-print dress and untied hiking boots. Leather straps make an X between her shoulder blades, some kind of harness or—it's a holster. Strapped to the back of her left shoulder is a dagger.

Well that can't be good. What kind of place gives weapons to ten-year-olds? I'm sure I could simply walk away and she would never know that I had been here, but the possibility of finding some answers is too tempting. What would Maia do? I know the answer to that before the question has even fully formed. I've been training for this moment since I was eleven. I don't have my star-shaped stickers, and the stakes are much higher than bragging rights, but I know I can do this.

Everything else around me fades away as I narrow my vision on my target. She's just a kid, but I can't go into this letting her have the upper hand. I've got to get that knife. I slip my sandals off again and leave them behind the tree. The soil is soft enough to cover the sound of my feet, and I'm not risking my shoes getting in the way this time.

The girl is still facing away from me, leaning over her lap and concentrating on something I can't see. I take a tentative step forward, knowing that I'm fully visible now and feeling like the yellow of my dress is shining like the noonday sun. If she were to turn her head, even a little bit... She doesn't. Another step. Another. I'm almost there when I realize I've seen this exact scene before; at Farmer's Market when Maia sent me on my spy mission. When I attempted to tag Red Polo Man, this is what I saw. My hand starts trembling, and I lick my lips. Keep it together. This isn't the first time I've seen something before it happens, and it looks like it won't be the last.

I reach out for the handle, scared the sound of my own nervous breathing will give me away. I hold my breath and take the last step, grabbing the handle of the blade and brandishing it in triumph. She gasps, standing and whirling around to face me in one movement.

That actually worked? Oh my gosh, that actually worked! Maia would be so proud. Even Sydney Bristow would be proud. That was pure awesome.

I'm so busy congratulating myself that it takes me a few moments to notice I'm threatening a child with a dagger. Her brown eyes are as wide as moons, the white showing all the way around the iris. She puts her hands out, pleading with me, terrified.

"Please," she whispers. "Please... I promise I won't do it again. Please don't hurt me."

Okay, definitely not how I was expecting this to go. "I don't want to hurt you," I promise, but I keep the knife pointed in her general direction nevertheless. It's heavier than I expected it to be, the wooden handle dark, the hand-carving worn smooth with age. "What do you mean, you won't do it again? Won't do what?"

Her eyes dart down to the rock where she was seated and my gaze follows. On a pillow of grass and dandelions, propped up as if on display, lies a scrap of paper no larger than the palm of my hand and a wooden twig with the end burned.

"What were you trying to do?" These aren't the questions I need to be asking, but my curiosity wins out.

Her eyebrows shoot up. "I was going to... to draw. For fun," she admits, close to tears.

I shake my head. "And that's bad?"

She looks again to the forest floor where her possessions are laying, as though questioning whether or not I can see what she sees. "On paper," she whispers, lowering her head in obvious shame.

I don't say anything, waiting for her to finish, but apparently that's all there is to this dramatic confession. I don't know how to answer her, but I have a hard time believing that this wisp of a girl who just wants to draw poses a threat to me. I lower the dagger to my side, and she ventures a look at me.

"You're not going to arrest me?" she asks, voice quivering.

"Arrest you? For drawing? Uh, no. No, I think I can let you go with just a warning." It's a lame joke, but instead of smiling, her shoulders visibly relax. What kind of place doesn't allow people to sketch? "What's your name?"

"Olive," she says, stronger now that she doesn't have the point of a blade aimed at her. Her eyes are roving over me, my appearance causing her brow to wrinkle. "I haven't seen you before. Who are you?"

"Paige," I say quickly. "My name is Paige." I need her to hear my false name again, as though that will make it sound more natural coming off my tongue. I have no idea how she would react to my real name. It would probably mean nothing at all, or she could start bowing or attempt to overpower me and take me to the Commander—draw a gun, or a pointy stick, or an ill-tempered badger. Of course, I am still holding her knife. I may have an advantage over a badger.

"Well, Olive," I say, looking around the clearing for a sign that anyone else may be near. "You want to tell me why you're out here all alone?"

She shrugs and shuffles one boot-clad foot over the grass. "I'm old enough to take care of myself. Besides, my village is just over the next rise, it's not like I wandered off to the Citadel or anything. I'm not dumb." She sticks out her little rosebud lips in a pout that's far more adorable than annoying. "I thought you were an Enforcer when you first found me. But you're not, are you? You're a Traveler." She emphasizes it in a way that leaves no doubt that the word is capitalized. Her candor startles me, making my mind go blank. How do I answer that? "It's okay," she offers. "My mom is a loyalist, but my sisters and I like the Travelers we've met. I hope I have the gift when I'm old enough so I can be the one to find the True Heir."

My heart skips a beat. "You know that story?" I ask.

"Everybody knows that story. My sisters and I play like we're Travelers, and we're gonna be the ones to find her. I'm the youngest, so I usually get to be the Heir."

"And what does that entail, exactly?"

She shrugs one shoulder all the way up so it squishes into her cheek. "Hiding mostly, and drawing. But never on paper; I promise I've never done that before. But I found a piece inside the stone dog, and I couldn't resist." She hangs her head again, biting on her lip and folding her hands behind her back. "I can put it back if you want me to. I barely made any marks on it."

So the drawing isn't forbidden, but the paper is? Forbidden paper. Loyalist. Stone dog? There's too much here, and I have no way of knowing if I'll retain any of this when I get back home. I pull my phone out of my pocket again and open the Notes app, balancing the dagger precariously while I try to thumb-type at the same time.

Olive's eyes go wide, and she takes a hesitant step towards me. "What is that?" she whispers.

Oops. Should have thought this through. "Don't worry about it, it's nothing." I wave a hand dismissively, the fact that I've just broken the Prime Directive not at all lost on me.

She takes another step, craning her neck out as far as she can so she doesn't have to step too close to me. "That's tech," she marvels. "You have tech—and it *works?*" She reaches a hand out towards my phone, wonderstruck. I pull it away instinctively and shove it back in my pocket.

"How do you know what that is? By the looks of things around here, it hasn't even been invented yet."

She looks at me like I'm crazy. "You don't have to lie to me," she pouts. "I know what tech is; I told you I'm not dumb. The grown-ups talk and I listen. I know things."

There's a rustling beyond the clearing that draws our attention, my heartbeat suddenly racing again.

"Olive! You can come out now!"

"Yeah, come out! We give up!"

I look to Olive and she looks to me, and I have no idea which of us is more scared. The voices are far enough away that I know I have a minute to make a decision, but close enough that I know it better be quick.

"Your sisters?" I whisper. She nods. "Look Olive, I have to get back home. I can't afford any more entanglements right now. I need for you to stay quiet about meeting me, okay?" She nods again, looking over her shoulder toward the increasing sound of the voices calling her name. I start to hand the dagger back to her but I'm struck with a thought. "Do you mind if I keep this? I'm pretty sure I'll be able to return it to you, and I have a friend who really needs some help right now."

"Okay," she says. "But be sure to bring it back, okay? It's my favorite."

A sweet little girl with huge brown eyes and a favorite weapon. I

417

decide right there that if there's anything I can do to help end this conflict, I'm going to do it.

"I promise." I use the sash around my waist, wrapping it around the hilt several times to secure the dagger at my hip. "Be safe, Olive. And keep drawing." I ruffle her hair the way Aidan does to me, and it makes both of us smile. Then I'm darting back to the tree where I left my sandals.

"Be safe, Paige," I hear her whisper as I duck out of sight.

I waste no time, but grab my sandals and head as quietly as I can back the way I came, trying to re-trace my steps to the path. As soon as I'm sure that I'm out of earshot of Olive and the villagers (which would make a great name for a girl band, by the way, if I had any musical talent whatsoever), I break into a jog, moving as fast as I dare over roots and rocks. I only bother to dodge the big limbs now, letting the small twigs swipe their stinging fingers across my face. Olive may only be a kid, and she may have left me with more questions than answers, but she just gave me a great idea for how to get home.

I curve off the path when I know I'm getting close, and follow the treeline around so that I can approach the cabin from the side rather than head directly to the front door. I duck behind the well and then the woodpile as I sneak my way closer. I can't tell yet if Hollis and Siobhan have returned, or if they're still out looking for me. There's only one little window on this side of the cabin, much too high for me to see into from the ground. I close my eyes and strain every muscle, trying to hear any noise or movement from inside. I hear nothing.

So option one: I dash inside, hoping they're still out, grab what I need and be gone in a matter of minutes. (Unless they are there, in which case my chance of getting out unscathed drops to absolute zero.) Or option two: I stand here and try to listen a while longer, just to make sure they're still gone. (Unless they are out, in which case I'm wasting precious, vital moments standing here with my ear pressed to a log.) Gah! My kingdom for a Magic 8 Ball!

Screw it. I'm going in.

I quietly creep up the same porch steps I quietly crept down less than an hour ago. Is that irony or just poor planning? Probably neither. I place my hand on the door handle, and take a deep breath before pushing it open with all the force I can muster. If they are here, I might as well have the element of surprise on my side. I step inside and crouch into what I hope is a suitable fighting stance all in one motion. It's dark and quiet. The blanket I used last night is still lying where I left it, draped halfway between cot and floor like a theatre curtain. The coals in the fireplace are dead, their glowing red eyes extinguished with the passage of the morning. And there above them, just as I remember it, is my best hope for getting home: a book.

I race across the floorboards, grab the book from the mantle and look around for my next necessity. There must be a pencil somewhere. A pen, a Sharpie, a piece of charcoal, anything! Wait... coal...

Kneeling, I examine the cold fireplace until I find a piece that suits my needs. I open the book to the very back and make a mark to test it. It makes a clear black streak across the page. It might be the most beautiful thing I've ever seen.

I fling the book onto the table and lean over it, drawing a rudimentary flower as quickly as my shaking fingers will allow. Five petals, stem, leaf —done. I take a breath, close my eyes and touch the drawing.

Nothing happens.

What did I do wrong? Think, Rennie! I grab a stray lock of hair and twist it around my fingers as I pace next to the table. What am I missing? I have a book, I have a sketch, it worked before, so what did I do wrong? Maybe Maia was the key in getting me here. Maybe it wasn't my drawing, but her influence that opened that portal from my sketchbook. She seemed to know precisely which sketch to ask me for.

Wait, maybe that's it. My sketchbook—those drawings mean something to me. They come from my own dreams, they filter my emotional clutter and redirect my fears. I need to create a sketch that *means* something. Something I have an emotional connection with. Or someone.

I clench my jaw, determination making my thoughts clearer. I lean over the table again and flip to another page of the book. The edge of my coal is becoming dull, but I don't care. It only makes my lines bolder as I sketch the one face I want to see more than anything else in the world right now. I know that if the process is going to work at all, then this will do it, because this one is coming straight from my heart without filtering through my head first. I know that, because to my surprise, it isn't Alex. And it isn't Maia. It's Claire.

Chapter Twenty-Nine

*T*ears flow down my cheeks, creating unexpected pools of shadow on Claire's otherwise lovely face. I draw her as I remember her best, unadorned and un-made-up, long hair hanging loose around her shoulders. A playful smile curves her features, like she's about to laugh out loud, and her eyes are looking directly at me. Each line I draw comes directly from my heart, as though my chosen medium were my own life's blood rather than a sooty piece of carbon. The huge gaping hole in my chest has re-opened as I allow myself to think about her like this. Oddly enough, as I come closer to finishing the drawing, I can feel a sense of closure that surprises me. I can think about her again, and cry over her now. It doesn't feel like healing. But maybe it's a Band-Aid.

I'm too absorbed in my own pain to remember that I'm in the cabin of my captors until it's almost too late. I hear footsteps on the porch and Hollis's voice rumbling before I snap out of my Pit of Despair. I grab the book and run to the door. Just as it's swinging open, I dart behind it so I'm hidden from their view. My pulse is pounding in my ears, and I look frantically around for an escape. There isn't one. Except...

I look at the open book in my arms, the portrait I've just created. It *is* Claire. There is no doubt what this means to me. Something wonderful and tragic, heartbreaking and strangely joyous. The lines at the top of her head waver a bit, like a breeze just blew through her hair. The shimmer dances down her face, so briefly that I could have missed it in the space of a blink. I smile as Siobhan closes the front door, leaving my hiding place completely exposed. She squeaks like the mousy woman she is and jumps over to grab Hollis's arm.

"What is it now?" he scolds. She points wordlessly at me, and his mouth drops open. "How... How did you..." He can't seem to finish that thought, but I'm not planning to stick around while he tries again. His expression changes from stunned to resolute, creases appearing in his dark skin as he takes a step towards me. "Paige, I don't think that we went about this in the right fashion, and we apologize for that. Now, how about we sit down and talk this over, real calm-like?" He's taking slow measured steps, reaching out a hand tentatively as he approaches, like I'm a wild animal.

"How about we don't?" I say evenly, then I flash them a smile and touch my hand to my big sister's face.

I land with a bump, the hard wooden floor doing nothing at all to ease my arrival. The smell of mildew stings my nostrils, such a harsh transition from the fresh forest air. It's so dark, I can't make my eyes adjust before I am full-on tackled by Maia's exuberant bear hug.

"You did it, you did it, you did it!" she stage-whispers, her arms around my neck (which is really awkward since her wrists are still tied together). She disentangles herself from me, zip-tie momentarily snagging in my hair, and she looks me over. "You're safe, and you're good and whole and everything? You know who I am?"

"It would take more than a little time traveling to make me forget you." I blink a few times rapidly, trying to make my eyes adjust faster. I can see the outline of her, and I can tell that there's a boarded up window on one wall that is letting in the very limited ambient light, but beyond that I'm lost. "Where are we?"

"I'm not sure. They completely freaked when you vanished. It was a little scary, but I wish you could have seen Donovan's face. He went totally white, then started turning red, then purple... as an artist, you would have been inspired." Leave it to Maia to try to make this situation as un-terrifying as possible. "Then they decided it would be safer to blindfold me, and they drove around for a while. I couldn't hear a whole lot, and I couldn't see anything, but I think they were arguing about where to take me. I guess they decided, 'cause here I am."

I get to my feet and look around. There are empty shelves around the walls, the cheap pre-fab kind with metal legs and semi-sturdy wooden planks across them. A steep, narrow staircase leads from floor to ceiling against the far wall, and that's pretty much it for the entire space. "You came in there?" I ask, pointing at the steps.

Maia nods. "Yeah, there was a laminated floor upstairs, and a counter with something heavy on it that we had to walk around. Then one of them opened a big square in the floor that led down here. I may have been blindfolded, but I didn't lose my super spy skills of observation." She flashes me a grin, and I realize my eyes must be adjusting if I can see that.

The boarded-up window is definitely our best bet for getting out of here, and I head over to check it out. I attempt to peek through the spaces in the makeshift barricade, but I can't see anything but bits of a brick wall across the way. Not helpful. I press my ear to the slats. "Is that running water?"

"Yeah," she says, joining me at the window. "I'm not sure if they brought me back downtown after all that running around, or if this is another part of it, but I'm pretty sure that's the creek. It sounds kinda far off though, so I'm not sure where we are. It runs through most of the town."

I dig my fingers into the side of the lowest board to see if it will budge. Maia reaches over to help me and I realize she's still zip-tied. "I have a present for you," I tell her, untying the dagger from my belt.

Her eyes grow three sizes. "Where did you get that? Did you… I mean, is it from… from the other side?" I nod and she just shakes her head.

"My best friend the time traveler. You are a freaking rock star!"

"Well, you got the *freak* part right anyway," I shrug and start cutting through the ties.

Her hands are free in no time and she throws her arms around me again. "Thank you." When she pulls back I can see in her face that, in spite of her efforts to lighten the mood, she's been truly frightened while I was gone. I hate that for her.

She tilts my face so that she can see better in the dim light. "Okay, we are going to get out of here, but while we're working on that, you need to tell me absolutely everything. Starting with why you have those scratches on your face. You *are* okay, right?" Her eyebrows knit together, and there's so much concern in her face, I can't help but smile at her.

"Those are only from tree branches; there are a ridiculous amount of trees there. But I am really truly okay. It was scary, and there were plenty of moments when I didn't know if I'd make it back, but I knew that wasn't an option. So here I am. And I'll tell you all the details as we work on getting out of here, but first I have another surprise for you." I cast an apprehensive glance towards the steps to make sure no one is about to come down here, then I bring my phone out of my pocket.

Maia gasps. "How did you get that? Didn't Parker take that from you in the car?"

I shake my head, already pulling up the phone and scrolling through my favorites list for Alex. "I think he meant to, but he was searching my bag for weapons and then, he just didn't."

Maia's eyes narrow with suspicion. "He *forgot?* They kidnap us and tie us up and dump me in here like it's a daily routine for them, but *that* he forgets? I don't buy it."

I pause before tapping on Alex's name. "What do you mean? You think he meant to have me keep it?"

"Well, he's also the one who left your bag with us, which had your sketchbook in it. And he's also the one who let me keep your bag *again* even after we got here. That didn't make much sense to me at the time, even though I was grateful for the oversight. But this? No way that was an accident."

"You think Parker's on our side?"

She shrugs, a smile playing with her lips. "I'm not anxious to put that theory to the test, but yeah. Either that or he's the worse agent ever."

I tap Alex's name and it starts ringing immediately. And it rings. And rings. Please pick up. Pick up pick up pick up.

Finally, just when I'm sure it's about to go to voice mail, a sleepy Alex answers with something that sounds like, "Runny time zit?" (Which I'm pretty sure translates to *Rennie, what time is it?*)

"Alex, thank God you're there. Maia and I were captured by Enforcers. Levi's working with them, and he brought them straight to us. There's a very long story and a very big kiss in your future if you can figure out how to get us get out of here."

Less than half an hour later, Maia and I have disassembled one of the shelving units and used the metal leg to pry off three slats of wood from the window. It's not easy, and I can think of numerous things I'd rather be doing right now, but it's getting the job done.

A quick glance at my Maps app told me our location, and it turns out Maia was right. We are right back downtown again, in the basement of a store on Higuera Street where only a few days ago I was sending Maia on a spy mission and no one was trying to kill us. Good times.

Alex drove past the storefront as soon as he could get here, and reported that no lights were on up there, but he was certain he saw the shadow of a man moving around. We've heard a few creaks and thuds that we had diagnosed as footsteps, so that confirmed it. No going up the stairs.

Maia and I are working on the next board as quietly as we can, when she murmurs, "Stupid Levi."

I can't disagree. "Yeah, I really misjudged him."

"Yeah, but you knew him for like five minutes. I've known him for months. I can't believe I could be so wrong about somebody. And to think that he has a crush on me? How sick is that after what he tried to do? I mean, for all he knows we're dead right now because of him. Oh, and you know what else? Talk about adding insult to injury—the theatre downtown isn't even doing *Into the Woods* this summer!"

"Way to focus on the important stuff, Mai," I whisper, using my hand to urge her to keep her voice down.

"I know it's not exactly on the same scale as handing us over to those creeps, but he still got my hopes up for nothing. I was willing to chalk it up to an honest mistake before, but now? Why even bring it up if it's just a big fat lie? What?"

Maia's words have frozen me in place. "It wasn't a lie."

"Um, yeah, it was. I checked."

I resume working with her on the stubborn board. "No, I mean, it wasn't a lie, it was a clue. Remember? He said that he'd given me a clue at the beach and if I'd followed it, he wouldn't have had to resort to turning us in. That was the clue."

"You lost me."

I shake my head, and try to work faster. "I told you about the crossroads, right? Well, in one direction there's the village. But the other direction leads..."

"Into the woods," she finishes. "Wow. If I wasn't so mad at him, I would say that's actually kind of clever."

"He wanted me to think, at least subconsciously, that I should go that direction, which would have led me straight to the castle."

The wood pops off suddenly, and I lean back to avoid getting smacked in the face. There should be enough room to shimmy out now. I convince the window to open (despite its best efforts to ignore my pleas), and lean my head out. There is nothing below us to shimmy out *to,* just a thirty foot drop to some rocks, the creek flowing by, and the shadowed form of a man.

"Alex?" I whisper into the dim light. "Alex, is that you?"

"It's me, you're safe. Caterpillar."

It's all I can do not to cry out to him, but I settle for waving and grinning like a fool.

"Stop flailing, you'll end up falling on your face and then no amount of Sephora time will be able to help you," Maia says as she pulls me back inside. But even though she won't admit it, she looks happy to see him too. "Did he just say *caterpillar?*"

"Inside joke."

Alex throws one end of the rope he brought up to us, and after about six attempts, I finally catch it. He's already tied a knot, so all I have to do is loop the end onto the leg of the closest shelving unit and pull it tight. Maia and I have loaded everything else we can find onto the shelves, hoping it's enough to anchor it, and we're ready to go.

A bell rings from somewhere above us. It's so incongruous, it makes us stop in mid-motion. And then we both realize what makes a bell ringing sound—the front door. Footsteps and voices confirm our suspicion: someone else is here.

"Hurry," I urge her, helping her to get her leg over the window sill.

"You should go first," she protests. "You're the one in danger."

"No way, I did not bust my butt to get back here to save you, only to chicken out at the last second. Now get out that window. I'll be right behind you." I give her a little push and she nods.

Alex has backed up the hill and tied the other end of the rope to a pipe, the theory being that with the rope pulled taught, and the angle not too unnervingly steep, we can slide right down. I found a pile of old rags in a box by the stairs earlier, and Maia has hers folded over the rope now, gripping it tight so she doesn't get rope burn. We hope.

Without another hesitation, she flings herself from the window sill. I watch as she flies down the rope towards Alex. It works. It really works! She lets go at the end to keep from crashing into the wall, and Alex helps to steady her. Then they're both waving at me to take my turn.

I grab my rag from the shelf and hitch my leg over the window sill, leaning low under the remaining planks. I try to ignore my racing heart and recall the bravery I felt earlier. I can do this.

And that's when the ceiling opens.

 Chapter Thirty

*A*t first, there are only feet. I never knew that shoes could be

terrifying. I don't hang around long enough to find out if pants can be

scary as well. I grip the rope with all my might and then I'm flying.

There are shouts behind me, overlapping cries of "Get her!" and

"Where are they?" and "How could you let this happen?" But they all

fade away as the wind rushes past me, and I'm only now thinking that

this wasn't a good idea in a short dress. But when it's modesty or my life,

I'm sure even Aunt Charlie would approve of this choice. At least I have

on cute underwear.

I drop to the ground and Alex is waiting for me. I point to the

window where Donovan is now hanging his head out, and shout, "Run!"

Maia takes off up the hill along the creek bed and Alex grabs my hand,

435

but I hold back. I take the dagger from my messenger bag and slice cleanly through the rope in one swipe.

Alex's eyebrows climb up into his bangs. "Where did you get that?"

I shake my head. "Long story. Come on."

There's a shrill metallic whine behind us, followed by a loud burst. A piece of the wall just behind Alex's head crumbles to the ground, showering dust all over us. I grab hold of him and look back to the window. Donovan has his gun pointed as us, and he's getting ready to fire again. Another whine, and we don't wait to see if his aim will improve any on round two.

We dash up the hill after Maia, and dive into the waiting car at the top.

"What took you guys so long?" Seth is behind the wheel of the black four-door Whatever-it-is and he doesn't even wait for the door to slam shut before leaving the curb. Alex falls against me with the sudden movement of the car, and I hold on to him as tight as I can.

I barely have a chance to catch my breath before his lips are touching my forehead, my cheek, my nose and finally finding my mouth. The ferocity of his kiss takes the air from my lungs, leaving me light-headed and giddy and greedy for more of him. It's only moments before I have to come up for air, and I lean my forehead to his, panting and grinning.

"Well hello to you too," I breathe.

He leans his head to my temple and pulls me in close so his words have an unobstructed path to my ear, his breath moving my hair. "I could have lost you," he whispers, voice cracking. "Between the Enforcers and the Traveling and Levi—I could have lost you." His hands are gripping my waist as though he's still afraid I might vanish at any moment.

I lean back so I can look into his eyes, and take his face in my hands. "I'm here. It's all okay now, I'm back and I'm safe."

"I wouldn't put money on that just yet," Seth says from the front seat, eyes harsh and cold in the rear-view mirror.

Alex clears his throat and sits up, his cheeks flushed. I guess in his excitement to see me again, he'd forgotten we had an audience. "Are they following us?" He looks out the back window of the car, but there's no one there. As soon as he opens his mouth to say this, headlights slide around the corner.

Maia gasps and grabs Seth's shoulder.

Seth swears under his breath, urging the car faster. "Any ideas?"

"Yeah," I say, "don't get caught."

"Gee, thanks."

We speed through a residential neighborhood, gingerbread Victorian houses blurring past us. My heart is pounding, and I'm holding onto Alex's hand like it's my lifeline. It's beyond the middle of the night and no one is on the streets. Seth flies through the intersections, not stopping for sign or signal, and the car behind us is still there. I steady myself with my other hand on the back of Maia's seat as we careen around one corner after another in an attempt to lose them. Where's a real cop when you need one?

I look back just as the Enforcers pass under a street lamp, and can see Donovan's enraged face behind the wheel. I've seen him angry, but this is a degree of rage I never knew existed. It sends a chill down my spine, and I silently will Seth to drive faster. "I have an idea," I say, speaking loudly so I can hear myself over the racket my heart is making against my ribcage.

"Yeah, I already heard your idea. I'm doing my best, okay?"

"No, a real idea. The next time you can get around a corner when they can't see us, turn off the headlights, make a quick u-turn, and kill the engine. With any luck, they'll fly right past us."

All eyes are on me, Alex and Maia's wide with surprise and Seth's narrowed, considering.

"That could actually work," Seth mutters.

"Of course it will," Maia says. "Do it."

"Okay, hang on."

We all hold on to whatever we can to brace ourselves, and Seth whips around the next corner. The street is wide enough that he can turn around right there, and we spin around. It's not quite like you see in the movies. The tires aren't squealing and we're not about to crash into a gas truck or anything, but even without that, it feels very James Bond. Seth turns the headlights off and quickly pulls the car into a small lot where there's a work truck we can park behind. He kills the engine and we all duck down.

My face is right next to Alex's and he reaches across to brush the hair out of my eyes. "Are you okay?"

I nod and give him a small kiss. Only a tiny peck of reassurance, but it's enough to send Seth over the edge.

"Hey, give it a rest you guys. We're fleeing for our lives, remember? Try to act like it."

"Sorry," I say, smiling at Alex.

"*I'm* scared," comes Maia's voice from the front seat, suspiciously close to where Seth's voice came from. "Feel like reassuring me any?"

I can't help but giggle.

We wait ten more minutes and nothing happens. We finally feel safe enough to drive home, but we take it slow and steady, not wanting to cause any unwanted attention. When we pull up in front of Maia's house, I'm leaning my head on Alex's shoulder and he has his arm around me. Now that the excitement is all over, I'm exhausted and I wish I could just sleep right here. I can't imagine there's any place I'll feel safer.

Aidan is waiting for us on the front lawn, pacing back and forth. Maia had texted earlier to say we were safe and headed home (so he didn't call out the National Guard or anything), but now that morning is almost here, it looks like he's well passed worried. For some reason, it doesn't seem to calm his fears any when we get out of the car with two boys in tow.

His jaw tightens as he marches over to us. "Seth, you have some explaining to do. And I assume you're Alex?"

"Yes sir."

"Don't show up with my girls at 4:00 in the morning and *yes sir* me. I want some answers."

Alex swallows hard, not sure how to proceed, but I jump in. "Aidan, I'm so sorry for all of this. I'll explain everything to you." Maia and Alex shoot me worried looks, but I just plow ahead, repeating, "Everything. But the part you need to know before you rip anyone's head off is that these two guys just saved our lives. And that's not a metaphor or hyperbole or any other device to gain your sympathy. We would actually not be standing here right now if it wasn't for them."

Aidan's eyes narrow, and his arms relax down to his sides as he looks us over. He takes in the state of my clothes, the scratches on my face, the red angry marks on Maia's wrists, and his jaw drops open. "You're serious." I just nod, and he scoops up Maia in a big daddy bear hug, then opens his arms for me to join in. "What happened? Who did this? It was those men who threatened you downtown, wasn't it? "

He doesn't wait for answers to any of his questions. He just releases Maia and I and solemnly steps over to the boys. "Thank you. If there's anything you need, anything at all…"

"It was our pleasure," says Alex, shaking Aidan's offered hand. "I'll never let anyone harm Rennie. You have my word on that."

Chapter Thirty-One

Once the boys are sent home (both of them decide to stay at Seth's house—much safer than tackling the streets again), Aidan asks Maia and me at least a dozen times if we're all right, and then he insists that we get cleaned up and go to bed. He says that he'll take care of alerting the authorities and anything else that needs to happen, and we can give him the detailed account later, but we should get some sleep. I don't argue. Every muscle in my body aches, my face is a mess of zig-zagged bloody scratches, and I'm covered in dirt from two different timelines. By the time I fall into bed, I'm already asleep.

It's taken roughly two-thirds of my life, but some of Maia's fashion sense may finally be starting to rub off on me. I'm getting ready to go downtown to meet up with Alex, and I actually look cute. I put on white shorts, cute strappy sandals, and a swingy trapeze-cut tank top in a pink floral that is perfectly girly without looking too Little House on the Prairie. Maia helped me to tame my hair, and she added two loose braids on either side of my face, tying their ends together at the back of my neck. I feel like an ad in Teen Vogue or an extra in a Taylor Swift video.

We're determined to put the horrors of yesterday behind us. Even though my hands won't stop shaking yet, and every time I close my eyes I see Donovan's wide scowling face, I will not cower in my room and let them win. I will make this a good day.

It also helps that I had another reeeeeeally great Ethan dream. Not one of the scary ones where we're running for our lives, but a good one filled with sweet promises and breathless kisses; the rush of adrenaline that only comes with knowing that time is not on our side. Seriously, if all of my recurring dreams were like that one, I would be one satisfied customer. Waking up is particularly annoying, though. Not only for having to end the dream, but also because for some reason, my subconscious still hasn't connected the fact that Alex is Ethan. I could be dreaming this amazing nocturnal tryst about my *actual* boyfriend instead of just the dream version of him.

But I think my favorite thing about the morning so far is that while Maia was helping me get ready, we were able to talk about every single thing that happened when I was on the other side, everything that happened last night, everything about Claire. It feels so good to be able to talk to her again; I mean really talk. It's a lot to take in, but as crazy as it all is, just being able to talk about everything makes me feel somehow normal. Or normal-ish, at least.

Now that Maia has dropped me off at the park, however, my nerves are starting to take over again. I pace back and forth between two shady trees, spinning my silver ring around and around my index finger and counting my footsteps for comfort. Why am I nervous? The Enforcers are nowhere to be seen. Maia knows everything. And I know how Alex feels about me. If I had any doubts, that kiss in the car last night sure cleared it up. He didn't change his mind overnight.

"Rennie!" All the butterflies in my tummy collide, forming a huge vortex of jittery wings at the sound of his voice. I turn, and he's there. I barely have a chance to notice how great he looks, or how the blue of his tee-shirt brings out the hazel flecks in his grey eyes before his arms are around me. He leans in, his forehead to mine. "Hi," he whispers.

"Hi," I whisper back.

"I missed you."

"You saw me seven hours ago."

He grins and kisses the tip of my nose. "I missed you."

He's brought us sandwiches from Gus's Grocery down at the end of the block, and we're sitting cross-legged on the park lawn just finishing them off as I fill him in on everything that happened on the other side. I try to recall every moment, but there's so much.

"That's unbelievable, Ren," he says when I'm done. "I mean, you told me some of the basics last night, but... wow. Tell me again about the girl?"

I smile, covering my mouth with a hand just in case I have avocado in my teeth. "Olive. She was adorable—biggest brown eyes I've ever seen—and so sweet. She's the one who told me about paper being illegal. Isn't that weird? Why would they do that? Poor thing was scared to death."

"And the dagger—that belongs to her?"

"Yeah. Where are you going with this?"

He gives a half-smile, but I can tell his mind is on a mission. "And the book you found in the cabin. You used that to get back here."

"Right. I remembered what you said about using a book to Travel, and my drawing worked to get me there, so I figured it must work in reverse too. Besides, I was highly motivated. I had you to come home to." I give him a shy smile, hoping that didn't sound as cheesy as it did in my head. Why don't I think about these things before I say them out loud? But he just blushes and smiles back.

"Rennie, I know this is all new, and you're still processing everything. But you do realize what this means, right?"

I nod as I start putting our trash into the paper sack. "Of course. It means I'm a full-fledged Traveler now, like you. And that if we accidentally cause a portal and end up over there, we have a way back."

He puts his hands on mine, gently forcing me to stop putting things away. I look up into his eyes, surprised by the wonder I see there. "No, Rennie. I mean, yes, all of that is true. But people don't *accidentally* Travel. It just doesn't happen. And then you made your own portal simply by drawing it."

I bite my lip, thinking about all that he's told me. "I didn't really think about it at the time. I needed a way home, and I knew that my sketch had worked before, so I just made it work again."

He chuckles and shakes his head. "Oh is that all?"

"Oh! And I made a list. You know, just in case I couldn't remember everything when I got back here, like you warned me might happen." I dig my phone out of my pocket and open the Notes app. I hold it up to show him, but he's looking only at me.

"You took your phone with you?"

"Well, yeah, I mean not on purpose, but it was in my pocket. Was that wrong?"

He presses his fingers to the bridge of his nose, squeezing his eyes shut for a moment before looking at me in that serious way he has. "It wasn't wrong. It was impossible. Rennie, the things that you're able to do—you shouldn't be able to bring anything through with you when you Travel, not the phone and not the dagger. Any kind of tech shouldn't work there, it shouldn't even exist outside of the Citadel. You shouldn't be able to create your own portals; *nobody* can do that. And you shouldn't be able to remember everything that happened on the other side, especially since you've only Traveled twice."

"Three times," I correct, pondering the whole list he's just given me, but unable to let the error just hang there being all wrong and stuff.

"What?" That tiny crease between his eyebrows has appeared, and I love that I know it means he's concerned about me.

"Maia helped me to remember yesterday that I've Traveled before; when I was eleven. We'd spent years telling people that I fell out of the tree in her yard, and that's what I believed too, but it's not true. I actually vanished, accidentally Traveling using a picture I had drawn. All these years she's known that I'm a freak, and she still stayed my best friend. Amazing, right?" I smile at him, but I notice that he's wearing his worried face again. "What did I say now?"

"You Traveled when you were *eleven*? With a portal that you made accidentally."

I nod, puzzled by the things he chooses to highlight when there are so many strange things happening.

A smile starts across his lips. "Well, all hail the True Heir."

I tilt my head at him, shaking it back and forth. "Oh don't start with that, you know I'm just me."

He shrugs, the cotton of his tee-shirt wrinkling over his chest. "*Hair of fire, eyes of ice...*" he quotes.

"Yes, I do have red hair, and I do have eyes that are barely even a color. But..."

"They're a perfect shade of blue. Ice blue," he amends, then continues. "*With her family she's all alone.* You told me you're technically an orphan, raised without mother or father. Just you and your aunt and your sister."

And my sister's gone. I haven't told him that part yet, but that does add to the orphan argument.

"She's been drawn in to a time forgotten... You said that sounded like Traveling, and you are one of us now. And the last line?"

"Her paper dreams will lead her home," I finish for him. "My dreams led me there. Putting them onto paper is what created the portal. Alex, you don't really think that I could be..."

He shrugs and takes my hand. "Maybe, maybe not. I'm not sure it even matters if you believe it or not, really. There are enough people out there who do believe it, and they're not going to stop looking for you."

I've read enough Chosen One stories in my life to know exactly what he's implying, but the thought of it applying to me? No, there must be another explanation. "I can't worry about what a bunch of strangers think of me right now," I state firmly. "There's really only one person's opinion I care about." I turn around and lean back so that my head rests on his thigh, smiling up at him.

He smiles back at me. "Well, this one person's opinion is very, very favorable. And I don't care who anyone else thinks you are, as long as you're mine." I look up into his beautiful eyes, and he softly sweeps my bangs out of my face with his fingers.

"There's something else, too, Rennie. What you told me before, about Traveling when you were a kid." He's running his fingers through my hair, root to tip, over and over and it's so completely intoxicating that I find I don't care if he's about to tell me that the park is on fire or that the giant alien mothership has arrived.

"Later," I murmur, as I close my eyes and swat lazily at a bee droning past us. "All of the craziness can wait a little while." It's time to tell him about Claire. I need to lower this one remaining wall between us, and then he'll know all of my secrets. I managed to bypass the details of the drawing that helped me to escape Hollis's grasp, but now it's time to let her story into the daylight. Maybe I'm still stalling for some reason, though, because when I open my mouth, that's not what comes out. "Tell me a story?"

I can hear him smile as he replies, "Always." He continues to draw his fingers through my hair as he collects his thoughts. Then, "Once upon a land, in a faraway time..."

"I figured out why you start that way," I interrupt, eyes fluttering open to see his reaction.

"Tell me why." He smiles, as though I'm teasing him. I'm not.

"It's because the land isn't the variable," I say, watching him. "Most stories start 'Once upon a time, in a faraway land,' but in your stories, it isn't the land that's far away. It's the time."

He's silent, eyes squinting as he mulls that over. "You're absolutely right," he says softly.

"You don't have to sound so surprised," I tease.

He leans down and kisses me. For someone who had never kissed a boy until two days ago, I seem to have taken to it quite well. It feels as normal and as necessary as breathing now.

"Hey," he says, sitting upright and brushing his fingers across my cheek. "Can I put the story on hold for a few minutes? There's something I saw earlier that I want to go get for you, okay?"

I shake my head, reaching up to put a fingertip on his smiling lips. "Everything I need is right here," I say, cheesy to the core. I guess it's best not to fight it.

He gently coaxes me into a sitting position and then stands, looking down at me with an impish smile. "You'll like it. Trust me."

"Always," I grin.

Chapter Thirty-Two

1 tilt my chin up and Alex leans down, steadying himself with one hand

on my shoulder. His lips brush mine once, twice, three times and then

we're both grinning. I giggle as he stands upright again.

"Be right back," he says, and then he turns and lopes across the lawn.

I hug my knees to my chest and watch him until he disappears around

the corner. With a sigh of pure contentment, I flop back into the grass,

staring up at the sky. What started out as a pretty crappy (and highly

unusual) morning has morphed into a great afternoon. The mysteries

and dangers all feel manageable now. No more lying to Maia, no more

hiding my grief of losing Claire. And so what if a few wackos from

another time think I'm this long-lost Heir person? Even the biggest of

problems feels small when I know that Alex is on my side.

I turn my head to see if he's coming back yet, a little embarrassed by how much I miss him already. There's a dandelion growing right next to my hand, and I pluck it out of the grass and hold it up, the blue sky shining through the fluffy white wishes. I spin it in my fingers and close my eyes, letting the sun warm my skin while I wait for him.

"Ethan," I whisper, the single word acting as both an acknowledgment of how lucky I am to have found him, and a wish for the relationship I feel certain is ahead of us. With a grin, I blow the white seeds into the wind.

"Well, that was pretty sickening," says a voice above me.

"Never made a wish before, Seth?" I reply without opening my eyes. "How sad."

"Not the dandelion. The public display of affection."

"Hm, that's odd. I don't remember inviting you to watch."

"Out here in a public place, it's kind of hard to avoid." I hear him sit on the ground beside me and I heave a not-so-subtle sigh in response. Guess he's not going away. I sit up slowly, deliberately taking my time to let him know what a pain he's being.

"What do you want, Seth?" Maybe if we cut to the chase, he'll leave before Alex gets back.

"Alex called me. He thought it would be a good idea to make sure you know what you're doing now that you're Traveling. Welcome to the club, by the way."

I suppose it's not that unusual that Alex would ask him to help me learn a few things given what happened yesterday. I guess they all have to look out for one another. I mean *we*. *We* all have to look out for one another. Weird.

"So you *are* a Traveler. I thought so," I say, looking him over to see if this fact makes me think of him any differently. Nope. Still a jerk.

"Since I was fourteen," he boasts.

I stop short of telling him that I have him beat by three years. Instead, I just nod. "Alex went over the basic rules with me. I guess there's five of them? But when I was there, they didn't seem to help me as much as I'd hoped. I mean, in order to navigate and talk to people, they didn't do much for me."

"The rules?" he scoffs. "I guess it's good that you know them, but that's kind of useless when you're first starting out."

I feel myself bristle at his criticism. "I asked him to put things in order for me, so he did that at my request. Why? What would you have told me that was so much better?"

He leans in, his response immediate and fierce. "I would have told you to hide. There's a map he should have given you of safe places to lay low, and you should have had that to start memorizing immediately. I would have told you to know your backstory. Have an alias ready and know the implications of choosing a name. The villages have a set list of names they can select from, and they're sorted by category. One village has nature names, one is gems and colors. You get the idea. Choosing a name identifies you with a certain people, and not knowing the consequences of that can be deadly. There are no nicknames, no last names. Someone asks you for a last name, it's a trick. But mostly, I would have told you to stay as far as you can from the Citadel."

I blink, startled at the ferocity with which he chooses to answer a simple question. "That actually would have been very helpful." The silence grows between us, and he's watching me like he's waiting for me to say something else. "So, thanks for bailing us out last night. I was surprised to see you there, but I was really grateful. Thank you."

"Yeah, I could tell. I guess it was just hard to say thanks when you were lip-locked with Alex, right?"

I open my mouth to reply, but I honestly don't know what to say to that. Maybe he's right? "Okay, fair enough. I'm sorry about that; we got a little carried away and that was pretty rude of us. It won't happen again."

He snorts in response. I guess it's up to me to get us back on track. "So, ummm... maybe you can answer something for me. I was told that I was supposed to form an alliance, and I've done that. But when I was on the other side, the people I ran into implied that my ally was supposed to be my sister. Do you know why they would think that?"

He nods. "There are some parts of the legend that are vague at best. People interpret them differently, and you end up with multiple variations of the same story." Seth yanks a blade of grass out of the ground and studies it, rolling it between his fingers. "So, you found your ally?"

I lean my arms back, tilting my face up to the sun. "Well, it's kind of a long story, but basically yeah. Alex, of course. I mean, unless I'm missing something I don't know about, it seems pretty obvious to me."

He looks at me, studying me for a moment in a way I don't like. "There seem to be a lot of things you don't clue into very quickly."

My whole body jerks back, like he just physically slapped me. "Well okay then. I guess that'll teach me to try to have a normal conversation with you. Thanks a lot."

"Look, you're a smart girl. If you wanted the real answer to that puzzle, you'd already have it. You don't need me to play along with your little game with Alex."

"What game? Alex and I aren't a *game,* we happen to be together. You could even say he's the man of my dreams," I say, proud of my little pun.

"The man of..." he starts to repeat, then shakes his head. "Yeah, that's exactly who he is all right." He picks up a rock and chucks it at a nearby tree, hard enough that it takes off a big chunk of bark.

"Hey, what's with you?" I demand.

"You're both idiots," he answers, face lined with anger.

I sit up straighter, flinging my hands in the air in surrender. "All right, I've had it. You caught me on the wrong day, Seth. You want to have it out? Fine, let's have it out. I'm sick of you being a jerk to me for no reason. You've known me for less than two weeks. Two weeks! What could I have possibly done to make you hate me so much?"

"Hate you?" His eyebrows climb up his forehead, and I can't tell if the surprise is real or sarcastic. "You think I *hate* you?"

"Well, let's see—you insult me every chance you get, you can't stand the fact that I'm dating your friend, and you seem to seek me out for the sole purpose of being a creep! So yeah, I'd say *hate* pretty much sums it up. Now I've had enough of the cryptic comments and nasty remarks. Just tell me what I did!"

"You want to know what you did? You really want to know? Fine, I'll tell you. You picked him. You picked *him*!"

It takes a few moments for the meaning of his words to catch up to me, like when you see the lightning but have to wait for the thunder to chase it to find out how bad the storm is. He's jealous? So much of me wants to dismiss this as more arrogance or sarcasm, but the look on his face won't let me.

"What are you talking about?" My voice is barely more than a whisper.

"Aren't you supposed to be sort-of dating my best friend?"

He has the decency to look embarrassed at that. "I like Maia. Probably more than I should, given the circumstances. But I *had* to get close to her, I didn't have a choice. You did."

"I don't know what that means, but I do know that there is always a choice. It may not be one you like, but there is *always* a choice."

"Look, I don't want to hurt her. She's a great girl, and things would be so much easier if I could just be with her, but I can't. And I'm sorry but, well, when the stakes are this high, there's bound to be some collateral damage."

My eyes narrow to slits, and my jaw drops open. "You did *not* just say that. You did not just say that breaking my best friend's heart is 'collateral damage'."

"You don't understand. I honestly don't want to hurt her. But wouldn't it hurt her even worse if I pretended to be something that I know I can't be? I realize that I haven't been great to you, and I've let my bruised ego do most of the talking. But, you have to know that the person you've seen isn't all of who I am."

"Oh good," I say, "so you're not really a self-absorbed, arrogant, jerkface creep who's hitting on his potential girlfriend's best friend?"

"Creep? Self-absorbed? Look, I've been laying the ground work here for six months, working my ass off like an idiot, putting all the pieces together so I'm at the right place at the right time, and for what? So you can choose *Alex*? Well, I'm sorry, but how *should* I react to that? You're

461

supposed to be with me!" His anger changes suddenly to a soft plea. "You're supposed to choose me."

I liked the anger better; I knew how to respond to that. My mind is reeling. What just happened? I get to my feet and he does the same, never taking his eyes off me.

"Seth, you're not making any sense. I have to find Alex, and if you have even half a brain under all that hair gel, you'll go find Maia and pretend like this conversation never took place." I turn to leave, but Seth grabs my arm and spins me around. He's holding my arms so tightly that my feet are barely touching the ground, and in three terrifying steps, he has me pinned to the tree behind me. He leans in close, his hot breath on my face, eyes wide.

"Rennie I'm sorry, this is not the way I wanted this to go down. But you have to hear what I'm telling you. Everything hinges on this, on *you*, and you're not making the right choices." He talks so quickly, I can barely make out his words.

"You're hurting me," I tell him, hoping that it makes a difference.

Startled, he lets go of my arms, but he keeps his hands on the tree trunk, one on either side of my waist.

"I'm sorry, I didn't mean to… I just…" he stammers, looking genuinely upset at the turn things have taken.

"Enough, Seth. I'm out of here."

"You owe me," he blurts out.

That stops me. "I what?"

His eyes are searching mine; I can tell he's scrambling for something to keep me here. "You said you know that rules. Rule four—I saved your life, I get to name my reward. My reward is that you hear me out."

I lean farther into the tree behind me and bite the inside of my cheek. I guess this is my first test to see if I'm really going to do this.

"Fine. I'm giving you exactly three seconds to tell me why I shouldn't knee you in the nuts and get out of here," I tell him levelly, way more calmly than I'm feeling at the moment. My whole body is trembling. Seth is *jealous?* That goes against every single thing I've known since I got here.

"Rennie, I…" He's clearly thrown off his game. I like it.

"One," I count, fully prepared to carry through with my threat.

"You don't understand what you're involved in."

"Two." Not only prepared to follow through, but kind of looking forward to it.

"Rennie, Alex isn't Ethan." My breath catches in my throat and my eyes fly up to meet his. "I am," he finishes in a whisper. "I'm Ethan."

My head starts shaking before I can even process what he's said. No. "You're lying." I try to say it with some strength behind it, but my voice cracks. "You heard me say that name in the cave, and you think you can use it to mess with my head."

"I'm not lying. You know I'm not."

"No! No, *you* are a jerk. Ethan is kind and sweet and comforting—he's saved me from every nightmare I've had for the past five months. He is everything that you're not." Even as the words leave my mouth, I'm rethinking them. Is Ethan all those things, or have I reassigned those attributes to him based on what I know about Alex?

"You've been trying to make the story fit what you thought you knew. But it hasn't been working, has it? There are pieces of the puzzle that don't fit." That part is true. I won't say that aloud just now, but he's right.

Why did I dream of Alex in one dream only, and Ethan in all the others? If they are one and the same, why won't my mind connect them?

"No, stop it. I don't know why you're playing this game, but I won't let you get in my head. Alex is Ethan. He would have told me if he wasn't."

"Oh right. 'Cause perfect angelic Alex couldn't possibly lie, could he?"

"That's right. He wouldn't lie; not about this."

He sighs, but stops short of rolling his eyes at me. "Listen, I told you just a minute ago that I've been Traveling for almost three years now. Three years. Do you honestly think that I don't know who I am by now? Give Alex the benefit of the doubt if you want to. Tell yourself that he was confused, and the memories were too slow to stick. But however you look at it, he's always known that I was Ethan. He has his own alias tattooed on his arm."

My head is swimming. "West," I whisper, feeling so so stupid. I look up at him, studying his pale blue eyes. Is he telling me the truth? How can I know?

"If that's all true..."

"It is," he cuts in, eager to convince me.

"*If* it's true, then why did I know him? Why does he feel familiar to me, and you don't?"

Seth grimaces, like I've just hurt him. "I wish I knew. I've been going crazy trying to figure that out. Best I can figure is that you two met sometime on the other side, and it must have been recently, or somehow significant. I don't know."

"And what about you? Why didn't you know me?"

"I did. I wasn't sure at first, but the only reason I went to the bonfire at all was to meet you. I mean, come on. The beach at night? The only reasons to go to the beach are soaking in rays and watching hot girls in bikinis. Neither of those happen at night, so what's the point?"

"Charming," I mutter.

"But I went for you. When I saw you, I still wasn't sure so I had to find an excuse to make contact. To touch you."

My mind flashes back to that first night at the beach. "You shook my hand," I remember aloud.

"I did, and I knew instantly that you were the one I'd been told to find. Then the night I saw you at the library, you hadn't even been here for two days and you were already holding hands with Alex, wearing his jacket and letting him kiss you. It was all I could do not to knock his head off. But he managed to convince me that you weren't showing any of the signs we'd been looking for, and that maybe I'd gotten my signals crossed. I believed him, too—temporarily. Then in the cave at the beach... you said my name, Rennie." His voice breaks, and he closes his eyes to regain composure for a second. It's like he's been waiting for days to tell me this. Or maybe much, much longer. I feel my heart go out to him, just a little bit. What he's saying may not make sense to me, but I'm completely sure that he believes it. "You said *my* name. And do you remember what Alex said?"

Of course I do, I'll never forget that day. My whole world changed that day. "He was facing away from me," I say, my voice getting thicker as I recall every moment. "And he said—he said it wasn't fair, that he wanted more time. He looked so sad."

"Yes," he affirms. "You said my name, you said *Ethan* and he thought that you'd figured it out. He thought you were talking to me."

And that's when I know he's telling me the truth. "That night when you came to my window, you weren't trying to tell me about Alex, or about Traveling. You wanted to see if I remembered you."

I allow my eyes to meet his, and he nods. "Yes," he breathes. He leans his head down closer to me, his cheek almost brushing mine, his lips so close to my ear that his breath sends a shiver through me. That familiar knot forms in my stomach again. All those times that it's appeared, I interpreted it as anger for how he was treating Maia and teasing me.

It doesn't feel like anger now.

"It's not too late, Rennie," he whispers, moving one of his hands from the tree trunk to my hip, gentler than I would have believed Seth was capable of. And more than that, it feels so very familiar. "You know the truth now, and it's not too late. You can still make the right choice."

I put a hand up to his chest intending to push him away, but my body betrays me. I close my eyes, my breath growing shallow. One kiss would tell me the truth.

"Seth, I..."

"Rennie? What's going on?"

My eyes snap open, my hand flying away from Seth's chest so quickly that I scrape my elbow against the tree bark behind me. Alex is standing there, bewildered and crushed. But I can't seem to go to him. In fact, watching him stand there, a fistful of daisies and a leather-bound book hanging upside down from his hand, all I can feel is my own hurt. Hurt and anger. Okay, hurt and anger and betrayal. But what I'm no longer feeling is confused.

"You lied to me." It comes out as a dare. Go ahead—deny it. (Please deny it.) "I had already chosen you, and you lied to me."

His eyes shoot to Seth, then back to me several times, and he licks his lips in an attempt to take in what I've said.

"Seth, what did you say to her? What have you done?"

"Nothing more than what you should have done from the beginning," he answers calmly.

I can see the moment that Alex accepts the implications of what Seth just said. "Rennie, I'm so so sorry," Alex pleads.

"Show me your tattoo."

He's startled into silence, hesitating. "Rennie, I..."

"Show me. Your. Tattoo."

His eyes never leaving mine, he reaches across and pulls up the short sleeve of his tee-shirt. I look down at the ink I admired, those marks I longed to trace with my fingers. Now it just mocks me. A permanent reminder of my gullibility.

"Seems like an introduction is in order, *West*." I spit the name at him.

He lets the sleeve drop and takes a step towards me. "I am so sorry. There are a lot of things I should have done differently. I know that. But the things I told you, everything I told you about myself, my ink, my family—it's all true. I did get the tattoo when my dad died and we moved out here. I just didn't tell you the part about choosing my alias for the same reasons. I guess I should have corrected your assumptions when they were off course, but I was always careful not to lie. I swear I *never* lied to you."

I push forward off the tree, and take a step closer to him. My hands are shaking, but there's no way I'm letting him see that, so I tuck them safely under my elbows, arms folded across my chest. "Well I hope that distinction brings you some happiness, 'cause I'm done."

He drops the flowers and the book to the grass, and crosses to me in a single stride. "Don't say that, Rennie. You know we belong together. No dream is as real as what we have, and you know that." He reaches up in an attempt to caress my face, but I push his hand away.

"Sorry, man," Seth starts, and I can tell he's fighting the urge to gloat. "Looks like she's picking me after all. Can't fight destiny."

"I'm not picking you; this isn't some ridiculous love triangle, so don't run out and get your *Team Seth* shirt just yet, okay? There's no triangle, there's not even a line right now, there's just a dot. A dot! Just a single, solitary, non-attached... And Alex, this is not about my dreams, or some strange saga of being in the right place at the right time and other weird time travel phenomena which I clearly don't understand yet. This is about us. You *knew* how important this was to me, how finding out that the Ethan from my dreams was alive and real and in front of me made me feel like I wasn't going insane. You had every chance to tell me the truth, but you chose to lie to me again and again, and I believed you!"

"Just let me explain. Please," he implores. "If you won't hear anything else, at least hear this. The connection that we have, it's real. I know if you just—"

"No." I hold up both hands, keeping him at bay with my sheer force of will. "No more of your stories." I turn my back on both of them, and take a step away before I stop again. "Don't follow me," I manage as the tears start flowing freely.

Somehow, I get around the nearest corner before I collapse against a black iron fence, sinking to the sidewalk and not caring that I'm still in public. My breath is coming in big gulping sobs now, my face buried in my hands and knees. Alex lied. He *lied* and I was so stupid and so desperate and so naïve that I believed him. Did he ever feel anything for me, or was it just some game to him? Some big keep-away match with Seth.

Oh man, Seth. I can't even... I just can't. Just when I'm finally able to tell Maia everything... *this*?

I wipe my palms across my face and they come away wet, slick with tears and snot. Lovely. I stop crying long enough to dig in the side pocket of my bag but there's no Kleenex. Naturally. Why would there be? Why would the smallest thing go right when it could go utterly disastrously wrong? I put my head to my knees again, burying it in my arms.

"Rennie?"

I tilt my head to the side, looking up at him through my hair. Not that I have to, I'd know his voice anywhere. "I asked you not to follow me, Alex. I can't do this right now." I push myself to my feet and turn to walk away from him, but he reaches out and takes hold of my arm.

I spin to face him, yanking my arm from his grasp. "Don't touch me." I need for it to sound like a threat, but it's a feeble plea instead. Pathetic.

He lifts his hands to show that he's harmless. "I'm sorry, I don't mean to upset you any more. I know you're still mad at me."

I can't reply. The tears are coming dangerously close again, the weight of them sinking into my chest.

"So I won't try to explain, not until you're ready to hear it. I know that would only make things worse."

"Then why did you come after me?" I risk a glance up at him, but it's a mistake. That little concerned crease is back between his eyebrows, and it hurts to know how genuine his pain is.

"You're crying," he says simply. "And when the girl you love is crying, you go after her. Even when she tells you not to."

I can't help it now, there's nothing I can do to stop the tears. Love? I have no idea how to respond to that. I don't even know if that makes

473

everything better or infinitely worse.

"I thought you might need a shoulder."

He holds his arms out—an invitation—and even though my head is telling me not to forget his lies and deceit, my heart wins this battle. I lean into his warmth, and let his arms envelop me. I don't even think about it, I just let him hold me.

"I'm still mad at you," I mumble into his shoulder, hiccuping through the tears.

His hand strokes my hair down my back. "I know."

Acknowledgments

What a journey this writing thing is! It can feel like a very solitary endeavor at times, but thanks to a great number of generous and talented friends & family, I've never felt alone.

Thank you, first and foremost to God (in all things, in all seasons). Everything else is shadow & echo.

Thank you to my family, those who have read (some multiple versions over multiple years!) and those who have been sideline supporters. I couldn't do any of this without you.

Thank you to Leslie Willis, artist and friend extraordinaire. Your cover art blew me away, and I continue to be amazed by your talent and generous spirit. MTFBWY, friend.

Thank you to Sam Nichols, who very graciously read and edited for me in my mid-stages, and helped me to move from premise to plot. Thank you for the push to get me to do more than dip my toe in. I'm not sure I'm swan-diving yet, but I'm wading with confidence. Opa!

Thank you to my critique partner, Rivkah Raven Wood, for your time, your energy, your wits, & your wit. For tirelessly answering my crazy emails and treating all of my bizarre questions and concerns as if they have actual merit. You're amazing, and I can't wait to attempt to return the favor.

Thank you to my many beta readers who have provided feedback for me. It was priceless to have your opinions and support as the story grew and transformed. I owe you so much (but in reality will probably just be hitting you up for more help with book two). Ali Miguel, Annora Lock, Becky Reser, Emily Cohen, Evan Piper, Jennifer "Z" Zornow, Joyce Stephens, Karin Piper, Katherine Rundall, Meghan Lastra, Michelle Herzan, Mindy Salango, Natalie Piper, Shelby Trett, Tika Viteri, and of course my amazing mom & dad. (And if I left anyone out, I'm so sorry!)

Thank you to Rod Trett for so many helpful suggestions and random "Does *this* sound better, or *this*?" questions; for the many hours of formatting help and for watching the puppy while I type in a quiet house.

Thank you to kevinandamanda.com for the generous free use of your incredible fonts. They are truly wonderful and I am happy to spread the word!

And lastly, thanks to YOU. Thank you for choosing to read my story, and for sharing in my characters' lives with me. I sincerely appreciate it! And if you've made it this far and you're still reading, I am truly humbled—and more than a little impressed.

About the Author

Sioux Trett was born and raised in San Luis Obispo, California (the setting of *Drawn In*). She graduated from college in Oregon, and now makes her home in the beautiful Ozarks. When she's not writing or reading, she can be found traveling, playing with the cutest puppy on the planet, or obsessing over things like Doctor Who, manicures, and Starbucks. Find more at her blog siouxtrett.wordpress.com.

Made in the USA
San Bernardino, CA
16 April 2015